About the Author

Gerry Moloney was born in Cobh, Co Cork, and now lives in Howth, Co Dublin with his wife Anne. They have two children and two grandchildren. He was an Executive Director of Allied Irish Investment Bank, and Investment Director of Enterprise Ireland. He has also worked internationally as an Investment Banking Consultant on Government contracts, and is currently an independent non executive director of a number of investment funds in Dublin's International Financial Services Centre. He received the Certificate in Creative Writing for Publication at the National University of Ireland Maynooth in 2013 and is a founder member of the Sapphire Writers Group at The Irish Writers Centre. *A Game of Consequences* is his debut novel.

For Katie and Harry

Gerry Moloney

A GAME OF
CONSEQUENCES

AUSTIN MACAULEY PUBLISHERS™

LONDON • CAMBRIDGE • NEW YORK • SHARJAH

ISBN 9781786937414 (Paperback)
ISBN 9781786937421 (Hardback)
ISBN 9781786937438 (E-Book)
www.austinmacauley.com

First Published (2017)
Austin Macauley Publishers Ltd.
25 Canada Square
Canary Wharf
London
E14 5LQ

Acknowledgments

Thanks

To my wife Anne and daughters Geraldine and Pauline for not only your proof reading and technology skills, but also your emotional support.

To John McKenna for persuading me to write the novel and also Patrick Semple and Orla Murphy at NUI Maynooth.

To all of the members of the Sapphire Writers Group at The Irish Writers Centre for your ceaseless encouragement.

To Susan Knight for putting the pen in my hand as it were, and to Patricia Prizeman, Michael Keohane, and Owen Dawson for giving me much welcome advice.

To the team at Austin Macauley for your professional help in converting my manuscript into the end product.

And most of all to Suzanne Power, my editor, for your insightful and constructive challenges and advice, and which you always delivered with endless patience and smiles.

I do of course accept full responsibility for the end result.

Chapter 1

Milo's grin had haunted Des all night.

He'd been sitting outside the boardroom when Milo swaggered out. The triumphant grin said it all.

It said: screw you Des. I'm the bank's new CEO, the new top dog.

It said: betcha didn't believe I could sweet-talk the board into passing you over and giving me the gig, did you?

It said: you've lost, but do feel free to kiss my ass anytime you feel like it.

Now, the image of Milo's grin flashed again as Des stood looking out the kitchen window with a mug of coffee in hand. He turned to Joan. She was looking tired and he realised he'd ranted on late into the night, venting his frustrations on her.

'There's definitely a storm brewing.' He watched her put down her newspaper.

'Storm? What are you talking about?'

'The weather of course. Look at it.' He turned towards the window and nodded at the dark clouds outside scurrying on the rising wind. 'What else?'

'I thought you might be talking about Milo's appointment.'

When he turned, she was sitting at the table watching him.

'Bloody Milo.' He threw the contents of his half full mug down the sink. 'I still can't get over the board appointing him. Incapable of engaging their brains.' He shook his head. 'That's if they had any in the first place.

Gobshites. Handing it to that jumped up snake oil salesman. Makes my blood boil. Conniving backstabbers.'

As he watched the dregs of his coffee cling to the plughole, he heard Joan get up and come over to him.

'Ah c'mon Des,' she said quietly, 'that's not really true. You know you're a much fairer-minded person than that.'

Yeah, he thought, maybe twenty years ago when we first met. I used to believe that "Do Unto Others" stuff once. Now if you want to succeed it's just dog eat dog. But it's not fair taking it out on her though. She's trying to be reasonable.

'Ah, I suppose you're right.' He shrugged.

'You knew Milo could get the job, didn't you? I mean he wouldn't have been in charge of marketing if he wasn't capable?'

'Look, I don't know. But you'd think they'd have seen my accountancy qualification as the deciding factor, wouldn't you? I mean, it's a bank we're running, not some shady second hand car outfit.'

'I'm sure they value your professional qualifications.'

'To say nothing of my twenty-four years of loyalty. You'd think a bank would value that above all.' He snorted and threw his eyes upwards.

'I'm sure things will work out just fine when they settle down, you'll see.' She smiled at him.

'Maybe. But it sticks in my craw they went for that counterjumper. It never occurred to me they could be so stupid. I mean the bloody fellow hasn't a bull's notion about the first principles of banking.'

'Ah Des, that's OTT surely. It can't be that bad.'

He looked at her raised eyebrows, her eyes pleading with him to calm down.

This ain't going to resolve anything. Stop taking it out on her. Just close the subject.

He looked out the window again.

'That weather could really turn nasty. I think I'll go for a walk on the pier before it breaks. Like to come?'

'Good idea. Just give me a few minutes to get my coat. Will you lock up?'

*****

When they got to Howth he parked the car and they started down the promenade of the pier. A strong south westerly swept them along under the upper tier wall. The grey granite glistened, angry spray whipping over it from the rollers on the incoming tide. In the relative calm of the dark sulky harbour, the navy and red lifeboat strained at its moorings. The wind ripped through the rigging of the sailing boats in the marina, their sheets beating mercilessly in a continuous dissonant rattle against their aluminium masts. By the wall a handful of battered trawlers huddled close. A couple of cider cans skittered by before becoming lodged in a heap of builder's rubble.

'Bracing,' Des mouthed to Joan with a grin. She nodded in acknowledgment, and buttoned the cape of her anorak more tightly around her neck.

At the end of the pier the unlit lighthouse was conserving its energy for the storm. Beyond it, the dark whale-like outline of Ireland's Eye was barely visible in the grey November light. A sudden gust caught them unawares, causing them to stagger. Exchanging glances, they turned back.

From force of habit he decided to return on the upper level, while she headed back the way they had come. The full blast of the wind was in his face but he battled on with spume from the breakers stinging his eyes.

The gale began to ease as he neared the lee of the mound on which the Martello tower stood guard. By the breakwater a flock of seagulls had battened down their hatches, as they faced into the wind with their heads buried under their wings. From the distant church belfry, the Angelus bell pealed dolefully.

When he descended the steps to meet Joan, he nodded to her in the direction of the Harbour Bar and she nodded back. Pushing in the door to its welcoming womb, his glasses immediately fogged up in the all enveloping heat. Removing them he ordered their coffees from the elderly barman perusing the racing pages of a newspaper spread across the counter. Moving to a table by the window, they struggled out of their heavy over-clothes and took their seats. The bar was deserted save for an old red setter sprawled in front of the glowing fire. He lifted his head lazily and looked at them with glazed curiosity before dropping it again and closing his eyes.

They sat in silence until the barman brought over the two mugs.

I can't leave this thing hang. It's not fair to her. Apologise.

'Joan, sorry about that outburst earlier,' he said, picking up his coffee. 'I was upset. Things were going just fine for me while Bill was the Chief Executive. I never even wanted his job, at least not then.'

'I know.' Joan gave him an understanding nod. 'You always said you two were a good team.'

'He led and I was more than happy doing the number crunching and making sure the paperwork was in order. But then I suppose there's little point in thinking about that since he popped off.' He felt calmer now and sipped his drink. 'Yeah, as the Yanks would say, it's a new ball game.'

'Yes Des, it is a new ball game now. You'll just have to move on.'

He watched her holding her mug to her lips in both hands and eyeing him over it.

'You know I don't think I'd have minded so much if they'd recruited someone from outside to run the show, but to end up having to play second fiddle to yer man.

Bloody whipper-snapper. Thirteen years my junior. God, it's asking a lot.' The image of Milo's swaggering grin returned and engulfed him.

'I doubt if it'll be that bad. Don't forget you still have a job to do in there.'

'I wonder. Milo and I have crossed swords over the past few years. It's not beyond the bounds of possibility he'll want me out the door. And I'll tell you something. If he tries it, I'll take him to the cleaners.'

'Ah Des.' She put down her coffee. 'Look, he might find *you* difficult to deal with at times. I mean, you can be rather pedantic when the mood takes you. But I doubt if it'd come to that. I'm sure he realises how much he needs you, even if he won't admit it to you.'

'Milo needs me? Don't get me going. Do you know the only difference between Milo and God?' He looked at her. She sat in silence, letting him continue uninterrupted. 'It's that God doesn't think he's Milo.'

'Steady on.' She pushed her mug to the side and leaned forward. 'Surely everyone has their doubts from time to time, don't they?'

He looked at her, smiling at what he presumed was intended as a rhetorical question.

'Oh no, not the Great Milo *Tiger* O'Toole. Sometimes in error, but *never* in doubt.'

She picked up her coffee.

'Oh have it your way, but I'm sure he'll appreciate a sound pair of hands backing him up to keep the show on the road.'

She's worried her dependable Dessie will throw in the towel. Which I might yet. But don't let her see.

'Ah, you're probably right. What's the point in getting worked up over it?' He picked up his mug.

'Give it time Des. You might see things differently when things settle down.'

'Maybe.' He rose. 'I'm going to get a refill. Do you want one?'

She's worried. It's not fair what you're laying off on her. Stop moaning.

'Are you worried about what Milo might do, is that it?' she asked when he came back.

'No, not at all. Naw, I can handle whatever he throws at me. That's one of the beauties of having a professional qualification. I don't have to do things by the seat of my pants.'

Not like *him*. Keeping just one step ahead of the posse.

'Good.'

He placed his replenished coffee in front of him.

'You know, I was probably overconfident of getting the job.'

'Maybe you were.'

'Yeah. Apart from anything else, Alan and the others said I was a racing certainty.'

The others. Oh God, the ignominy of it all. The loss of face when I meet them.

Joan was looking at him as she stirred her fresh coffee.

'You don't need me to tell you that you shouldn't pay too much attention to what others tell you about things like this. They could well have been saying the same to Milo.'

'Ah no Joan, that's not fair.'

But it is, isn't it? Admit it. It's one of the realities of corporate life. To be certain of being on a winner, best back all horses. She's right. Trust none of them.

'Anyhow, I'll be okay,' he added.

'You sure?' She seemed to force a faint smile.

'Sure I'm sure. And anyway, now is not the time to entertain doubts. The bank needs me more than ever. Someone they can rely on if they run into choppy waters.'

Ha, that's a good one. *If* they run into choppy waters? The real question is *when*?

'Good.'

'No, I won't allow this set back to screw up my career in there. I told them at the CEO interview that I'd guarantee we wouldn't lose our top spot in the Second Division of banks. No, not on my watch. And even though they didn't give me the job, I'm still going to do my damndest to keep it that way.'

'That the right attitude to have Des.'

The right attitude. The very words Jack used when he gave me the bad news. *We know you won't let this little setback upset you. Your day will come. You have the right attitude.* For all the bloody good it's done me.

'But you know what they say Joan, it's a long road that has no turning. I'll bide my time. The board will eventually realise they've made a botch of the appointment. They'll turn to me to dig them out of the mess, a mess for which I might add they've only themselves to blame. Of course Jack is a useless Chairman anyhow. The blind leading the incompetent. For God's sake, imagine putting a marketing man in charge of a bank. I ask you?'

'Well just make sure you don't do anything dishonourable along the way.'

He looked at her clutching her mug.

She's seriously worried. Reassure her.

'Whoa. I never said I would. No, I'm in there for the long haul. Even the best run companies have temporary setbacks. A bad year, a profits dip. Life is full of hiccups. No, don't worry. I won't do anything dishonourable. I'm a loyal company man. Loyalty always pays off in the long run you know. So for now, it's going to be a matter of knuckling down,' he paused a moment. 'Even if it's going to be with gritted teeth.'

Joan was watching him intently.

'So what happens next? Business as usual?'

'Quite honestly, I don't know. As I said, there is the possibility he'll want me out of the place. Anyhow, he's asked me to have lunch with him on Friday. The

Shelbourne if you please, whatever he's up to. I guess I'll get a much clearer picture then of how the land lies.' He spread his hands out. 'Just have to wait and see, I guess.'

'I'm sure it'll work out just fine for you.' She leaned across the table and put her hand on the back of his and gave it a light squeeze.

When they went outside, the waves from the incoming tide were now crashing over the pier wall and washing across the promenade. Des pulled up the collar of his coat.

Yes, a storm is definitely brewing.

Chapter 2

To:	*All Staff*
From:	*Milo*
Date:	*22nd November 2003*
Subject:	*Going Forward*

Dear Colleagues
You have heard of our board's decision to appoint me as your CEO and I feel both honoured and humbled by it. No doubt you are all aware of the very significant challenges ahead, but I know I can rely on each and every one of you to ensure that we optimise our combined strengths and together take our bank to even greater success.

I have informed our board I will bring forward to the December meeting a Strategic Plan to cover the next three years. With this in mind I intend to carry out an immediate review of our strategy, operations, and structures. In this regard I will be having detailed discussions with our senior management team, and I hope you all will contribute to this thought process. My commitment to you is to keep you fully informed of our progress towards the common goal of our team: WINNING! M.

*****

Des pushed open the swing door of the Old Stand. He immediately spotted Alan at a table.

Another *Jackson Pollock* tie. Fancies himself. More for after hours than in the bank though. Must drop a hint to him sometime.

'Ah, there you are.' Alan moved over to make some space on the bench seat. 'Sit down and I'll get a menu.'

Des angled his way in.

'No need. I doubt if they've suddenly gone mad after all these years and changed their cuisine offering. I'll have the fresh salmon salad,' said Des, looking around the bar.

Usual lunchtime crew. Two guys at the oval counter, a barstool between them. Suits, striped shirts, golf club ties. Rag trade from South William Street. One tucking into burger and chips, crossword and biro at the ready. Other idling with a coffee and the *Irish Times* property pages. Red faced, middle aged guy in the corner. Sports jacket, check shirt. Tweed cap pushed well back, looking pleased with himself. Easing bottle of tonic through a few lemon slices into clinking glass. On the skite. Probably up from Kildare or Meath for the day. Table there by the back wall under the photograph of Kevin O'Higgins' funeral. Two freshly coiffured women. Uncertain age. Engrossed in conversation, glasses of red in hand. Bottle of *Fleurie* standing to attention, corkless. Shopping bags on floor, *Brown Thomas, Richard Alan, Marks and Spencer.* Retail therapy they call it. Any excuse. Concept of an honest day's work beyond them.

'Well, what do you think?' asked Alan bringing Des out of his reverie.

'Think?'

'Milo's missive.'

Milo. Bloody Milo.

'Hey Alan, you're our go-to guy on the communications front. If you don't know, who does?'

'Yeah, but what do *you* think?'

I think I know better than to tell you what I think.

'Too early to say. It'll take a few weeks before we'll know for sure which way the wind's blowing.' Des shrugged.

'All the same, did you notice the bit in it about reviewing structures? Do you think he's got some of us up for shaving?'

Didn't think he'd feel threatened.

'To be honest, I think there's little point in speculating. I'm having lunch with him tomorrow. Might know a bit more after that.' He nodded to Alan with a brief smile.

Which doesn't mean I'll share it with you.

'And I wonder what he has in mind for you?' Alan murmured leaning forward.

Good question. The Shelbourne. One o'clock. More apposite if he'd made it High Noon. Shoot out. Just make sure to wear your bullet-proof vest, Dessie boy.

'Just have to wait and see. Won't I?' He looked at Alan, his face expressionless.

'You know I was sure you'd have got the job. I don't know what the board was thinking.'

Des felt his stomach lurch. Don't trust any of them, Joan warned. But play along.

'Ah, they probably had their reasons.' He nodded through a forced smile. 'Anyway, the world hasn't fallen in.'

'Well he certainly needs you, why, it's obvious you're indispensable to him.'

Indispensable? No, Alan, the only one indispensable to Milo is himself. Keep this guy at bay.

'Hope you're right.' Des managed another smile. 'But you'll be fine. Milo needs you. Keep his PR profile spinning. Sure, he was absolutely over the moon with the coverage you got him in *Finance* magazine. What was the headline? *The Year of the Tiger.* Nice pun on Milo *Tiger* O'Toole and the Chinese New Year. Well done.'

Alan acknowledged the compliment with a modest smile.

'There's the barman. Let's order.'

When they had done so, Des turned to Alan.

'Yeah, Milo needs you to help him oil his way around the press hacks. No one knows better than you how to fob off those felon setters. And you're pretty adroit with the brokers' analysts too. How do you do it?' He winked in a conspiratorial manner.

Alan smirked, touched his finger to his nose, and remained silent.

'It must be your innate Northside cuteness. Fair play to you. Quite honestly, it would drive me cuckoo.' Des shook his head.

'Des, it's my job. It keeps the dog in biscuits. But you're right. We'll all know soon enough what Milo has in store for us in his brave new world.'

*****

Des looked about him when he reached the Shelbourne Hotel.

Departing guest entering taxi. Liveried porter. *Have a nice day.* His trailing hand collecting tip and sliding it into his trouser pocket. Does he get his tailor to strengthen them? Inside, a blaze of an outsize flower arrangement on a side table. Ostentatious. Impresses Americans probably. Raised decibels coming from the Horseshoe Bar. Popping cork. Wedding party. Having a jolly good time. Suits at low tables in hushed conversation in the Lord Mayor's Room. Planning another property wheeze. By the door, a youngish woman, glasses perched on head. Prodding laptop keyboard with intent. Pale blue shirt and striped navy trouser suit. Tailored package.

'Can I help you, Sir?'

He glanced. *Olga* her badge proclaimed. He nodded in the direction of the Saddle Room.

'I'm meeting someone for lunch.'

At the entrance to the restaurant an elderly maître d' with shined head and clipboard enquired if he had a reservation.

'Yes, I'm meeting Mr O'Toole.'

He consulted his reservation list and smiled.

'Of course. Table for two. Please follow me.'

Des advanced across the chessboard patterned floor. Which piece am I? Better not a pawn.

The maître d' bowed as he drew a chair out at a window table.

Must find obsequiousness pays.

'Can I get Sir something to drink perhaps?'

'No, thank you. I'll wait.'

Outside on Kildare Street, the traffic rumbled past. Some lunchtime girls hurried by and turned in the direction of Grafton Street. Three chortling suited men with loosened collars and ties clutched polystyrene coffee cups and *Subway* bags.

That was me once. Footloose and fancy free. Me now?

He looked around the dining room. The chandeliers reflected brightly on the copious wall mirrors hanging over gold studded leather booths. At one of them the wine waiter stood as he poured a generous ball of malt from an overloaded drinks trolley. A distinguished looking bishop slid diagonally into his seat, nodding to the server in acknowledgment.

Bishop's pawn. They also stand who only serve and wait.

The tall figure of Milo approached.

New charcoal suit, sky blue stripe shirt, silk navy tie. The sweet smell of success.

'Hope I didn't keep you waiting?' Milo's face was radiant.

Doesn't give a toss. At least that grin has gone.

'No, no at all. Just got here in fact.'

'How's the money market this morning?'

Since when did he give a damn about the money market? *En garde.* Opening gambit before he gets down to his real agenda. My heave ho?

21

'A bit cheaper. The outlook continues to look like lower rates.'

'Good. In fact, it's one of the things I wanted to talk to you about.'

'Interest rates?' Des raised an eyebrow.

'No, the market. Its appetite for lending money. It's early days yet, but I have big plans to push the boat out. Being top of the Second Division of banks is all very well, but the time has come to play with the big boys.'

What sort of crap is he on about?

'Yes Des, time to move into the First Division. For a start, we'll need to spearhead an expansion drive on our lending book. Where the real profits are. So, to do this, we'll need to get more cash under our belt. My question for you is: how?'

Not in the job a bloody week and already wants to swim out of his depth.

'Well Milo, for a start we could try to increase our deposits.'

'But?'

What's he playing at? Knows all this already.

'Milo, we know we've a very good solid client deposit base. And loyal. We have a policy of paying them a fair rate, not too much and not too little. If we increase the rate though, it'll eat into our profits.'

'Yeah.' Milo half smiled, half nodded. 'If our punters are too lazy or stupid to shop around, why should we reward them by paying them more?'

Punters. You're talking about the bank's customers.

'We could of course borrow more in the interbank market.'

Milo shrugged, outstretched his hands wide, and put on an innocent expression.

'Des, I'm a simple marketing man and this is a bit beyond me. Explain to me why we haven't been pursuing this course of action more aggressively?'

Oh God. That line. A simple marketing man. Does he think I fall for his claptrap? Does anybody? Always plenty of dopes around of course.

'Well, it's pretty expensive money, so our margins get squeezed.'

'Yeah.'

Of course you knew. So why are you asking me?

Milo was silent for a few moments and then scratched his head.

'But something is puzzling me. It seems to me we might be missing a trick here. We know it's a badly kept secret,' he looked over his shoulder and dropped his voice, 'a badly kept secret that a couple of foreign banks are sniffing around with a view to coming into our market. They'll be totally reliant on the interbank market to raise their funds. So, how can they make serious money out of it if we can't?'

'Well, we can, but it's really a matter of how far we go. We've to be seen to be acting prudently. And of course there are regulatory constraints.'

'Let me be clear about this.' Milo sat back and looked at Des closely. 'Are you telling me we're limited because our margins will get squeezed, or because the Regulator won't let us?'

'Both factors come into play. It's a question of the extent to which we do it.'

'How d'you mean?'

For starters, Milo, your normal bull in a china shop approach is a no-no.

'To be successful, it would require careful planning, and subtle execution.'

'Right.' Milo's eyes narrowed. After some moments he leaned forward.

'Des, I'd like you to do a theoretical exercise for me. Just how far could we push this boat out? What's the maximum we could borrow before our friend the

Regulator starts jumping up and down, and what would it cost us?'

Des shifted in his seat.

Milo doesn't do things in theory. This is for real. But why is he asking me if he's going to heave me? What's he up to? Best buy time by playing along.

'Sure, Milo.'

'Good. I want you to make this your top priority,' said Milo, looking directly into his eyes.

'No problem.'

'How long will it take?'

That's it. He wants to get my last drop of blood before he fillets me.

'I should be able to have a first cut early next week. You say it's a theoretical exercise?'

'Well, it is.' Milo seemed to consider the question. 'But you see I've promised the board we're going to expand aggressively. I've committed to taking us into the First Division. So I need to develop some options. Right?' His eyes showed that he considered his logic reasonable.

So he's deadly serious. Good God. That's out of our reach. And Jack fell for it. So that's how he landed the CEO job.

'First Division?' Des repeated.

Lash the loans out to the Celtic Tiger nouveau greedy. Wave Lady Prudence goodbye. And of course ignore the inconvenient fact chickens always come home to roost.

'Yes. That's where we're headed Des. And I intend to get us there sooner rather than later.' He flashed his triumphant grin again, and waved to the waiter. 'I presume your roast beef on the trolley is up to your usual standard?'

The waiter nodded.

'Shall we both have the beef?' asked Milo as he turned to Des.

Don't let him steamroll you. Ask for anything else.

'Actually I was thinking of having fish.'

'No, no, Des, you must have the beef. It's always excellent.'

It probably is, but feck him, dig your heels in.

'I'd prefer fish.'

'Des this is my treat. I insist you have the beef.'

Right, I'll have the roast bloody beef.

Des nodded his agreement. He watched in silence as the waiter carved, served and moved off.

'You do realise, Milo, this will bring us into unchartered waters?'

'Of course I do. I want expansion, but it must be controlled expansion.' He started into his main course. 'Excellent.' He looked at his plate and tapped his knife on it a couple of times. '*Bon appetit.*'

Hope you and the board have a *bon bloody appetit* for the high risks you're hell bent on pursuing.

'Milo, you realise if we go down this road, we could end up in the Regulator's sights.'

'Good point, the Regulator. Actually, I've been thinking about our petty bureaucrat friends.'

They're not petty. They take their responsibilities seriously, even if they irk us sometimes.

Milo put down his knife and fork.

'This is as good a time as any to mention what I really want to talk to you about.'

Here it comes. He's recruited a new team. Goodbye Des, nice knowing you.

'I hope you weren't too upset you didn't get the CEO job. But the bottom line is the board wants the bank brought forward in an aggressive way, and they've tasked me with making it happen.'

Here comes the guillotine.

'This market is ripe for exploitation, Des. The bigger players are fat and lazy, had it too easy for too long. That's why the foreign vultures are circling. But if we get our act together, we can scoop the jackpot. That's where you come in.' He pushed his plate towards the centre of the table and looked squarely at Des.

What the...? This doesn't make sense. Keep calm.

'Where I come in? I'm just your numbers man.' Des looked at Milo, puzzled.

A broad smile spread across Milo's face.

'That's what I like about you, Des. You aren't the mere bean counter some think you are. You've got the breadth of vision to understand complexity. You understand banking. You know it isn't black and white. You can see success involves juggling a lot of balls in the air and making sure you don't take your eye off any of them. You can see around corners. And where we are going there are going to be plenty of corners. Are you with me?'

Beware insincere praise.

'I appreciate the compliment, but I'm not sure I am. What are you saying exactly?'

'Look, I've given this whole matter quite some thought. Our bank is about to set out on one hell of an exciting voyage.' He spread his arms. 'We need to think big. My core strength is the vision to chart us forward. What I need is a strong details man to keep a steady hand on the tiller. Right?'

Des wasn't sure he understood but nodded anyway.

'And I know you're not the type of guy to harbour ill feelings towards me just because I pipped you to the post in the CEO stakes, are you?' Milo added in an apparent conciliatory tone.

You couldn't be more wrong. And, you feckin' know it. But play along and see where he's going with this.

'Right Milo. Mind you I was a bit disappointed though.'

'Naturally Des. But let me tell you about one of my first decisions. I've decided to create a new post by appointing a Chief Operations Officer. To be my deputy.

And I want that COO to be you. What do you say?' He beamed across the table.

Good God! COO. New post. Up another rung. More money. More status. Me? He wants me to do it. Wow. Why? Only the other day he was mocking me with that grin. Now he's welcoming me like a long lost relative. What the blazes is he up to? Best play safe.

'I'm not sure I know what to say Milo. I wasn't expecting this.' Think fast. No time. Ask.

Des cleared his throat.

'What exactly will be my responsibilities?'

'You'll be in charge of all day-to-day operations. I'll focus on strategy and be the public face. We'll get a new marketing guy, and get you some support for your old finance role. But basically the day-to-day running of the shop: Finance, Administration, IT, HR, Risk, Compliance, all yours.'

Christ, this is a serious promotion. It'll be a hell of a challenge keeping him under control, but there'll be a hefty pay increase to make it worth my while.

'Thank you Milo. I appreciate your vote of confidence. And what have you in mind by way of...?'

'Oh, compensation? Don't worry about that. I was thinking in terms of raising your base salary by a third to two hundred K. I also intend to get board approval for a new results related bonus scheme. More importantly I've flagged I want a generous share option pool for key executives. As my deputy you'll be the second largest holder. And you can be rest assured I intend to make sure the options terms are generous. And I'm certainly not going to sell *myself* short.' Milo chuckled and winked to Des. 'I take it this is acceptable?'

Good God, an extra fifty K. Seems excessive. Increase alone is more than twice we pay graduates. Could do with a drink. But if it's the going rate in the First Division? Maybe I'm just in the right place at the right time. Mind you it will be hard earned with this bastard in charge.

'Of course.'

'Good. And I bet you enjoyed the beef after all, eh?' He grinned. 'Shall we order coffee?'

That triumphant grin again. Better fasten your safety belt Dessie boy.

'Sure. Thank you.'

*****

When they got back to the bank, Milo asked Des to come into his office. Milo's personal assistant, Orla, rose from behind her desk when she saw them come in.

'Hey you're looking smart,' Milo grinned at her, 'but then you always look smart.'

Smarmy bastard. That dress she's wearing looks new. Wonder what the chemistry is?

'Thanks.' Orla smiled cheerfully. 'Jack's looking for you.' She turned back towards her desk.

No. Just being pleasant. Keeping him at arm's length.

'Okay, check the share price for me and then get him on the phone.'

'They're still at 100.'

'Not for much longer, they won't be.' He winked to her before continuing. 'I just need a word with Des now, but put Jack through when you get hold of him.' He gestured to Des to join him in his office and closed the door behind them. 'Jack's a royal pain in the arse, so I need Orla to filter his calls.' He rolled his eyes towards the ceiling.

Nice attitude towards his Chairman I don't think.

'Now Des, I'd like you to let me know what additional resources you think you may need for this new COO job of yours?'

'Milo, I haven't really had a chance to think about it yet.'

'Of course.' The telephone rang. Milo picked up and listened. He mouthed 'Jack' to Des, and waved to him to take a seat.

'Jack? Hi. We lunched together just now. He's agreed to take on our COO post.'

Des gazed around Milo's office as he listened to the crackle of Jack's voice. Two filing cabinets stood behind the door, a table with some chairs over by the window that looked out on to College Green, and, hanging on the wall over a drinks cabinet behind Milo's Victorian desk were three Malton prints: Trinity College, the Custom House, and Dublin Castle.

Milo leaned back in his chair and twiddled a pencil.

'Well Jack,' said Milo, putting his finger to his lips and shooting a warning glance at Des, 'to be honest he took a bit of persuading. It was really only when I pointed out the bright prospects we have, together with his remuneration package, that he came round.' He put his hand over the mouthpiece and whispered to Des, 'got to keep him under pressure,' and winked.

'Yes Jack, our new share option scheme clinched it. I'll have to fast track my plans for it. I take it you're still in full support?'

The fecker hasn't even got approval for what he just promised me.

'But Jack we discussed this already. It's essential all key executives participate.' He shook his head in frustration across the desk to Des. 'Perhaps I didn't make myself clear. I regard you, Chairman, a key executive for the purposes of this scheme. Naturally I'll discuss my recommendation in advance with you about who will participate and how many options they get.'

Ah. Cutting Jack in for a slice of the pie. So that's the rabbit he pulled out of his hat to get the nod for the CEO job. Bloody conman.

'No, Jack, I haven't fixed on the option price yet. Promise to keep you in the loop though. Okay, enjoy the weekend. See you Tuesday.' Milo hung up. A smile began to form on his lips. At first it was almost imperceptible, but it gradually spread to his entire face. He looked across at Des.

'Sorry about that. This is the sort of crap I've to deal with now. You need the patience of Job dealing with that fellow. He appoints me CEO, but he just can't let go.' He pulled his chair up to his desk and looked up. 'Now, where were we? Oh yeah, I just want to be certain that you've sufficient resources to carry out your new responsibilities. Understood?'

'Understood.'

Understand only too well what I'm dealing with and there won't be any room for near misses. Still, I know my onions, and for the higher status and extra money I'll take my chances.

*****

'What did you think? Honestly?' Joan asked.

'I don't think I was with it most of the time,' Des shrugged.

'Don't worry about it. Beckett isn't exactly everyone's cup of tea.'

They were sitting in a wine bar at the harbour. It was her birthday and he'd asked her what she'd like. She knew he'd get her some jewellery, but she really wanted to see the latest production of *Krapp's Last Tape*.

She knows me only too well. Still, she accepts me for what I am. She knows I only suggest the theatre to amuse her, knows I've little interest myself. Maybe I'm a bit too predictable for her. My phone call earlier. Let her bring it up. It's her evening.

'Did *you* enjoy it?' he asked.

'I found it riveting. I particularly liked the way the lighting engineer managed the contrast of light and darkness. It worked really well.' Her lively eyes reflected her enthusiasm.

'But why did Krapp keep disappearing offstage? Surely it's sort of odd for someone to do that in a one-man show?'

'What you've got to understand is Beckett is exploring immortality.' He watched her put down her glass to free her hands. 'Krapp is celebrating possibly his last birthday. Reminiscing on one thirty years earlier. Examining his own life. His 'disappearing', as you put it, is a metaphor for moving between life and death.'

'God, why can't Beckett just *say* that if it's what he means?' Des spread his hands, his face a question mark.

'He's trying to make his audience think for themselves.' She picked up her glass.

'Well, I have to confess it did nothing for me. Too far removed from reality for my taste. Beckett in his arty-farty world might like to paint things black and white, but he's wrong. The real world is all grey. Anyhow I hope *you* enjoyed it. Happy Birthday!' He raised his glass.

She leaned over and kissed him.

'I did indeed. It was most thought provoking. And thank you for the treat.' She sipped her wine and replaced the glass on the table. 'Now, explain to me what you were saying on the phone earlier about the new job Milo has given you?'

Knew she hadn't forgotten.

'Ah, explain. There's the rub.'

'I don't understand.'

'You know Milo, right?'

'Mmm. I've met him a few times.'

'Well you know what I think of him. So what do you make of him?'

'Oh he's confident. Charming in his own way I suppose.' She shook her head, non-committal.

'Would you trust him?' Des asked.

'Let's just say he wouldn't be my type. I suspect his sincerity is a bit on the shallow side.' She looked at him. 'But why are you asking me about him. I mean I hardly know him. You work with him. You're the expert.'

'To be honest I think Milo's heart is as big and as warm as the crematorium above in Glasnevin.' He was silent for a moment. 'You know I was listening to a Northerner being interviewed on the radio this morning. He was some sort of paramilitary and he was asked by an American reporter to explain why people in a civilised society feel the need to acquire guns.'

'Paramilitaries up North. What have they got to do with Milo?'

'Let me finish. I can remember the Northerner's answer. I can also still hear his strong Belfast accent. "For those who understand the sit-ye-eh-shen, no explanation is necessary, and for those who don't understand the sit-ye-eh-shen, no explanation is possible".' He sipped his wine. 'When you're dealing with Milo, you either understand where he is coming from or you don't. It's not easy to explain.'

'Okay, try me.'

'You know I don't really trust him. I'm not saying he's crooked, but for him all boundaries are challenges. They're there to be stretched to the limit, the absolute limit. And even then, his idea of a limit is pretty flexible. I also think he's devious. When he was in charge of marketing, I could largely ignore him, but now he's my boss. He wants to make significant changes to the way we do business. With me so far?'

Joan nodded.

'We'd lunch today and he told me he was creating a new post. COO. His deputy, right hand man. He's asked me to fill it.'

'But only yesterday you didn't have a good word for him. So why would you take on this?'

Don't tell her about the money or she'll say I'm being bought. Not now. Another time.

'As I see it, whether I like it or not, he got the top job, I didn't. I've got to accept reality. The new job he's created is extremely attractive. A significant step up for me. I mean even if I said no, I'd still have him as my boss. So why not take it?'

Joan looked at him askance.

'I suppose it sounds like a well-deserved recognition of your ability.'

'Well I think I should give it my best shot.'

'In this case, congratulations, well done.'

Des looked at her. She was smiling and had raised her glass to him. I think she's bought it. No point in alarming her by telling her things aren't going to be that simple.

'Thank you.' He smiled to her.

Her eyes twinkled and she leaned over to him. She dropped her voice to a murmur.

'Now, let's finish off that bottle of wine. I can't wait to get home to enjoy the really *best* birthday present you can give me.'

Chapter 3

To: *All Staff*
From: *Milo*
Sent: *3rd December 2003*
Subject: *Structure Changes*

Dear Colleagues
The first three weeks as your CEO have been both challenging and rewarding. I've been reviewing our corporate structure and as a result I've decided to implement two key changes. Firstly, I'm creating the new post of Chief Operations Officer (COO) who will have responsibility for overseeing all the day-to-day operational activities of our bank and will report directly to me. I am delighted to announce our Chief Financial Officer, Des Peters, has agreed to take on this role in addition to his existing responsibilities.

Secondly, I believe it is essential we have an effective forum responsible for the new Strategic Plan which we are developing, so I've decided to create a Management Committee to assist me in driving this forward. Joining me on this Committee will be:

Des Peters, COO.
Ed Feeney, Head of the Branch Network.
Jerry O'Herlihy, Head of Credit.
Head of Marketing, (expected to be announced shortly).

As I've already advised, I intend to present our new Strategic Plan to the board later this month, so in the meantime, please keep your suggestions coming in. M.

Des arrived in the boardroom ten minutes before the appointed time for the first meeting of the committee. Ed and Jerry were standing by the sideboard helping themselves to coffee.

'Ah, here's the man who'll be able to tell us what Milo's up to,' said Ed.

Look at him. Trying to look important in that ridiculously wide grey pinstripe. Thinks it gives him an air of gravitas. Delusional.

'Up to?'

'Yeah,' Ed answered. 'You're in the inner sanctum now, in the know. This new committee. What's it for? I mean we all know Milo. I doubt if he really wants a committee to advise him, does he?'

Thinks the bank should revolve around him. Best maintain a distance.

Des gave an easy smile. 'Let's just wait and see how he's going to operate it.'

'Well,' said Ed, making an imaginary adjustment to his cufflinks, 'as long as he doesn't intend to try to interfere in the way I run the branches I'll give him any assistance I can.'

You mean you'll carry on as you always did, doing your damndest to frustrate us all.

'I'm sure Milo's well satisfied with the tight ship you run here already.'

Des looked over at Jerry who was quietly observing the interchange.

'Well, you all set?'

'I'm a bit like yourself,' said Jerry. 'I'm keeping my powder dry. I don't think Milo'll have any complaints with my end. Our bad debt experience is the best in town.'

Good old Jerry. Old school banker. Conservative. Won't be spotted in a watering hole with the Louis Copeland suits.

'I see Milo says he intends to appoint a new Head of Marketing soon,' said Jerry. 'Do you think he might have Alan in mind?'

'Obviously not,' Ed butted in.

Jerry looked puzzled. 'Why do you say *obviously*? I don't see anything obvious.'

'You don't get it, do you?' Ed shook his head. 'If he was going to give the job to Alan he'd have done so. And anyway, if you read his email again, Milo uses the word expect, not intend.'

'Intend, expect, what's the difference?'

'The same difference between a girl intending to have a baby and expecting to have one,' said Ed, rolling his eyes to heaven.

'Ah.' Jerry nodded to himself.

'Who's expecting a baby?' asked Milo from the doorway.

Ed watched the CEO enter the room. 'Hi Milo. No one. Just a figure of speech.'

'Right,' said Milo, 'let me grab a coffee and then we'll get cracking. Okay?'

They drew their chairs up.

Milo glanced at some brief notes on his jotter and then looked up.

'Right. I thought as this is our first meeting, it might be a good idea if we started out with a few ground rules. The three executives nodded.

Silence for Herr Fuhrer.

'I want this to be a free forum for open discussion. We know the board is ultimately responsible for the affairs of the bank.' He opened his eyes wide and smiled. 'But, of course, we all understand the day-to-day running is down to ourselves, the management team. That's why I'm establishing this committee. We'll have collective responsibility. Okay?'

Collective responsibility my bum. Milo does what he wants. Takes any credit going and blames the rest of us for any problems.

Ed cleared his throat.

'Just for clarity, I notice we have no one from our Secretary's office here to keep minutes?'

A written record? You must be joking.

'Excellent observation, Ed. You're always a good man to make sure we follow the correct procedures,' said Milo, with more than a hint of irony. 'I thought for the moment we'd operate without minutes. It will help the free flow of constructive ideas.'

Jerry coughed.

'I can see how collective responsibility would work in theory, but surely in practice it might be a bit difficult. I mean I'm not really qualified to second guess Ed on how he runs the branch network.'

Milo looked at the three of them and gave a patient smile.

'A very good point Jerry. But I want you to be free to ask any questions you feel appropriate.'

Better play along. Ask something non-threatening.

'Milo, do you want us to focus on operational matters or the more strategic issues?'

'Excellent question Des.' Milo's smile returned. 'As I said in my email, our immediate priority is the three year Strategic Plan.'

Una duce, una voce. He needs to sell his plan to the board. Committee provides his cover. No records of any reservations any of us might have. No interest in operational matters. Will stitch me up for any problems on that front.

'If there are no other questions,' Milo continued, 'I think it might be a good idea if we spent some time considering the challenges we face. And before we start, let's remind ourselves of the basics. Banks make their money by borrowing cheap and lending dear. We don't pay our depositors any more than we have to, and we charge our borrowers as much as we can get away with. Right?' He looked around the table.

Ed leaned in across the table. 'It's a bit more subtle than that, surely?'

'Of course it is, Ed,' Milo nodded in apparent agreement.

Don't be stupid Ed. He means what he said.

'Okay,' continued Milo turning to Jerry, 'let's start with you.'

Jerry straightened himself in his chair.

'Well, the key to good lending is do it as safely as we can, meaning, aiming to get all the money repaid along with interest as it falls due.'

'And the challenges?' asked Milo.

'Twofold. Identifying who we really want to lend to, and making sure we do comprehensive credit checks before giving it out in the first place.'

'Thanks Jerry, succinct and to the point.' He turned to Ed. 'And you, what challenges do you see at your side of the house?'

Ed sat up straight.

'Running a tight ship in the branches by controlling the overheads.'

Des noticed Milo was watching Ed.

'And do you have any views on the interest rates you pay our depositors?'

Ed shook his head.

'That's not my decision, Milo.'

Milo's eyes narrowed.

'Yes, yes, I know the board decides what rates we pay, but are they not persuaded by your recommendations?'

Ed shifted in his seat.

'I appreciate that. In practice we keep a close eye on what the competition are paying, and usually match it.'

'And what about the challenges?'

'The real challenge is from the outfits who offer tax dodges to win new business. Bogus addresses, offshore accounts. But we all know this is going on.'

'I don't know that we do, Ed.' Milo frowned. He scribbled in his jotter.

You know damn well it's going on Milo. Just trying to have it both ways, aren't you?

Milo looked at Des. 'And what do you think? The challenges we face?'

Des was conscious Ed and Jerry were looking from Milo to him and back again.

For God's sake, we all know the challenges. Better play his game though.

'Two fronts really. Ed is right about gathering the money in. But the bigger threat is going to come on the lending side from the foreign banks. They see big opportunities in our booming economy.'

'Just a minute,' Milo rose and refilled his coffee, taking what seemed an inordinate length of time, then returned to his seat. 'Gentlemen, I think Des has hit the nail on the head. Whether we like it or not, the ground rules are changing. The foreign banks. Let's assume they're going to attack our market aggressively, so let's think outside the box here. Let's assume they want to make serious inroads, how would they go about it? What d'you think Des?'

This is a bloody re-run of our conversation in the Shelbourne. He already knows the answer. Getting this committee's cover for what he's going to do anyway.

'Borrow to the hilt in the interbank market and target their lending on the big corporates, property developers, personal mortgages, and credit cards.'

'And do you think they'd succeed?'

'They'd certainly make big inroads. Think of the demand already there from property developers alone. Falling over each other driving up land prices.'

'Fair point,' Milo agreed. He looked around the table. 'Gentlemen, whether we like it or not, this is the market in which we're going to have to compete. And I've asked Des to have a look at the implications for our Balance Sheet. His eyes fixed on Des. 'So, if we wanted to say double the size of our loan book, what are our options?'

Des cleared his throat.

'Well one obvious option would be to double our share capital. Of course if we have to convince our shareholders to write cheques, we'd have to promise them we could at least double our profits. That would be pretty challenging.'

Milo scribbled, and then looked up.

'And what about the option of borrowing more in the interbank?' Milo looked to the others. 'I've asked Des to figure out how far we could push that boat out.'

Des glanced around the table.

'I've been doing some calculations. I wouldn't recommend it, but if we were to stretch things to the absolute limit we could get close to doubling our loan book. It would of course mean a quantum leap in our risk profile.'

Milo scribbled in his jotter and then looked at Des and scratched his head.

'Des, you've just put two options on the table, both of which involve doubling the size of the bank. Are they mutually exclusive? I mean could we put both in play and be four times our current size?'

Des sank back in his seat and felt as if the blood was draining away from every part of his anatomy.

I refuse to believe it. The man can't be serious. Prudential risk in tatters. How do I respond? The others are watching. I'm the new COO. Can't argue with him in front of the children. I've got to appear constructive.

'That could be a logical deduction, Milo. But only on paper of course.'

Milo put down his pen and held Des in his gaze. 'You say on paper, but surely it could be in practice too?'

I've somehow got to buy time to frame reasoned arguments against this madcap idea.

'That's a bit of an over-simplification, but yes, Milo, you're right.'

'So what's stopping us?'

'It would be well outside the scope of our lending policy,' Jerry interrupted.

'Yes Jerry.' Milo put his head in his hand for a moment and then looked up. 'I know what our lending policy is. But is there any reason why we can't change it?' He gave Jerry a withering look.

'It's a prudent policy that's been approved by the board and has served us well.'

'Hold your horses there. There's no need to go on the defensive.' Milo leaned forward. 'All we're doing here is exploring what a new competitor might do.'

Oh no we're not.

'I was merely pointing out,' Jerry responded, 'our policy contains various lending restrictions, that's all.'

Fair play to him. Won't be bullied by yer man.

'Internal rules can easily be changed.' It was clear from Milo's tone that he was making a statement, not a question for discussion. He looked about the table again.

'Gentlemen, it seems to me we've identified a mechanism that could quadruple our present size. That's of course if we've the courage to go for it.' Milo's eyes seem to glaze.

Courage isn't the word I'd use. But having bought Jack with those share options you shouldn't be slipping him in the first place, there's nothing to stop you, is there?

Milo looked around the room again. Now his eyes were bright with sharp intent.

'Gentlemen, I'll need to think about this a bit more. We'll need a full scale planning meeting soon. In the meantime, you might all think about how you can contribute to a quantum increase in profits.' He looked around the table. 'Unless there's anything else, our meeting is adjourned.'

'There's just one other matter I'd like to raise if I may?' Ed cleared his throat.

'Shoot.' Milo paused in picking up his papers.

'I was wondering if you'd made any progress with the new position?'

'You mean as Head of Marketing?'

'Yeah.'

I wouldn't go there now if I was you Ed.

'Yes, Ed, but sorry I can't give you a name yet. We're still finalising the paperwork but I expect to be in a position to confirm the appointment very soon.'

'I presume that means it'll be an external appointment. Can you at least tell us where he's from?'

Milo rose and picked up his jotter.

'In strictest confidence, it's not a he, but a she. Her current job is Vice President of Marketing at Tesco.' He walked to the door and turned. 'See you, gentlemen,' he said, and left.

The silence in the room was broken by Ed muttering, 'Sweet Jesus.'

Des looked at Ed's dropped jaw and the colour rising in his face.

'Sweet Jesus,' Ed repeated and shook his head. 'He's going to appoint a supermarket check-out girl to be in charge of our marketing. To think the bank has sunk to this.' He shook his head again.

Chapter 4

'Tough day?' Joan asked Des as she turned the television to mute. She had heard him bang the front door and drop his briefcase in the hall, before he threw himself into his armchair.

'Ah, just Milo at it again.' He ripped a magazine from under him and fired it on the floor.

'And what's he at this time?' She put down the remote control on the table and turned to him.

'He's invited us to a Christmas dinner with some of the board next week.'

Forced smiles and endless drivel.

'An invitation to dinner? Oh.'

Feigning interest, probably.

'Well he says it's an invitation. The senior management team. Sorry, but we don't really have a choice in the matter.'

Joan nodded in brief understanding.

'Where? A decent restaurant I hope?' A faint flicker of a smile crossed on her lips.

'No chance. Arthur's bloody club. It's going to be a boring night, with boring food, in boring company, in boring surroundings. Sorry, love.'

'Oh I doubt if it'll be that bad.' Her faint flicker faded.

'At least the joint has a decent wine cellar. But that'll be about it.'

'Speaking of wine, let me pour you a glass while you tell me who'll be there.' She rose and moved to the sideboard.

'The usual crew. Milo, Ed, Jerry and Alan. Jack, of course, as chairman, and Arthur, as our senior non executive director. I'm not certain about the wives. Milo's Alison will probably be making it obvious she's the boss's wife. I expect Lorraine won't led Ed go without her, and Jerry's Gretta. Jack is, as you know, a widower, and I doubt if Arthur would force his wife to endure the evening.'

'What about Alan's wife?'

Des looked at her with an arched eyebrow.

'I'm not sure all is well in that department. I don't know the story and I don't ask. Don't raise the subject if he's solo on the night, right?' He nodded to make sure she understood.

'I get it. But I thought you two were buddies. You say you don't know his set-up?'

'Yeah. Look, men don't discuss that kind of thing. If the other guy wants to raise it, fine. Anyway, I suspect he's a bit of a gadfly when it comes to the opposite sex.'

'You mean he has the ladies in your bank in competition?' She laughed.

'Oh God no, I wouldn't think so. No, Alan's too smart to do "doo-doos" on his own doorstep.'

'That bloody bank. Always competing. Making more money. And sport. Do you ever talk about anything else?' She shook her head and looked away.

What's the point in answering? She's heard it all before and still doesn't understand. If you don't keep focussed, the other guy will get the jump on you. You don't deliberately set out on that road, but before you realise it, the job is a 24/7 obsession. Winning the chase becomes everything.

'There're times I just don't understand men,' she answered his thoughts, taking a sip from her glass.

'As the fellow says, you're not meant to.' Des chuckled to himself.

'But I mean, why can't you guys get a life?'

Good question, fair play to her. Why don't I? Why don't we get more of a life together? Why am I sucking her into my love-hate relationship with the bank? I need to create some space for us. But when? How?

'As you say, you don't understand. For some of us the bank is our life. Anyhow, this dinner's likely to be one of those evenings where you're going to have to listen to a lot of bullshit about our esteemed organisation.' He threw his eyes at the ceiling.

'I'll survive. Anyhow I get on well with Gretta. And Alan is always easy company, wife or no wife.' She sipped her wine.

'I wonder what your take on it will be,' he said, thinking aloud.

'My take on it?' She looked up. 'But Des, you can hardly expect me to understand the dynamics of the evening – whatever is going on?'

'Well there's so much change right now and I'm very wary of where Milo's leading us, and if Jack has any control over him. You might keep an eye and ear out for straws in the wind.' He picked up his glass. 'Anyhow, how was your day?'

'One of the students is doing some research into Bartholemew Mosse, the guy who founded the Rotunda. Oscar Wilde's father wrote his biography. He had access to Mosse's diaries but lost them.'

'Sounds like that line in one of his plays,' Des tittered. 'Something about carelessness.' He looked at Joan who wasn't amused by his crack. 'Sorry, anyway, you were saying?'

'So, I'm giving her a hand reassembling a profile of Mosse's life from the bits of the jigsaw she has.'

'A paper-chase. Don't you find it very frustrating?'

'No. In fact I find it very absorbing. A combination of being able to help someone starting off and self-learning. Can be very rewarding. Maybe a bit like you feel when your number crunching produces the results you'd hoped for.' She smiled.

'You're probably right. Anyway, I hope your efforts don't lead you down too many blind alleys.'

'I'm thinking the same about your efforts, Des.'

He noticed her smile wasn't her usual one.

*****

A northerly wind bearing a flurry of snow was funnelling up from Grafton Street. Des and Joan clutched their coats around them as they alighted from the taxi. A crowd of Thursday night office workers and suburban housewives wearing multi-coloured layers and bearing assorted shopping bags and hot whiskey smiles, milled about the entrance to the Stephen's Green Shopping Centre. Des watched a makeshift choir singing carols, and rolled his eyes when he saw fluorescent clad charity collectors walking backwards in front of passers-by.

Trying to lighten their wallets. Same every Christmas. *And the Boys from the NYPD were singing Galway Bay* belched noisily from a record shop. Shane McGowan and Kirsty McColl. They've a lot to answer for. Romanian standing on upturned beer crate mangling *The Fields of Athenry*. Country cousin further along with sonorous trumpet bum-noting his way through a dreary dirge. Here and there beggars loitering in doorways with crumpled polystyrene coffee cups. Courtesy of Ronald McDonald. The Great American Dream. Supplier to the Universe of Quarter Pounders. Slurring vagabond staggered towards the open taxi door, hand extended. 'Merry Christmas'. Des placed his hand in the small of Joan's back and propelled her up the Arcadian steps to the imposing front door of the Dublin and County Club.

In the hallway, they were welcomed by a blazing turf fire. The sound of breaking glass followed by a burst of raucous laughter indicated the location of the gentlemen's bar to the rear of the premises.

'And you are with?' The hall porter asked from his nook. He bore the demeanour of a retired not so senior army officer and wore an aged face and matching uniform.

'We're guests of Arthur Harford.'

'Oh yes, the Chairman's party. He's upstairs waiting for you in the Captain Bligh Room.'

They ascended the broad staircase which spiralled around a large, elaborately decorated Christmas tree. At the open door, they were greeted by the tall frame of the beaming, flush-faced Arthur gripping a gin and tonic to his chest.

'Des, you're the first.' He held out his hand, and turning added, 'and Jane, good to meet you again. And looking very well if I may say so.'

'It's Joan,' murmured Des to Arthur.

'Oops, apologies, I sometimes get my names mixed up, but never a pretty face.'

Oily smile. Watch him. Milo supporter. Still, slick cover-up of faux-pas.

'Now let's see what can we get you?' He motioned to a bored looking waiter. In front of him was a small table on which sat an assortment of bottles and glasses. 'A G and T? Some wine perhaps?' Arthur waved vaguely.

'Yes, a glass of white would be great,' said Des.

'I'll have the same please,' said Joan.

Joan looked about the room.

'The Captain Bligh Room,' she said. 'Is there a Mutiny on the Bounty connection?'

The question brought an instant beam to Arthur's face. His demeanour reminded Des of a kindly uncle about to indulge a five-year-old nephew.

Condescending old fart.

'This building was built in 1757 when Stephen's Green was being laid out by Lord Iveagh. Subsequently presented it to the city, in fact,' he said, taking a drink.

Yawn, yawn.

'And when did the club acquire it?' continued Joan.

Fair play to her. Probably couldn't care less but knows how to play these jokers along.

'We opened here in the 1810. Many of our men were anxious to fight for King and Country. They joined the various forces and went overseas – India and the Malayan peninsula. Usual trip was three years duty, followed by three months furlough. So they needed a place to hole up before they went back East.' Arthur drank again.

What a crashing bore.

'Did they not stay with their families?' asked Joan.

'No. You see often their families had emigrated. So they formed this club. As it happened, Captain Bligh was in Dublin supervising the construction of the North Wall and he became our patron. So we named this room after him.' He downed the rest of his gin and tonic, and nodded to the waiter for a top up.

'How interesting,' said Joan shooting Des a glance.

Just then Milo and Alison arrived. Arthur turned to greet them.

'We're just ordering some refreshments,' and nodded again to the waiter.

'Could I have a word in your shell like?' Milo murmured to Des. He turned to the others.

'Excuse us for a moment.' He caught Des by the elbow and drew him into another room across the landing.

'Wanted to nab you before the evening starts,' he whispered. 'Board meeting earlier, and we had a very interesting development I expect you'll be rather chuffed with.' He glanced over his shoulder.

'Yeah?' Des looked at Milo.

'I didn't want to raise your hopes, but I saw my opportunity.'

What's he up to now?

Des laughed nervously. 'Are you going to tell me or do I have to guess?'

'They've bought the Strategic Plan.'

Wonder what's in it?

'I'll need to flesh out a few details of course,' Milo continued, 'but I don't think there'll be any problems there. Anyhow, they're really excited. Could see it'll make us a serious player. They wanted to know how they could help, so I saw my chance and talked about strengthening the board.'

Ah get on with it.

'I took the bull by the horns and proposed...' he paused and glanced again over his shoulder.

Oh for God's sake cut out the schoolboy stuff. There's no one else in the feckin' room.

'I proposed you be co-opted. Told them you were crucial to the Plan's success. Strictly between ourselves, there was some foot dragging. But I persuaded them in the end.' He grabbed Des's right hand and with a broad grin shook it vigorously. 'Congratulations Mr Fellow Director. We'll make a great team.'

Des took a step backwards, his thoughts in turmoil.

'Jesus Milo, I wasn't expecting this.'

Out of the blue. The board. Hey that's just great. Or is it? A catch? Yeah, getting me further inside his tent, compromising me. Deal with that stuff later. Money.

'I, eh, presume there'll be some sort of financial...?'

'Of course, Des, of course,' Milo, still grinning, cut in. 'There'll be the usual director's fee. Forty K. I haven't sorted out the share options pool bit yet, but it's agreed to in principle. Trust me.'

Trust *you*? Pull the other one.

'Sounds great. I'm really going to enjoy my dinner.'

Meaning, I might if I could figure out what you're really scheming.

'Oh, not a word to the others for the moment. Jack wants to announce it himself. So act dumb. You know we'll make a great team you and me. We'll be in it together. Now let's go back and join the others.'

We'll be in it together. In what though? Thank you, God.

'Sure, don't worry,' said Des, 'I'll keep quiet until Jack makes the announcement.' He smiled and Milo threw his arm around his shoulder as they headed back to the Captain Bligh Room.

The rest of the party were seated at the rectangular table. Beneath the gleaming chandelier, crystal wine glasses glistened on the starched linen table cloth. Each place was set with king's pattern cutlery embossed with the club's coat of arms, together with the napkins and china side plates also bearing the club's insignia. At the head of the table sat Arthur.

'Ah here they are,' he said, rising. 'Milo, I've placed you there between Joan and Lorraine,' and pointing to his right, 'and you, Des, over there between Jerry and Gretta,' nodding to the other side of the table.

Joan immediately caught Des's eye, her eyebrow raised in question.

He mouthed 'surprise' to her, but didn't think she understood.

'Before we start,' Arthur began, 'I'd like to welcome you all to my club. It's both a pleasure and an honour for me to have you here as my guests, and I hope you don't find it too stuffy.' He laughed at his own witticism. 'As this is a new departure, I just want to say, enjoy the evening, and, *bon appetit.*'

Arthur eased himself into his carver and immediately the diners fell into conversation. There was a tap of a knife on a wine glass and Milo rose.

'Sorry to interrupt, but I'd like to say, unaccustomed as I am as your new Chief Executive,' he paused to chuckle, 'I'm delighted we can be here this evening. I really appreciate the efforts all of you have put in to support me since my appointment.'

Pass the puke bucket.

'I also appreciate the support of the ladies.' He smiled benignly around the room. 'And as a small token, there's a small gift for each of you on the table. Thank you all.'

Des watched Lorraine pick up the box, pull the bow and tear open the paper.

A small crystal clock. Wonder what expenses account he ran them through?

'Oh,' she said examining it, 'the bank's logo's on it.'

Crookstown Crystal. That dodgy client. Must've twisted his arm. Embossed. She's unimpressed. Can't flog it to a pawnbroker or even give it away. Joan will play along though.

'Why, Milo.' Joan turned to him smiling. 'What a very thoughtful idea. I didn't realise yer man there,' she nodded across the table at Des, 'was such a poor timekeeper,' she added in mock seriousness.

'It's just a token of my appreciation.' Milo responded, feigning sheepishness.

'I assure you it's much appreciated. I think the effort some people put into things these days doesn't get the recognition it deserves.'

Des glanced at Milo to see if he had picked up on Joan's innuendo, but he was already refocusing his attention on his next topic of conversation. The waiter was moving around filling up wine glasses. Another two waiters served plates of smoked salmon and prawns.

'So what are your plans for Christmas?' Des asked, turning to Jerry.

'The two lads are off from college so they'll probably condescend to break bread with us on the big day.' He shook his head and smiled ruefully.

'I'm sure it's not that bad.' Des's words hovered between a statement and a question. 'So what are they into? The lads. Dermot and...?'

'Dermot and Oisin. Dermot is as wild as ever. Loves the rugby and all that goes with it. Turns up every now and again but I think it's just for a change of laundry.'

'Not that bad surely?'

'Oh yes. The only time I meet him some weeks is in the front drive when I'm on my way to work and he's coming in, usually in a rather dishevelled state. The Business Studies takes a back seat, between the rugby, the pub, and the women.' Jerry shook his head again.

'Sounds like a well-adjusted young man to me,' Des laughed.

'Hmph. And Oisin's studying economics. Hoping to make Auditor of the Debating Society next year. Just loves an argument.' Jerry rolled his eyes. 'Loves the cut and thrust.'

'Like Milo over there.' Des nodded indicatively across the table and laughed.

I shouldn't have said that. I'm now a director. Must be more discreet.

'Speaking of our Milo,' Jerry leaned over, 'I'm a bit concerned with the tone he adopted at our committee meeting.'

'How d'ya mean?' Des asked, going on full alert.

'Well, his general attitude to our lending policy.'

'You think so? I didn't think he was finding fault.'

'Maybe not exactly. But I'm worried our existing lending policy could be seriously compromised if he pushes the boat out too aggressively.'

Worried? Better gee him up.

'You might be right, Jerry, but let's cross that bridge when we come to it shall we? Don't worry, you're a sound banker. That's a great comfort to me and I'll be in your corner if any curved balls come on the lending front.' He managed a reassuring smile.

In Jerry's corner. You sure you will be Dessie?

The waiters were clearing the plates and replacing them with the main course of turkey and ham. Des turned to Gretta.

'And how's Gretta these days?'

'Great thank you.'

Des glanced at her. Getting on, but making an effort. Looks like she's been to the hairdresser today. Red dress suits her blonde shading. Nice cameo on the lapel.

'Great to have a night out,' she continued. 'This time of the year is so busy, what with trying to get everything just right for Christmas.'

'From what Jerry was just telling me, Dermot's hardly about much to help out.'

'Don't be talking to me. I don't really mind him coming in at all hours of the night. I just wish he'd keep his room a bit tidier. I'd swear half of those country pals of his living in bedsits take more care of them.'

'Ah, boys will be boys.'

'Of course you don't have any...' she paused, 'any children. Isn't that right?'

Des felt a slow lurch in his stomach.

'No.'

An awkward pause was interrupted by the hovering waiter. Des placed his hand over his glass.

Gretta cleared her throat.

'Do you mind me asking you something about Jack?'

'Sure.'

'It's just when I came in here this evening I was having a conversation with him. We were talking about nothing in particular, and out of the blue he asked me if everything was alright at home.'

'Everything alright at home?' repeated Des.

'Exactly his words.'

Clown doesn't even realise he's irritating the wives.

'Oh don't bother yourself about it. Jack sees himself as a sort of father figure. The bank is his life. Sees us as family. But sometimes he takes it too far.'

'Actually if it was only myself to think about I'd have said something, but I wouldn't want to let Jerry down.'

'I'm sure he finds you a great support, Gretta.'

*****

53

Around the table, the buzz increased. Des looked over at Alan and Lorraine who were paying rapt attention to some anecdote Milo was relating.

Homage to Janus. Scanning his troops under hooded lids and bonhomie. Updating his files. Wolf in sheep's clothing. Who's he got next up for shearing? Beware the Ides of Milo.

Des noticed Jack slip from the room. The waiters were serving Christmas pudding and coffee, and placing decanters of port at each end of the table.

When Jack returned, he didn't resume his seat but stood behind his chair and tapped a glass with a spoon. The conversation trickled off.

'This is not a formal occasion so there will be no speeches,' he started. 'However, I feel I can't let this occasion pass without saying a few words. The first is to thank you all for coming here, and, if I may say so, particularly the ladies, looking lovely as always.'

Des leaned over to Gretta and murmured, 'see what I mean?'

'Hear! hear!' said Alan.

Too loud. Had a few snifters before he got here.

'And if I may say so,' continued Jack, 'we would not be here if it wasn't for Arthur's generosity in inviting us to his magnificent club.'

Milo clapped his right hand on the table three times to Arthur, who shrugged back with a false modest smile.

'As I said, this is not a formal occasion,' Jack continued, 'but it's the first time we've met since Milo's promotion, so I know I speak for all of you in congratulating him. Milo, you'll have our full support.'

Des glanced around the table. All were looking intently into their coffee cups.

'And of course,' Jack was in full flow now, 'it would be remiss of me not to wish all of you a happy and peaceful Christmas.' He smiled to the room. 'And we can leave the business of prosperity in the New Year in the capable hands of Milo.'

'Hear! hear!' Alan repeated.

There was a short round of applause which Jack cut short by holding up his hand.

'I haven't quite finished yet. There is just one announcement I have to make before I sit down, and a very pleasant duty it is too.'

Here we go. Assume modest demeanour.

'Forgive me, ladies, for bringing some business onto the menu here. We had a board meeting today and one of our decisions was to co-opt a new member.' Jack paused and looked around before continuing. 'I'm delighted to announce our new director is none other than dependable Des here. Congratulations Des.' Jack beamed.

A spontaneous burst of applause followed. Des did his best to adopt the expression of a boy at his own party when his guests sang *Happy Birthday To You*.

Milo rose and lifted his glass.

'A toast to our new director.'

The waiter glided around the table with a port decanter.

Mock servility. Eye on his slice of the Staff Christmas Fund.

Des stole a glance at Joan. She was looking at him and wore a smile, but her brow was furrowed, her eyes questioning.

*****

When they left, the snow flurries had ceased. A dark muffled figure lay prone on the steps under some cardboard. A disorderly queue of revellers stood under the gaze of two burly doormen at a nearby entrance from which reggae music escaped. Des pictured a scene in the basement of heaving intertwined bodies engulfed in a fug of sweat and alcohol fumes.

He hailed a passing taxi.

'You never mentioned a seat on the board,' Joan began. 'Were you expecting it?'

'No. Came out of the blue actually.'

'You seemed very calm when Jack announced it?'

'Milo tipped me off when he arrived.'

'So that's what the huggermugger was about.'

'Yeah, he couldn't wait to tell me.'

An ambulance was parked awkwardly outside a nightclub on Tara Street. Two paramedics were hoisting a girl onto a stretcher.

'So, are you pleased?'

He glanced across at her but couldn't read her face in the darkness.

In no rush to congratulate me.

'Oh yeah. Up another rung on the ladder. Two in two months. Helps make up a bit for the disappointment of not getting Milo's job.' He looked at her again. 'Are you happy?'

'If you are, so am I.' She leaned over in the taxi and kissed him. 'Well done.'

'Of course I am. Why wouldn't I?'

'I don't know. It's just you give so much of your time to them. I wonder do you ever think about what you really want in life?'

One of my life's ambitions, a seat at the board table. More cash. Enjoy for now. Analyse negatives later.

'Joan, the bank's my life. I like working in it.'

'Exactly. But don't you think some people can get so engrossed in what they're doing, they become blind to alternatives?'

A puzzled look crossed Des' face.

'Like what for instance?'

'It could be anything really. A job, a marriage, a vocation, a sport. We all need to take a step back now and then from our daily routine and consider the alternatives.' She looked over at him to check he was listening. 'Focus is one of your strengths Des, an admirable trait. But what I'm saying is I hope you take stock sometime of where it's all leading you.'

'A fair point. Must remember.'

Some other time.

The taxi reached The Five Lamps. One was unlit. Underneath, a group of young men and women swayed uncertainly, laughing and giving each other high fives.

'Tell me, what did you think of the rest of evening?' Des broke the silence. 'I know you met them all before but not since Milo got the leg-up.'

'You mean apart from your latest recognition? I suppose more or less what I expected. Certainly not as boring as you made out it would be.' She laughed. 'Mind you, the speeches were a bit windy.'

'Par for the course. By the way who did you get stuck with when I was with Milo?'

'Let me see. Oh yes, Ed and Lorraine. I was amused when Ed wandered off the first chance he could get to ingratiate himself with Arthur.'

'Good old Ed. Likes to act as if he's independently minded, but really he's an arse licker. So what was she like on her own?'

'Lorraine?' Joan shook her head. 'Wanted to find out if you'd anything to do with recruiting the new marketing woman. Told her you don't discuss office stuff with me.'

'Yeah?'

'Ed's really worked up about it. Thought it bad enough recruiting a woman in the first place, but someone from a supermarket really stuck in his craw. Something about it being beyond him how Milo thought selling baked beans qualified her to work in a bank.' She laughed softly to herself.

The taxi slowed as they approached the Bull Wall. A blue flashing light signalled a Garda checkpoint. Their taxi was waved on.

Des sat quietly for a while looking across the Sound and after some moments mumbled, 'bloody Milo.'

Joan sighed.

'I always thought he was rather pushy but he's absolutely brimming with confidence now. I think you're right to be wary of him.'

'I know.'

Forget about him Dessie for now or you'll screw up her Christmas as well.

'Tell me,' he turned to her, 'what did you make of Arthur and his club history spiel? Pedantic old bugger don't you think?'

'Actually I wouldn't be too sure. An expression of my mother's came to mind.'

'Yeah?'

'If you bought him for a fool you'd get a bad bargain.'

Des chuckled.

'I think what he was saying about the club was all an act,' Joan continued. 'You know, playing his sound independent director part but really would prefer to be somewhere else. If you ask me he has his own private views on the lot of you, probably not very flattering ones.' She paused and he was aware she had turned towards him. 'Just be careful.'

She's the sitch well sized up, as usual. Should listen to her more. Better close down this discussion.

He turned to her, chuckling.

'You know, you make it sound like I'm working in a nest of vipers.'

'Hmm. Maybe closer to the truth than you might care to admit.'

Yeah. Things are moving faster than I'm comfy with. Can't let her see I'm worried though. Need time to figure out. Engage bluster option.

'Don't fret, I'll heed your advice.'

'You just make sure you do that,' said Joan as the taxi reached their house.

Chapter 5

To:	*Des*
From:	*Milo*
Date:	*19th December 2003*
Re:	*Meeting*

I hope you and Joan enjoyed last evening. Congratulations again on your election to our board. I know you're planning on taking a break in New York over Christmas and I guess are trying to clear your desk, but I'd appreciate it if you could drop by before you go home this evening – I'd like to fill you in on a couple of board matters. Let Orla know if 5.30 would be okay. M.

Des read the email with irritation. So this is how it's going to be. Beck and call. Still, no gain without some pain. God only knows what he's at. Get it all over with. Better than coming back to the unknown. Let Joan know I'll be late.

The telephone rang. Ed was on the line.

'Did you see our share price this morning?' he asked.

'No, I haven't looked at it yet. What's up?'

'Up is right. Another three.'

Des flicked on his screen. Sure enough, 112.

'Thanks for letting me know.'

'What's happening do you think?'

Oh for God's sake. Give him a non-answer and get rid of him.

'Someone's buying, Ed. Talk to you,' he answered and hung up.

*****

Milo's desk was covered with files, newspapers, and coffee cups when Des walked in. His boss looked up.

'Good, there you are.' He got up with a file in his hand. 'Let's sit over here at the table. There are a few things I want to brief you on.' When they sat Milo glanced at some handwritten notes in his file. 'Let's get the formalities out of the way?' He looked up at Des, who nodded in acknowledgment.

'First, I told you about the director's fee. Forty K. Okay I presume?'

Des nodded.

Further recognition of my worth. Loyalty pays. Top up pension pot. Take Joan on autumn break. Whiff of nose in trough? Still, everyone else at it. A price later? No matter.

'Second, your Letter of Appointment.' Milo reached into his file, picked it out and glanced at it. 'You'll see it's short and simple. Arthur drew up a standard letter a few years ago. Three year term, renewable. Nothing you wouldn't expect. Pure formalities.' He thrust it into Des's hand with a nod. 'Okay?'

Des read the one page letter.

'Yeah, looks fine. Thanks.'

'Third,' Milo looked straight into Des' eyes, 'as fellow directors clearly we're in this together. However, as CEO, I don't want any misunderstandings between us about how I intend to manage the board.'

We're in this together. Reminding me. Don't say you haven't been warned.

'I take the view if for whatever reason the bank doesn't perform,' Milo still held Des's eyes, 'it'll be my ass that's exposed. Therefore, I don't want *any* board members interfering in the way I run things.'

'But is not the board responsible for...?'

'Hold on there, hear me out.' Milo raised his hand. 'As far as I'm concerned the board is responsible for high level strategic decisions, but when it comes to the day-to-day running of the bank, that is management's responsibility, *not* the board's. Understood?'

'Understood,' said Des somewhat hesitantly, 'but presumably the difference is not always clear cut?'

'Maybe so, but one of the things they're paying me for is to make those decisions. Do I make myself clear?'

Des shifted in his seat.

What's clear to me is you're a dab hand at the linguistic version of the three card trick. But I can't just roll over.

'Of course Milo. By the way where are we at with your Strategic Plan?'

A flash of irritation crossed Milo's face and he leaned forward suddenly.

'Our Plan Des, *our* Plan.'

'Sorry Milo. Of course. Our Plan.'

'I've a copy here to take away with you. Essentially the board's approved it and appointed a subcommittee of Jack, Arthur, yourself, and myself to sign off the final version.'

'A subcommittee?'

'It's the way I intend to get things done around here from now on. Most of the board know sweet FA about banking, so I'm not going to waste my time involving them unless I have to. Know what I mean?' He gave Des a man-to-man look. 'It's a sort of outline planning permission from them to fire ahead. You and I'll sort out any wrinkles with, of course, Jack and Arthur.' He winked. 'Shouldn't be any problems on that front.'

You've everything nicely rigged, haven't you?

'Okay, I'll study it while I'm away and get back to you with my thoughts.'

'You're flying out on Tuesday, right?'

'Yeah. I'm taking Monday off to get organised.'

'Oh.' Milo looked firmly at Des. 'I was rather expecting you could look at it over the weekend and talk to me about it before you go.'

Not a request. A bloody demand. All in the course of duty. Ah what the hell, I'll be in Manhattan with this behind me soon enough.

'Understood, see you Monday.' Des picked up the file and put it under his arm.

'Good. Let's say at ten.'

*****

'You're not reading those office papers still, are you?'

Des put them down and looked over at Joan.

'I probably shouldn't have, but I promised Milo I'd give him feedback before we left.'

'But you said you were taking tomorrow off?'

The evening news had ended and Joan was tidying the Sunday newspapers lying in a heap on the floor.

'I know, sorry love, but I only got them late Friday, and it's in my own interest.'

'And when may I ask do you intend to pack?' She was now standing over him with her hands on her hips.

'I'm meeting him in the morning. So even allowing for some wrinkles, I should be home by early afternoon.'

'God, you and the bloody bank.' She shook her head. 'And tell me what's so precious about those papers, not that I really want to know?'

Worked up ahead of the holiday. Just reason with her.

'Milo's so-called grand plan for the next three years. Very far reaching implications. It's long on aspirations, but very short on detail. In fact, there's feck all detail. Upshot is, he's giving himself far too generous a licence and I need to figure out how to control him.'

'Surely it's not all down to you to keep the bank's CEO on the straight and narrow?'

'There's the rub. He's formed a board subcommittee to finalise the details. I'm on it. The board will be looking to me to anchor it down. So will the Regulator.' Des stopped as the implications of what he had just said dawned on him.

Joan shook her head again.

'I just hope you know what you're doing.'

Meaning, you don't think I do. And do I?

'Of course I do. I just need to be on top of things.'

'Well, watch yourself.' She started to head for the door and then turned. 'Okay. I'm off to bed. You coming or are you going to spend half the night reading that?'

'I need to go through some of this again. You go ahead. Night.' He pressed his lips together in an attempted sheepish smile to her and picked up his papers.

She left the room rolling her eyes.

'Don't stay up too late.'

Pushing my luck. She won't jack up before the trip. But expect a kickback at some stage.

*****

The next morning there was an email from Alan asking him to call as soon as possible.

'Hi, Alan, Des here. You looking for me?'

'Thanks. I know you're trying to get away and you're in just to see Milo, but it's about the share price. It's up again this morning. Only another two cent which is nothing itself, but the Stock Exchange have been on and want to know if there's anything happening they should know about.'

'Leave it with me. I'll talk to Milo.'

Christ. We're being overtaken by events.

'I couldn't get hold of him. It's just, you know, if there's anything going on we'd need to tell them,' said Alan, the concern his voice clear.

'Thanks. I'll get back to you.' Des put down his phone and headed for Milo's office.

'Hi Des,' Orla said, 'packed and ready for your trip? I'm sure Joan has her credit card topped up?' She smiled broadly.

'Well not quite packed yet, but nearly ready. Just got to clear this bit of biz with Milo and then I'm done. Are you doing anything special yourself?'

'A few of us are taking a skiing chalet for a week.' She raised her eyebrows, but this time her smile was enigmatic.

A few of us. Hardly a girlie Christmas break. Doubt if there'll be too much skiing either. Wonder who? None of your business Dessie. Enough on your own plate. Don't pass a risqué remark.

'Sounds great. Is himself...?' he nodded to Milo's closed door.

'Oh yeah, he's waiting for you.'

He tapped on the door and walked in. Milo was on the telephone and waved him to a seat by the table. Des put his file down and gazed out across College Green at the Bank of Ireland. A porter was opening the gates of the customers' car park. Buses, taxis and delivery trucks were lined up at the traffic lights waiting for green. A Garda dismounted his bike and stood, legs apart, waiting to ensnare errant motorists in the restricted zone. And a Merry Christmas to you too.

Milo was speaking into his phone.

'I appreciate you might like to have more time, but I think we need to press on.' He looked at Des as he spoke and mouthed *Jack*. 'But the board has already approved the general thrust.' He drummed his fingers on his desk and shook an exasperated look to Des. 'But Jack, we've already agreed the subcommittee can finalise the details.' He put his hand over the mouthpiece.

'Sorry Des, be with you in a mo', and then removed his hand.

'Actually he's with me right now,' he paused, listening. 'Yes, Jack, that's precisely what we're about to discuss.'

He rolled his eyes.

'Jack, when we're done, I'll flesh out the detail and we can meet up with Arthur and finalise things. Okay?' He paused again listened intently. 'Yes, I'll have the detailed proposals for the share option scheme agreed with Arthur by then too.' Rolling his eyes again he listened. 'Yes, Jack, your name is on my list. Bye, talk to you soon.' He hung up.

Milo shook his head vigorously.

'Christ, that fellow can be a right royal pain in the arse sometimes. I mean, he knows the board's agreed the Plan in principle. The subcommittee's only there to rubber stamp the details. Now the bloody fellow thinks the board should see the final version for sign off.' He threw a biro he had in his hand across his desk. 'No, no bloody way.'

'No,' Des agreed in a distracted manner.

'As far as I'm concerned, apart from some minor adjustments, details, we've got board approval.'

Minor adjustments my backside. There's feck all details in it to adjust.

'If we're to conduct our business like Jack seems to want, we'd never get anything done. I'm going to start the way I intend to go on.' He got up from his desk and joined Des at the table. He grimaced. 'Apologies for the rant. Okay, the Plan. You've reviewed it. Thoughts?' He looked at Des.

Better sound positive or I'll be here all day.

'Good clarity on the direction in which you intend to lead the bank.'

'Thank you,' said Milo nodding. 'Any particular points you'd like to raise? I know that you're heading off in the morning.' He was watching him with wary eyes.

Have to hand it to him. Trying to make sure I can't come back with reservations later. Speak up.

'Perhaps we could look at the action points, make sure I understand them, you know.'

Like it would be useful if the Plan actually dealt with them.

'Sure.' Milo sat back and crossed his legs, keeping his eyes on Des.

'Well, let's start with the big one, the one that's most immediate. Increasing our share capital.'

Des had kept his voice steady, unsure what the reaction would be. He was surprised to see Milo begin to smile at him.

'I thought you'd start there.' Milo uncrossed his legs and leaned in to the table. 'As you might guess, the idea came to me at our management committee. Simple one really. If we want to be a Division One player, we must have more share capital under our belt.'

'Fair enough Milo. It's always useful to have spare capacity to exploit market opportunities. But, doubling it. Surely a bit aggressive?'

Meaning, I'm telling you I think it's bonkers.

'Good question.' Milo nodded in calm agreement. 'The way I look at it is, the market doesn't like it when companies keep coming back to tap their shareholders for relatively small amounts of extra cash. So I thought, let's go for a biggie now.' He opened his arms wide and shrugged his shoulders. 'I don't see why not?'

Good God, he really *is* serious. Some stunt for a Second Division bank to pull on the market. Still, he's bought off Jack, so there's really no one to stop him.

'Yeah, not an unreasonable argument,' said Des as he struggled to identify a coherent rebuff. 'But it's still very big for a company our size. I mean can the market swallow it? You'll have to pitch the price at a pretty low level if the shareholders are to reach for their cheque books, won't you?'

'*We*, Des, *we*. Of course we will. The today price is 114. I was thinking we might fix it at 90. The greedy buggers wouldn't be able to resist an offer of over twenty per cent off. If we make a positive statement about our outlook, we'd be home and dry. Tell me, am I right or am I right?' Milo was smirking now.

Greedy buggers. Of course you're only talking about the bank's owners.

'Yeah Milo, it's probably doable all right. But we'll have to be very careful about what we say about the outlook though, or we could be in trouble with the Exchange. As it is, they're chasing us for an announcement.' Des furrowed his eyebrows.

In trouble with the Exchange. I'll be in trouble with Joan if I don't get out of here pretty soon.

'Of course Des. We wouldn't want to upset our friends in the Exchange would we? Always pretty high and mighty about anyone breaking their rules, unless, of course, they're cut in on the deal themselves.' He gave a low laugh.

'You do appreciate if we propose to double our share capital, we'll have to rework the numbers, give the market some guidance on the implications for our profits next year, the dividend we intend to pay and so on?'

Milo sat back. 'Des, you're the number cruncher around here. But c'mon, we went through this at our committee. Doubling share capital equates to doubling profits, give or take.' His nod sought Des's acquiescence.

That was an assumption *you* just pulled out of the air.

'Steady on Milo.' Des frowned. 'In theory we could, but it would be a mega leap for us.'

Milo sat back in his seat and extended his arms again.

'The past is history. We're in a new ball game now Des. It's dog eat dog. Johnny Foreigner is coming and is already flirting with my wife. I can live with that, but I'm damned if I'm going to let him bed her.' He folded his arms and studied Des.

'Maybe, but it'll still take time to double our profits.'

A slow smile developed on Milo's face.

'Des, if I didn't know you better, I might even believe you hadn't already squirreled away some. What's the term you bean counters use?' He looked up at the ceiling and then back at Des. 'Sandbagging isn't it?' His eyes were twinkling. 'No. I don't think we'll disappoint market expectations about doubling our profits. I know I can rely on you to produce the goods if push comes to shove, can't I?' He winked. 'I don't think you need me to tell you how to do your job, do you?'

Des grimaced.

'Really Milo, I don't know what you mean. Our accounts have always been prepared in line with recognised accountancy standards. And, as you know the auditors certify them as giving a true and fair view. It's standard auditor terminology.'

'Yes indeed, a true and fair view,' Milo grinned. 'I can never work out if that's a euphemism or an oxymoron. The auditors certify that the accounts give a true and fair view and everyone's happy.' He paused and chuckled. 'Anyhow, in the unlikely event an issue with numbers arises, that's way down the road.'

God dammit, he's absolutely determined. Produce the numbers to back up his profits forecast. Flog the shares to the unwashed who haven't a clue about the risks. Still, if no rules are broken?

'Okay Milo, let's proceed with the share issue. Obviously we'll have to get our broker on board. Now, we'll need a fresh position on our lending policy. Presumably you'll be developing a paper?'

Milo appeared to relax.

'Of course. I'll talk to Jerry, get him to do a first draft. My bet is you and I are going to have to beef it up quite a bit though.' He nodded co-operation.

Doesn't give a hoot about it now that he's got me onside with his share issue.

'Okay, let's see what he comes up with.'

'Anything else?' asked Milo.

'The other thing I noticed is the Plan is silent on specifics about the new marketing person.'

'I expect we'll have Dawn on board early in the New Year. She's very savvy, a real self-starter and a seriously high achiever. I've no doubt she'll hit the ground running. The reason the Plan is short on detail is I want to give her plenty of scope to deliver what's needed.'

Des shifted uneasily in his seat.

'Can I ask you something Milo?'

'Sure.'

'Can I ask you do you have any concerns there could be a clash between Ed and her?'

Milo laughed.

'You may well be right there. But let's just say I think we need to inject a strong sense of oomph into building our book of deposits. She'll definitely deliver on this. I just hope that Ed, for his own sake, doesn't try to spike her guns. What d'you think?'

'Hopefully not.'

'My guess is he'll come around. One of Ed's problems is he takes a very narrow view on how the bank should be run, so initially he'll be wary of her. But when he sees his share options quids in and rising fast, he'll be far less inclined to throw sand into her gearbox.' Milo sat back with a satisfied look.

Gave options to Ed as well as Jack to buy off resistance. And to me because...?

'Is there anything else?' Milo asked raising an eyebrow.

I need time to think all this through.

'Yeah, just one other thing. Where are you at with the share option scheme?'

'Ah yes, the options. The bottom line is the board has agreed to issue up to five million to key executives and asked me to make a final recommendation to Arthur. Shouldn't be a problem there as he agrees we need to attract and lock in the best talent. Wouldn't have got Dawn without them.'

Bought her as well.

'So when will you be...?'

'Oh sorry Des, didn't mean to keep you in the dark. I've you down for a million. Hope you'll find that satisfactory?' He beamed at his rhetorical question.

Good God. Could be worth a stack. Why that many? Work it out later.

'That's great Milo. Much appreciated. Thank you.'

Will keep my nose to the grindstone for a while. Slowly slowly catchee monkey trap? Later.

'Twenty per cent per annum, usual five year qualifying period. I'll eat my hat if the share price hasn't at least doubled by then.'

'Fair enough. How are you going to go about setting the strike price?'

'I want to fix a low price naturally.' Milo laughed. 'Maximises the incentive to all of us to produce the goods for our shareholders. Right?'

'Well, of course. But you do know it can't be below the market price?'

'So Arthur told me.'

'And speaking of the share price, it's been steadily rising,' said Des. 'The Exchange want to know if there's anything going on they should know about.'

Milo put his hands up and laughed. 'It wasn't me, Your Honour. But seriously, it's the market that decides on our share price, what are we meant to do about it?'

'The market may be anticipating our fundraising.' Des was frowning. 'So I think we should announce it ASAP, the next twenty-four hours. Doesn't give us much time to crunch the numbers. Let me see. We can release some headline stuff like the terms, one for one at ninety cent or whatever, and say something about our prospects, what we may do with the dividend, that sort of thing.'

'Okay, I agree. Can you sort out the announcement with Alan?'

'Sure. We also need to find out who's been pushing the share price up. We don't want any insider trading investigations landing on our doorstep.'

'Insider trading?' Milo looked bewildered.

'Yeah, just in case. The recent sharp rise. We need to be sure no one's dabbling.'

'But hardly anybody knows any of this yet?'

'Milo, whether you like it or not, lots of people know. For a start, the board has seen the Strategic Plan. They might have talked to pals in the golf club or wherever. We just need to eliminate the possibility of anything sticking to us. Don't worry, for peace of mind I'll get Alan to check with our broker.'

'Okay, if you say so.' He stood up. 'That it?'

'You didn't tell me what price you're going to fix the option strike price at.'

'I was thinking of 90.'

'But Milo, I told you we couldn't issue them below the market price. That's now 114.' Des looked at him sharply but his face was deadpan.

Milo smiled enigmatically.

'You're forgetting that we'll be selling our new shares at 90, the price we'll be telling the Exchange. That's the price we'll be asking Aunt Nellie to pay, and if we think it's a fair price for a slice of the cake for her, in my book it's also a fair price for us.' He paused and looked at Des. 'Couldn't be more transparent, don't you think?' He nodded. 'Have a great trip and enjoy Christmas. And of course,' he added with wink, 'prosperity in the New Year.'

'And to you too.' Des picked up his file and set out for his office.

When he got there, he closed his door and tried to analyse his thoughts.

First Milo. You resent him because he got the job you thought you were entitled to. But board backed him, not you. So you can like it or lump it. Nothing to be gained by letting it eat away at you. If you walk away they'll say you're a bad loser. And anyway, he's the guy who promoted you. More status, more money. That counts for a helluva lot in your own self-worth calculations, right?

Second, these options. I'm up twenty four cent on a million right now. It's only a paper profit of course, but is it excessive? Well, it was the board, not Milo, who decided to introduce the scheme. So it's not a question of Milo trying to buy me. Therefore, it's okay to participate. But why is Milo being so generous with my allocation? Hasn't asked for anything in return. Must be to justify an even bigger dollop for himself. But again it's the board, not Milo, who decides the split. So, if they regard it as fair and not excessive, why should it concern me?

Third, the Strategic Plan. I think it's too aggressive, but that's just my view. The board has been appointed by the shareholders who want a higher share price. Fair enough. Times change and they've appointed a new CEO with an express mandate for a change to a bolder market presence. Nothing wrong there, provided, yes, I've got the key: provided risks are controlled. That's the potential Achilles heel. Risk, with a capital R, and that's *my* responsibility. *That's* what I'm being paid to control.

Des re-ran his analysis and couldn't fault it. He rose and prepared to go home.

Must tell her the good news about the options. Wait. She might overreact if I tell her now. Better to wait until she's sitting back tomorrow afternoon somewhere over the Atlantic.

Chapter 6

'Is there something wrong?' asked Joan.

She was sitting in the Business Class Lounge in Dublin Airport, watching Des with raised eyebrows. He had a preoccupied look when he clicked off his phone.

'Milo. At it again. I wish he'd consult me a bit more before shooting from the hip.' He was shaking his head.

'But you were with him yesterday. So what's happened now?'

'We were discussing a rather large deal. Very large by our standards. To do with raising our share capital. It's all very market sensitive.'

'I thought all banking business was sensitive? Why is this one a problem?'

'He's sent an email to all the staff saying a big deal's imminent. Jumped the gun. The Exchange will go crazy. All market sensitive stuff has to be disclosed immediately to the public, not just to a select few. Upshot is I've Alan working on an announcement we've to rush out. We'll have to grovel to the Exchange and have our wrists smacked, but that's the easy bit.'

Joan put down her newspaper.

'So what are you going to do?' She glanced at her watch. 'Our flight leaves in fifty minutes.'

'I think we better get out of here and clear immigration. I'll talk to Alan again then.'

*****

Thirty minutes later, Des pulled his mobile out.

'Alan, I'm about to board, but I need to know how you're getting on?'

'I've just started working on Milo's bullets.'

'Listen, you're going to have to get the thing finalised and out pronto.'

'What's the rush? Why not first thing in the morning?'

'We can't wait. Milo's email's likely to leak, leading to rumours impacting our share price. You'll just have to get him to clear it. What have you in it now?'

'Hang on there and I'll scroll through it.' There was a pause on the line and then Alan resumed. 'Okay, here it is. To capture benefits of exciting new opportunities… board decision to expand capital base… rights issue of one new share for every existing share… issue price ninety cent… directors confident… blah blah… enhanced earnings forecast… dividend to be maintained on increased share capital… offer will close on twenty first January. That's the gist of it. I'm just putting it into plain English.'

Des felt his heartbeat rising. He glanced at his watch.

Christ, can't I get away with Joan for a few days in peace? Must I do *everything* myself?

'Read those bits again about the new opportunities and the dividend.'

As Alan read the relevant pieces back, Des could hear the tannoy announcing the final boarding call and saw Joan who was the last remaining passenger at the gate signalling to him.

'Alan, got to go. But for God's sake tone down the stuff about the exciting new opportunities. We don't want to give the market the impression we've just struck gold.'

'Gotcha.'

'And another thing. Make sure you drop the bit about maintaining the dividend. We haven't run numbers on next year's profit forecast, never mind thought about the dividend.'

'Are you sure Des?'

'Yes, kill it. Oh, and get Orla to send me on a copy. I'll look at it when I land.'

He switched his mobile off and joined Joan in the tunnel down to the plane.

*****

'I rather like turning left when I board a plane. Thank you for the treat.' Joan put her hand on his as they sat together with champagne glasses awaiting take-off.

'I know,' Des nodded. 'We should get away together more often. And flying Business Class once in a while won't break us.' He sipped from his glass. 'And boy, do I need it after the last twenty-four hours.'

'Yes, you were rather whacked when you got home yesterday.'

A question, not a statement.

'Ah, stuff I just had to deal with. Milo isn't a details man. He makes sweeping statements and generous promises. I've to try to analyse them and assess the risk implications. And his email this morning left me with no option but to intervene. Anyway, Alan is sorting it out.'

'I'm sure he will.'

'But it's not him I'm worried about. It's Milo's ability to throw his weight about. If there are any issues, he'll bully Alan into having his own way.'

Joan leaned over and squeezed his hand. 'There's nothing you can do about it now. You're on your holidays. And remind me, which night have you booked for the Met?'

Des gazed in front of him lost in thought. He then shook himself. 'Sorry. Oh, yeah, the Met. That's Saturday. *Aida*. Domingo is in it. Should be good.' He sipped again.

When they were airborne, he turned to her.

'Sorry about bringing that banking baggage on board with me. But you know what they say,' he waved out the window, 'every cloud has a silver lining.'

'Oh I like silver linings.' She turned to him, her curiosity aroused.

'Yeah, yesterday. When I was with Milo he told me he was awarding me some share options. Could net a nice profit for us down the road.'

'Share options?' Joan put her glass to her lips but immediately put it down again. 'I read somewhere they foster a culture of greed?'

'Ah no. The press hacks love to peddle misinformation. They're just a bunch of begrudgers because they don't get them. No, the whole idea behind share options is to align the interests of key staff with those of the shareholders.' He smiled to himself.

'So, how will it work for you?'

Des looked around, leaned over, and dropped his voice. 'The board have created a pot of five million.'

'I thought you said Milo gave them to you?'

'Well, he recommends how the pot is divvied out.'

'Put that way, it sounds like a bribe.' She pulled her head back slightly and eyed him.

Wish she wouldn't think like that.

'Ah no, you don't understand. Most companies now have them. It's just to motivate and reward extra effort beyond the normal course of duty.'

That's the party line of course. But is it really true? It's a heck of a lot of money for doing my job. Stop Dessie. You thought this through before you came home last night and decided you only needed to concern yourself with looking out for red flags on the risk front.

'But five million sounds rather excessive motivation, no?' She picked up her glass and sipped.

Hard to argue with that. Better shift emphasis.

'It's a sort of loyalty thing as well, so there's a catch. You're locked in for five years.'

'Pretty thin line between earning loyalty and buying it,' said Joan under her breath.

'What's that?'

'Oh nothing, just talking to myself. Des, are you sure about this?'

'Of course I am. It's totally above board. Sure the whole country's at it in some shape or form.'

'Not the country I live in.'

'Well, maybe not librarians, but it's normal practice for bankers who get them as part of their reward for oiling the wheels of commerce and providing the money making opportunities for anyone who wants to play.'

'Oh I know my salary wouldn't pay for Business Class.' She looked at him. 'You sure you're not doing anything wrong? You say loyalty, but surely loyalty can be blind?'

Loyalty can be blind. Not now. Let the festive season do its work.

'Joan, come on, you know I've played it straight all my life, even to the point of it probably costing me the CEO job.'

'Okay. But tell me as a matter of interest, how do they decide how to divide out the five million?'

'It's really down to Milo. My allocation's a million. I presume he's getting even more himself.'

'A million?' She looked at him her eyes goggling. 'That seems obscene.'

God. This is meant to be a good news story. You've got to calm her down.

'It depends on the way you look at it. He's dividing them between seven of us I think, and well, I'm the Number Two in there.'

She sat back with a puzzled look on her face.

'But surely five million of these options, divided between seven people, must offend some code of ethics?'

'It's pretty well standard in banking.' He shrugged his shoulders.

'Be that as it may, it doesn't seem right to me.' She fell silent for a few moments. You see no problem going along with this?'

He felt a flash of annoyance.

I'm entitled. It's legal. A measure of my self-worth.

'Look Joan, both the shareholders and the board have, or will have, approved it. What do you want me to do? Quit and join some other firm, where my rewards for doing my job will be a fraction of what I'm earning now?'

'You know that's not what I'm saying. It's just that, well, what you might have to do to justify it.' Again she fell silent for a few moments before continuing. 'Are these options going to be handed to you just like that?'

'Ah no. Before anything happens, Arthur has to sign off Milo's recommendation. Then the board has to consider it before they approve it.'

Rubber stamp it more like.

'Arthur? Why not Jack? I mean he's the Chairman, isn't he?'

'Arthur is our senior independent director. Jack's conflicted because he's getting some as well.'

'Sounds like the old chestnut about the Unionists up North who say they're loyal to the Crown and the cynical observers who say their real loyalty is to the half-crown.'

'I don't get it. What's this got to do with our option scheme Joan?'

'I'm thinking of where Jack's real loyalty now lies. It seems like whenever Milo will ask him to jump, he'll ask, "how high"?'

'That's a bit unfair.'

'Maybe Des, but time will tell.'

Just then the steward came by and offered refreshments. Des had him pour a half glass of wine, and then picked up a paperback. He was about to open it when Joan turned to him.

'Just one more question before you start into your book. You say the key staff are in on this option pot. That includes Ed and Jerry I suppose?'

'Presumably. And the new marketing lady, Dawn. Maybe Alan as well.'

'That'll make Lorraine happy. I told you that she thinks Ed is undervalued.'

'If nothing else it might calm him down. His nose is out of joint over Dawn's arrival. Making money on those options will make him pause before he mouths off.'

'A few weeks ago you said Milo is very political. Machiavellian seems a better word.'

'Sorry?'

'Can't you see? It's all part of a pattern. He's managed to compromise his Chairman, and now you're saying he's shackled Ed.'

'Ah, steady on.'

'Do you remember your Virgil from your boarding school days? *Timeo danaos et dona ferentes?*'

What the hell is she on about now?

'No, I forget.' He shook his head. 'Tell me.'

'The guy looking at the wooden horse at the gates of Troy. *I fear the Greeks. They bring gifts.*'

Des sat quietly for a moment and then began smiling.

'Okay, I get it Miss Smartypants. But don't worry. That shyster salesman would need to be ringing on my gate very early in the morning to put one over on me.'

'Well, as long as you're aware of what you might be getting into.'

Des detected the doubt in her voice.

'Don't worry, Of course I do.'

But do I?

*****

They sat back in the yellow cab as it overtook and weaved its way on the crowded Van Wyck Expressway.

On the other side of the grill, the driver was having an animated conversation on his hands-free phone with a plumber who'd obviously not turned up. Times, dollars, and obscenities were tossed about in a storm of intermittent outbursts and blaring horns. Des looked at Joan and smiled at her visible discomfort.

'Welcome to New York,' he murmured.

She rolled her eyes and tried to tighten her seatbelt further.

The sharp rays from the low December sun slatted their way between bare trees. Christmas lights winked and blinked from the windows of the squatting bungalows, their doors bedecked with seasonal wreaths. Road signs flashed: Flushing Meadows, Shea Stadium, La Guardia.

When the Manhattan skyline came into view Des nudged Joan and nodded to the skyscrapers. The Empire State, the Chrysler, and the Met Life jostling each other, as if straining their necks for the best view. Trump Tower lording it over Central Park. Further off, the Wall Street blocks forlorn in the absence of their sentinel twin towers.

The cab suddenly dived into the Midtown Tunnel beneath the East River, and surfaced only to be engulfed by the Manhattan mayhem. The driver honked his way through the straightjacket of Forty Second Street, hemmed in by near grid-locked traffic and towering buildings. On the sidewalks, beanie topped traders were selling handbags and tourist tat.

They turned up Fifth Avenue, its lights ablaze. A steel band was playing *Mary's Boy Child* to a reggae beat. At every junction shoppers clutched multi-coloured bags as they waited to cross. Pedestrian signs flashed, *Walk, Don't Walk*. Adrenalin charged traffic cops shrilled their whistles and gesticulated wildly. Stopped at the junction of Forty Fifth Street, a wave of human flesh surged across antlike in front of them. One-man Salvation Army bands and Santa Clauses hogged the sidewalks, rattling cans to strains of *Hark the Herald Angels Sing*, and *Ho Ho Ho*.

Hordes of muffled last minutes shoppers barrelling into Louis Vuitton, Zara, Tommy Hilfiger.

A choir in altar boy regalia stood on the steps of St Patrick's Cathedral singing cherubically. *Christ the Saviour is Born.* A few dozen law officers were lounging nearby, gloved hands on hips and fingers inside holstered belts, their back-up paddy-wagons in the side street. It was not yet four o'clock, but the sun was setting. Opposite FAO Schwarz the cab turned and circled Bergdorf Goodman and the Plaza Hotel.

On Central Park Lane horses and buggies were lined up, their drivers in mufflers and their horses laden with seasonal regalia. The signs said fifty dollars for twenty minutes. Out of towners hoisted their charges on board, camcorders and cameras whirring. Street sellers, portrait painters, tour bus touts and hustlers of mixed nationalities meandered through the throngs.

'Wanna be taken for a ride Buddy?'

Their cab pulled in at the Helmsley Park Lane Hotel. 'Sixty-seven dollars,' the unshaven driver growled through the grill.

Taken for a ride.

'Mr and Mrs Peters,' said the hotel receptionist, 'we're expecting you. Hope you'd a great flight.' She handed them their room key adding, 'oh, and here's a message for you. Came in a couple of hours ago. Have a nice stay.'

In their room, Des tore open the envelope and pulled out the pages. They were headed *Stock Exchange Announcement.*

'I'll need to deal with this first love and then I'll be with you.'

He moved to the large window overlooking Central Park. The horses and buggies were circling through the Park to Columbus Circle and back by Grand Army Plaza.

'Damn it,' Des said, as he read.

'Something the matter?' Joan paused from unpacking.

'This.' He waved the pages before her. 'It's precisely what I told him not to do. Damn, damn, damn.' He chucked them on the nearby table and slumped onto a chair, running his hands through his hair.

'What's the problem?'

'I asked him to tone it down and he hasn't.' He scratched his head. 'Must call him.'

Joan looked at her watch. 'You do realise it's now after nine in Dublin?'

'I don't give a goddamn what time it is.' He reached for his mobile and dialled.

'Alan. I just got your message.' Des was glaring at the pages in front of him.

'Do you know what time it is?'

Des closed his eyes and mouthed 'Jesus.'

'Yes Alan, I know what time it is. Where are you? I can hardly hear you. Can't you get somewhere that's a bit quieter for God's sake?'

'Eh, O'Neills. You're not the only one who's off for Christmas.'

'Okay, sorry.'

'Did you get the Exchange announcement?'

'Jesus Alan, I asked you to tone it down.'

'But I did tone it down, well, a bit.'

'Not as much as I wanted. But listen, the dividend. I specifically asked you drop the reference to maintaining it on the increased share capital.'

'I know.'

'So why in God's name didn't you do it?'

'Because Milo insisted on keeping it in. Des, you weren't here.'

'Milo! Jesus. I know I wasn't there.'

'Des, what's done is done. Calm down.'

'Okay, I'll calm down. Has this gone out yet?'

He picked up the pages and began to scan them.

'Yeah.'

'Can you get it back?'

'No. Sorry. It was released this afternoon.'

'Shit. Looks like we've to live with it then.'

'Now that you're on Des, there's one other thing I need to tell you.'

'Yeah?'

'You asked me to check on dealings in the shares. Our broker says one of our staff has been buying.'

'What?' Des jumped up from the chair. 'When did this happen? Were there many shares involved? Have they told you who?'

'No, not yet, but I should know by the time you're back here.'

'Right, let me know as soon as you find out. Hey, Alan? Sorry to disturb you. Have a good break.' He hung up and collapsed back into his chair.

'Trouble?' asked Joan who was sitting on the bed and watching him.

'Yeah, a right bloody mess. I told Alan before we left what to say, or to be precise, what not to say in the bloody announcement. Anyhow, when you and I were somewhere over the Atlantic, Milo stuck his nose in and overruled me. Cooked our goose rightly. And just to put the tin hat on it, it looks like we might have an insider trading case on our hands.'

'Well, he's the boss. So it's his problem surely if anything goes wrong?'

'In theory, you're right. Trouble is the bloody eejit has over-egged market expectations and will expect me to sort it out. There was no need for it.' He shook his head.

'But surely it's Milo's the one who authorised the announcement?'

'Look, if push comes to shove at the end of the year, Milo will want the numbers to reflect what he's promised. Some aspects of accountancy aren't pure science, although God knows we like to think it is.'

'I'm not sure I follow. Surely the whole point is accountancy *is* very precise. The numbers either add up or they don't?'

'Joan, it's really quite simple. Milo's just told the market, formally, what numbers to expect. Period. But I'm responsible for producing them and he seems to think I've some sort of black box I can produce them from. Like a rabbit out of a hat. He's no interest in how I do it as long as they meet his expectations.' He glanced at his unopened suitcase and outside at the gathering darkness.

'Bugger that. Come on, let's go and get some air.'

*****

At St Patrick's Cathedral on Christmas Day, the choir was in full voice singing *Angels We Have Heard on High* at the end of Mass. In the grey daylight it was snowing lightly on the departing congregation, as they greeted each other under the sheltered gothic portico.

'Is that what is called pulling out all the stops?' asked Des with a grin. 'They rather let their hair down when they got to the end.'

'They certainly did,' Joan said with a broad smile. She reached over and kissed him. 'Happy Christmas, again.'

Let's get organised. Too nippy to hang around here.

'Just after one,' he said, checking his watch. 'I've booked dinner in the Plaza for seven so we've a few hours. Why don't we go over there to the Rockefeller Centre and get a coffee. We can watch the skaters.'

'Sounds good.' She took his hand.

They crossed Fifth Avenue and strolled towards the pedestrian zone which was crowded with holidaymakers. NYPD officers stood around chatting to each other good humouredly. A giant Christmas tree, smothered with tinsel and lights stood tall over the packed ice rink. Onlookers hung over the viewing platform with flashing cameras recording the happy faces of loved ones. Des looked around.

'There's one there,' he said, pointing to a cafe overlooking the rink.

Inside, their senses were assailed by the bubbling cauldron of colours, heat, heavy aroma of freshly roasted coffee, multi-lingual accents and perpetual motion.

'Sorry there aren't any tables free,' said a server.

Des slipped him a ten dollar bill.

'Oh here's one by the window,' the now smiling server pointed.

When their coffee arrived Des poured in some milk and stirred slowly. Right, quality time. He looked across at Joan.

'You were on to your folks this morning. All well?' Des nodded his interest.

'Oh yeah. They'd just finished eating. Bart answered. Sounded a bit squiffy. But Mummy was tip top. I promised her I'd bring her over to Lynda in Brighton before Easter.' She looked at him, checking.

'Before Easter?'

'Oh don't worry. You don't have to come. I presume that's alright with you?'

'Sure. You decide on when you want to go. Be able to get time off work I assume?'

'Oh yeah, I'm way ahead with my hours.'

He picked up his cup and began to sip it.

'Speaking of work, how's the job going? You were helping someone research someone.' He paused, 'Some medical guy.'

When she looked at him, her face seemed to have tightened.

'You don't remember his name, do you?' She shook her head. 'Bartholemew Mosse.'

'That's it. I forgot.'

He was aware she was looking at him closely.

'Yes you did forget, didn't you?'

'Sorry love. I guess I've been a bit distracted of late.'

'So I've noticed.'

In the silence that developed, he put his coffee back on the table and stirred it again.

Women.

'Look Des,' she continued after some moments, 'I don't want to be a spoilsport on our break, but I'm getting really concerned you're getting far too caught up in that bank of yours. You're coming home late, you're leaving early, and I don't think you're sleeping very well. You hardly ever talk to me, and when you do it's little more than a perfunctory politeness.'

'Ah that's a bit unfair.'

'It isn't really from where I'm sitting. Look, I don't want to harp on about it, but you really need to consider where it's all leading you.'

'Well it is my job. And anyway, I'm quite sure the problem is just a short-term one. I'll be able to work through it alright.'

Joan was holding her coffee in her hands with her eyes fixed on his.

'Maybe,' she said.

Move it along.

'Promise it won't last.' He managed a contrite smile and sipped his coffee. 'But to go back, just how is your job going?'

'Both Mr Mosse and my job are fine,' she replied her face softening. 'Mind you I was tempted to apply for a new post lecturing at Trinity College, but I let it pass.'

Good, that's over. She's made a fair point though. Must think about it a bit more when I get the chance.

'Yeah?' He pulled his chair closer to the table and leaned towards her.

'It had its attractions. More money and shorter hours to name two.'

'But you decided against having a go at it?'

'Yeah. I rather like what I'm doing. The challenge of helping people research projects is very satisfying. I wasn't convinced I'd find lecturing as personally rewarding.'

'Fair enough. But then,' he laughed lightly, 'you've always enjoyed a challenge.'

'Oh I do. As long as it's not beyond my reach.'

He tried to analyse her smile. More than a hint of a message there?

'And you?' Joan continued. 'You were on the phone to Helen. How's your Mum?'

'Much the same. The Alzheimer's is taking its toll. At least now the nursing home's looking after her, I don't feel too bad.'

'And how are the rest of them?'

'Oh Helen has the house full. The lads are all at home. I'd say the place is upside-down. We were right not to accept her invitation. She just doesn't have room for us.'

Joan eyes began to twinkle.

'You know I rather like being over here with you.'

She leaned over and took his hand.

She's happy. She likes New York at Christmas. Wonder how things would have been if we'd been able to have kids? But it wasn't to be. She accepted the facts when they told us. Still, it must still hurt at times.

'Tell me,' she asked, 'did you enjoy your Christmas Mass in St Patrick's?'

'Oh, I didn't think you'd be interested. Hardly your cup of tea is it?' He leaned forward, suddenly curious about her interest.

'Hey, just because I'm not into organised religion doesn't mean I can't visit a church once in a while.'

'Yeah?' his eyes questioning.

'Of course not. Going into one of them doesn't mean you must sign up for the package on entry, no more than going into Weirs means you're committing to buying one of their watches.'

'That's a bit cynical.' He peered at her, puzzled.

'I don't think I'm the cynical one around here. I like to think things out for myself and I find it very helpful to take other people's views on board before I draw conclusions.' He noticed her self-defence, and felt a pang of guilt for being the unintentional cause.

'Oops. Didn't mean to suggest that. Sorry.' He paused. 'But going back to that Mass, what did you make of yer man's homily? It was rather odd I thought.'

'Why?'

'Well, I thought given that it's Christmas Day he'd be preaching about the Bethlehem stuff, not the corny parable about the shepherd and the lost sheep.'

'Corny parable?' She looked at him with arched eyebrows. 'That's a rather odd view for someone educated in a monastery to take.'

'My education has nothing to do with it,' he replied, flustered. 'Okay, maybe corny isn't the right word. Irresponsible is more like it.'

'Irresponsible?'

'Yeah, leaving the ninety-nine sheep to fend for themselves. What if a wolf attacked them? Surely any shepherd worth his salt should have been prepared to write off one stray, a bad debt if you like, in the interests of the greater majority? I mean, I thought the whole Christmas message was about saving as many souls as possible.'

'You and writing off bad debts.' Joan shook her head. 'Can you never get away from boiling everything down to pounds, shillings and pence?' She sat back. 'Actually I thought he was onto a very sound idea. My guess is he'd reckoned quite a few of the congregation turn up only once a year, the strays as you call them, and it was them he was trying to reach. I mean if even a handful of those strays were listening to him, he'd consider his effort a success.' She looked directly into his eyes. 'Don't you think?'

He put his elbow on the table and cupped his chin in his hand. He nodded to her.

'Put that way, I guess you're right. You know I suppose if I'm honest with myself, I'd have to admit I wonder at times about my own motives for attending. I often think it's no more than an automatic exercise, like paying my life insurance premiums.'

'Des, we all have to do what we think is right. The important thing, as far as I'm concerned, is to try to make sure our decisions are informed ones.'

Wonder if that was meant for me? Either way I should practice it myself a bit more.

'And a bloody good fist you're making of it too. C'mon, let's go,' he added pushing back his chair. 'Let's stroll around a bit.'

'Sure.' She stood up and put on her coat. 'You know, I'm look forward to dinner at the Plaza.'

'Me too. To say nothing of Domingo in Aida at the Met on Saturday.'

Chapter 7

Des slumped into the chair at his desk and stifled a jet lagged yawn. He hummed a few bars of *Celeste Aida* as he glanced at his screen and saw the share price had risen to 120.

Back to work Dessie, Radames has been buried alive and the Fat Lady's stopped singing.

He reached for his keyboard and typed.

Alan, we need to talk urgently.

What now? Not much point banging on about the announcement. Damage done. Still, better give him a rollicking. Can't let him off altogether for ignoring my instructions. Even if it wasn't his fault.

An incoming message popped up.

Des, I'm free. Shall I come up now?

Knows he's overstepped the mark. Good.

Yes.

There was a gentle tap on his partly open door and Alan stuck his head around it, eyebrows raised.

'Come in,' Des nodded to the vacant chair by his desk. 'Did you have a good break?'

'Most enjoyable,' Alan said smiling, 'but much too short. And you? How was New York? Joan enjoy it?'

He's cool. Must realise I'm about to have a pop.

'Yeah, it was great. Thanks.' He looked Alan in the eye. 'Right, let get me get straight to the point. The announcement. I'm sure you understand I was, shall we say, unhappy?'

'Let me explain,' Alan began.

I doubt if you can.

'I tried to amend it as you asked Des, but the bottom line is Milo overruled me. He insisted the original text about maintaining the dividend be kept.'

Judas washes his hands. No, that was Pontius Pilate. The old trick of when you're caught out. Blunt the attack by accepting responsibility but blame the other guy.

'But I stressed I wanted it removed, to say nothing of dampening down the profits forecast. I mean if you weren't going to change the goddam thing, you should've let me know.' Des frowned.

'With all due respect, I would have if I could.' Alan raised his hands and spread them in a helpless gesture. 'But you insisted it had to go out before the break. And as I couldn't contact you, I'd no option but to send out Milo's version.'

'Well, I want you to know I'm not at all happy. If you and I are to work together, this better not happen again. Understood?'

'Understood.' Alan had a resigned look on his face.

Fair play to him. Knows when he's beaten, but he still held his ground. Didn't apologise either, didn't say sorry. I like that in him. Must remember to adopt the same tack in my dealings with Milo.

'Okay. Let's move on, shall we? The share price. You mentioned on the phone our broker knew something about unusual activity. What did you find out?'

'Not unusual activity as such. They say the market is guessing Milo's going to do his damndest to inject some sex into our operation, so they've been recommending it to their private clients. A few institutions are building positions also. So the price can only go up.'

'So, we don't have to concern ourselves about the share price. That's what our broker is saying?' Des raised his eyebrows and tilted his head to the side.

'In effect, yes.'

Des noticed Alan was looking elsewhere.

Something not computing here. Keep digging.

'You know I was sure our fundraising would hit it. But I see they've actually gone up even more.'

'You do appreciate, don't you Des, it's because of our dividend forecast.' Alan coughed lightly.

There was a sharp intake of breath from Des.

'Yeah, of course. Milo's unnecessary and bloody insane forecast. I suppose we'll just have to live with it.'

'Well, if that's it?' Alan rose.

Why does he want out of here so fast?

'No, hang on a minute.' Des motioned to Alan to sit down again. 'I want to know what our broker told you about who's been buying our shares?'

'Well, they pointed out of course they're not in a position to identify precisely who's behind every deal.'

'Yes, but you told me on the phone one of our staff had been buying. Who?'

Alan shuffled in his seat and coughed.

'Orla,' he said.

'Orla?'

'Yes. Apparently, she bought fifty thousand.'

'Fifty thousand? Where in the name of God did she get that kind of money?' Des looked about him, distracted. 'Oh, that doesn't matter.' He put his head in his hands. Insider information? Oh God. He looked up.

'When did she buy them?'

'The broker said the seventeenth, the day before we'd dinner in Arthur's club.'

'For Chrissake Alan, never mind Arthur's feckin' dinner. What's much more important is that it was the day before our board meeting. She must've got hold of the board papers, the Strategic Plan, and put two and two together. Oh God.' He looked about his office wildly.

'Maybe she didn't have access to the board documents.' Alan's eyes sought to placate.

'Maybe. But why then *did* she buy the shares?'

Alan shrugged his shoulders. 'I don't know. Who knows? Maybe Milo told her to.'

Suddenly Des felt numb. Insider Trading. A nightmare engulfed him. Charlie Bird and the television camera lights blazing, Gardai dawn raid, Milo being yanked off to the Bridewell. Evening Herald headline: *TOP BANKER ARRESTED.* Delight of the great unwashed. Joe Duffy's Liveline switchboard jammed. *'And tell me Mary why don't you feel sorry for him?'* Barstool know-alls, drooling over their pints. *'Do you know what I'm going to tell you? Did you see yer man O'Toole being bundled into the squad car on the box last night? Oh a right bowsey. Of course all bankers are just a shower of bastards.'*

'Christ Alan, if this gets out, there's no knowing what damage it could cause.'

Alan remained silent.

Des put his elbows on his desk and dropped his head onto his hands again.

'Right, I'll need to think about this.' He looked up with a weak smile. 'Thank you Alan, that will be all for now. I'll call you when I need you. And close the door behind you.'

He rummaged among the papers on his desk and waited until he heard his door click. He then picked up the phone and dialled.

'Arthur, I appreciate it's New Year's Eve, but I wonder could I pop over? Something I'd like to bounce off you. Good. At three you say? Thanks.'

*****

The gloomy post-solstice sky gave Ely Place a dismal appearance. It failed to bring cheer to the dirt brown Georgian buildings, despite the attempts of a few rays of sunlight to clear the chimneys of the deserted hospital in Hume Street.

Discreet location, nothing loud or brash. Just right for dealing with clients who don't want to be seen consulting legal eagles. Arthur doing a nice line in securing court orders, judgments, discreet divorce settlements, recalcitrant debtors. Gentlemen and Ladies all, of course. Hacks from the press never think of hanging out around here for a lead. No, wouldn't be able to pass Doheny and Nesbitt's over there. Filling their notebooks with economic forecasts and juicy weekend titbits. *'No Minister, I won't quote you, just informed sources'.* Locality also rather handy for Arthur with his club only a short sideways stagger across the Green after a port fuelled Friday lunch. No, no fool Arthur. Joan had him in one.

He rang the doorbell at number eighty-seven and was buzzed in.

'Des Peters,' he announced to the receptionist.

A lady of a certain age. And a certain religious persuasion. Shirt stiffly starched, buttoned to the neck. Collar must nearly choke her. Won't reveal any of Arthur's secrets.

'Mr Harford is expecting me.'

'Oh yes, please take a seat and I'll let him know you're here.'

From the reception room he could see the Gallagher Gallery, its concrete and glass façade looking dreary in the December dusk. A few magazines lay scattered on the table in front of him, *Horse and Hound*, *Country Life*, *Punch*, and a few newspapers. He picked up one, and pretended to read it. Eventually he was shown in.

'Ah, Des old man, good to see you,' Arthur beaming as he rose from behind a large mahogany file laden desk, 'and how are we today?'

Ruddy face. Good lunch. Club tie. Should get rid of those wine stains. Can get away with it in the circles he moves in I suppose. Probably finds it amusing to have to deal with lower mortals like me. Focus Dessie, You're on a mission.

'Just fine Arthur, just fine. It was good of you to...'

'Not at all. Please take a seat.' Arthur waved towards a chair at his desk. 'Good Christmas? How was New York? Jane enjoy it? Can't say I've been there myself since my student days.'

I told you in your club her name is Joan. But you were too busy boring her with your Captain Bligh crap.

Arthur laughed lightly.

'I prefer to hunt at this time of the year.' He paused. 'Now to what do I owe the honour of this visit, eh? Oh, and congratulations again on your elevation on the board. Good idea to have one of the staff help us in our deliberations.'

God, really establishing the demarcation lines. Just get on with it.

'Thanks Arthur. And I really appreciate you agreeing to see me at short notice. In fact I wasn't sure you'd be in today, what with the public holidays and all.'

'Not at all. Glad to be of service.' He beamed again.

Cliché slid in with the ease of a judge's pre-lunch custodial sentence.

Des leaned forward, his right elbow on the desk.

'It's probably only a niggle really, but I find this insider trading stuff a bit of a grey area. I'd appreciate it if you could give me some clarity?'

'Nothing, eh, nothing the matter at the bank, is there?' Arthur's eyes opened wide.

'Oh no, just a theoretical question.'

Arthur still studying me. Knows bloody well that's not true. But he won't thank me for making him aware formally there's jiggery-pokerry going on.

'Insider trading. Bloody stupid law if you ask me Des. No one wanted it except a few crackpot independents in the Dáil. Cranks. Only ones who'll be caught will be a greedy minnow or two. Mark my words. The bigger fish are always smart enough to hire themselves a decent lawyer and get off scot-free.' Arthur sat back and waved a dismissive hand.

Bigger fish like yourself.

'Quite. But I was wondering about the offence itself. What exactly constitutes insider trading?'

Meaning, what I really need to know is what I should do about my current suspicions.

'Well, as you know, in general terms the law makes it an offence for anyone to misuse privileged information, information not generally available to the public,' said Arthur nodding, professional to professional. 'The tricky part is interpreting some of this. That's what keeps me and my colleagues in the legal profession in business.' Arthur smiled to himself. 'And of course anyone found guilty of an offence could be facing a fine, or a jail sentence, or both.'

As Arthur spoke, Des was acutely conscious that he was being sized up.

'Des, this can be a delicate subject.' He paused. 'But if, for the sake of argument you were concerned someone in the bank had bought shares based on such information, there could be a problem.'

He knows.

'Oh no.' Des cursed himself for cutting in a bit too quickly. 'I was just wondering if such a case arose, how I should deal with it.'

Arthur's eyes hooded, alert. Like a cobra's.

'I see. Well the first thing you need to establish are the facts. Who dealt, when did they deal, and did they have access to privileged information?' Arthur nodded once more to Des.

'I see. Establish the facts.'

'Quite. These of course may not be easy to come by, so my advice would be to confront the individual concerned and record the outcome.'

Cover my ass. Mission accomplished.

'Record the outcome?'

'Exactly Des. Nine times out of ten there'll be no substance to your suspicions. But you never know. So just jot down a note of your conversation and keep it on file, as a purely precautionary measure. You never know who might come sniffing around at a later date. The Regulator for one.' He tilted his head back a fraction, his eyes fixed on Des. 'Just as well it's only a theoretical question.'

Those cobra eyes again. Knows bloody well I'm not giving the full picture.

'That's right Arthur. It's purely theoretical.' He tried to sound calm.

'Oh, and that's another thing Des. If by any chance those guys ever call you in, a word of advice.'

'Yeah?'

'Just answer the questions they ask. No need to volunteer anything over and above. Otherwise they'll feel obliged to dig deeper. Okay?'

'Okay. Thanks. Well, I'll be on my way then,' said Des as he rose.

'And a happy and successful New Year to you. Des.'

As they walked to the door, Arthur put his hand on Des's shoulder.

'You know I'm really delighted about your appointment to the board. Please feel free to drop in anytime you'd like a chat.' He paused. 'Anytime, Des.'

Come into my parlour, said the spider to the fly.

'Thanks Arthur, I appreciate your offer. I'll definitely take you up on it,' said Des resisting his impulse to run.

When he stepped out onto Ely Place the remaining sunlight had gone, and a chill north wind from Merrion Street hit him in the face.

*****

Des walked briskly along the dimly lit Hume Street and onto Stephen's Green. The park gates were already locked for the evening. Through the bar windows of the Shelbourne Hotel, he could see animated patrons raising champagne glasses and slapping backs.

He hurried onwards and down Dawson Street to avoid the shoppers and buskers, and pulled his scarf tighter. He knew he must confront the issue and had nothing to gain by procrastinating.

When he arrived at his office he called for Orla.

Need to tread carefully.

'Hope you'd a good break?' He smiled as she came in and motioned her towards a chair by his desk. 'How was the skiing?'

She was wearing an outfit he hadn't noticed before with the skirt cut well above her knees. He wondered if he had imagined she had an extra bounce in her step, but her eyes seemed wary.

'Oh we didn't do too much of that.' She laughed and crossed her legs.

We. Didn't do too much of that. Of what then? Don't even think about it Dessie.

'Good. Well whatever you did, you're looking great.'

'Thank you.' She laughed again.

A hint of nervousness there?

Des shifted uneasily in his chair.

'Orla, there's something I need to ask you. It's, eh, a little delicate.'

'Ye…ss?' Her smile dissolved into a slight frown.

'Don't worry. It's nothing personal.'

She looked at Des, her eyes questioning. 'I'll help you if I can.' She uncrossed her legs and tried to tug her skirt over her knees but it was too short.

'It's eh, come to my attention you bought some of our shares recently.' Des felt his shirt collar grow tight.

'That's right. Is it a problem?' She furrowed her brow.

'Hopefully not. It's just there's potential for an issue. It's probably nothing, but I'm afraid I have to ask you some questions.'

'Go ahead.' She was now looking at him intently.

'My information is you bought fifty thousand. Is that correct?'

'You've got your facts right. I did.' She folded her arms across her chest and was looking warily at him. 'Anything else? You're wondering where I got the money, are you?'

Des tried to look at her without catching her eye.

'Where you got the money to buy them is your business. I doubt if you robbed a bank.' He laughed nervously.

'No I didn't. No, it was money my aunt in Boston left me in her will. She died last summer you may remember.'

'Oh yeah, I'd forgotten.' He immediately regretted disclosing he'd thought about it. 'It's just you bought them immediately before we announced our share issue.'

'Yeah, I was lucky. I got them at 104. They've gone up a nice bit since then.'

'You were indeed fortunate,' said Des as he wrote in his pad.

Bought 50,000 on 17th @ 104. Board 18th!

Cut to the chase.

'Orla, sorry, but I have to ask you one other question. Did you have a specific reason to buy them?'

'Because Milo advised me to.'

Des felt his heartbeat increase and his palms become clammy. He looked again at the papers on his desk trying to calm himself. He looked up.

'Orla, we need to be clear here. Are you telling me Milo advised you to buy our shares the day before the board meeting?'

'Oh no.' She paused to think. 'It was a week or two before. I didn't have the money then. I only bought them when it arrived in my account.'

'I see.'

No, I don't. Could be true or false. Steady Dessie. Did she know about the share issue when she dealt?

He turned over a few pages on his desk in an effort to steady himself. 'Remind me, who exactly sees the board papers before they go out?'

'Well last month I collated the pack, the stuff Milo gave me. The management report, the financials, your report. Then he added more stuff of his own.'

Ah ha.

'Like what?'

'I didn't really see it, but I think it could have been his Strategic Plan.'

'So, you're telling me you haven't actually seen what's in the Plan?'

Orla shook her head. Des sat back looking at her.

Can't be certain she's telling the truth, but assume for now at least she is.

'Good. That's helpful. And thanks for the clarity.' He nodded to indicate their conversation had ended.

She stood up and headed for the door. When she got there she turned around.

'Des, I hope you don't mind me asking, but did I do something wrong?'

'No, I'm pretty sure there isn't a problem. It's just this inside information stuff. I need to be sure no one inadvertently broke any rules.' He forced a smile to her as she left the room.

Reasonable story. But still, whiffy. Milo. Shit. Another fine mess. Without the Laurel and Hardy humour unfortunately.

He reached for the phone and dialled.

'Milo, we need to talk.'

'Sure, but I'm a bit busy. Can it wait 'til Friday?'

'Not really.'

'Well I'm tied up right now but I'm being picked up here at eight for a New Year's Eve party. We could meet at say seven?'

'Seven it is then.'

*****

Milo was tidying away some files when Des arrived.

'Sorry for button-holing you like this Milo, but I need to clear up something.'

'Anytime. Shoot.' He gave Des a warm genial smile.

'There's no easy way to put this,' began Des and hesitated.

'Come on, out with it. We're 'in lodge' here anyway. What's on your mind?'

'It's about dealings in our shares ahead of our Stock Exchange announcement.'

'Yeah?' asked Milo with a quizzical look.

'It seems Orla's been buying and making herself some money along the way.'

Milo beamed.

'Good for Orla, smart girl. So where's the problem?'

God he's cool. Surely he realises. Cast your fly gently.

'There isn't necessarily a problem. It's just it doesn't look good. You know, market abuse, price sensitive info floating about, CEO's PA turns a fast buck, sort of thing?'

'Hang on, back up. You mentioned price sensitive info floating about. Like what?'

'News of the share issue. Orla bought ahead of our announcement.'

Milo furrowed his brow. 'I fail to see the connection. Sure she knew nothing about it.'

'Maybe she didn't Milo, but you did.'

'So?'

'Orla says you told her to buy them.'

Milo scratched his head, looked up at the ceiling and then at Des.

'I did?'

'Yes.'

'I don't remember telling her to buy them. When was I meant to have told her? Did she say?'

'She said a week or two ahead of the board meeting. You do realise this could be construed as a tip off?'

'A tip off? I don't see how it could. Let me think.'

Des watched Milo pace up and down the room.

I've one hell of a cool customer here. Certainly acting the innocent. Hope for all our sakes he is. Or is he trying to concoct an alibi?

Milo stopped and turned back to Des. 'I have a vague recollection of making some casual remark to her about the shares being a good buy. Let me think. You say a week or two before the board?'

'Look Milo, we've got to get the facts straight here. This has the potential to be serious. I mean we could be looking at an infringement of the insider trading law.'

'Oh for God's sake Des, don't make an inquisition out of it. You've got this out of all proportion. I told you I can't remember if I said anything to her. And even if I did, how the hell could it be construed to have anything to do with insider trading?' He scowled.

'Let's look at the facts. She says she bought them on your advice. Next thing we make an announcement on the Exchange. The price jumps. She makes a tidy profit. How do you think it looks?'

Milo's eyes narrowed.

'I don't give a goddam how it looks. Are we talking here about facts or about you jumping to conclusions? You're the accountant around here. You like facts. So let's stick to them.'

Des took a deep breath.

'Milo, the facts simply show that when you were in possession of insider information you encouraged her to buy the shares.'

'Hold on there. If, and I stress the if, I advised or encouraged her to buy the shares a couple of weeks before the board meeting, there's no way it could've been based on insider information.'

'Why not?'

'Because I only got the idea for the share issue just a few days before the meeting, not a few weeks. And even then I got the idea from you. You brought it up at our committee meeting.'

This is like trying to nail jelly to a wall. It was a hypothetical question I was answering, and thanks to you we've no minutes.

'*I* brought it up? No I didn't.'

'Yes, you did. It was when I was exploring how we should respond to a foreign bank coming in here.'

I'm being side-tracked here.

'Okay, let's park the reasoning behind *why* the decision was made.' Des paused to check Milo was in agreement. 'What I want to know is, are you sure you only formulated the capital raising plan just a day or two before the board met?'

'Absolutely.'

'So the possibility of the share issue simply didn't exist whenever Orla says you spoke to her?'

'Of course, I'm sure. Absolutely.'

'Good.'

'Des, let me be clear, I never, repeat never, will do anything illegal. I know at times I push boundaries but at least give me credit for not transgressing the law. Right?' Milo spoke in measured tones, his confidence evident.

Back off. He has you fair and square.

'Sorry for pushing you,' said Des nodding agreement with a weak smile. 'But you'll have to appreciate a key part of my job is to make sure we're clean as a whistle.'

'Precisely why I value you Des. I know your first loyalty is to the bank.' Milo returned Des's truce with a smile. He then looked at his watch.

'Okay, I'm glad we've cleared that up. I better be off. Enjoy your dinner and a Happy New Year.'

Des watched Milo spring from his seat and stride out of his office.

Your first loyalty is to the bank.

*****

'Home comes the hero.' Joan got up from her computer and kissed him. 'How was your re-entry? Better than you feared I hope?'

'Ah, could have been worse, I suppose.' He threw himself into an armchair and forced a smile. 'Sorry I'm a bit later than I thought I'd be.' He nodded to her computer screen. 'I thought you'd be getting ready to go around to the Doyle's. What time are we expected?'

'It won't take me very long.' She began to close down her computer.

'I was just doing some research for work. Need to re-engage brain myself.' She looked at him again. 'It wasn't really a good day for you, was it?'

'Bad enough, to be honest. I'd to try and sort out a problem with insider trading.'

'Sounds pretty serious.'

'Yeah, it certainly has the potential to be serious. It's one of those things where you have to start from a position where you think there might have been a murder, and until you can prove otherwise everyone's a suspect.'

'That *is* serious.' She hit the off button on her computer and looked directly at him.

'Yeah, I decided to consult Arthur on it.'

'And did he solve the problem for you?'

'Well it's not straightforward. I had to talk to him in riddles. I didn't want to name any names.'

'Why not? I mean going to a solicitor is like going to confession is it not? If you don't reveal all, you can't reap the full benefits?'

Only if you can trust who you're opening up to.

'One way of putting it I suppose, even if it's not absolution I need.' He smiled wistfully. 'Trouble is, Milo's on the fringes of it. I don't know who I can trust.'

'Sounds messy.'

'It is. Anyhow Arthur has advised me what to do.'

'Good. Well done.' She stood up and smiled.

'Yeah.'

Easy for her. Sees it as an open and shut case. Move on to next item on the agenda.

'Oh, and another thing. Remember we were talking about loyalty? Milo remarked that my first loyalty was to the bank.'

He watched Joan's smile fade.

'But you say it yourself, don't you?'

'Maybe. But I didn't like him having that view of me.'

'Did you think it was some sort of veiled threat?'

'Ah, I doubt it. Milo doesn't do veiled threats.'

No, he doesn't stab you in the back either. He just comes at you full frontal with a hatchet.

Chapter 8

Des was reviewing the December Risk Report when he heard a polite cough at the door. He looked up. Alan.

'Coming?' He asked.

'I thought the meeting was ten thirty?' Des glanced at his watch.

'No Des, ten. Milo wants to introduce the new marketing dame.'

Mmm. He'll have a hidden agenda, but too soon to expect any clues.

'Okay.' He rose and they went to the boardroom where Ed and Jerry were standing by the sideboard drinking coffee.

'Ah,' said Ed replacing his cup on his saucer. 'I was just saying to Jerry I don't see why Milo couldn't let things settle down a bit before he foisted his new *femme fatale* on us.'

Starting his New Year itching for a row. Probably got his belly full of domestic grief over Christmas.

'Hi guys,' Milo called from the doorway, 'can I introduce you to Dawn?' A smiling blonde in her early thirties followed him in.

Attractive. Good figure. Black well-tailored suit, cream silk shirt. Ed's supermarket check-out girl label definitely a misnomer.

'Hello,' she said with a Northern accent looking at the gathering.

'Why don't we all top up our coffee and sit over and then we can get down to business?' said Milo and introduced the team. He then asked Dawn if she would like to introduce herself.

She looked at each of them in turn before beginning.

'I guess you can tell from my accent, I'm from the North, Rostrevor in fact. I got my post grad at Queens and my Masters in Marketing from the London Business School.'

Matter of fact. Not boastful. Business-like.

'I did a two year internship with Bank of America in New York, and since then I've been with Tesco. Working on their expansion in the States.' She looked about the table at each of them.

Confident. Thought she'd be. Milo ain't stupid.

Milo gave the gathering a benign *that's my girl* smile before turning to her.

'Dawn, I'm sure the team would be interested in why you decided to leave your trans-Atlantic job to come and work with our modest bank?'

God, did no one ever tell you, Milo, you can't do modesty?

'A good question. I really enjoyed the challenge, but quite honestly the weekly commute was getting to me.' Des watched her looking around the table, assessing as she spoke how her arrival was being received. 'So when I heard on the grapevine you guys were on the lookout for a new Head of Marketing, I threw my hat in the ring.' She laughed and looked at Milo. 'When I got to the interview stage, I was very impressed by what you have to offer, and, well, here I am.'

Oh God. A mutual admiration society. Still, give her a chance though.

'Thanks Dawn. Now I'm sure there are lots of questions here.' Milo looked around the table. 'Who'd like to start?'

Wearing his bet-you-won't-catch-me-out-with–this-cookie smirk. Okay, start the ball rolling.

'Dawn, you're obviously welcome here, and I hope you enjoy the experience.' Des smiled and nodded to her.

'Why, thank you Des, I'm looking forward to it.' She returned his friendly gesture.

'I was wondering what your analysis of our bank is?'

'That's a pretty tough opening question on my first day,' she said with a false laugh. 'I think it'll take me a little while to understand how all your cogs mesh.'

Streetwise. Probably has done her desk research, but buying time until she gets a handle on the soft stuff. Yeah, politically astute.

'Fair enough, but what are your initial impressions?' Des pressed.

'Fair question. Well, what strikes me most is this is a solid if somewhat conservative bank. Steady growth suggests a loyal customer base. Your bad debt provisions are below average so you have a strong handle on your risks, or,' she laughed, 'your bad debt provisions are understated.'

'You need have no concerns on that front,' Jerry interjected, looking aggrieved.

Touchy, touchy. Ed's the one who should feel threatened. Maybe we're all vulnerable.

'Sorry Jerry. Didn't mean to imply…' She looked at him, her eyes contrite.

Ed coughed. 'So, would you put us in the *if it ain't broke don't fix it* category?'

'A great question Ed, so why try to fix it, indeed?' She looked at Milo, who nodded to her. 'But we need to analyse our market. If we're happy it's stable, great, there's nothing for us to fix. But if we suspect it might be changing, we need to consider how we're going to react.'

'As far as I'm concerned,' interjected Milo, leaning forward, 'there's a seriously important issue here. The board is now of the view we need to become much more market responsive, meaning, be better attuned to what our customers want. This neatly leads to the question of what business we're in.' He turned to Dawn. 'You have some views on this you might share with the team?'

The board is now of the view. You mean you've persuaded them to change their position.

'Sure.' Dawn drew the sleeves of her jacket up a couple of inches. 'The relevant question is, what business are we in?'

About to hit her stride.

There was an exchange of glances around the table.

'My guess is you're thinking the answer is pretty obvious, we're in the banking business. Right?' She paused for effect. 'But what does that mean?'

'Loans. Deposits. Cheque books.' said Ed, sharply.

'You've just listed our three main products Ed, right?' Dawn asked.

'Yes. It's what our customers want, why they deal with us.' He sat back, his eyes radiating exasperation.

'Are you sure?' She paused. 'Or maybe they deal with us because what they really want is a new car? Or they want their savings to be secure? Or they want to pay their bills with the minimum of hassle?' She looked around the table. 'My contention is what we offer is not itself what they want but the *means* to what they want.'

'It's a kind of odd way of looking at it if you ask me,' said Ed, sitting back and folding his arms.

Milo sat looking on twiddling his pen, a ghost of a smile playing on his lips.

'Look at it another way,' continued Dawn. 'My friends in the insurance business tell me people don't buy life insurance. It has to be sold to them.' She looked around the table and laughed. 'Of course calling it *life insurance* must be the greatest mislabelling of all time. But then I suppose if it was called death insurance, which is what it really is, it would be a pretty hard sell.'

Milo gave a that's-my-girl chuckle.

She's smart. Clever boxing here. Wonder where she's going with this?

'Charles Revson, the guy who owned Revlon, the cosmetics outfit, was once asked what business they were

109

in and his answer was "in our factory we manufacture cosmetics, but in the stores we sell hope".'

'It strikes me as a rather cavalier way for a respectable Scandinavian manufacturer to talk about his business,' said Ed, his voice rising.

Milo put down his pen.

'Ed, I think Dawn's message is we should be looking at ourselves as our customers see us, not from the inside as providers of products.'

'Exactly,' said Dawn, 'because if we don't, we run the serious risk of missing out on new opportunities, opportunities for greater profits.'

'Can you give us an example of what you have in mind?' asked Milo.

As if you don't know.

'My view is that if we're to get a bigger bang for our buck, well, for a start, we should ask ourselves are we optimising the potential of our branch network? Maybe we should expand our customer offer.'

'Such as?' Milo asked.

'Offer life insurance and pensions?' Dawn appeared to consider her own question.

'But,' said Ed, his face becoming agitated, 'our staff are trained bank officials, not greasy insurance salesmen.'

Bloody fool can't even see he's being ensnared.

'Ed, my point is if it's a financial service and our customers want it, why shouldn't we sell it to them if it improves our bottom line.' Dawn exuded reasonableness. 'I mean that's why we're here, isn't it?'

'But it's not banking,' Ed said with determination through gritted teeth, and shook his head.

'So, let me get this straight,' Milo cut in, 'Your argument, Dawn, is we should think of ourselves as being in the financial services business, not just pure banking?'

You might be fooling the others with your Punch and Judy show guys, but you ain't fooling me.

'Exactly,' Dawn nodded vigorously. 'In a nutshell, we're talking about providing the best financial experiences our customers could wish for.'

Oh God. We're now into providing experiences. An experience in marketing bullshit more like. But still, there's a good idea behind it.

Milo looked at his watch.

'I suggest we take a break. I need to make a few calls. Shall we reconvene in say forty minutes? We can then look at what this means for our different business units.'

Discussion closed. Neat double act though. Redefine the business, and the customer better make sure he *caveat emptors*.

*****

Des was on his way back to the boardroom when he met Alan and Orla having a confab in the corridor. Alan immediately caught him by the elbow.

'A word?'

'Sure.'

'I've a request from one of the journos. Noel Nash of the *Daily News*. Wants to do an interview with you.'

Reporters. Untrustworthy shower. Play safe.

'Why me? Why not Milo? It's his domain surely?'

'No, he wants you. He's probably the sharpest in the finance space. Knows the difference. Doesn't buy the usual spin. Thinks he'll get a better angle from you than from Milo.' Alan nodded. 'Do your image no harm Des. "New COO takes the helm", stuff. Yeah?'

'Hmm, I'm not sure.'

One false move.

'Noel's really anxious to do it. You can trust him, which is more than I can say for some of the other hacks. I'll sit in if you want.'

'But where's the upside for us in it?'

'Well it's always a good idea to keep a positive image out there. The real risk is if we don't play the game, they might think we're trying to hide something. C'mon, you'll be fine.'

'Okay, I'll do it. But tell Noel it'd be helpful if he could give some pointers in advance of the issues he wants to cover.'

'Right, I'll set it up. Thanks.'

*****

'My young daughter came home from school the other day and asked me how do you eat an elephant?' said Milo when the meeting reconvened. He looked around the table. 'And you know what her answer was? You cut it up into little pieces.'

Des fought to contain a smirk, as he watched Ed roll his eyes.

'The point is,' continued Milo, 'the board has approved our Strategic Plan which involves quadrupling our profits, and we've got to figure out how we're going to deliver. They've done their bit and doubled our share capital. Now it's our turn, quadrupling profits.' He looked at his jotter, and then around the table again. 'As a starting point, I'd like to suggest as a first cut at our elephant we set a twelve month target of doubling our bottom line, and then push on from there. Okay?' He rubbed his hands and looked at Jerry. 'So, let's start with our loan book. Double it over the next twelve months. Thoughts?'

'I'd say it was virtually impossible.' Jerry's voice was calm, but his face betrayed shock.

'Impossible? Which bit, doubling our loan book, or the time frame?'

'Lending the money out would be the easy bit, that is if we ignored our credit assessment criteria. Getting it back would be a different kettle of fish though.'

'Surely that's a rather sweeping statement?'

For a moment, they held each other's eyes in silence.

112

Jerry was about to respond when Milo held up his hand to stop him.

'Going back to what Dawn was saying earlier about our customers' personal needs, there must for instance be scope to squeeze extra profits through expansion of our credit card business.'

Uh-uh, show time.

Jerry seemed to consider.

'Maybe.'

'I mean, just how often do we review personal limits?'

'When our customers request them.'

'And do we turn down many?'

'Very few.'

'So if we're looking for a quick boost to profits, it seems to me we should say, double existing limits across the board?'

'But we just can't go around increasing credit card limits without our customers asking us to,' Ed interjected, his face flushed.

'I don't see why not?' Milo responded with a dismissive shrug. 'They don't have to take us up on it if they don't want to.'

'But we can't act unilaterally just like that.'

Milo looked at Ed, his frustration obvious. 'Ed, I think you told me your lady wife Lorraine has a Clancy's charge card. I don't know what her limit is, but are you telling me they couldn't double it they wished? Or for that matter, do you think she'd object if they did?'

Des noticed Alan trying to stifle a titter.

'Milo, you can't compare us to Clancy's. For God's sake, all they do is sell jumpers and lino. This is a bank we're running here.' Ed's eyes were dancing.

'They mightn't be a bank, but they seem to be generous offering out credit to anyone who walks in off the street.'

Surely you can't get merchandise on tick just by asking for it?

Milo looked around the silent table.

'I believe I've made my point,' he said, and looked across the table to Jerry.

'This is your area, so I'd like you to review the implications of doubling the limits.'

Jerry coughed lightly.

'It'll take a little time.'

Milo had shifted his attention to his notes but immediately looked up.

'Well we don't have the luxury of time, and this action point is a priority.' He turned to Dawn. 'You might give him a hand. I need this done as a matter of urgency.'

Des noticed an exchange of glances between them.

'Fine.' Dawn picked up her biro and took some notes. 'Incidentally, I was thinking of another angle. Market research supports the view that credit card holders don't pay attention to the interest they're charged. In fact, very few of them can actually quote the rate.'

'Aha.' Milo looked up. 'So you think there could be scope to increase our charges then? Law of Economics stuff, supply and demand?'

How to teach a parrot economics? Get it to repeat supply-and-demand.

'Yeah. Of course we'd have to tell the customers we were doing it, but my guess is very few of them would go so far as to cancel their card.'

'Good point,' said Milo smiling. 'Jerry, can you do some sensitivity analysis on how much extra we could get away with?'

As W C Fields said, "never give a sucker an even break".

Milo scribbled some notes and then looked up again.

'Now, let's move on shall we? I was thinking when Dawn was talking earlier about her friend the Swedish cosmetic guy selling hope in his stores. Customers always want new cars, but we don't give out that many car loans, do we Jerry?'

'Not really. Most of them avail of deals offered in the showrooms.'

'And I presume it's a reasonable guess the showroom guys get an extra commission for selling a loan with the new car, right?' Milo was nodding to Jerry seeking confirmation.

'Em, right.' Jerry sat back, his face resigned.

'So, what I'm thinking is, if we offer the salesman a juicier kickback than our competition, he'd steer loan business our way, yeah?'

D'Artagnan calls for his musketeers.

'But you're forgetting it would push up the monthly repayments.'

Milo snorted.

'Jerry. I doubt if anyone buying a car would notice. Anyway, we could muddy the waters by changing the other numbers.' He paused. 'If we lengthened the term by say a year, the monthly repayments would actually look cheaper. Indeed, we could bump up our interest charge as well. Everyone would be a winner.' He sat back.

Not the poor sod paying more than he should be. Yep. W C Fields got it in one.

'Let's make this the second action point.' Milo turned to Des. 'Can you run some simulations and see what might be feasible? Dawn, you might do some research on breaking into the motor dealers market directly.' He looked at his watch and shook his head.

'Now can we move on, *please*? Right, I want to look at our lending for property development. Jerry, I think it is fair to say we're not a significant player. I take it that you agree?'

'Sure. To be one we'd need a deep pocket so that we could follow our money if a problem arose. Otherwise we could be washed out of a deal.'

'But our increased share capital should be a big help?'

'In a way, yes. But you still have the question of risk, and our appetite to take it on.'

Fair play, sees what's coming, but not going to roll over too easily.

Milo seemed to consider Jerry's response. 'But maybe our low risk appetite's hurting our profits?' He raised a querying eyebrow to all present.

Was that a wink he gave Dawn?

'It depends on how you manage your risk,' said Jerry.

'Okay. Let's talk about security cover. What's the norm now for a development?'

'It varies, depends on who, what, and where.' Jerry shrugged his shoulders. 'But I'd say typically a loan is for sixty-five to seventy per cent of the value of the property.'

'Why not higher? Seventy-five to eighty per cent?'

'Higher risk obviously.'

'Surely if the security for a loan is backed up by a valuation by a reputable estate agent, our risk is minimal, if not downright non-existent?'

Reputable estate agent. Definitive oxymoron.

'Maybe. But we also have to consider who we're lending to.'

Sound man Jerry. Still sticking to his guns.

'Yeah, but at the end of the day if the borrower defaults, we don't care who he is. We simply seize the property, and clear the debt by selling it to the highest bidder.'

'Milo, you have to appreciate what we're talking about here is prudent lending.' A flash of anger crossed Jerry's face.

'One man's prudence can be another man's opportunity,' said Milo waving his hand. 'I'm thinking of what's in the best interests of our shareholders.'

Which neatly coincides with the value of your share options, Milo, doesn't it?

Milo rolled his pen between his fingers for some moments before speaking again.

'Okay, here's what we'll do. Another action point Jerry. We'll get in the bigger players for a series of lunches.' He glanced at Dawn. 'You might join us as well. This'll give us a good handle on what we must do to crack the market.' He looked at his watch. 'I suggest we take a break and resume here at, say two?' He nodded to the team and rose.

*****

Des was going over the meeting as he sipped a coffee in The Oval Bar.

Interesting point Dawn made. Looking at things from the customers' perspective. They see us as solving their problems. Good conundrum. Is selling a car a means to making money on a car loan, or is a car loan a means to making money selling a car? And the discussion on credit card limits. Milo must be wrong. The issuers can't be that lackadaisical, can they? Why not test the water Dessie?

He finished his coffee and stepped out onto the street.

In Clancy's furniture department he was looking at a dining room suite when he heard a voice at his elbow.

'Very serviceable, Sir. Is it for a house or an apartment, if I may ask?'

Des glanced up at the salesman.

'Eh, an apartment I'm buying. I'm just checking things out at the moment.' Des nodded towards the suite. 'Yes, this one looks about the right size. Four chairs is it?'

'The table extends to accommodate six place settings should you need them.'

'Good. I see the price is marked down to fifteen hundred in your sale?'

'Yes, Sir. A particularly good bargain if I may say so.'

If it was, you wouldn't be flogging it at half-price.

'Yes, so it seems to be.' Des pursed his lips. 'Tell me, I was wondering if it would be possible to open a charge account for it perhaps?'

'You'd have to fill out a form,' said the salesman eyeing Des's business attire. 'But I wouldn't think you'd have any difficulties, Sir.'

'I don't suppose you'd know how much credit I could get, would you?'

The salesman looked over his shoulder, and dropped his voice.

'Once you confirm you've a regular income and the right address. I'd say they'll give you all of it.'

'You know,' Des paused, 'it would be very handy if I could get some furnishings here as well. Curtains, maybe the carpet. Do you think I could include those on my charge card?'

The salesman gave Des a knowing wink.

'Oh I'd say so, Sir.'

'Umm, say, three thousand. Do you think I could push it to seven, if I kitted out the bedrooms also? Buy the lot here?' He smiled broadly.

The salesman's eyes moving like fruits on a slot machine. Commission must be worth a week in the Canaries to him.

'Sir, we try very hard to make our customers happy. I'd say you're good for seven. Just let me get you a form to complete and I'll look after the rest.' He retreated, smiling as he went.

I'll look after the rest. Probably already singing *Ole Ole Ole* in anticipation of sitting in front of a large jug of iced sangria, and ogling topless nymphs.

'Oh, just one last question,' asked Des when the salesman returned. 'What interest rate do you charge?'

The salesman shook his head.

'Interest? Oh no, we don't charge interest, Sir.'

'No?'

'Oh no Sir, we value our customers too much. We're not like bankers you know. There is, of course, a small administrative charge, but it's just to cover the paperwork.'

Des put the form in his pocket.

'I'll have a look around your carpet department and be back to you. Thank you, you have been most helpful.'

Good God, Milo's right. Seven grand credit just like that. All you've got to do is ask for it.

*****

When he arrived in the boardroom the others were assembled. Milo looked up from his notes.

'I think we've covered most of the ground, so let's see what we still have to clear up. Des, how are you getting on with your analysis of the interbank market stuff?'

Needs another week. Probably not acceptable to Action Man here. Just take a few short cuts.

'Two or three days should do it.'

Milo scribbled.

'Right, that's our fourth action point.' He looked at Ed. 'We're now over to you. Our deposit book. What can *you* do for the cause?'

'Our branch network works very diligently at securing a loyal and satisfied customer base. Mind you it isn't easy at times with the competition poaching our business with offshore tax schemes.' Ed spoke as a man who didn't underrate his self-importance.

'I appreciate that Ed, and we're eternally grateful to you and your colleagues.'

Milo, your irony is lost on yer man.

'But,' Milo continued, 'I want to hear your thoughts about how we're going to get our numbers up.' He turned to Dawn. 'Have you any ideas to help Ed with this?'

'We could pay a higher rate to win new large deposits. Of course we'd run the risk of cannibalising some existing business, so we'd need to be very selective how we do it.'

'If we're prepared to pay higher interest rates,' interjected Jerry, 'why not pay it to everyone?'

Milo sat up with a start.

'Ah lads, be realistic. If you go up to a fast food joint in Grafton Street and ask for a burger and chips, they're hardly going to say "If I were you I wouldn't do that. Go up to the Shelbourne and they'll give you a much more nourishing meal".' He glared around the table.

Jerry and Ed looked on with stony faces and Alan spluttered a laugh.

Dawn leaned forward, arms on the table.

'Well, my view on this is simple. We should seriously consider any initiative where borrowing from depositors costs us less than whatever Des has to pay in the interbank.'

'But surely we have to factor in the costs of running the branch network?' asked Ed.

Milo threw his biro onto the table.

'Oh for God's sake Ed, your branch network is a fixed overhead we're stuck with. It's clear as day Dawn is making a fair point.' He picked up his biro and scribbled some notes. 'Right, we've spent enough time on this. What I want is for you Ed, and Dawn, to produce a proposal which will allow us to be more flexible on the deposit rates we pay. Understood?'

'Understood,' said Ed, scowling.

'Right, are there any other issues we should look at before we wrap up?' Milo looked around the table, and his eyes rested on Dawn.

Uh-huh. Hidden agenda?

'Just one if I may,' said Dawn.

'Shoot,' said Milo.

Dawn looked around the table and her eyes finally rested on Des.

'Have you ever considered offering offshore deposit accounts?'

Des felt an onrush of blood. He struggled upright in his seat trying to frame a coherent response.

'You're asking about us offering offshore accounts?' he managed.

Christ. That's a stick of dynamite she's just chucked in. Why he hired her? Think.

'No,' he continued, 'the bank's policy is not to offer offshore facilities.' As he spoke, he could feel his heartbeat rising.

'Why not?' Dawn persisted. 'I mean Ed has already said he's losing deposits to them.'

'Dawn,' said Milo interjecting, 'have you something specific in mind?'

Just what have they cooked up? Oh God.

'Well, it seems to me that it would be a heck of a lot easier for Ed to build his deposit book if he had access to *some* offshore facility.' Her eyes were defiant as she looked around the table. They eventually settled on Milo. 'If it helps I could do a bit of digging. I think I should be able to come up with something we could at least give some consideration to?'

They've concocted an offshore tax wheeze. We could land in serious do-dos with both the Regulator and tax man. Dessie you're responsible for risk, so you're going to have to nail this good and proper. But how? Best if I don't go in with my hobnailers until I understand the detail or I could blow my chance. Here's what I'll do. Analyse and deconstruct the proposition, and then shaft it with a persuasive argument at the board.

'Dawn, all suggestions that help to dissect our elephant are welcome.' Milo scribbled. He then looked around the table with a patriarchal smile. 'So thank you all for your contributions. We've a few really constructive action points here, so I think we're well on the way to filling in some of the blanks in our Strategic Plan. The meeting is closed.'

There should be a skull and crossbones on the cover of that bloody Plan of his.

Chapter 9

'I've just been talking to Noel,' said Alan, pulling up a chair beside Des's desk.

'Noel?'

'Yeah, Noel Nash the journo I was telling you about. He suggests coming in later this week. How would that suit you?'

Des looked at his diary.

'Would four on Thursday suit d'you think?'

'Oh he'll make himself available.'

'You were saying he's good?'

'Yeah. Can be a bit off-putting at first. Quite casual, acts the gobdaw a bit, but don't be put off. Worked on Wall Street in his early days.'

'Oh.'

Hope I'm not walking into something here.

'Is there anything in particular I need to bone up on?'

'Not really. What he's interested in is your take on the strategic stuff. Where the whole banking industry is going. I can ask for it be off-the-record if you like. You'll be fine.'

'Right. I'll put it in my diary.'

*****

Des sized up Noel when he arrived the following Thursday.

Dishevelled. Could do with a haircut. Jacket crumpled. Alan said not to be put off.

Alan introduced them, and Noel gripped Des's hand.

'Thanks. I appreciate you agreeing to this.'

Kerry accent. Cute boys those.

'Not at all. When Alan here asked me to meet you, I was more than happy to oblige. Now, how can I help?'

Noel opened his satchel and took out a notebook.

'I thought we'd start with your share issue,' the journalist said.

'Sure.'

'Your press release referred to *exciting new opportunities*. I'm wondering if you're thinking of buying another bank, maybe overseas?'

God. In your face from the off.

'Ah no, no. It's just with Ireland being the fastest growing economy in Europe, we want to be ready for the inevitable good lending opportunities that will arise.'

'Good opportunities, you say.' Noel laughed. 'Sounds like code for mixing it with the big boys? Is that not a bit out of your league?'

Slow this guy down.

'I wouldn't put it in those terms.'

'But you've just doubled your share capital. It seems to me a logical next move?'

He's watching me closely. Keep calm. Shift focus.

'Our first duty is to optimise shareholder return.'

'Are bigger profits a dirty word? No, ignore that, not a question.' He laughed as he jotted down some notes. 'And do you intend to focus on any particular sectors?'

'Ah now, I can't be letting you in on trade secrets.'

'Fair enough. But if I suggested you'd an eye on say, property development, or personal borrowing, would you contradict me?'

Des looked to Alan who cleared his throat.

'We'd prefer not to comment on specifics. But you wouldn't be too wide of the mark if you speculated those sectors might be included in our list of potential targets.'

Noel jotted down more notes. He scratched his head.

'You mentioned the economy has been the fastest growing in Europe. Some might argue this growth rate is not sustainable, so maybe now is the wrong time to be upping your lending?'

Be careful. This Kerryman worked on Wall Street. Could be using Colombo's trick of asking a question to confirm the answer he's already figured out.

'We can only take our market as we find it. If we're presented with sound lending opportunities by trusted customers, we'd be foolish not to give them serious consideration.'

'So, you judge each new loan opportunity on its individual merits?'

'Of course,' Des nodded his agreement.

'And you don't operate any limits on any one borrower or market sector?'

This guy understands the first principles of banking. Maybe better than we do.

'No, I didn't mean to imply we'd be imprudent. Of course we take these factors into account. In fact, sometimes we've been accused of being over-conservative.'

'Yeah, but that was then. You've put "Tiger" in charge now.' He laughed to himself. 'A marketing guy through and through. Presumably the big share issue was his idea?'

'That would have been a board decision,' said Des, glancing at Noel as he scribbled.

Good God, several pages filled. Watch your step here.

'But Milo would have proposed it, yeah? I mean they'd hardly have pushed it through without his say so?'

'Fair comment.'

Noel scribbled some more and then looked at Des.

'I understand you'd thrown your hat in the ring for the CEO job. Were you surprised when Milo got the nod?'

Des felt his stomach heave. The image of Milo's triumphant grin flashed again.

'That's a leading question and I don't think we need to answer it,' said Alan interrupting. 'C'mon Noel, you agreed you'd play by the rules.'

'Okay, sorry, won't do it again,' said Noel, with a smirk. 'Your press release also said you'd pay the same dividend on your increased capital. Pretty ballsy commitment, isn't it?'

'You're not quite right there. It was more like hope to maintain the dividend level.'

'Ah lads,' Noel laughed. 'You might fool some people with such lingual gymnastics, but the three of us know it really means the same thing. If you don't follow through on your promise, the market will assume your bank is in trouble. So, to give your profits a quick boost, you've no real option now other than lend aggressively.'

This shagger's done his homework alright. Play cool.

'I wouldn't agree with your choice of words. As I said earlier, we're naturally prudent in our lending practices. And as for maintaining our dividend, yes it will be challenging, but the board's confident we can deliver.'

Noel put down his notebook and scratched his head.

Another Colombo trick.

'You keep referring to the board. But you're on it now, the decision making process?'

'Of course. The board has collective responsibility.'

'But you yourself, Des. You're Milo's Deputy, right?'

'Correct.'

'So if he walks under a bus in the morning, you take over, right?'

Des became aware he was perspiring and his tie felt tight. He tried to laugh.

'I don't think Milo is planning anything along those lines at the moment.'

'But if he did,' persisted Noel, 'it would be up to you to run the show, right?'

'That would be a matter for the board.'

'Of course.' Noel looked at him directly. 'But it would be reasonable to assume they'd look to you, yeah?'

Des felt he needed a drink of water but didn't want to appear to be under pressure.

'In the first instance, of course.'

'Of course.'

Noel scribbled for a couple of moments and then looked up.

'And as COO, what are your other responsibilities?'

'Why, the general operations of the bank.'

More like firefighting while Milo gads about.

'That presumably means you're responsible for risk?' Noel was looking at him closely.

'Yeah.'

'And compliance?'

'Yeah.'

'And internal audit?'

Setting me up?

'Noel, if you don't mind me saying so,' Des frowned, 'this feels like an inquisition, not the interview I thought you wanted.'

Noel put his hands up.

'Sorry, didn't mean it that way. I'm trying to understand your role. I'll put my question a different way. If the Regulator has any questions to ask, you're the "go to" guy. Right?'

Ouch.

'Noel, let me put all this in context. As a matter of policy, we take our responsibilities very seriously and are prudent in the way we conduct our business. As for communications with the Regulator, yes I'm the usual contact person.'

'Of course, the Regulator. Our friend with the light touch. So light I wonder does anyone even notice if he exists anymore.' Noel smirked. He held up his hands. 'No, I'm not asking you to comment.' He closed his notebook. 'Thanks Des. I really appreciate your time.'

'Sure.'

As they walked to the door Alan turned to Noel.

'You know you wouldn't want to pay too much heed to the naysayers who'd have you believe the Celtic Tiger will self-destruct.' He laughed.

'Maybe not, but some commentators out there, you know, the Doheny and Nesbitt School of Economics types, think the whole thing is wildly overheating. They think the financial services system has become one giant casino, and it'll all end in tears.'

Alan raised his hand.

'Ah now Noel, there are flyboys around in every industry, but we're talking here about a solid bank. We don't get hoodwinked by cowboys.'

Noel laughed.

'Yeah, everyone knows Milo wouldn't take prisoners.'

'Yeah,' said Des as he shook Noel's hand.

Des was looking out the window when Alan returned.

'So, Des, what did you think?'

'I didn't like him trying it on about the succession stakes. A bit out of order I thought.'

'Ah, he can't resist trying to take a rise. That's just Noel. But otherwise?'

'A little too close for comfort really, zoning in on our lending plans.'

'Don't worry about it. Any half clued in journo could work out the only way we can make our numbers is by bumping up our lending. No, Noel's much more interested in you.'

'How do you mean, me?'

'What he's really trying to work out is how you're going to manage Milo.'

'How I manage Milo?'

'Yeah Des. If you're strong enough to keep Milo's excesses under control.'

'God, you think so? Is it that obvious?'

'It's been pretty obvious to all of us ever since you were appointed COO.'

*****

Des sat in silence at their dining table, slowly chewing a piece of meat. Joan was drinking a glass of wine and watching him.

'Something on your mind?' She asked.

'Sorry.' He put down his knife and fork.

'It's really something I have to think through. Something occurred to me during an interview I was doing today with a journalist.'

'You don't usually do press interviews. How come?'

'Alan set it up.'

'Why didn't the journalist ask Milo?'

'Oh he said the journo particularly wanted me.'

Joan hesitated before she spoke.

'Sounds a bit odd to me. I mean Milo is very much your front of house man. Are you sure Alan didn't have some ulterior motive?'

Never thought of that. Don't show.

'Ah no. Probably just trying to ingratiate himself with me.' He nodded in self-confirmation. 'Anyway what I was going to say was the exercise made me uncomfortable.'

'In what way?'

'For starters, I didn't like his line of questioning.'

'How do you mean?'

'He seems to have worked out pretty well what we're up to.' He shrugged.

'But you're not up to anything as you put it, are you?'

'Em, no. But I was uncomfortable fobbing him off with the party line. Wanted to sound a lot more confident about what we're doing than I really am.'

Joan sipped her wine.

'Like what?'

'Well at one point I was trying to emphasise our prudence, but I doubt if he was really buying it.'

'Why not?'

'He's worked out we're going to have to lend out a hell of a lot more money. That's a pretty accurate assessment, but I can't admit it because it raises questions around our tolerance for risk.'

'So why are you doing it if you shouldn't?'

'It's not my idea, its Milo's. If he gets his way, he'll have us like hamsters on a treadmill. To hit our profit target, we've to lend more. To lend more, we've to take more risks. And when the risks keeps going up...' He trailed off and shook his head.

Joan topped up his glass, studying him as she did so.

'Would it be fair to suggest it's not so much the interview that's got to you as the fact you're uncomfortable with the direction the bank is taking?'

How does she manage to keep zoning in on the kernel of things?

'I'm not sure if it's that, or my role in it. But one thing I am sure about. The interview has brought home to me some realities I've been pushing back on.'

Joan took another sip.

'Sounds like there's a gap between what you're doing and what you think is right.'

'Yeah, you're right.' He picked up his glass and put it down again. 'You know at one point the journo implied we were turning the bank into a casino.'

'Quite a few of people think that about banks in general,' she said, matter of factly.

'And me a croupier?' He tried to smile, but he knew it lacked conviction.

'Of course not.' She put down her glass and looked him in the eye. 'Look Des, I'm concerned about you ever since Milo took over. You've become extremely restless. It's not like you at all.'

'Sorry, I'll do my best to manage that. At least he's paying me well so I shouldn't complain.'

Joan looked at him for some moments before she spoke.

'The money might be fine, but I think you're in danger of becoming detached from the Des I know.'

'How do you mean?'

'Your old self, what you value, is getting pushed aside by the excitement of the chase.'

Never thought of that.

'A fair point. I'll bear it in mind.'

'Do that.' She looked at him in the eyes. 'You do realise if things don't change, you may have to consider your position in there?'

'Ah now, I can hardly turn my back on the place.' Des shook his head. 'Forget Milo, I owe it to the bank, particularly now.' He picked up his glass and looked at her. 'I'm indispensable to them.'

'Des, the graveyard is full of indispensable people,' she responded, looking at him to make sure he was listening to her.

'Ah, you don't understand.'

'Maybe not. But if you feel at any stage things are getting out of hand, you can always turn your back on it. We'll get by alright.'

'Ah it won't come to that.'

She doesn't really get it. I can't just walk away and leave everyone at Milo's mercy.

Chapter 10

'I was wondering,' Dawn asked Des on the phone, 'if I could drop by? I want to run something by you.'

'Sure.'

'Sorry about this,' she said, when she arrived with a bundle of files, 'but I'm trying to get my head clear on this offshore idea, Project Coral we're calling it.' She placed her papers on Des's desk, sat, and crossed her legs.

We're. Milo's bought in.

'I'd like to get a steer from you before I put anything on paper to the committee.'

You mean Milo's told you to make sure you've got me sucked in.

'Sure.' He smiled as he looked at her.

New outfit. Does her figure justice. Probably has a string of suitors.

'Well,' Dawn began, 'the problem we're dealing with here is really very straightforward. Our depositors hear on the grapevine they can avoid tax on their nest eggs if they have an offshore account. Our competition offer them, but we don't. The upshot is we're being creamed.'

'Go on.' Des nodded.

'What's really hurting us is that it's the very cheap money we're losing.'

He sat back watching her.

'So, have you come up with a solution?'

'The obvious thing to do is to set up an offshore subsidiary. That way, any tax issues would be the customer's problem, not ours.'

Don't show your hand until you find out more.

'So you think that's the route to go?'

131

'Actually, I don't.' She shook her head.

So what's she got up her sleeve?

'No?'

'Because apart from the fact we might prefer not to have to look for approval from the Regulator, we could have our auditors jumping up and down.' A faint smile formed around her lips. 'But, I think I've identified another option.'

Aha. Getting there.

'Another option?'

'Yeah, Des. We'd put in place a warehousing arrangement with an existing offshore bank.'

Distinctly whiffy.

'A warehousing arrangement? I'm not sure I follow.'

'We'd be an agent, a middleman. We'd steer the deposits to an offshore partner bank, but we negotiate an introductory fee from them for the business.'

You mean a hidden kickback. This stinks, and I'm being set up. Dig more, but don't show your hand.

'Presumably it's not like that Ansbacher scheme a few years ago, that ended up with names being named in a High Court report?' Des asked the question in what he hoped was a casual tone.

'It might look a bit like it at first glance, but this scheme is different,' she said leaning forward and putting her elbows on the desk.

What they all say before they're caught.

'The Ansbacher scheme,' continued Dawn, 'was orchestrated by an accountant out of a private office.'

Semantics.

'And why do you think, if it was being run by a bank, it would be different?'

'There'd be no transaction trail on our books for a start. And anyway, we'd make sure we had a cast iron legal opinion we weren't doing anything improper.'

Maybe. Better see the small print before condemning it though.

'Surely there must be some catch?'

'Not really. But the only way we can be sure is to talk to our potential partner.'

'I see. And have you identified who such a partner might be?'

'Not yet, but I think someone located in the Caribbean would be best.'

This needs to be strangled at birth. Assemble arguments. Devil in the detail.

'Okay. This seems to have distinct possibilities. Let me see. You say you need to do some more research. How long will it take?'

Dawn smiled.

Thinks she's won. No harm, buys me more time.

'I should be able to table a proposal in a couple of weeks.' She started to gather her papers.

How far has Milo been drawn in?

'Okay, why don't you do that.' He looked at her. 'By the way, given the sensitivity of this, I'd appreciate it if in the meantime you didn't discuss this with anyone else.'

'Well,' Dawn hesitated, 'I've given Milo the broad outline.' She shifted in her seat.

'Oh. But not the details?' Des tried to look surprised.

Not that he gives a monkeys about details, but it's where I'm going to nail this harebrained idea.

'No, I haven't worked them out yet.'

'Right Dawn, I get the picture. You might get back to me when you've completed your research and we'll see how to position it for the committee.'

And kill it once and for all.

'Thanks for your support Des. I really appreciate it.' Her eyes shone and she uncrossed her legs slowly. 'You know I think we're on to a really exciting development here.' She gathered up her papers and left.

*****

'Hiya Des, long time no hear,' said a strange voice on the phone.

'Who am I speaking to?' he answered, puzzled.

'Ginger. Remember me?'

'Ginger?'

'That's right, Ginger McHugh. Surely you haven't forgotten? Ginger from Rossallen.'

Rossallen. Boarding school. Five years. A blur. Chapel, Class Room, Study Hall, Dorm. Ginger? Got him. Pockmarked face, sucking fag butts behind the Pav. Smart aleck, never liked him. Still, let bygones be.

'Of course I remember you Ginger. God. It's a long time since those days. I heard you were in the licensed trade?'

'Right. And you're a banker now I hear?'

'Someone has to oil the wheels of commerce you know. So, you tracked me down?'

'Yeah. Listen, we're organising a class reunion. It's thirty years since we sat the Leaving, so we thought we'd do it for old times' sake. Should be fun. Would you be up for it?'

'Em, when's it on?'

'Saturday the seventh of Feb. In the Rossallen Arms. Dinner and overnight. Visit the College. Myself and Rosser are organising it. You remember Rosser? He's in Galway now. Estate agent slash property developer.'

Rosser. Bloody mountebank.

Des laughed. 'Rosser. Plush offices on Eyre Square?'

'But of course,' chuckled Ginger, 'always wanted to be top dog.'

More like a bloody mongrel.

'The seventh you say?' Des opened his diary and saw the date was blank. 'I'm not sure if I can make it. How are you doing on numbers?'

'Twenty-three definite at this stage, so we should hit about thirty. Joe's coming over from New York and Tom from Melbourne. Should be good craic.'

'Okay, I'll see if I can rearrange my diary. Leave it with me and I'll get back to you, okay? Just let me take a note of your number.'

He wrote it down and took a deep breath.

*****

'Good, I was hoping to catch you on your own.'

Ed was standing alone in the boardroom when Des arrived for the meeting.

'Yeah?' Des raised his eyebrows.

'I was wondering what you make of Milo hiring Dawn. They seem hell bent on cutting right across how I run the branches although she doesn't put it that way.'

'Well she makes a good point about our changing marketplace, and inevitably this means we've to make adjustments, even if we'd prefer not to.' Des tried to sound reasonable.

'Does that mean you agree with what she and Milo are proposing?' Ed asked with arched eyebrows.

Testing whose side I'm on. Doesn't trust me since my promotion.

'They haven't proposed anything yet. We'll have to wait and see how things pan out.'

'I still don't like it,' Ed snorted. 'If you ask me, they're sacrificing our high standards in their pursuit of short-term profits. They won't be happy until they turn the bank into a hypermarket, buy one and get one free. Hurry, hurry while stocks last.'

He's on the money there. But I'm COO now and have to discourage dissention.

'Ed, you have to remember where our loyalties lie. The board decides policy, and our job is to implement it. They're hardly going to ask us to do anything imprudent.'

'I hope you're right.'

Ouch.

The other members of the committee began to arrive and take their seats around the table. Milo called them to order.

'Right, let's get down to business.' He opened his jotter and rubbed his hands. 'We've some action points here from our last meeting.'

Straight in at ramming speed. No need for going through the gears.

'The first action point was our credit card limits. Jerry, you've looked at this for us?'

'The credit history is actually pretty good. About ninety per cent of the users keep within the repayment terms.'

'So,' Milo jotted some notes, 'we could increase their limit without too much risk?'

'But you can't just do that out of the blue,' said Ed, cutting in excitedly.

'Ed, so you said the last day.' Milo glared at him. 'Of course we can if we want to. But if they don't want to take up our offer, we're no worse off. Anyone else have a view on this?' He looked around the table. 'Des?'

He's using me. But then, I suppose he's paying me well. He was right about Clancy's. That salesman.

'If our delinquency rate is as low as Jerry has said, I don't see why not. So yeah.'

Milo smiled broadly.

'And Jerry,' interjected Dawn, 'what about raising the interest rate. Is it a runner?'

'I looked at it, but to be quite honest I wasn't able come to a satisfactory conclusion.'

'Do you think a hike of say, two per cent, might prove damaging to us?' asked Milo.

'Possibly.'

'Okay, so here's what we'll recommend to the board. Double the limits for Jerry's non-delinquent ninety per cent brigade.' He scribbled some notes. 'And raise our interest margin by one per cent all round.'

'Can we be clear here. Milo, are you saying we do this without consulting our customers?' asked Ed, his tone challenging.

Milo exhaled noisily and threw his biro on the table. 'No, Ed, this is a matter for the board to decide. I'll let you know the outcome. Now let's move on, shall we?'

Simple. Present board with recommendation of committee. Highlight boost to profits. Board only sees dollar signs and rubber stamps.

'Our next action point,' Milo continued, 'was around car loans. Des and Dawn, you were going to look at this?'

Dawn nodded to Des to go ahead.

'I was to do some simulations, and they just confirm the obvious. If we lengthen the term of the loan, the monthly repayments drop, even if we increase our profit margin.'

Dawn came in.

'I've had a few preliminary discussions with some motor distributors. They'd definitely be interested in promoting a four or five year loan plan.'

Milo beamed.

'Excellent work. Tell me, was their interest driven by the longer repayment period, or was it the possibility of paying them the higher cash incentive we discussed?'

For Chrissake Milo, they're car salesmen. It's all folding stuff in their back pocket. Period.

'They found both features of our proposed scheme equally attractive,' Dawn answered, nodding. 'I'd say we're definitely on to a winner here.'

'Then we'll pursue both.' He looked around the table. 'I take the silence as agreed.'

Neat. Decision made with no discussion.

'Our next action point,' continued Milo, glancing again at his notes, 'was to do with increasing our lending for property development. Dawn, could your brief the meeting on how our lunches went?'

'Sure. They were all very positive. They particularly liked our willingness to consider being more flexible than the competition with the sixty-five per cent loan to value yardstick.'

Bloody sure. Why wouldn't they?

Milo nodded to her in acknowledgment.

Jerry coughed.

'Just one question Milo. Have we thought about what the cost of our funding for this will be? I mean, is this whole thing doable?'

A puzzled look came over Milo's face, and he turned to Des.

'When we were talking about foreign banks, didn't you say if they have twice our capital they could be four times our size? So we've doubled our capital, so I can't see where the problem is?'

Snap goes the trap.

'Well,' Des answered, 'we were talking theoretically at that stage.'

'Christ Des, you're not now telling me it can't be done, are you?' Milo had raised his voice and leaned suddenly across the table staring at Des.

Bugger. What did Joan say? As long as you know what you're doing. Steady the ship.

'No Milo, I'm not. But we'll have to get the credit rating agencies, the Regulator, and others onside first.' He fought to keep his voice and appearance calm.

Milo sat in silence, looking around the table.

'Right,' he said after a while, 'I think we'll leave the sorting out of the technical details with our COO.' He glared again at Des. 'I *can* leave it with you, can't I?'

Meaning, or do you want me to hire someone else to do your job? Oh God.

'Yes Milo.'

Milo wrote some more notes before continuing.

'This brings us to our deposit rates. Ed, you and Dawn were to look at when we might pay a premium rate to select depositors. What have you come up with?'

Neat sleight of hand. Shift focus to "when we", not "should we".

Ed picked up one of his documents.

'Yes, we've looked at this and though I'm not against the idea per se, I still have serious concerns about cannibalisation.'

'Dawn, what's your take?' asked Milo turning to her.

'Yeah, it's a risk of course.' She caught Milo's eye. 'But if we don't do something, we could end up with Des having to pay top dollar for the money in the interbank.'

'So what are we going to do about it? Des, do you have a view?'

Des, here's my noose. Be a good chap and just stick your neck in there.

'I think the arguments are finely balanced. Perhaps we should consider giving Ed the flexibility to increase the rates on deposits over, say, a hundred K.'

'A hundred K,' repeated Milo. 'Okay, let's run with that for a test period of six weeks and we'll look at it again.' He scribbled in his jotter and then looked around the table.

'There was one last action point. Dawn's idea about an offshore facility We've codenamed this Project Coral. She's told me she's not ready to table it yet.' Milo looked at his watch. 'So we're finished. Thank you all for being so constructive. Meeting closed.'

We're finished. Quite. Right, Dessie, time to make your move.

He followed Milo to his office.

'Milo, I'd like to have a word with you about this Coral business?'

'Certainly Des.'

'It's just that, as your COO. I'd like to know a bit more about what's going on.' He noticed Milo seemed unfazed by his question.

'Des, I've asked Dawn to keep you in the loop so you know as much as I do. You appreciate, of course, that we must keep things hush hush until we're good and ready to break cover?'

'Yes, but it's important that as a fellow executive director I'm up to speed.'

'Of course. Couldn't agree more. I'll make sure once Dawn completes her homework, you'll be the first person I'll discuss it with. After all I really value your input in these matters.' He put his hand on Des's arm. 'Don't worry, rest assured Project Coral will go nowhere without you on board. Okay?' He smiled to Des.

'Okay.' Des nodded.

No, it's not bloody well okay. And that insincere smile of yours scares the hell out of me.

Chapter 11

'Grab a seat' said Milo, when Des arrived at his office a few days later. He was sitting with Dawn at the table looking through some papers. 'Dawn's got her Coral proposal developed and has a copy here for you,' he nodded at a presentation document. 'I know you'd like to go through it in detail later, but I thought it'd be useful if she gave you a heads up.'

Heads up my granny. Suck me into the quicksand more like. Things moving apace. Look for opportunity to make decisive move.

'Sure,' Des replied, pulling up a chair.

'So, my starting point,' said Dawn, pushing up her cuffs and handing Des his copy, 'was trying to be clear about what we're aiming to achieve here.' Her tone was business-like. 'As I see it, our depositors' primary need is to place their money where there's no disclosure to anybody. Anybody.' She looked at Milo for affirmation.

'We understand.' He nodded to her. 'No need to say any more on that front.'

'It follows therefore we'll have to be careful about the jurisdiction in which we locate the business. I'll come back to that. The other issue we must decide on is the mechanism we use.' She looked at Des to make sure he was engaged.

Milo nodded to her again.

'So, for this I've been working on the assumption that we don't want any records appearing on our books. That way we won't be a party to any tax evasion issues. I also think our preference should be an offshore warehousing arrangement. Des, I mentioned this to you the other day and you didn't see any problems.' She exchanged glances with Milo.

They're watching me like hawks. *Entrapment*. That's what DeLorean claimed when he was stung by the IRS.

'Good. Carry on Dawn, a warehousing arrangement?' Milo waved his right hand to her to continue.

Des watched her push her cuffs further up her arms.

'It would work out a bit like when an insurance broker sells a policy. He doesn't actually hold the customer's money on his own books, but simply washes it through.' She glanced at Milo as she finished.

'Seems to me to be a distinctly encouraging road to take,' Milo said, nodding, 'go on.'

'So, if we keep the money off our books, what's in it for us, you might ask? Well, our customer's primary concern is secrecy, not the interest rate he gets. That means our partner bank needs to only pay the customer a token rate. As a result, they generate a juicy profit margin on the deal. So, we need to negotiate a chunky share of that margin for ourselves.' She was now looking intently at Des.

They know I'm the only one who can really block this. Wait for the details.

'Oh, I forgot. Help yourselves to coffee.' Milo waved at the cups on the table. 'So, Dawn, how do you propose we proceed?'

'Two steps. First, we've to negotiate our cut with our offshore partner, and second, we've to establish a nominee company through which we channel the cash.'

That means a paper trail.

'I though you said there wouldn't be any records in our books?' asked Des.

'That's precisely why we should establish a nominee company. It enables us to move the cash but without actually owning it.'

Of course. Off Balance Sheet. Fair play to her. It's legit, but surely an abuse of a recognised practice? Buy some time while you think.

'But surely we'll have to have records somewhere?' Des shot Milo a meaningful glance.

'Ah no, not here.' Dawn shook her head. 'All records will be offshore and covered by local secrecy laws. That way our customer wins and our offshore partner wins.' She looked to Milo.

Here comes the punch line.

'And most important of all,' Milo laughed, '*we* win.'

'But wait a minute,' said Des. 'If we cannot access the records, how will we know what's happening to our customers' money?'

'That's where our nominee company comes in. Let's call it Coral Nominees.' Dawn leaned forward, earnest. 'We'll own Coral Nominees, but all their records will be kept offshore, and they can only be accessed by Coral's officers.'

Definitely sounds like Ansbacher. Just keep digging.

'And who'll be the officers?' Des scratched his head.

Dawn looked to Milo.

'A very good question Des. You and I need to talk about it because quite frankly I don't have the answer.' He picked up the coffee pot and offered a refill.

Quite frankly I don't have the answer. He's lying.

'So what are the critical issues, Milo?'

'Obviously we can't have the information sloshing around, so it's got to be restricted to a very small number of people. Apart from anything else, if some crank who had a grudge against us got hold of it, he could cause us a lot of trouble. Whistleblowing and the like.' Milo opened his hands and tilted his head as he held Des in a steady gaze. 'It's a tricky one.'

He appears to want my help. But be wary.

'So what options do you think we have?' asked Des.

'What I'm thinking,' said Milo clearing his throat, 'is given that we must keep this thing watertight, we should restrict all client facing data to the people we nominate directors of Coral.

'The Coral directors will be our nominees?'

'Yes Des, we can delegate the record keeping stuff back to our offshore partners, but we'll be nominating two of our own people to the board. It will be our company after all.'

Keep going Dessie.

'And who have you in mind to appoint?'

'Has to be at senior level. People we can trust.'

Des noticed Milo was shifting in his seat and had dropped his eyes.

A trap. Flush him out.

'Ed maybe?' Des suggested, with tongue deep in cheek. 'He's our main customer contact.'

Milo had a steely look in his eyes when he looked up.

'No, Ed's far too rigid in his views. No, this calls for someone with a more flexible approach, someone who can see around corners. I was thinking of Dawn here, but she hasn't been here long enough to have our detailed corporate knowledge. I've told her this already.'

Don't let go.

'So where does that leave us?'

'It's led me to conclude it should be you and me.'

Shit. This is a poisoned chalice. When the solids start to fly, the Regulator will string me up first. Think.

'I see. I can understand a certain logic there. But there might be an argument for separating some functions here.'

'How do you mean Des?' Milo knitted his eyebrows.

'It strikes me as I'm the one who'll be interacting with the authorities here, it might be better if I'm not privy to the details of our offshore activities. If I wasn't a director of Coral, I'd be genuinely unable to supply them with any detailed information they might request.'

'But as the bank's COO, wouldn't you want to know the details anyhow?' Milo scratched his ear.

'Presumably Coral will have its accounts audited. which should be good enough for me.'

Milo appeared to mull this over. Dawn stayed silent. Des waited. Eventually Milo spoke.

'You know, you could have a valid point there. Of course it would still need a second director.'

A win. A small win, but a win.

'And you definitely want to rule Ed and Dawn out?'

'Yep.'

'Well, it certainly narrows down your options.'

'Maybe it's not my place to make a suggestion,' Dawn interjected, 'but would you consider one of our non-executives? Arthur or Jack maybe?'

Not my place to make a suggestion. A rehearsed double act?

Milo turned to Des.

'What do you think?'

Definitely choreographed.

'If you're thinking along those lines, I'd go for Jack. It might be as well not to have Arthur on that board.'

'And your logic is?' Milo seemed puzzled.

'Well, it's just if anything unforeseen was to happen and we needed legal advice, if Arthur was a director, he'd have a conflict of interest and couldn't act for us.'

Even if it never stopped him before.

'Good point, Des. It hadn't struck me,' Milo responded. 'Okay, Jack and I will do the necessary. Now Dawn, what else do you need from us?'

'We need to decide where Coral is domiciled. We can't have any near misses here on the secrecy front. My research points to the West Indies The next step is to identify a suitable partner out there.'

'And have you identified someone?'

'Yeah, a crowd called BWI, the Bank of West Indies. I've checked them out. They provide the service we want, and I'm told they're extremely reliable.'

'Have you explored the financial implications for us?' asked Des.

'Only in a preliminary way, but I'm confident it will be more than self-financing.' Her smile radiated confidence.

'So what next?' Milo poured himself another coffee.

He's relaxing. Thinks he's got it over the line.

'It now just needs us to go out there and negotiate the details.' She looked at Milo and he in turn looked at Des.

'I assume you'd like to go through Dawn's written proposal. You might come back directly to me if you've any issues. If there are any, let's iron them out before the committee sees it. And the board, of course. That okay to you, Des?'

Milo's smile. Amiable. False. Time to throw some grit into the engine.

'Yeah. Seems fair enough. But there's one other thing I wondered if you'd thought about Dawn?'

'Which is?' She looked at him with apparent surprise.

'Marketing. How are we going to sell this new service. I don't think the authorities would be amused if they thought we were promoting an offshore tax avoidance scheme.'

'Whoa there,' Milo cut in, in a stern voice. 'Back up. Nobody said anything about us promoting any kind of tax avoidance scheme.'

'Okay, maybe I should have chosen my words better.'

'Christ Des, we're not playing Scrabble here. So what *did* you mean to say?' Milo made no attempt to hide his annoyance.

'Sorry. What I meant was how exactly is anybody going to know about our, our new, eh, deposit facility, if we don't promote it?'

'Des, we sometimes provide services to our customers which we don't promote. Share dealing for instance. So, if one of our managers becomes aware that a customer is going to close their account to move their money offshore, he can simply provide that customer with additional information to help inform his decision.'

'To avail of our Coral facility?'

'As an option we make the customer aware of.' Milo paused. 'Look, Des, I've made it clear on more than one occasion I won't condone or have us involved in anything illegal in this bank. And I might add, I intend to get Arthur's legal advice on any new initiatives. Do I make myself clear?'

Seems reasonable, but it still smells. I need more time.

'Thank you for clarifying that. I'll get back to you when I get through the presentation.' Des picked up Dawn's document and left.

When he got back to his office, he sat at his desk and smiled when he thought at least he'd outfoxed Milo's attempt to nominate him as a director of Coral. And then, his smile faded when it occurred to him, maybe Milo hadn't wanted to appoint him in the first place, but had stage-managed the whole conversation to divert him from focussing on the formation of Coral itself. Had he just jumped out of the frying pan into the fire?

A flash of sunlight hitting a passing vehicle in College Green, distracted him for a moment. When he settled down again he realised he could no longer continue to ignore the full implications of Milo's succession to the CEO job. Milo was simply doing whatever it took to accelerate the bank's profit growth, and would continue to do so, regardless of the inherent risks, and he'd stop at nothing in pursuit of his Holy Grail.

A logical consequence was, Des now realised, he was exposed in a way he hadn't fully grasped before. The Regulator for one would show him no mercy. And it would be extremely naive of him to rely on Milo's assurance about not transgressing the law. He felt he needed to talk through the issues with someone, but the only people who would understand them were in the bank and he could hardly discuss it there. One thing he was certain about however - time wasn't on his side.

*****

The aroma of freshly ground coffee greeted Des and Joan when they stepped from Grafton Street into Bewley's. He glanced around the room and spotted an empty table.

'The usual?' Joan asked him when the waiter approached. He nodded. 'A large cafetière of coffee and two scones please.'

The waitress took their order.

Most of the tables were occupied by Saturday morning shoppers and students. At a large table by the window two single men were reading newspapers. At the table beside them two twenty year olds were sharing a croissant.

'So did you tell your folks you flunked your Michaelmas exams?' One of them asked the other. 'Not yet. I used your trick and told them they'd been delayed.'

Des leaned over to Joan.

'Trinity.'

'How do you know?'

'Look at their clothes. Students in the other colleges don't wear labels.'

She rolled her eyes. The coffee and scones arrived and she turned to Des.

'Something I must ask you. You may remember I mentioned at Christmas I thought I'd bring my mother over to Brighton.'

'Eh, yeah,' said Des, who'd been wondering if he should air with Joan his latest joust with Milo.

'It's just things are a bit quiet at work this time of the year. I thought I'd go the week after next. There's no need for you to come. It'll only be a few days. I presume that's okay with you?' Her eyes and a slight nod sought his confirmation.

'Of course,' Des smiled.

'Any travel plans yourself?' She pushed the plunger down in the cafetière and started to pour.

'Not really. I'm toying with an idea though.'

'Oh?'

'No big deal really. I'd a call the other day from one of the guys I was in boarding school with. Himself and another guy are organising a reunion. Our thirtieth. Asked me to come along.'

The Chapel. Sermonising Monks. Ginger sucking cigarette butts behind the Pav.

'You'll go I presume, won't you?' said Joan, her voice almost eager.

'I'm not sure.' Des picked up his coffee and shook his head.

'What's involved?' she asked, holding her cup in mid-air awaiting his response.

Des wondered why she seemed interested.

'Basically it's a Saturday. Travel down to Rossallen, meet up, steak and chips or whatever, and overnight. Backslapping and speeches. That sort of thing.'

'And why wouldn't you go? Could be interesting.'

'Oh I don't know. Not sure I want to spend a day with thirty grown men misbehaving like schoolboys.'

Joan laughed.

'What's so funny?'

'I was going to say it would at least make a change from your office routine, but on second thoughts...'

'Ha ha.'

He picked up his knife and buttered his scone.

'On one hand,' said Des, 'it could be a right pain in the ass. But then on the other, it would be interesting to see how some of lads turned out. I haven't really been in touch with any of them since I left.'

'Do you mean you'd find it amusing to see how they got on? Or would it be a kind of one-upmanship thing? I know girls' schools reunions are.'

'No, it's not that. No, it's just I've this theory lads who go away to boarding school at an early age build a sort of shield about themselves. A self-defence mechanism. The real person hides behind their mask. But outside it, they present a different self to the world. I'd be curious to see if thirty years on they've yet revealed their real selves or if they're still in hiding.'

'Sounds a rather unusual reason to attend a school reunion. But why not? Go for it.'

Des fell silent for a moment.

'You know, you're probably right. I think I will. Why not indeed?'

She poured them more coffee.

'Of course before you go down there, you'll have to figure out something for yourself.'

'What's that?'

'Which Des Peters is going to turn up.'

'Sorry?'

'Which mask will you wear.' She laughed lightly. 'Only pulling your leg.'

Maybe she is, but she's closer to the bone that she realises. Change subject.

'By the way,' he said, 'any progress on your research into Bartholemew Mosse?'

'Ah, you remembered his name this time.' She smiled. 'Thought you might forget again. You seem so distracted these days.' She picked up her coffee. 'It's at an interesting stage actually, a sort of crossroads that doesn't have a signpost.'

Sounds too bloody familiar.

'Sounds a bit frustrating. So what are you going to do?' He put his elbows on the table and leaned forward.

'I think the best thing to do when you find yourself in a dilemma is just to work harder at finding the solution.'

But if there's no one you can turn to for help in resolving your dilemma, what then?

'So which road are you going to take now to find your friend Mosse?'

'Research can lead one in many directions before one finds the right one. In this case I'm going to explore a completely new angle and try the Royal Irish Academy.' She smiled.

Explore a completely new angle. Sounds so simple.

'I see. Well, good luck.' He looked at his watch. 'Right, you want to do some shopping. I'm going to get myself a haircut and head out to the rugby in Castle Avenue. See you at home at about six?'

'See you then, and enjoy the game.'

He put twenty euro on the table, kissed her, and headed out onto Grafton Street.

*****

Des stood looking out the window of his office, when a sudden squall sent pedestrians dashing for cover under the portico of the Bank of Ireland opposite. Others clung grimly to their umbrellas, waiting impatiently for the traffic lights to change. A fleet of buses swept past splashing them as they tried in vain to escape.

He walked back to his desk and glanced at the open newspaper. He looked at the photograph of himself alongside his interview with Noel, and smiled as he thought about its contents.

Reads well. Markets always evolving... Good lending opportunities... Prudence. Fair reflection of interview. Must thank Alan.

His thoughts were interrupted by the phone ringing.

'Des, Milo wants to see you,' said Orla.

'Okay, give me ten minutes.'

'Sorry, but he asked me to get you immediately.'

Damn. Must be really itching to get Coral onto the launch pad.

Milo glared at him when he came in to his office and waved his newspaper at him.

'What in the name of God to you think you're playing at?' He sprang up and threw Noel's article in front of Des. 'Jesus, I know you can be a bit of a woodener in the real ways of the world, but this... this interview. I just don't believe it.' He started to stomp up and down his office.

'Sorry Milo, you've lost me. I thought it read quite well. Those references to prudence and collective responsibility and so on. What's the problem?'

'Are you a complete imbecile? What's the problem? Never mind all that prudence shit. I'm not talking about *that*. I'm talking all your coded references to being after *my* job. *That's* what's wrong.'

What the hell is he on about?

'I'm sorry, Milo. I still don't understand.'

Milo stopped pacing and turned on Des, his nostrils quivering.

'You don't understand? Do you think I'm a total bloody gobshite?' He grabbed the newspaper and started to scan the interview. 'Okay, take this bit. You just tell me what this is meant to mean. *'The Bank's COO stated he was ready to take over from Milo O'Toole as Chief Executive.'*

Des shifted in his seat.

'You've got it wrong Milo. That was in answer to a casual question about what would happen if you walked under a bus or some such.' Des held out his arms protesting his innocence.

'Goddam it Des. I don't know about the question being casual, but your answer certainly is casual, that is if I was minded to put a charitable explanation on it, which I'm not.' He snorted and started to look at the article again. 'And here's another bit. *Appointment of Peters designed to keep Regulator at bay.* Have you taken leave of your senses? In the name of God, what conclusion would any rational reader come to? What does it say about the way I run this place?'

Des felt his heart thumping.

'That's not what I said. What I said was...'

Milo raised his hand.

'I couldn't give a flying fart what you said or didn't say. The only thing that matters is what the papers say. There are people out there who believe the kind of crap the papers print. God, I can't believe you could be so stupid.' He fired the paper down on his desk.

Des felt his collar tighten. Keep quiet, he commanded himself, you'll only make things worse.

Milo picked up the paper again and started to read it. He then looked up and glared again at Des.

'And you couldn't resist the final thrust of the dagger into me could you?'

Des looked at him, waiting.

'No, you couldn't,' Milo continued and began to read. *'Peters agrees O'Toole doesn't take prisoners.'* He flung the paper back on his desk and sat down, his head in his hands. Eventually he looked up. 'Can I ask you a simple question. Have you taken complete leave of your senses? What were you thinking when you said that?' He paused. 'I mean why on earth did you decide to give that bogman from the MacGillycuddy Reeks an interview in the first place? Was your sole purpose to assassinate my good character?' He sat back. 'I'm waiting, and your explanation better be good.'

Dessie you've somehow got to get control of this.

'For a start, I didn't say anything about you not taking prisoners. Noel did.'

Milo jutted his head forward.

'And did you disagree with him?'

'It was a joke.'

Better not tell him I laughed at it, or he'll go mental.

153

'Some joke.' Milo shook his head. 'Go on.'

'And I gave the interview because Alan asked me to and I thought it was in the bank's best interests.'

'Alan!' Milo jumped up. 'Oh for God's sake. There are times when I think I'm running a bloody crèche in here. He above all people knows that effing puck goat is hell bent on destroying my reputation. Alan. By God I'll settle his hash in my own good time.'

He took his handkerchief out and wiped his face and sat down again. He allowed a long silence develop and then he spoke in measured tones.

'I hope you realise Des this is one gigantic cock-up you've created. If you ever wanted to destabilise a situation, just talk to those journos. They're lazy, they're spiteful and they're vindictive.' He shook his head and then looked at Des. 'Just answer me one question. Why did you decide to stab me in the back? I mean after all I've done for you?'

He looked at Des, but when there was no answer forthcoming continued.

'Right. I realise you can't undo the damage you've caused, so here's what I'm going to do. I'm not a vindictive man as you know, so for now, I'm willing to let the hare sit. But if you *ever* do anything again that challenges my authority, I'll have your ass out the door so fast you won't remember you were *ever* employed here. I take it I make myself clear?'

Des began to feel his blood pressure easing.

'Yes Milo.'

'Good.' Milo looked at his watch. 'I've asked Dawn to come here in twenty minutes to discuss Coral. Be back here by then.'

Back in his office, Des reflected what had happened. He knew his own behaviour was faultless, even if Milo had gone ape. Had Alan set him up? Joan had asked him if Alan could have had an ulterior motive on the insider dealing problem. Could it be that he himself was the meat in the sandwich?

From now on Dessie boy, trust absolutely no one.

*****

When he arrived back at Milo's office Dawn was already there.

'Ah here you are,' Milo smiled. 'You've looked over Dawn's presentation?'

All smiles. Nothing has happened. Not half. Just don't push him over the edge. And Dawn, she's eyeing me. Wonder if she's been filled in. Only disagree if you really have to.

'Yeah, I'd a good look, and Dawn's quite correctly highlighted the two aspects we need to focus on. The establishment of the facility and how we implement it.'

'Agreed.'

'On the first, the establishment of the scheme, I don't see any particular problem.'

'Good.'

'Provided of course we take sensible precautions.'

'Precautions? What sort of precautions?' Milo's smile faded and he leaned over his desk.

'Yes, Milo, precautions,' He nodded to affirm he had chosen his word with care. 'Once we form Coral Nominees, we'll need to be able to establish it's a totally legitimate part of our business. We cannot afford to slip up on any technicalities so we must be certain we identify all the potential pitfalls. You've already said we should run it past Arthur and I agree, even if only to get his written views for our files. For our own protection.'

'Yeah, of course. I'll get Arthur to give us an opinion everything is above board. Does that cover everything off for you?' He signalled to Dawn to take a note.

Well done Dessie, one box ticked.

'I think it would be as well to get the auditors onside as well. Just in case, you know.'

'I'll get Arthur to cover that off in his opinion to us. Now, you also said that you want to discuss the implementation phase?'

Good. Another box ticked.

'Yeah. Remember you said we wouldn't actively promote this to our customers?'

'Correct.'

'Milo, the Regulator can be tricky if they suspect something we're doing doesn't pass the smell test.'

'Go on.'

'They expect us to operate by the spirit as well as the letter of the rule book.'

'I'm not sure I fully understand your point?'

'Look, Milo, it'll be vital that Ed doesn't have his managers selling this under-the-counter with winks and nods to our customers.'

Meaning we both know bloody well there's a fair chance it's going to happen, but I need to cover my ass.

'Like porn? Ed?' Milo smirked.

'Milo, this is a serious issue. It isn't funny.' Des looked directly into his boss's eyes, determined to ensure that his message was understood.

'Sorry, Des. I understand the point you're making, and couldn't agree with you more. I'll make it my business to ensure that Ed and his musketeers are kept in line.' He sat back. 'That it?'

'For now, yes.'

'Right, this is what I'll do. I'll make sure Arthur gives us the written opinion we need. Then, we'll run it through the committee and have the board endorse it. Okay?'

This is a stitch up. But at least I've my boxes ticked and Arthur's letter to cover me.

'Okay.'

No, it's not bloody well okay, and that insincere smile of yours scares the hell out of me.

Chapter 12

Des drove past Newlands Cross and watched the countryside unpeel before him. Morning sun glinted over the frost at the foot of the hedgerows, and glistened on the thawing runway at Baldonnel. He was having second thoughts about agreeing to attend the class reunion, having lost touch with the lads. While he really didn't care much what had happened to any of them, he was nevertheless mildly curious.

It was in Rossallen he'd honed his survival instincts. He'd left home when he was twelve and was boarded there with a few hundred others, for months at a time. Studying and passing examinations was the easy bit. But getting involved on the playing field was essential if you were to protect your vulnerabilities. Business was like that, too, of course. He now realised it was in Rossallen he'd learned how to handle the Milos of this world and where he'd mastered the art of fighting his corner.

Was it Wellington who said the Battle of Waterloo was won on the playing fields of Eton?

There was also, of course, the more subtle side to the Rossallen education agenda. The students were encouraged to explore and understand a meaning in their lives and to take personal responsibility for their actions, all of which was backed up by the inculcation of a solid grounding in moral values.

Now as he drove, he reflected on how much had happened since his boarding school days. Getting qualified, getting a job, starting in the bank. And meeting Joan of course. He smiled to himself when he recalled it was Joan who'd encouraged him to go to the reunion. Joan who in reality knew very little about his early life and yet seemed to think he should attend. She'd been amused by her own quip, about which Des Peters was going to show up. She was probably concerned about his irritable moods of late and thought meeting some old school friends might cheer him up. Fat chance. Still, she meant well, as always.

He turned on the radio. Another stabbing in Rialto... Victim known to Gardai... Car crash in Inishowen... Two joy riders critical in Letterkenny General.

He flicked a button.

'I put it to you there are people out there who think the government could solve the problem by stimulating employment in the West by...' He hit the off button.

Absurdities, twaddle, sound bites, opium to the masses. Self-styled economics experts. Probably attended half a lecture on some quango course for the unemployed.

He saw the turnoff signs for the various towns. Naas, Newbridge, Kildare, Monasterevin, Portlaoise, all bypassed now. In his boarding school days he used to think of them as the five sorrowful mysteries. The trip back after Christmas holidays each year was the worst. Incarcerated in a lugubrious limestone sepulchre on the edge of the Bog of Allen, there was nothing to look forward to until Easter. At least He'd been able to escape from His tomb after three days. Rosary and Benediction every evening. And Mass at seven in the morning. Two on Sunday. The High Mass in the Monastery, the entire community in full voice. *Credo in unum deum.*

He reached the turnoff for Rossallen and recalled Ginger saying he'd be at Devine's at one. The reunion was starting with Mass in the college chapel at three. He glanced at the time.

Noon. Why did I come? Procrastinate.

He headed for the Slieve Blooms and drove uphill mile after endless mile of deserted mountain road until he reached The Cut where he pulled over and stepped out. His gaze was drawn in a slow panoramic sweep spreading outwards and downwards from his afforested surroundings to the enormous boglands on the lower slopes and beyond. Here and there giant concrete power stations slumbered, Gulliver-like, oblivious to the cloying quagmire into which they were slowly sinking. And away to the west, a long narrow strip of fog enveloped the comatose Shannon with a grey opaque shroud. He sat on a low wall, entranced by the view, and soaking in the silence.

It was after two when he parked outside Devine's. Once inside, his attention was immediately caught by a loud guffaw at the counter. Three middle aged men stood there beside plates containing the remnants of ham and cheese sandwiches. Coffee cups rested in front of them.

'Well, if it isn't the man himself, Des Peters. We thought you were lost.' Des looked at the shaven head and broad grin of the speaker who was placing his cup back on a saucer. He held out his hand. 'Great you could make it,' and sensing Des's hesitation, 'Ginger' he added.

Ginger! God, is this what thirty years can do if you don't look after yourself?

'Sorry, didn't recognise you. Good to see you again.' Des shook his hand.

'You mean without my crop of red hair?' Ginger laughed. 'I've been in the wars with the big C. But the chemo is taking care of that.' He looked around and waved at the others. 'You remember Rosser and Dermot? Will you join us for a coffee, or would you prefer a drop of the hard stuff?'

'Oh, sorry to hear, but you look well on the mend now. Well done.' He smiled to Ginger. 'Yeah, a coffee would be great thanks.'

He glanced at Rosser.

Look at him. Gone to the dogs. Fat as a fool. Connacht rugby club tie. Blazer just back from the cleaners. Still looks a shiftless waste of space. Delighted giving the two fingers to authority. Always getting us into trouble. Loudmouth.

'Wise man Des, plenty of time for the other later, eh?' Ginger looked at Rosser, who nodded with a dutiful leer.

'You're right there, Ginger, plenty of time.'

'So tell us, what have you been up to?' asked Ginger. 'You're a big wig now in that bank of yours, wha?' He nudged Des in the ribs, winking to the others as he did so.

So it's going to be like this. But you knew before you came. C'mon Dessie, make an effort.

'Yeah,' Des forced a laugh, 'I always felt I'd a bit of a head for figures, so it's no surprise really I ended up in a bank I suppose.'

'Good for you. Feeding the Celtic Tiger? I hope he's feeding you as well,' said Ginger grinning. 'Or at least if he's not, you're getting your share of the grub stakes?'

Rosser smirking. Barfly. Dermot smiling. Neat understated dress. Signed up to be a monk but jumped ship somewhere along the way. Got on well with him. Pity I lost touch. Find out more later.

'Oh, I forgot your coffee.' Ginger called the barman.

'Sorry I was a bit late,' said Des. 'Got delayed getting out of the house. You know how it is sometimes.'

'Ah, she who must be obeyed delayed you, wha?' Ginger sniggered.

'Begod, getting your Saturday morning oats still, eh?' Rosser winked with another leer.

Knew he'd never grow up. Calls for a vacuous teenager's response.

'Whatever.' Des shrugged.

'We'll need to be getting out of here pretty soon.' Ginger was looking at his watch. 'Benny's saying Mass in the chapel at three.'

'Benny?' Des asked with a raised eyebrow.

'You must remember Father Benedict? He was our Dean of Studies.'

'Oh yes, Benny. I'd forgotten.'

'They made him Abbot after we left.'

'He's the Abbot?'

'No, not any more. Now the ex Abbot. They've to hand over the reins when they hit some age.' Ginger looked at Dermot who was standing slightly away from the others.

'You'd know. You're the religious affairs expert around here. *And* you were in the A Class. How old do you have to be when they defrock you?' Ginger laughed again. Rosser guffawed.

'I wouldn't put it in those terms,' Dermot said. 'They're like bishops. They must retire at seventy-five.'

'Anyway, let's finish this stuff off and get ourselves over to the College. After the Mass there'll be a group photo and we get to meet some of the monks who are still alive and kicking. Then back here to enjoy ourselves, wha?' He clapped Des on the back. 'You can leave your cars here lads. I'll do the driving.'

Mistake coming here. Why *did* Joan encourage me? Ah, I'm committed now.

*****

The laurel hedging had been removed from the long narrow drive. The tall beech trees were still there, bare but for a few copper leaves clinging on steadfastly. They rounded a corner and the college came into view, its forbidding stone edifice squatting on the hill top.

'Look, a golf course,' said Ginger pointing as he drove. 'Wonder where they moved the rugby pitches to?'

'Begod, times have changed from our day,' Rosser said rubber-necking.

'The tennis courts and the Pav still holding up, I see,' said Dermot.

'You and your tennis,' muttered Ginger. 'Weren't you college champ in sixth year?'

'Yeah. It was the only thing I was worth a damn at.'

'Did you keep it up?' asked Rosser.

'Ah no. In the monastery it wasn't really a practical option.' Dermot laughed lightly. 'Playing tennis didn't quite fit in with their concept of strictest observance.'

'Temptation of mixed doubles hanky-panky, eh?' guffawed Rosser. 'Challenge the chastity vows, would it?'

Oh for God's sake. This juvenilia.

'Did you stay in there long Dermot?' Des interjected.

'Just over two years. I left just coming up to Christmas in Seventy-Six.'

'It's nearly three,' said Ginger glancing at his watch as he pulled up. 'We better head straight down to the chapel. There'll be plenty of time for catching up later.'

'I've got to see a man about a dog,' announced Rosser as he scampered around a corner.

God only knows what the bloody fellow is up to.

*****

There was a low murmur, emanating from about twenty others, in the chapel when the three of them eased their way into a pew. Two fat candles bisected by a silver chalice squatted on the stark marble altar. Weak sunlight struggled its way through the plain gothic windows and settled on some of the Stations of the Cross. Des shivered and pulled his coat tighter around him.

Ginger nudged Des and stood up. The rest of the gathering did likewise when a slight figure emerged from the sacristy. At first Des didn't recognise Benny. Gone was the authoritative figure who ruled the Study Hall with unbending discipline. Here was a stooped, older, feebler man. When he got to the altar he stopped and faced them with a sheepish smile.

'You are all indeed most welcome. I'm very pleased you've decided to start your reunion celebrations with the Holy Sacrifice of the Mass. I'll have a few words to say to you later.' He walked around behind the altar and commenced the service.

Des listened vaguely. The Gloria. The Epistle. The Gospel. He watched the congregation kneel and stand when prompted. Some enunciated the responses, some mumbled, others were silent. *I believe in God... Creator of Heaven and Earth... Rose from the Dead... Life Everlasting.*

He began to wonder if those around him believed in what was going on, about this God who went around preaching and got himself crucified for His troubles. Did these guys believe all of this? Had they their fingers crossed when they joined in the recitation of the Credo? Or were they just going along with it? Surely they didn't believe the life everlasting stuff? Were they plain lazy or just didn't want to rock the boat? How many of them had taken the trouble to think for themselves on matters of religion since they left?

And me?

The Mass was coming to an end when Benny came around the side of the altar and spoke to them directly.

'Our gospel reading today is about the farmer who goes out to sow seed. Some fell on stony ground, some fell among thorns and some fell on rich ground, and the consequential effects on the harvest. It is of course a parable used by Jesus to get across His message about salvation and redemption.'

Here we go again. Treating us like schoolboys who cannot figure things out for ourselves. Idiots' Guide to the Meaning of Life. Next he'll be feeding the stuff about it being is easier for a camel to squeeze through the eye of a needle. It's alright for you Benny. You made your bed over sixty years ago when you decided to opt out of the real world.

'Some of you might think this gospel tale is a bit trite, but you have to bear in mind that the vast majority of His followers were simple people with little education. He had to talk to them in a language that they could understand, but one that did not dilute the powerfulness of His teaching. They could choose to follow His message, or they could choose to let it fall on stony ground, or have it choked off by what might appear to be more attractive alternatives.'

Good marketing pitch. Show the punters both sides. Then sell the sizzle, not the sausage. Dawn would like this. Her Revlon guy. *In the stores we sell hope.*

'We read out earlier a list of the those dearly departed from this life, who were here with us thirty years ago. Today we hope and pray when they passed on they found the rich ground and are with The Lord in Paradise. But this afternoon I'd like you to consider for a moment what the gospel message is saying to you individually.'

Ah ha, good old Benny, still our Dean of Studies, still dishing out our homework.

'At the beginning of our ceremony I said I was delighted you'd decided to start your reunion with this Mass. Maybe you're all regular churchgoers and accept the church's teachings.' He smiled. 'But I suspect not. Some of you probably believe in God, and some of you may not. Hopefully, for at least some of you, His message has fallen on rich ground. But some of you may have elected to let it to fall on stony ground. You are all mature men. That is your prerogative.'

Umm. Somewhere along the way he's pulled on a velvet glove over that iron fist of his.

'But I suspect there are others of you, possibly the majority of you, may have chosen to allow yourselves to be choked off like the seed falling amongst thorns in the gospel, and have pursued the gods of wealth, power and social status.'

Pity Milo isn't here to hear this.

'Perhaps some of you have allowed your Christian values to be diluted and who may have strayed, unwittingly perhaps, to worship instead at the altar of the Celtic Tiger.'

A movement caught the corner of Des's eye. Rosser was advancing up the side aisle with carefully measured steps. He slid into a vacant pew.

What the hell has he been up to?

'Those of you who might identify with such a description might expect me to preach to you on the error of your ways, and return to what we call *The One True Faith*. Yes, I hope you'd do that. But even if you've decided for whatever reason such a path is not for you, I'd ask you to consider the deeper question of why you're here, and what your values are, and what you stand for?'

Fair play to you Benny. Like your man in St Patrick's in New York. Make the most of your chance with your captive audience.

'I've been in this world for over eighty years, and I haven't met anyone to tell me that this is a practice run we're on. So I invite each of you to ask yourself this question: do you really believe the pursuit of the Celtic Tiger should be an end in itself? Is it *really* what you want out of life? And does it matter to you how you achieve it? Is *any* price worth paying to get it? Can you be certain that no one is getting hurt along the way, or may be hurt whenever the Tiger's own day comes, and come it surely will? Just how much at peace are you with your own value system? Are there any steps you can take to improve it?'

My value system. Nothing wrong there. But think back Dessie. You used to believe there was more to life than status and money. What happened since? *You used to be a fair minded person.* That's what Joan said one day when I was ranting on about Milo. You've changed Dessie, that's what. And you haven't even noticed it.

Des looked at Benny more closely. He had indeed the body of a man in his eighties, but the light in his eyes contradicted his feeble appearance.

'You're all men of the world. Whether you choose to believe in God or not is your business. But please never forget the values that we tried to instil in you when you were here in Rossallen, the values of truth, morality, and justice. And remember, you should always be man enough to openly and proudly live by those values.'

He stood in silence for a few moments, and then slowly raised his hands in blessing.

'Our Mass has ended. Go in peace. Enjoy the rest of your reunion.'

*****

As Des came down the stairs in the hotel for the pre-dinner reception, the clamour of voices and raucous laughter from the bar told him where to head. Ginger stood at the well laden counter with three others, regaling some anecdote to their obvious amusement. Further along, another group with loosened ties sat on bar stools clutching pints to their chests and wearing broad beery grins. Scattered at a number of tables around the room were the others in animated conversation. Des approached the counter close to where Ginger was standing. An elderly barman queried Des silently with raised eyebrows.

Ain't my scene, but I'm stuck. Go with the flow.

'A glass of red, please.'

'Watch it lads, the bank manager's here. All on best behaviour now.' Ginger laughed to his group. He eyed Des. 'Only kidding. Here, let me pay.' He shoved some notes and change lying on the counter in the direction of the barman. 'Look after my father here.' He laughed again and the group joined in unison.

'You shouldn't, but thanks,' Des acknowledged.

'I was just telling the lads here, I met Nedser over in London a couple of years ago. You remember Nedser?'

'Yeah?' Des responded. 'I wondered what happened to him after he disappeared that night?'

'He was accused of stealing a tenner from one of the juniors. He told me he was framed by I won't say who.'

Wouldn't be surprised if it was Rosser.

'Anyhow when our beloved President, The Booby,' he looked at the others and was rewarded with knowing grins, 'do you like that, *our Beloved President*, eh?' He continued, 'when The Booby found out, he gave him a right hiding. Nedser told me he just decided to do a runner there and then. Went to London. Never came back.'

Rough justice. But that's life sometimes.

'You mean he went to London straight from Rossallen and stayed there?'

Ginger nodded.

'Yeah. Told me he hitched to Dublin, and bunked his way onto the ferry and train to London. Signed up for the army. Lied about his age, but they were only interested in hitting their recruitment targets and didn't look for proof. He stayed with them six years.'

'So what's he doing now?'

'Oh he met a young one and they settled down. They've two kids. Her father has something to do with Billingsgate fish market, and got him set up in an office job there.'

'He didn't think of coming over for the reunion, did he?' Des was curious now.

'Nah. Told me he feels he got a rather shitty deal at Rossallen. Had moved on. Didn't want to be reminded. Poor auld Nedser.' Ginger fell silent for a moment and then looked around. 'Lads, your glasses are nearly empty.' He called to the barman. 'Same again, please.'

Wonder how much of the yarn is true. All the world's a stage. Actors, all of us.

A waiter appeared clanging a bell. 'Dinner is served,' he announced.

'That was rough on Nedser all the same,' said Des.

'When you find yourself dealt a poor hand, the best thing to do is cut your losses,' said Ginger, picking up the remaining banknotes from the counter and putting them in his wallet.

They picked up their glasses and joined the movement to the dining room. Ginger put an arm around Des's shoulders.

'I've put you on Table One with Benny. Hope you don't mind. He won't stay long and then you'll be able to enjoy yourself.' He patted Des on the shoulder, gave him a wink, and moved off.

The tables in the private dining room each had a flag of the school colours, and a centrepiece floral arrangement flanked by bottles of red and white wine. Thirty year old photographs jostled with each other for position on the available wall space. At Table One he found his name card beside Dermot, who was already seated to his left. Benny's name was on his right, but he had not yet arrived.

At least I can talk to Dermot. One of the saner ones.

'Ah, we meet again,' Dermot said, smiling.

'Indeed.' Des pulled out his chair. 'Have you kept in touch with the lads, or are you like me? It's the first time I've come to one of these.'

'Me too. Ginger persuade you with his silver tongue?'

'Yeah, something like that.' Des laughed.

Dermot glanced over both shoulders and leaned over to Des.

'To be honest I wasn't going to bother coming. I lost touch when I joined the monastery, and then when I left, well, I wasn't really in the frame of mind to renew acquaintances with anyone.'

'I'm afraid I don't have that excuse Dermot. I just didn't bother. Got caught up in my own life. Getting qualified, getting a job, into the rat race, got married. Rossallen just faded away.'

'Still you're here now. I've heard you're doing rather well in the banking business. Going well for you?'

'It's going very well actually. Got a decent leg up a few months ago.' Des nodded in self-confirmation. 'Mind you, there's the odd wrinkle I've to iron out, but then so have most jobs.' He laughed. 'And yourself?'

'After I left the monastery I'd to do a bit of thinking about earning a crust. Anyway, you may remember I was also pretty useful at the maths and commerce, so I decided to train to become an accountant as well. Not your Institute, the other one. Anyway, my Da knew an accountant in Drogheda and he took me in.'

'Who took you in?' Rosser announced his arrival at their table and dragged a chair back with a screech on the parquet flooring. He sat on the other side of Dermot.

Dermot looked at Rosser.

'Oh we were just catching up. Sharing accountants' stuff.'

'Of course. Both of you are in that racket.' Rosser threw his head back and laughed. 'Begob you're the boys to keep those Dracula's in Dublin Castle away from us law abiding tax payers, eh?'

'You know what they say. Having to pay tax is one of life's two certainties.' Dermot smiled. 'And yourself Rosser? I hear you're a big wheel estate agent?'

'That right. Galway. And next year I'm going to have a crack at Kings Inns. I rather fancy the idea of being called to the Bar.'

Called to the bar is right. Skewed tie. Over sloshing that wine into his glass.

'Yeah, I started shifting residential stuff, but I now concentrate on property development. Lots of activity in the market in the West. You guys on the East coast don't know what you're missing. Great opportunities to make serious money over there.' He touched his nose. 'For those in the know, that is.'

Ginger rose at the next table and banged a piece of cutlery on his glass.

'Just to let you know, Father Benedict has been delayed and wishes us to start without him. So please tuck in, and we'll have some speeches later. Enjoy.'

Des turned to Dermot.

'Drogheda, eh?'

'Yeah. I'm the junior partner in a small practice.'

'And how do you describe a small practice?'

'Oh, annual audits, VAT returns, a bit of financial advice. Mainly small businesses and some private family money. Not in the big league like you.' His smile was modest.

'A lot to be said for what you're doing, I often have thought. The big league, as you put it, isn't always what it's cracked up to be. Has its own pressures.'

'I'm sure it has. Still, it has good financial rewards.'

'You don't look like a guy who'd want much more.'

'To be honest, not really. I'm pretty much in control of my own destiny. To my way of thinking that's more important than more money.'

This guy is interesting. Straight talker. Wonder why he decided to...?

'Eh,' I hope you don't mind me asking, and tell me I'm out of line if I am,' said Des, 'but I'm curious about your vocation to join the monastery and then leaving?'

'Not at all. Vocation you say.' Dermot chuckled. 'Who was it said, *I fear those big words*? It's quite simple really. Maybe it's the way I was brought up, but I always had a strong desire to do the right thing, the decent thing if you like. So when we were in Rossallen, I was impressed with the life the monks led, so joining them seemed a logical next step.'

'But, if I may ask, what caused you to leave? Did your priorities just shift?'

'No, Des, my priorities didn't shift. It's just after a while I came to the conclusion it wasn't necessary to live the life of a hermit in order to stick to what I valued. Or to put it another way, I felt I could realise my potential more fully outside.'

'Fair play to you. It must have taken some guts all the same to up sticks.'

'Not once you're sure you know what you want.'

Why does this seem like a recurring theme? I warned myself to trust no one, but this guy is surely okay?

'I don't find myself in Drogheda that much,' said Des, 'but if you were ever in Dublin and fancied a bite of lunch, I'd be delighted to have a chat. My treat.'

'I might take you up on that.' Dermot nodded.

The noise in the dining room was rising steadily. The waiters had cleared the dishes after the first course and were now serving a choice of fillet steak or salmon. Rosser was calling for more wine for the table.

Dermot turned to Rosser. 'So, do you confine your business to Galway city?'

'Ah no, Limerick, Sligo. Anywhere in the West in fact. Whenever a serious proposition crops up I like to take a look. Can't buy property off a map you know. Got to kick the tyres, walk the land.' His was gesticulating, waving his hands in broad sweeps.

'Must involve a lot of travel then?'

'I've a driver. Gave up driving myself a few years ago. Makes things easier I find.'

Sounds more like you've been put off the road. Maybe there *is* such a thing as justice in this world.

Rosser leaned across Dermot.

'Des, that bank of yours. You've a new guy running your Galway office. I haven't met him yet. Could you set up an introduction for me?'

'Sure.'

'Strictly between you and me, I have a nice juicy financing opportunity coming up.'

Strictly between you and me. And Dermot. And the wine waiter. And...

'I'd like to do an old school pal a favour,' Rosser continued. 'First crack at the lending side of it. I presume you'd be interested, eh?' He gave Des a knowing wink.

Do an old school pal. Don't say he didn't warn you.

'Of course Rosser. Give me your card. Our man there is Ted Garvey. I'll call him and ask him to get in touch.'

Play the game. Keep smiling. Chummy.

'Great. Don't forget. You won't regret it.'

'I'm sure I won't. Glad to oblige, and thanks for giving us the opportunity.' Des smiled. Rosser handed him his card. 'I'll definitely make the call Monday.'

I'll call Ted alright, and warn him not to touch this shyster with a bargepole. Our bank subscribes to the rather old fashioned view about loans: we like to get our money back.

Des heard the empty chair on his right being pulled back and looked around to see Benny sitting down.

'Apologies, I didn't mean to be late.'

'You've missed the starter Farther Benedict, but let me order you something.' Des looked around for a waiter.

Benny raised his hands in protest. 'Please don't. I had supper with the community already, but I wanted to come along to represent them here.'

'You've eaten? Oh.'

'Yes. I got delayed. Someone I wasn't expecting came to see me. Had a bit of a problem he wanted to talk through with me.'

'Isn't it a bit late on a Saturday evening to be at someone's beck and call, Father? Didn't you mind?'

'It's the path I've chosen. I like to think if I can be of help to anyone, I'm available. Sometimes people just want a listening ear. Sometimes a bit more than that. I do what I can.' Benny smiled.

'It's a very Christian way of living. Loving your neighbour and all that.'

'Oh, one doesn't have to take the love bit too literally. Love after all is a pretty ethereal concept. But comfort, support, charity, yes. And often most important of all is providing hope and direction when the going gets tough. Giving is easy enough. All it really takes is to make a little effort.'

'You say easy to give. Surely it depends on one's other commitments?'

'Actually it's more about priorities, getting them in the right order.'

Des looked at the frail and seemingly simple man who clearly not only had strong beliefs, but also lived by them.

'I must remember that.' Des smiled. 'Incidentally, I was rather taken with your homily.'

'Thank you. On occasions such as today, I try to make what I have to say relevant, so it's nice to know someone was listening.' He smiled.

Joan was right about that homily in New York.

'There now, I've said it,' Benny continued. 'Pride is one of the seven deadly sins. I need hardly remind you.'

'Come Father, surely you're not about to tell me sinning is something of concern to you and your colleagues in the monastery?' Des gave a teasing smile.

'Well I can only speak for myself, and the negative bits don't bother me. No, I'm a great believer in focussing on the positive. Doing the right thing.'

Des was conscious Benny was looking at him directly as he spoke.

'No,' Benny continued, 'the God I believe in doesn't demand I keep a list of my failings on a slate.' He shook his head, and then smiling continued, 'but now you've aroused my curiosity. Tell me what aspect of my homily appealed to you?'

Not sure I should open up here. Ah just go for it.

'Father, I'm in the banking business. Maybe all of us are not quite the nasty money changers in the temple you guys hold us out to be, but...'

'Hold on there,' Benny interrupted. 'I never said bankers are nasty anything. I don't believe in putting labels on people. We're all individuals. How we choose to behave is up to each one of us alone.' He looked directly at Des. 'Anyway, you were saying?' He leaned forward, waiting.

He expects a coherent answer, so don't try to bullshit the man.

'Well, for instance you were encouraging us to live by the values that were instilled in us here in Rossallen, justice, morality and so on. It seems to me if one was to embrace your concept fully, we have a responsibility to intervene in the interests of the greater good, even in situations we are not directly involved in ourselves.'

'Yes?'

'In the business world, such situations are not always clear cut. A lot happens in an amorphous grey area. What struck me about what you were saying, is that applying your logic in practice could have far reaching consequences.'

Just then Rosser gesticulated, knocking over a bottle of wine. It broke a glass, and the red wine spread in an ever widening patch across the white linen tablecloth. Benny had been observing the action and after a few moments looked back at Des.

'Far reaching consequences indeed.' He smiled and nodded at the table. He cleared his throat. 'So, I did have someone listening to me. I don't know if you'd be interested, but we often get people coming down to us just to take some time out. For a day or two to reflect on things.' He glanced at Des. 'I'd be more than happy to arrange it if you'd like to come.'

'You mean, come on retreat? Morning Mass, Confession, Benediction, the whole caboodle?'

'No, no, no need for that. Well, you can do the full retreat if you want to. No, I was just suggesting if you ever felt you'd like to talk something through with someone who was at a distance from the action as it were, I'd be delighted to provide a listening ear.'

'Well Father, thank you very much. I'd never thought of doing a thing like that. I appreciate your offer. You know, I just might take you up on it.'

Dessie, you know bloody well that's exactly what you should do. You just have to trust *someone* and this wise old owl fits the bill perfectly. You'd have nothing to lose.

Chapter 13

Des was reviewing the February numbers when he heard the familiar ping.

To: *Des, Ed, Jerry, Dawn, and Alan.*
From *Milo*
Date: 8th March 2004
Re: *Management Committee Meeting*

Following a very successful visit to the Bank of West Indies by Dawn and I last week, we have now signed a Heads of Agreement with them on establishing our new operation, Coral Nominees. I expect to get board approval for this next week. I am planning on launching this new service on April 1st, so I'm organising a meeting in the boardroom tomorrow morning at nine to discuss. M.

Didn't realise he'd move so fast. Heads of Agreement. Euphemism for done deal? Bloody fellow is capable of anything. Have to find my moment to kill this off. But if I jump in too early though, I could self-destruct. Best assemble the facts, do some clinical analysis, and when time is right, go for the jugular.

The phone rang and he picked it up. Orla.

'Des, it's a call for you from a Mr Swales at the Regulator's office.'

'Who?' Des frowned.

'Mr Laurence Swales. Wants a word with you. Shall I tell him you're at a meeting?'

This isn't normal. What's he latched on to? Only one way to find out.

'From the Regulator's office? No, better not. Put him through.' The phone clicked.

'Des Peters here, how can I help?' His tone was tentative.

'Laurence Swales. I was wondering if I could have a word with you?'

Accent? English. Public School?

'Of course.'

'It's just something has come across my desk, and I was wondering if you could help clear it up for me?'

Des went on the alert and wondered if despite the apparent simplicity of the question, it masked something more complex.

'I will if I can. Eh, what is it?'

'I'd prefer not to discuss it over the telephone.'

Des felt his stomach tighten.

Something's wrong. The share issue? Market announcement. Orla's deal? God, it could be anything.

'Oh dear, this sounds rather ominous.'

'No, not really. It's just something I'd like to clear up,' said Laurence, insistent.

Just face the music.

'So when would suit you? Sometime next week?'

'It shouldn't take long. Half an hour should do it.'

Means now in Regulator-speak.

'How about sometime this afternoon?' Des noticed he was beginning to perspire.

'Could you drop over at say two-thirty?'

Des looked at his diary. It was blank for the afternoon. Don't show.

'Sorry, no, not two-thirty. Could you make it a bit later, say three-thirty?'

'Great, see you then. You know where we are,' said Laurence and hung up.

What the hell does he want? Can't be Coral. Doesn't know about it yet. Nothing ominous, he said. Probably would say that, wouldn't he? Don't buy it. This isn't a courtesy call. He's onto something and I'm the go-to man for the answers. And if I don't, it'll reflect badly on me. Better take a burst around College Park and clear my head before meeting him.

The phone rang again.

'All set for our Coral meeting in the morning?' Milo's query sounded normal.

'Sure.' Des frowned, as he wondered what his boss's real agenda was.

'Just thought you might like to kick it around with me beforehand?'

Checking to see if I intend to cause trouble so that he can neuter me.

'No, I think I'm fine. By the way, I've just got a call from the Regulator. Some guy called Swales. Wants to see me this afternoon.'

'Never heard of him. Must be some minion. What's he want to annoy you about?' A tetchiness had crept into Milo's voice.

'Damned if I know. Wouldn't say on the phone.'

'Christ, have those guys have nothing better to do than bug us? I mean, it's not as if we're doing anything out of the ordinary.'

Des allowed himself a smirk as he had a mental image of Milo glancing across his desk at his Coral file.

'Ah, it's probably something routine, maybe a return misfiled. Anyway, I'll sort it.'

'Rr...ight,' said Milo, with a falter. 'But Des?'

'Yeah?'

'Give me a call as soon as yet get back and let me know the story.' He hung up.

He's worried. And if he is, so should I.

*****

As he mounted the steps outside the Regulator's office, Des glanced at his watch: three twenty-two. Just right. The reception area did little to camouflage the tired appearance of a building that had seen better days. A makeshift cashier's booth to handle commemorative coins and out of date currency had been installed to one side. By the door a security man in an ill-fitting uniform asked him gruffly what he wanted before directing him to the reception desk a few paces away. Behind the desk, another security man was studying *The Racing Post.* Beside him, a receptionist looked up with a practiced enquiring eye.

'I'm here to meet Mr Swales. Laurence Swales.'

'And you are?' she asked as she reached for her Visitors Log.

'Des Peters,' he said, surprising himself with the weakness in his voice.

'Please take a seat.' She wrote in his details.

He picked up a newspaper and gazed at it, conscious he was feeling on edge. He recalled advice he'd once got as a trainee accountant, about dealing with someone in authority: if you want to stay in control and they ask you awkward questions, don't feel under pressure to respond straight away, just take your time. He glanced over the top of his newspaper and saw the receptionist putting her phone down and turning to speak to *Racing Post*. He glared across the lobby at Des, rose and came over.

'You're here to see Lar?' he asked sullenly.

'I've an appointment with Laurence Swales.' Des tried to convey an air of authority.

'This way,' said *Racing Post* nodding in the direction of the lifts.

They entered and travelled upwards.

In his office, Laurence rose from his desk and shook Des's hand.

Early forties. Too much time in the sun. Short, plump, hair thin on top.

'Glad you could make it. I don't think we met before? I only took up my post here a few months ago, still getting around to meeting my clients.'

English accent alright. Hasn't got his plummy tones right though. Probably minor public school. And we're not your client, Lar, even if we pay your wages.

'Pleased to meet you, Laurence.' Des smiled, and nodded agreeably.

Laurence picked up a file and walked across the room. He sat back in his chair, folded his arms and crossed his legs in a manner that reminded Des somehow of a schoolmaster who was about to administer a distasteful punishment and wished to delay it.

'Yes, I was with the Regulator in Singapore, but when this opportunity came up in Dublin, I thought it would be a good idea to get back closer to home. Kids in boarding school on the mainland and all that.' He smiled again.

Ingratiating small talk. Mainland. It's just another bloody island like this one.

'Well, I hope you enjoy your time in the Republic of Ireland.' Des returned the false smile.

'Thank you. Now I must apologise, but I can't offer you anything. Tea is served at three here, so I'm afraid you've just missed it. If you'd been able to be here at hour earlier, I could've done something for you.'

Cut the crap and get on with whatever it is you want to see me about.

'That's no problem, in fact I just had a cup before I left, thank you,' Des lied.

'Now, I'm glad you could drop in. This COO job of yours. It's a relatively new position in your bank I hear?'

'Yes.'

'You must find it a change. Taking on a broad portfolio of new responsibilities? Quite some challenge, I'm sure?'

'Oh yes, but it has its compensations.'

'Good for you.' Laurence began tapping his foot on the floor.

Oh for God's sake, spit it out.

'Desmond, I won't beat about the bush. I'd like you to help clear up something for me please?' The false smile had now disappeared and the tone was serious.

'If I can.' Des leaned forward, nodding, empathising.

'I've been looking at the movements in your share price over the past few months, and well,' he gave Des a meaningful look, 'without going into the detail of the numbers, it's outperformed the market by quite a bit. Would you care to comment?'

'Yes, it has indeed outperformed quite handsomely. A few of the pundits put us on their recommended buy list for 04. Indeed our broker thinks they're in for a good run.'

'And are they?'

This isn't what he wants to talk about. Bat it back.

'Have a good run?' Des shrugged. 'Only time will tell, but it's what our broker seems to think.' He managed an easy smile, two professionals in mutual agreement.

'And you think the movement is solely down to that?' Laurence furrowed his brow.

He hasn't called me in for this. Keep the answers vague until he breaks cover.

'Obviously the buyers are outnumbering the sellers.' Des shrugged.

'Obviously.' There was a hint of displeasure on Laurence's face. 'But come now, you must have some opinion of your own about this sudden buying interest?'

'In fact I do. Our last Stock Exchange announcement was in December when we were doing our share issue. We expressed confidence in our trading prospects. It was interpreted by the market as a positive.'

'You say expressed confidence. Surely a bit of an understatement of what you actually said. Would *strong* confidence not be a bit more like it?'

Des appeared to consider this.

'Yes, I agree we sounded pretty bullish.'

'Desmond, you are the COO and a director of the bank. Are you happy that statement fairly reflected the true situation?'

It was bloody Milo's doing when I was in New York. Can't admit. Shift the focus.

'Let me be clear. Our board's announcement was designed in part to reflect the current trading position and ensure a false market didn't develop in our share price.'

'And do you believe the current price fairly reflects your trading prospects?'

'It's the market's view of our trading prospects, and it seems fair enough to me.' Des extended his hands as much to say "and I'm a reasonable man".

The phone rang, and Laurence crossed to his desk to pick it up. He listened for a few moments, and then told his caller he'd ring them back in thirty minutes.

I was right. Full agenda not yet on table. Don't drop your guard.

Laurence came back to the table.

'Where were we? Oh yes, glad to hear you believe the price is fair. That's the kind of answer we regulators like to hear.' He looked at Des closely.

Des waited. He became aware of a clock ticking somewhere on a wall behind him.

'Oh, now you're here, there's just one other thing.' Laurence picked up the file on the table. 'Did you feel pressurised into making that announcement when you did?' He glanced at his notes. 'Yes, here it is the twenty third, the last trading day before the Christmas break?'

Why is he uncomfortable about this?

'I wouldn't say pressurised. But the share price had been rising, and we were anxious not to be seen to be sitting on what might be regarded as price sensitive information.'

'You had price sensitive information, you say.' Laurence began to tap his foot on the floor again. 'Yes, we had noticed. So we decided to examine the share deals immediately before the twenty third. One purchase in particular caught our eye.'

'Yeah?'

'Ah yes. A Ms Orla McGinley. She's one of your employees, is she not?'

Christ, he's spotted it.

'Orla? Yeah.'

'And what is her position in your bank?'

'She's personal assistant to the Chief Executive.'

'Personal assistant to the Chief Executive. Would I be right in thinking that would give her access to price sensitive information?' His eyes were now firmly on Des.

Keep calm. Easy does it.

'At times she does, and at times she doesn't.'

'Desmond, I don't know if you are aware, she bought fifty thousand shares a few days before you made your announcement. The question is, did she know it was about to be made or not?'

Des looked straight at Laurence.

'A very fair question. Indeed it's the very one that I asked myself at the time.'

'So, you were aware she bought them ahead of your public announcement?'

'Yes. As COO I have a responsibility to make myself aware of such issues. When I picked up on it I queried her. I went through the chain of events, and satisfied myself she wasn't aware we were about to make our announcement, never mind what was in it.' Des pushed his chair back from the table and crossed his legs.

Laurence continued to look at him closely.

'So, you're confirming there wasn't a breach of any Insider Trading Laws or Codes?'

'I am. Incidentally I've made a file note of the sequence of events and my conversation with her. If you'd like a copy I can send it over to you.'

Put that in your pipe and smoke it.

'I don't think that'll be necessary.' Laurence looked defeated. 'I'm sure we can rely on your assurance everything's above board and there have been no regulatory breaches.'

Laurence signalled the meeting was over and walked Des to the lift. 'I'll see you out, security, you know.'

In the lobby, *Racing Post* was holding a mobile phone to his ear and tearing up what looked like a yellow bookmaker's docket.

'Thank you for dropping over,' said Laurence. 'I think it's always good to clear up these little things. Can save misunderstandings later.' He smiled.

Just let me out of here.

'Not at all.' Des returned the smile.

When he got back to his office, he picked up the phone to Milo.

'Just back.'

'What did nosey Swales want?' The aggressiveness in Milo's voice was obvious.

'Wanted to know why our share price was doing so well. Implied we overegged our announcement.'

'Must have nothing better to do than stir shit.'

'Actually I think it was a cover he was using. At the end of the meeting it transpired he'd been trawling through the dealings in our shares. Spotted Orla's deal.'

'Oh for God's sake. What did he think was wrong with that? Christ, we've been through all this bullshit before.' Des pictured Milo's rolling his eyes at the ceiling.

'I think he was of the view we might have an insider trading case to answer. Didn't quite say that though.'

'I presume you saw him off the patch alright?'

'Yeah. Told him I'd investigated it and was satisfied everything was above board.'

'Which of course it is. Good man yourself.'

'Yes, Milo, of course.'

Well, it was this time, but it was close. But next time?

'Still, I suppose these petty bureaucrats have to be seen to do something to justify the exorbitant fees they charge us for dreaming up new regulations and wasting our time. Can't they find someone else to screw around?'

We mightn't like it, but it's a job someone has to do.

'Anyhow,' Milo continued, 'you'll be along tomorrow morning I presume?'

'Sure.'

Old bravado back. Orla's fifty grand is peanuts. Don't know which should worry me more about him: when he's praising me or when he's baring his teeth. Each encounter seems to be a roll of his dice. Got to be well prepared for the day when the wrong number comes up.

*****

As the committee members were gathering around the boardroom table the following morning, Milo was glancing at his watch.

'We're a bit behind time, so let's get started. Dawn, perhaps you'd brief us on where we are with Coral. And before you start, I'd just like to remind you all this is strictly confidential for the moment. Understood?' He looked at each of them with steely eyes.

Not the time to cross him.

Milo gave Dawn a slight nod, and she picked up a bundle of handouts and passed them around.

'Thank you,' said Dawn. 'In summary the position is as Milo said in his email. We're nearly there. We've signed the Heads of Agreement and we just need board final approval.'

Wasting no time. Just wants our rubber stamp. This could get tricky. I'll need to choose my intervention extremely carefully.

Ed butted in.

'Excuse me, but I'm a bit confused already. How can we have signed an agreement without our board approving it first?' He looked at Milo with accusing eyes.

An expression of frustration crossed Dawn's face. She said nothing but looked at Milo. He nodded to her and then he turned to Ed.

'The board has already signed off on our Strategic Plan. This is purely an operational matter which is management's responsibility. Does that clarify matters?'

Framed as a rhetorical question. Neat three card trick there, Milo.

'More or less, but don't they sign off on this as well? I mean Dawn was just saying...'

'Ed, I know what Dawn just said,' Milo interrupted impatiently. 'Rest assured I'll ensure all the board's needs will be met on this issue.' He signalled to Dawn to continue with her presentation.

'Next is to explain what this facility is.' She pulled up the sleeves of her shirt slightly and leaned forward. 'Our new subsidiary, Coral Nominees, will be managed on our behalf by BWI, the Bank of West Indies. Coral will keep track of the deposit flows, and each depositor will have a separate numbered account.' She spoke assuredly.

Fair play to her. Confident, backing herself on this.

'But if the deposits leave our books,' asked Alan, 'doesn't that mean we lose control over them?'

'Good question. We'll continue to have control, but through Coral. Remember Coral is our company and it gets a cut of any business under our BWI agreement.'

This just might work alright, but still seems close to that Ansbacher dodge. Better do a line by line comparison if I'm to develop a killer objection.

Ed decided to interject again.

'But surely if we plunge into this, we could end up in a situation where our depositors would shift all their money off our books?'

Milo looked exasperated.

'Ed, no one is plunging into anything. And may I remind you part of your job is to hold on to our existing deposits. Coral is merely an extra weapon for you to use at your discretion if you think any deposits might walk out the door. Do I make myself clear?'

'Understood,' said Ed, clearly unhappy.

Jerry cleared his throat.

'I think what we're proposing here is a pragmatic solution to a problem we have. But surely if our deposits shrink, we'll have less money to lend out, and that'll hit our profits from another angle.'

'Thank you for raising this Jerry,' said Milo. 'What Dawn has outlined is what I regard the first phase of the Coral initiative. However, I've signalled to our friends in BWI we'd like to explore possible recycling opportunities with them.'

Recycling! Jesus, He means Coral lending money. Sounds like a bank within a bank. Coral's not authorised to do this. Can't let it pass. But not in front of the children.

'So where does this leave us now?' Jerry persisted.

Dawn glanced at Milo before continuing.

'We intend to go live with the Coral deposit facility on the first of the month.'

Milo placed his hands on the table and looked at Ed.

'It'll be up to you, to brief your managers on when they should offer this new facility. Dawn will fill you in on any of the operating details you feel you may need.'

'I'm going to have my work cut out for me.' Ed was shaking his head.

Milo glared at him for a few moments. When he spoke, his tone was cold.

'Ed, that's what I'm paying you for.'

He looked around the table at each member of the committee in turn.

'I'm sure none of you need reminding, but you all have options to buy shares in the bank at considerably below the current share price.' He looked around the table and made sure to catch the eye of each of those present. 'And the bottom line is our share price is determined by the amount of profits we make. So, you are in control of the value of your own personal nest eggs.' He looked around the table again. 'I presume my message is clear?'

He watched each of them nod their heads.

'Now, are there any further questions?'

Alan coughed lightly.

'Just one if I may. What do you want me to do about communicating this externally?'

'Good question. In this case I want you to keep the lid on Coral. We don't want to draw any more attention to it than is absolutely necessary.' Again Milo looked at each of them in turn.

'But there'll be enquiries from our friends in the media.' Alan persisted tentatively with an edge to his voice. 'They're bound to find out about it.'

Milo dropped his head into his hands and ran his fingers through his hair. He then looked up.

'Alan, you're the communications expert. Just work out some line or another about bank secrecy and customer confidentiality.' He smiled enigmatically. 'I don't think you need me to tell you how to fob them off and send them up blind alleys.'

He does need you to tell him Milo, but you're a real slither, and you're too cute to say something incriminating that can be quoted back to you later, aren't you?

Milo looked around the table. 'Okay, let's leave it there? Des, could you stay on?'

*****

When the others left the boardroom, Milo looked over at Des.

'What d'you think?'

Got to work myself up for this.

'Looks like Dawn's done her homework. Obviously I'd like to go through the full proposal. Make sure there's nothing there to trip us up.'

'Good. I don't want anything to turn around and bite me on the arse here. In fact, I think it would be a good idea if you flew out there and checked things out for yourself.' He nodded to Des. 'I'm pretty sure everything is rock solid, but I'd like you to be happy too.'

You don't give a toss about me. A trap? Where? Think quickly. If I go, I'm implicated. But if I don't, he can say I didn't rate Coral as a risk.

'Yeah,' said Des, 'it might be no harm.'

'So let's organise it. I'll ask Dawn to set it up. In fact I think she should go with you, do the introductions and so on.' He nodded his CEO-in-charge-of-everything head.

'Eh, sure.' Des sank back in his seat feeling browbeaten.

'Tell you what. You've been busting your ass here since you took on the COO job. Take Joan. Caribbean beaches are not the worst place in the world to spend a few days. I'm sure I can find some space for an extra airfare in my expenses budget.' He grinned.

'Oh, thanks Milo. I'm sure she'd like that.'

Stop stalling.

'By the way,' Des added, 'you were talking about using Coral to recycle money back to our customers. What exactly have you in mind?'

'Don't concern yourself about that.' Milo threw an arm in the air. 'It's just a vague idea I haven't thought through. Don't worry, I'll go through it all with you if it looks like being a runner.'

'Yes,' Des felt his heart pounding, 'but when you were talking, well, it may be the terminology you used, but there's a risk of it being seen as a bank operating within a bank.'

189

'Yeah?'

'If that construction was put on it, we'd have a regulatory problem.'

Milo looked at Des, his face expressionless.

'Thanks Des, nothing has been nailed down yet. But I take your point. I'll have a word with Arthur about it and close that off. Okay?'

'Okay.'

Actually it's not. It's another brush off. This can't go on Dessie. You know bloody well this whole business could get completely out of hand and you've simply got to put a stop to it. You've just got to assemble all your arguments coherently and then have a rational discussion with him. And the board if necessary.

*****

The phone was ringing in Des' office when he got back. Ed.

'Des, I just want you to know I'm not at all happy with this Coral business.'

Bloody cry baby. *You're* not happy? How the feck do you think I feel? Fend him off.

'Yeah? In what way?'

'We'll it's all a tax dodge, isn't it? It's taking us into unknown territory.'

Tax Dodge. Don't even think those words.

'I agree it would be a new departure. But Ed, we've all got to accept we've a new Chief Executive now.'

'I know, but what really worries me is where he's leading us.'

You're not on your o-nee-o there.

'Ed, you've got to understand the board appointed Milo to do the job. They've agreed the Strategic Plan. Their sign off on the Coral Heads of Agreement is next.'

'And are you yourself supporting it?'

Des took a deep breath. I can't tell a downright lie.

'Ed, I'm sure you'll appreciate when I'm wearing my director's hat, I'm not at liberty to discuss such matters with you. However, I can assure you, I consider the interests of all of our stakeholders when I make my contributions at board level.'

Whatever that gobbledegook means.

'Okay, if you say so. Thanks Des.'

*****

When Des got home that evening, Joan was getting ready to go out to her Bridge evening.

'How was your day?' he asked.

'Very interesting. Remember the research student I was telling you about, trying to get information about Bartholemew Mosse?'

'The one who was going up to the Royal Irish Academy to find out more?'

'Yeah. Anyhow, between the jigs and the reels, she's discovered a descendent of the great man is living down the country. She's got in touch, and hopes to meet him.'

'Sounds good.'

'It's better than good - it's great. It just goes to show if you really apply yourself and stick single-mindedly to a task, the journey can be very rewarding.'

He watched her brushing her hair in front of the mirror in the hall.

'And how was your day?' she called over her shoulder as she brushed.

Wait until I've my ducks in a row.

'Oh interesting as well. But then it's never dull with Milo around. The usual caught piggy-in-the-middle between him and the troops. All in a day's work.' He shook his head.

'Well you knew that when you took on the Deputy job didn't you?'

I thought I did, but totally underestimated the political intrigue I'd be embroiled in. Don't admit that until I find my way out though.

'Ah I suppose so,' said Des, forcing a laugh. 'Anyway, it's always interesting, always something new.'

'Yeah? And what was new about today?'

'Oh, apart from other things he wants me to go to the West Indies. to run my eye over a new operation we're establishing there.'

She continued to brush her hair and began to smile.

'So when are you going?'

'Actually it's 'we'. He's proposed we both go. A trip to the sun in March would be pretty alright, eh?'

She put down her brush and turned around to face him. He noticed her smile had disappeared.

'Des, let's just be clear about something here. I've no doubt you're excellent at your job, and I'll support you in any way I can. But I want to have minimum dealings with Milo and his cronies, and I certainly don't want to be the beneficiary of any jollies he wangles up. By all means, you go wherever your work takes you, but just leave me out of it.' She faced back to the mirror and patted down her hair. She then turned to him again. 'I must fly or I'll be late. Should be back by eleven. Bye.'

He watched her go out the hall door and close it behind her. He was reminded of a train journey he'd taken a couple of summers earlier from St Pancras to Gare du Nord. It had begun with a series of tunnels which got progressively longer and darker. And then the train had gone down into a really long one. It seemed endless.

Chapter 14

Some days later, Des sat brooding in his office ahead of his meeting with Milo and Dawn, to discuss his upcoming visit to the West Indies. He was still thrown by Joan's refusal to accompany him. Apart from feeling she would have enjoyed the trip, he hoped to avail of the opportunity of a few days away from the office to think and talk through his predicament with her. One moment he wondered if he was being paranoid about Coral, after all it had board support and wasn't illegal, and the next he wondered if he was being compromised by his sense of corporate loyalty, or even the rather generous financial rewards he was getting.

He rose and walked down to the meeting.

'So everything's organised?' asked Milo.

'Yeah,' said Dawn. 'We fly out to Queenstown on Tuesday. Everything's booked.'

Milo looked at Des.

'Joan looking forward to it?'

Des felt a yearning heave in his stomach.

'Unfortunately no, they're rather short staffed at the library. Some of them are on midterm break. She couldn't get the time off.' He surprised himself with the ease he'd rolled off the lie.

'Oh bad luck. But I'm sure there'll be another time.'

As if you give a monkey's.

'Yeah, hopefully,' Des replied.

'Now, you guys got your programme fixed?' Milo continued looking from Des to Dawn.

Dawn leaned forward.

'What I've told our friends is this is really a familiarisation visit for Des. I also want to see if I can explore the Phase 2 possibilities, the recycling idea.'

So it hasn't gone away. Must keep a close eye on this.

'I presume you're meeting with Bob?' Milo looked at Des. 'Bob Chandler is their CEO. A very agreeable guy. When it comes to doing a deal, he cuts through the bullshit. Doesn't allow the lawyer pedants to get into the driving seat. A man after my own heart.'

You mean he doesn't let facts or technicalities get in the way of a fast buck.

'Yeah, I'm looking forward to meeting him,' Des nodded. 'And indeed the others who Dawn says would be worth meeting.'

'Yeah, I've asked Bob to line them up.' She exchanged glances with Milo.

There they go again. This thing is going ahead with or without me. I badly need to identify a deal breaker.

'Good,' said Milo smiling. 'Give you a chance to raise any questions you might have.' He smiled at Des. 'I want you to be comfortable with all aspects of this initiative.'

As comfortable as a mouse eyeing up a lump of cheese in a trap.

'Oh I'm sure everything's been looked after,' said Des, returning the insincere smile. 'I'm looking forward to the opportunity to see things first-hand for myself.'

Milo sat back and crossed his legs.

'I think you'll find the arrangements are well set up. Our friends out there are used to this, so their systems are well tried and tested.'

'That's good to hear. Still, it'll be no harm I see exactly how Coral will work,' said Des, maintaining his amiable demeanour.

Milo turned to Dawn.

'Now, you said something about jollying them along on the recycling side. Where are we on this?'

Pay attention.

'Well, you remember when we were out there, it was suggested I should explore this a bit more? What opportunities there might be to boost our profits?'

This thing is definitely getting legs. Time for action.

'Who suggested this?' asked Des.

Dawn glanced at Milo, who cleared his throat.

Good. At least they know they're on thin ice with me on this.

'Bob mentioned some of their other bank clients do this, and thought we might like to do the same. I showed an interest in pursuing the idea.'

Whoa!

'Are you saying Coral could be in the lending business?' Des's tone was sharp.

Milo uncrossed his legs and leaned forward.

'No, certainly not. I told you Des I'd have a word with Arthur about this. I don't think any of us would have an appetite for going down that road. Indeed, I specifically told Bob any lending would have to be on the strict condition it was done by BWI, not Coral.'

I'd like to believe you, but I don't really.

'Very wise.' Des nodded.

'Bob didn't see a problem in principle with this. However, he made the valid point if borrowers were totally unknown to them, he'd want some sort of comfort from us.'

He's up to something.

'So how could we satisfy his needs?' Des looked from Milo to Dawn and back.

'I don't have the answer but it's where we are at the moment. Dawn's trying to find a solution. Right Dawn?'

'Exactly Milo. We don't have any firm proposition from them yet about how it would work. It's still at the discussion stage.' She sat back glancing from one of them to the other.

I don't trust either of them. But without a concrete proposal on the table, there's nothing for me to oppose. No option but to bide my time.

'I see,' said Des. 'Let's wait and see how your discussions pan out.'

'Yes, we'll have to wait and see,' Milo nodded. 'And don't forget, any agreement will have to be approved by the board.'

Board approval. That's it. He'll have to produce a document with a recommendation at some stage for that and then I'll get my chance to scupper it. Problem solved.

'Seems fair enough,' said Des.

'Good. So you're flying out Tuesday. I'm sure Bob will look after you very well. Let me know how you get on.' Milo switched on his salesman's smile. 'Enjoy.'

Enjoy what? Building sandcastles?

As he stood up to leave, he noticed Milo had jettisoned the three Malton prints from over his drinks cabinet and replaced them with a modern pop art picture.

'Oh, I see you've installed a Roy Lichtenstein print,' he said to Milo, nodding towards the wall. He laughed lightly. 'A shift from the traditional to the modern in line with our new direction, is that it?'

Milo looked at him, his face expressionless.

'Yeah, something like that. But it's not a Lichtenstein print, it's an original.'

Good God. Must have cost a fortune. Hope the shareholders don't find out what he's blowing their money on.

He walked in a daze on unsteady legs to the door.

*****

Des gazed at the idyllic Caribbean scene which was straight out of a tourist brochure: sun shining from a cloudless sky, calm sea, and the white spotless beach. A few early morning joggers were gliding along by the seashore. Beyond them, some brightly coloured fishing boats were putt-putting towards the horizon.

A waiter was rearranging large plates of mixed fruit at a table across the veranda. About half of the tables were occupied, couples in bright summer wear, and some business people like himself in white shirts with long sleeves, prodding laptops. Two waitresses drifted between the tables with coffee pots.

'Ah, there you are. Had a good night's sleep?' said Dawn, pushing her sunglasses back on her head and pulling a chair out from the table. She looked the full business-woman-on-a-mission part in a silk shirt and lightweight tailored business suit.

'Tip top.' He stretched his arms over his head and gave her a broad smile. 'And you?'

'Ah, I never got used to changing time zones. Woke early. Anyway, it gave me a chance to go through my notes for today. All set?' she asked, eager to get their business underway.

Des smiled.

'Yeah, all set. Mind you I find myself in an unusual position. Going on a fact-finding mission. I'm usually the one answering the questions, not asking them.'

'In which case you're well equipped to identify the ones to ask, the ones that you'd prefer not to be asked yourself.' She laughed.

'We're hardly going to get into a cross-examination session are we?'

'Ah no, I'm only kidding. No Des, these guys are straightforward and business-like. What you see is what you get.'

'Good.'

She waved to a waiter and ordered orange juice and coffee, and then looked at Des.

'You have to bear in mind their business is not exactly rocket science. Their service is essentially administration, record keeping. Bob's okay. He'll do what he's told.'

'Sounds easy. However, it must meet our own needs as well.'

'How do you mean? You're not about to throw a spanner in the works, I hope?' Her face clouded.

Why is she so defensive? Must be under orders from Milo to chaperone me.

'Ah no. It's just we need to be certain this new service we are going to offer meets with all of our legal and regulatory obligations.'

'Of course. Sorry Des, I was taking that as a given.' She lifted her hands in token surrender. 'I think you'll find everything is kosher on that front, but if you come across any issues, let's try and sort them out while we're here. Okay?'

Hmm. We don't want to be going back to Milo and telling him we've a problem, do we? She's a smart cookie alright. No wonder he hired her.

Des looked at his watch.

'If you'll excuse me.' He rose and folded his napkin. 'When do we leave for the office? Do we need a taxi?'

'We're due to meet Bob at nine. His office is not far away but it can get a bit sticky walking around, so I'll book a cab for say eight-thirty. See you at the front door then?'

'See you then.'

*****

'Impressive,' Des remarked to Dawn.

They were looking out the boardroom window on the eighth floor of Colonial House. The panoramic view of Queenstown and its harbour immediately commanded attention. Colonial House itself was the tallest building in the area, challenged only by a string of resort hotels along the coast out to their right. Close in to the harbour, a giant cruise ship was preparing to dock, whilst three more stood by, waiting their turn.

Des glanced around the boardroom which was equipped with modern office furniture. A few nondescript paintings, presumably by some local artist, reminded him vaguely of Gauguin. On a sideboard were a number of coffee pots, fruit juices, and plates of cookies.

'Dawn, good to see you again,' said a voice from the door. 'Had you a good flight?' A small thin man in his late fifties crossed the room. He shook hands with Dawn.

'Good to see you too, Bob. Let me introduce you to our Director and COO, Des Peters.' She flashed her winning smile.

'Delighted to meet you.' Bob bowed slightly.

'And I'm pleased to meet you too.'

'Let's help ourselves to some coffee.' Bob waved to the array on the sideboard. 'How's Milo?'

Des looked at Bob's smile. It reminded him of a fawning waiter hoping to influence the size of his tip.

'Fine fettle as always,' Des nodded. 'Sends his very best regards.'

'By the way, how long are you over for? I hope you'll be taking some days to see our wonderful country?'

'I'm planning on seeing the island tomorrow and then getting the overnight flight back.' Des looked over to Dawn. 'You've been here before. You're planning to take a couple of days in Cuba aren't you?'

'That's right, I always wanted to see it, so I thought this is my chance.'

'Well, I hope you both enjoy your time here. Now, are we all set for our new venture?' Bob sat and motioned to them both to do likewise.

Dawn took charge.

'Sure. We thought it'd be a good idea if Des could familiarise himself with the set up here. He's our director who has to liaise with the Regulator and the auditors, so he obviously would like to be able to answer any questions they might ask him.'

'Right,' said Bob, nodding. 'What I've arranged is a session for you with each of the heads of our banking, services, and operations departments. I've organised lunch for noon and I'll rejoin you then. So if you've any questions for me, we can deal with them then. Sound okay to you Des?'

'Sure. Sounds just fine.'

'Good. I think you'll find the arrangements we are putting in place for Coral will be to your satisfaction. Milo will have told you we've similar arrangements with other European banks.'

'I'm glad to hear it.'

'Now, Dawn, you'd like to spend the morning getting to grips with the arrangements we're working on the lending side, right?' Bob looked at her.

I'll deal with that later.

'Right.'

'We ourselves haven't got to a final position on it yet, so I think it best if you and I thrashed it around a bit more. I've asked our in-house legal adviser to sit in.'

'Sounds good.'

Bob rose.

'Fine then. Des, come with me and I'll introduce you to our team.'

*****

A dull ache enveloped Des, as several mental images from the day jostled for attention. The obsequiously smiling Bob, the recurring references to the as yet undefined lending proposal, the inexperienced Dawn's determination to drive though the entire project, and the certainty that behind it all was the Machiavellian Milo and his triumphant grin pulling the strings. And overarching all of these, he could still see Joan walking out their hall door, telling him she wanted no part in the bank's intrigues. He'd been shaken, but he knew he couldn't fault her reasoning. He was also conscious he somehow needed to get his own reasoning straightened out. Urgently.

'Not a bad way to spend an evening in March, eh?' said Dawn, snapping him out of his thoughts.

He looked over at her. They were again sitting on the hotel veranda. It was still warm, despite a gentle sea breeze. At the other side of the swimming pool was a long buffet counter, covered with in a spotless white table cloth, and crammed with a seemingly never ending display: salmon and lobster, meats and mangos, chicken and chowder, pineapples and oranges, beans and beets, salads and salamis, presented a kaleidoscope of tropical rainbows. Beyond it, on a platform under some palm trees, a steel band belted out calypso songs. A few couples were dancing. The tables were occupied by laughing guests in brightly coloured garb, fighting to be heard above the incessant beat. *Come Mister Tally Man, Tally me Banana.* White jacketed waiters and waitresses slipped gracefully between the rows of tables, bearing drinks trays above their heads.

'Yeah, a different world,' he managed returning to his immediate surrounds.

'Beats the weather back home. I could get used to this life.' With a grin she nudged her plate of scoured lobster shells towards the centre of the table.

'Except if you were working here, you wouldn't be doing this every night.'

'True.' She pushed her chair back and crossed her legs displaying an expanse of thigh. 'So tell me, what did you make of Captain Bob's crew?' She idly picked up her wine glass.

'They seem a competent lot. If Bob is anything to go by, I don't think they'll set the world on fire. But then, that's not what we want from them, is it?'

'Yeah, Milo also thought so.' She drank some wine.

Is she just being agreeable or is it a veiled warning?

'Mind you, processing paperwork is not my idea of job satisfaction.'

She looked at him over her glass.

'For me neither. But they seem quite happy. After all, they'll be getting good money out of us without having to work particularly hard for it.'

Their waiter arrived and offered more drinks. Des looked over at the band. Some swaying dancers were joining in singing *Work all Night on a Drink of Rum.* They ordered coffee and liqueurs.

'So you'll be supporting the final agreement with the board?' she asked.

Watch her. Working 24/7. Milo's lapdog. No, much more than a lapdog. Far too astute. Probably under instructions to make sure I toe the line. Choose your words carefully.

'Oh yeah, I don't see any issues at this end on the deposits front.'

'So do you think there could be some at our end?' Her question was sharp and specific.

'It's going to be down to how we market this. Neither our Regulator or tax authority will be amused if they see us promoting a scheme leading to funds moving offshore.'

'But we wouldn't be breaking any laws, would we?' She frowned.

Under instructions to have me signed up before I leave here?

'Em, maybe not, but pretty close.'

'I don't see how. I mean it's not as if we'd be actually *promoting* the service.'

'Yeah, but sometimes the perception can be greater than the reality. We're just going to have to be careful.'

'Fair enough. But the process is under our control.'

'True. What it boils down to is, we'll just have to invest considerable time with Ed on the various scenarios about when he should and shouldn't inform customers about Coral.'

'You think so?'

'I do Dawn.'

'Then let's do it.'

Good. Seems to satisfy her. Might back off a bit now.

Dawn called for the bill when the coffee and drinks arrived. Most of the diners were now out dancing and singing along to *Six Foot, Seven Foot, Eight Foot Bunch..*

Des looked at Dawn. She'd uncrossed her legs and was swaying gently to the throbbing beat in her light summer clothes.

Very enticing. Must have a lover, boyfriend at least. God, there's a thought. Milo? Surely not? He noticed an extra button on her blouse was open and her breasts were free. A surge of desire caught him by surprise. He noticed she was watching him closely. Is she coming on to me? Steady on Dessie, get a grip. Talk biz.

'And how did you get on with the recycling idea?'

'Not there yet, I'm afraid, but getting close.'

Press on.

'So what's the problem?'

'It's relatively simple. Bob's up for it and happy to put the loans to our customers on his books. But he doesn't know them, so he needs some sort of comfort from us.'

'You mean he wants us to guarantee them?'

'It would be his preferred option of course, but I told him it was a non-runner. Milo's clear about that. But if we're to get a slice of the action, we're going to have to provide Bob with some sort of comfort. From his point of view it's not an unreasonable stance,' she nodded.

'Yeah, I can see his point of view. So what *are* we going to do about it?'

She picked up her drink and appeared to consider the question.

'It's a bit of a conundrum really.' She sipped her liqueur. 'If we're to get a share of the profits, we're going to have to give something, even if it's not the guarantee they want.'

'Like make a concession?'

'As I said, I don't know. Coral will have to make some sort of commitment. I think the best thing to do is to talk this through with Arthur.'

'Arthur?'

'Yeah. He's our legal advisor after all. We need to find a mechanism that'll satisfy Bob, and at the same time make sure we're not exposed.'

'You mean exposed if any of our customers welsh on their debts to Bob?'

'Yeah, that's about it.'

She's trying alright, but doesn't seem to realise she's playing with fire. Technicalities of lending money and getting it back are not straightforward. Her 'Pile 'em High and Sell 'em Low' experience, as Ed colourfully called it, doesn't translate to banking.

'Well, I agree we should get Arthur's opinion.' He picked up his glass and sat back.

Dawn was looking out over the top of her glass at the band. The dance area was now crowded as they joined in singing *Day, is a Day, is a Day, is a Day, is a Day, is a Day-O*. Des looked at an enigmatic half smile on Dawn's lips, and felt vaguely disconcerted.

'And how are you finding things with us?' He asked. 'Glad you signed up?'

She shook herself out of her reverie.

'Oh yeah, I'm really enjoying it. A great challenge, to say nothing of good people around. Yeah. I'm really enjoying it.'

'Great.' He sipped his drink. 'And you're heading for Havana tomorrow?'

'Yeah, thought I'd have a look-see. Castro's getting on and won't be able to keep the lid on it much longer. One of the last bastions of communism. How they sell stuff without marketing support intrigues me.' She eyes twinkled. 'Pity you couldn't come.'

'Ah, I need to get back. Speaking of which, anything I can do for you when I get there?'

'No, it's okay. I'll send an email to Orla to set up a meeting for me with Arthur.'

'Ah, Orla, nice girl. Very efficient. I've always had a bit of a soft spot for her.'

Dawn turned quickly and looked at him.

'You're going to have to take your place in the queue, behind Alan, aren't you?' She laughed.

'What?' He said, unable to contain the surprise in his voice. 'Alan and Orla?'

'Oh, I thought you knew. Yeah, they've been an item since before my time.'

'Didn't realise.'

An item since before my time. Would make it from sometime last year. December. Jesus. Orla's purchase of the bank's shares. She didn't have direct access to insider information. But Alan did. Shit. And I've given my personal assurance to the Regulator I'd investigated things fully and everything was clean. Oh God.

Des closed his eyes. The steel band played on. Dawn watched. The patrons danced. They sang along.

Daylight Come an I Wanna Go Home.

*****

Des woke up with a start.

He was dreaming he was back in Rossallen, sitting in the classroom. A teacher was out sick and Benny came in and asked them to write an essay on *Damocles* which he had spelt out in large sloping backhand writing across the blackboard. As soon as he left a general rumpus developed. Ginger started into a much exaggerated strutting impersonation of Benny, to the shouts of encouragement, while Rosser squatted on the teacher's desk, smoking a cigarette butt. Suddenly the classroom door was flung open and Benny reappeared, his face puce. Ginger dived back into his seat and Rosser sprang into an oversized wicker waste paper basket behind the door. A deafening silence descended under the Dean of Studies' sweeping glare. Then someone began to titter and everyone's eyes were drawn to wisps of smoke escaping from Rosser's hiding place. In one movement Benny whirled around, whipped out a sword from under his monk's habit, and plunged it into the wicker basket. There was a scream, and when Benny removed his sword it was dripping with blood. He ordered the class one by one to stand over by the wall, directing them at close range with his bloody weapon. Then, just as Des's turn came and he rose from his desk on rubber legs, the bell for the end of class rang.

Opening his eyes, Des looked around him and breathed a sigh of relief when he realised the ringing bell was coming from his hotel alarm clock.

*****

After his breakfast, he decided to take a local bus to Jamestown. He sat at the front and looked out at the coastline. After they passed the Royal British Country Club, the road swung inland and through a neglected sugar plantation, and then uphill until it reached a cliff top on the other side of the island. A spectacular view unfolded of a raging sea, crashing against the rugged shore and throwing up a vast cloud of spray.

Alighting at Jamestown, he strolled the short distance to a small harbour. A few boats lay overturned on the foreshore. Three men were mending a fishing net at the water's edge. Over by the breakwater, a cluster of screeching gulls was scavenging among a low pile of lobster pots.

A rough track led him to a beacon on a hilltop. When he got there he sat on a wooden bench and absorbed his surroundings. The gentle breeze of his hotel was replaced by an incessant force coming in off the Atlantic, its waves battering the coast.

An involuntary shudder passed through him when he thought about the personal assurances he had given Laurence about his incomplete investigation into Orla's insider deal. The self-protecting file note he'd composed on Arthur's advice seemed scant consolation. He knew in his heart he'd compromised himself because of his lack of thoroughness.

And then it occurred to him it could be part of a pattern. Was he an unwitting player in an amoral game? Was it too easy to merely disapprove of Milo's standards and the way he operated? Was he himself not also tainted and seduced by power and financial rewards? Was he just sleepwalking his way through it all?

Benny's words came back to him. Benny hadn't preached religion, or spoken out of both sides of his mouth. He'd simply appealed to the individual's better nature, to embrace and practice truth and honesty.

Arriving back at the harbour, he saw a hostelry beside the shore line. Outside it there were some inviting benches on a crude patio, beneath a cluster of palm trees. Presently a girl in her twenties, in a loose floral smock and flat sandals, emerged from the open door and ambled over.

'And how are we today?' She gave him a broad smile.

'Very good, thank you.'

'Hey, do I hear an Irish accent there?' Her eyes danced mischievously.

'Eh yeah, but how did you know? There can't be many Irish around here.'

'I think you Irish have been coming here for over two hundred years now. You guys were the first slaves here you know, you and the Scots.' He felt her watching him.

'You mean even before the African slave trade?'

'Right. You can check it out on the tombstones in the graveyard over there.' She nodded towards a low walled area nearby. 'Now what can I get you this beautiful day?'

'A cold beer would be great.'

'What's your name?'

'Des, and yours?'

'I'm Rosie.' She flashed her eyes and threw back her head. She was grinning now.

'Your second name isn't Scenario by any chance, is it?' He couldn't help it.

'You know if I'd ten bucks for every time I've been asked that question, I'd be the richest girl on the island.' She laughed.

'Sorry.' He put his hands up in mock apology.

'It's okay. You over here on holidays?'

'No, just a quick business visit. I fly back home to Ireland tonight.'

'A pity. This is a great place to chill out.'

'I'm sure. You work here all the time, Rosie?'

'Sure. Work isn't too hard. Not too many customers during the week. The money keeps me going, but you don't need that much of it around here. I've enough for my needs.'

'Never tempted by the bright lights of Queenstown? Or Miami maybe?'

'Oh no. I don't need to chase dreams. No, I'm content with my lot here.' She laughed and started for the building and called over her shoulder, 'One beer coming up.'

I don't need to chase dreams. I'm content with my lot.

When she came with the beer, Des sat back and closed his eyes and tried to blot out thoughts of the confined flight home, and the upcoming war of attrition he was going to have to wage with Milo. Eventually he heard the toot from the returning bus, and, looking up, saw the girl waving to him from the door of the hostelry. Waving back with a grin, he put a five dollar bill under his glass for the beer, and then a ten dollar one for Rosie Scenario.

Chapter 15

To: **Management Committee**
From: **Milo**
Date: **4th June 2004**
Re: **Project Coral**

Coral Nominees has now been up and running for two months, and I think it would be useful if we could set aside our meeting scheduled for next Monday morning (7th) to review progress. It will also give us an opportunity to take whatever preparatory steps we think may be judicious in advance of preparing our half year Accounts. M.

Davy Byrnes was doing a brisk Friday lunch trade. A motley assortment of office workers, shoppers, and tourists were taking a break, before gearing themselves up for their afternoons. Des and Alan entered from Duke Street, found a table, and ordered the plate of the day.

'How're you getting on with our friends in the West Indies?' Alan asked.

'A good question. I'm not entirely sure myself, but Milo's giving us an update on Monday.'

'From what I can make out, it's well ahead of expectations.'

They were interrupted by the dishevelled appearance of Noel.

Danger.

'Ah, I wonder what conspiracy you two gentlemen are hatching up?' The journalist asked with a mischievous smirk. 'Mind if I join you?' Before either of them could reply, he pulled up a stool and sat down.

'Do we have a choice?' Alan asked chuckling. 'Can we get you a drink?'

'I'll have a coffee but won't stay. I need some dirt for the weekend.' His eyes darted around the bar as he spoke.

Alan signalled to the waiter.

'Dirt?' Des asked as he felt an uneasy hollow feeling in his stomach.

'I'm short of copy for Sunday and my editor is on my back. I need to plug a hole with a few hundred words hatchet job on something or someone. You guys must know of a juicy piece of skulduggery in the financial world I can expose, eh?' He laughed.

He may be a serious journo but his antics certainly can throw the unwary off guard.

'Sorry Noel, can't really help you.' Alan shook his head. 'We're up to our eyes these days, no time to tune in to gossip.'

Noel looked at him and then at Des.

'So I hear. My Deep Throat was telling me your Caribbean caper has got off to a flying start?'

'Keep your feckin' voice down,' Alan cut in looking over his shoulder.

'Ah.' Noel looked vaguely around the bar. 'They're all too busy with their own petty gossip. Anyway, I hear it's going gangbusters.'

'C'mon Noel, you know we can't talk about that sort of thing,' urged Alan.

'Now lads, you wouldn't want me inventing something from scratch and getting the wrong end of the stick, would you?' He smirked.

Stay quiet.

Alan looked at Des, and then back at Noel.

'We're off-the-record here, right?'

'Of course.'

'We need you to keep clear of this for a while. If you do, I'll try to see my way to giving you the first heads up on it, before the competition. We need a bit of space to get our own ducks in a row. Okay?'

Alan, trying to keep a foot in all camps. For all the good it'll do him.

Des watched Noel drink his coffee.

Took copious notes at the interview, but was sizing me up all the time as well. What he printed seemed innocuous enough, until Milo twisted it.

He suddenly realised Noel was talking to him.

'You're very quiet Desmond. You're the COO in there. I presume that makes you the organ grinder of this offshore lark?' He picked up his coffee without taking his eyes off Des. 'Or is it the Great Milo?'

'I'm not sure...' Des began, as he glanced at Alan.

'C'mon Noel,' Alan interrupted. 'I've promised you I'd give you the inside track on this when we were ready to go public. If you jump the gun now, you'll have your arse hanging out the window. You'll be going off at half cock and running a major risk of getting your facts wrong. So just lay off it for a few weeks.'

'Okay.' Noel nodded his agreement. 'But mark my words, this West Indies racket of yours is going to end in tears.' He pushed his stool back and stood up. 'Right, I'm still short a story for Sunday. I better check out another hostelry or three, while there's still time. Ciao lads. Thanks for the coffee.' He grinned and waved goodbye.

Des watched him disappear into the throng in the back bar, and then turned to Alan.

'Jesus, yer man gives me the creeps. It was great you were here to handle him. He's a bloody loose cannon. Where in the name of God does he get his information?'

'I don't know how and there's little point in trying to find out. But he's good. Acts the gobshite a bit, but don't be taken in. It's the Kerryman in him. He's very sharp. Great reader of a situation. Doesn't get fobbed off by press releases, mine or anyone else's. Does his own digging. Anyway, relax, he won't run anything on us, at least not this Sunday.'

'You sure?'

'I'll call him this afternoon and make bloody sure.'

Am I the organ grinder? And if it's Milo, wouldn't that make me the monkey?

*****

Milo called the committee to order.

'Right, I want to focus on our Coral operation. Our half year end is approaching and we need to see if there are any steps we need to take before the month end.'

You mean to window dress the accounts before the public see them. Prefer to term it Balance Sheet management myself.

'Dawn, maybe you'd kick off with what has been happening on the deposits front?'

'Well, the information we have is rather limited. They're not on *our* books, you know.'

'Of course,' Milo nodded impatiently, 'but how much money did we pass through?'

'Last month we doubled April's seventy million.'

'Can I be clear here,' Jerry cut in, 'are you saying we've opened offshore deposit accounts for over two hundred million in just two months?'

'No Jerry, it isn't what I said.' Dawn was shaking her head in frustration. 'That's the whole point of the scheme. All we did was transfer the money to Coral.'

As Frankie Carson says: *It's the way I tell 'em.*

Milo looked at Des.

'You've looked at this arrangement. You discussed it with Arthur. I take it you agree with Dawn's summation?'

Ensnaring me again.

'Yeah, I've talked to Arthur. He advised us the arrangement we've set up is entirely compliant with our regulatory requirements. However, we need to be cautious about attracting publicity to what we're doing.'

Like Noel having another cut at you one of those Sundays, Milo.

'But you're confirming Arthur says there's nothing illegal about what we're doing?' asked Milo as he checked to ensure everyone was listening.

'That's correct,' said Des, despite his discomfort.

Pontius Pilate's line: *What is truth?*

'Good.' Milo turned to Ed, satisfied with Des's confirmation.

'And how are you finding things in the branches? From what Dawn says, it looks like word's spreading?'

This is one of our weak links.

Ed paused for a while, before answering.

'Yes. You said you didn't want the scheme promoted aggressively, so we kept it low key. However, once word got around, we've begun to attract quite a bit of money, even from people outside our core client base.'

'Ed, can I clarify something,' said Des, intervening. 'How exactly does our offer differ from the competition?'

'They oblige their clients to actually open the offshore account in their own name. As you know, our mechanism just gives them a Coral numbered account. The clients' financial advisors are advising them this is a more efficient way to do things.'

You mean efficient in dodging tax.

'And what about the interest rates they're getting?'

'Oh, the rate's not an issue. The clients rarely even ask what it is.'

'I don't think we need to discuss the rates the clients are getting any further,' Milo interjected. He looked around the table. His demeanour was stern.

In other words, we know we're screwing them, but the subject is not for discussion.

'So Ed, what sort of number do you think we'll be looking at by the end of the month?' Milo continued.

'Hard to say really,' said Ed, shrugging his shoulders. 'But even in the first few days we've seen strong inflows. We could be looking at a figure in the three fifty to four hundred million range.'

Milo smiled, and then looked at Dawn.

'I know the fee matrix is a bit complex, but what sort of blended return do you think we'll make on this?'

'As a rough rule of thumb, I'd say we should clear over four per cent on it.'

A broad smile came to Milo's face. He looked around the table in the expectation it would be shared.

'If we can keep this momentum up, it'll give our profits a real boost at the year end. And it won't do the share price any harm either. Or the value of our share options.' He glanced at his notebook. 'Right, let's look at where we are with Coral and the lending front. Dawn, can you lead in?'

Dessie, you might have to move in hard here. But hold your fire and see first how far they've progressed it.

'So, there was a slow start on this. It really only got off the ground last month but it's up and running now. My understanding is that BWI has lent just over forty million so far.'

Jesus. The lending phase is up and running. How the hell could it? He confirmed specifically to me he'd get board clearance first and he hasn't. Dessie, you can't sit idly by. Wait, Ed's coming in.

'What exactly is our involvement in these loans?' Ed asked.

Dawn shifted in her seat.

'Technically speaking, we're not involved at all. The loan is between BWI and the borrower, who at another level is our client. However, because BWI doesn't know the borrowers, Coral steps in and provides a vetting service.'

'But how does Coral do this?' Ed persisted.

'It employs Arthur to check the security, and he gives the all clear to the Coral board.'

'And how do you cover your risk off?' Ed asked Milo furrowing his brow.

Milo seemed to consider how to answer the question.

'The bottom line Ed is, if the borrower defaults, the security which Arthur has approved kicks in.'

This simply won't do. The board has not authorised it. Dessie, you've got to move.

'Sorry to cut in Milo,' said Des, 'but when do you expect *our* board will be considering this proposal?' He could feel his heart thumping and he was aware of Dawn's eyes darting from his to Milo's.

Milo glared at him.

'Des, this lending business is Coral's affair. The bank's board is not involved.'

Not bloody half.

'But Milo, you told me that the board would be considering it.'

Milo forced a smile.

'I think Des there must be a misunderstanding here. Of course it has been considered at board level. By the Coral board, that is. Now I can't tell you anymore.' He looked around the table. 'We've got to comply with local secrecy laws you understand. Our bank is not involved in any of the lending we've been talking about.'

Misunderstanding? No there bloody well isn't. We're up to our necks in this lending, and I don't give a damn how you choose to present it, even if you've caught me out on a technicality. Still, I can't let this go. I'm just going to have to regroup.

'Des,' said Ed, eyeballing him, 'do you see these loans yourself at any point?'

'No.'

'You don't? Why not?'

Because I didn't know the blasted scheme was up and running in the first place. I'm caught in the middle. This isn't the forum to sort this out. It has to be between me and Milo only.

'Essentially it's because I'm not a director of Coral. Obviously, it wouldn't do if I was in breach of the local secrecy laws, would it?'

Milo looked relieved with Des' reply and leaned forward and looked around the table.

'Anybody got anything else they want to raise? No? Okay, thank you all for coming.' He glanced at his watch. 'Oh, is that the time, must rush.' He stood up and left.

Knows bloody well things are about to get seriously hot and heavy between us.

*****

'I've been waiting to hear that from you for some time,' said Joan, her relief palpable. 'I don't claim to understand the intricacies of your job, but I don't have to be a genius to figure out it's been getting to you for some time now. So fight for what you believe in, and I'll be with you all the way.' She came around the table and hugged him.

A strange feeling came over Des as he reflected on what had just happened. He had just told her he'd decided to make a stand, the outcome of which being far from clear because he realised there could be negative consequences. In his experience bureaucracies didn't like challenges, particularly from within, and were liable to engage in exceedingly rough tactics in order to prevail.

Having decided to make his move, his main concern was Joan might balk at the risk of a negative outcome. Whatever his arguments, it seemed improbable the board would not continue to support Milo, one possible consequence being he himself heading for the exit and minus his secure and lucrative income stream. But she didn't seem bothered by the prospect, in fact very much the opposite, judging from her reaction just now. Elation swept over him.

Over dinner he'd been venting his frustrations to her. Initially it was to do with Milo, but the conversation moved on when she expressed puzzlement with how there seemed to be a high degree of vagueness about the ground rules of how banks operated.

'I thought they'd be pretty clear,' she'd said.

'In theory, they are. The trouble is, rewards are high for the guy who can spot any loopholes and exploit them.'

'And who pays for this, this exploitation?'

'That's the point. It's a sort of so called victimless crime if you like, like insider trading I guess.' Thoughts of Orla and Alan's share purchase came back. 'So on one level it costs nobody, but if you think about it has to cost someone, somewhere.'

Joan took the lid off the casserole dish in front of them.

'Another spoon?

Des nodded.

'So who is this someone?' she continued.

'Impossible to say really. No one in particular. Society at large I guess. Take for example people who dodge tax by sending money out of the country. Who's pays for that?' He shrugged his shoulders.

'Presumably the other taxpayers who have to make up for the loss of revenue to the State coffers.' She looked at him directly.

She knows I'm uneasy and she's trying to push me into action.

'Ah ha. It's not that simple. The State has options. It can either raise the lost tax from another source, or simply cut planned expenditure instead.'

'On what for example?'

'Roads, medical cards, increases in social welfare allowances. It's not only the taxpayer who has to pay the price for the dodgers.'

217

'So what you're arguing is if someone evades their tax, it always costs someone else money?'

'Precisely. And anyone who helps them is in effect complicit in what is at best sharp practice.'

'C'mon Des, are you not being a bit hard on yourself there?'

'I guess I'd have thought so a year or two ago, but I'm not so sure now. You see now I'm in a position of greater influence in the bank, I find I'm being pressed more and more into supporting these, what should I call them?' he paused. 'Dubious practices, I guess.'

'Surely banking was always a bit that way?'

'I don't agree there. Before, the customer could rely on the banks to offer him a fair deal. Now it's far from clear who the banks are working for, themselves or their customers.'

'Lack of transparency?' asked Joan pouring the coffee.

'Yeah. The customer thinks he sees what's going on, but doesn't really. Even if he doesn't quite trust the bank he assumes the law is protecting him. However, if the bank has a clever lawyer, well, the apparent safety net can be a mirage.'

'I see.' She stirred her coffee. 'Of course behaviour doesn't have to be illegal to be unacceptable.'

'Yeah. You know I think the real problem is the opaqueness of it all.' He fell silent.

'So why doesn't the Regulator do something?'

'Ah, he does up to a point. But if no rules are technically broken, his room for action is limited. In the old days he only had to indicate his displeasure. Everyone knew if he raised an eyebrow, it equated to a yellow card in sporting parlance. But such subtleties count for little or nothing anymore.'

'So, where does all of this leave you?' she'd asked, the concern in her voice obvious.

'To be honest I'm struggling to find the answer. At our committee meeting today for instance, Milo asked me questions on two occasions around clarifying something on the bank's policy. As the only other director in the room, I felt I'd no option but to toe the party line. But I felt very uneasy doing so, even if my answers weren't technically untrue.'

'Leaves you in a rather awkward position then, doesn't it?' She scratched her temple.

Des laughed nervously.

'The philosophers will tell you when you find yourself in an intractable situation, you have two options. One is to accept things as they are and just get on with it. The second is to stand up and fight and try and change the situation.'

'Change the situation. But can you?'

'Joan, I've reached a turning point. I'm damned if I'm going to accept any longer the status quo. Apart from everything else, it'd be moral cowardice. I've got to stand my ground and try to change things. So now the question bothering me is precisely how?'

'So what are you thinking of doing?'

'I'm not sure. But if I'm to have any chance of winning, I'm going to have to identify the critical issue I'm going to fight on, and then resolve to go to battle on it.'

'Have you thought about the possibility you might lose? What happens then?' Joan had leaned forward, her voice deep with concern.

'I now believe the important thing is to stand up and be counted. It won't be easy, particularly with Milo. I'll have to be prepared for all possible outcomes.' He forced a smile.

It was then there was a complete change in her demeanour and she'd said her piece, about fighting for what he believed in, and what she'd been waiting to hear.

Suddenly Des realised the extent of the worry he'd caused her. He knew he could do nothing about the past, and he'd at last made the right decision.

'I'm sorry,' he said, looking into her eyes, 'for being so selfish and putting you through all of this. But we'll be okay whatever happens next.' He finished his coffee and pushed his chair back. 'Now, let me tidy up and maybe you'd fancy a walk over to the village and we could stop off for a nightcap?'

Chapter 16

'I need to talk to you straight away,' said Milo, with an urgent tone in his voice.

Des had promised Joan they'd go to Laytown for a walk on the beach, before having dinner in The Lobster Pot. He was getting ready to leave when the phone rang.

'Can it keep to the morning?' Des pleaded. 'I'm just on my way out.'

'No, it can't. I need you right now,' Milo insisted.

Feck him. Must be something really serious. He can only have got in from the West Indies. Joan won't be amused. Maybe I can sort it out quickly.

'Right Milo, I'll pop down,' he said, with an ominous feeling coming over him.

When he got to the CEO's office, he was taken aback at Milo's appearance. His face was drawn and haggard, his loosely knotted tie was askew, and his shirt and trousers were badly crumpled. A weekend bag was thrown on the floor, and his desk was strewn with files.

'Bad flight was it?' Des asked looking around.

Milo was rummaging through his files, and glanced up with a wild look in his eyes.

'Good, thank God you're here. I hope you didn't have to cancel anything important?' It was clear from Milo's agitated state his question was perfunctory.

Something is seriously amiss alright.

'It's okay. I rescheduled.' Des started to pull up a chair to the desk with mounting foreboding.

Milo picked up a bundle of papers from the clutter.

'Better sit over here away from the mess.' He plonked down in one of the chairs and waved to an empty one.

'I take it there's a problem?' Des looked at his boss with raised eyebrows.

'Yes, and a serious one to boot.' He sighed. 'I need to talk it through with you.' His voice was weak, devoid of its usual confidence.

'Right.'

'Before we start,' Milo said, dropping his voice, 'I've to warn you that this has the potential to become a very serious issue and could possibly end up in the courts.' He clasped his hands and leaned towards Des. 'We could have to swear affidavits as to what we knew and when we knew it. Do you understand?' He looked directly into Des's eyes making sure his message was received and understood.

'Ye...ss. But you better fill me in.' Des cupped his chin in his hand, while maintaining Milo's eye contact.

'It concerns Coral. You know your access to information on it is on a limited basis, so I don't want to compromise you.'

That would be a first.

'You realise, I won't be able to help you much if you can't give me all the facts?'

'Look Des, I know, God I know. But let's see how far we can get in playing it by the book. Okay?'

'Okay.'

Milo picked up his jotter from his bundle of papers. Flicking through some pages, he settled on one and then looked up at Des, making sure he had his full attention.

'Right, let me try to sum up what's happened. Coral's been supporting lending by BWI to our customers. However, although Coral doesn't actually lend the money, it provides comfort to BWI for those loans by vetting the security on them.'

'Yes Milo, I know. We discussed it at the committee. Arthur makes sure the bank isn't running any risks.'

Milo grimaced.

'We'll come back to Arthur's role in this. For the reason I've given you, I don't want to give you any details. However, what I can tell you is one of the loans, a rather large one, is for a major property development. I'm now virtually certain we've a mega problem with it.'

'I presume the board of Coral knew about this loan?'

'It did, but that's not the issue. The problem is I've reason to believe the loan is at very serious risk, and Coral is probably on the line to take a big hit.'

This just doesn't make sense.

Des scratched his head.

'But how could we if Arthur clears everything in advance? You're not going to tell me he screwed up the security are you? Did he not get the title deeds for BWI?'

Milo leaned over the table and put his head in his hands and ran his fingers backwards through his hair. When he looked up, his eyes had a haunted look.

'The short answer is no. That in itself isn't the problem though. It's not uncommon in property transactions for the lender not to physically hold the title deeds. Instead, they accept a Letter of Undertaking to deliver them from whoever is acting for the borrower.'

'Maybe I'm missing something here, but presumably Arthur has such an undertaking?'

'He does.'

'Look. I'm sorry Milo, if that's the case, I don't see the problem. Why are you getting worked up about it?'

'Because I think we've been duped by the borrower's agent – an estate agent cum rogue legal eagle. Let me explain. I was free yesterday afternoon and went out for a round of golf. I teamed up with a guy who works for one of the banks that's trying to enter our market here. To cut a long story short, he was bragging he'd pulled off this great lending deal in Galway.'

Estate agent. Rogue legal eagle. Galway. Rosser? Nah, just a coincidence.

Des watched as Milo picked up a biro, and then threw it back down.

'Christ, I could do with a drink.' He got up and opened his cabinet and took out a bottle of Jameson and two glasses. He glanced at Des. 'You'll have one?'

Des nodded affirmation to the non-question.

Milo poured two generous measures and brought over the glasses.

'From what I could work out, they're financing the same development as we are. If I'm right, it means the borrower has taken out two different loans, secured by identical Letters of Undertaking on the same property.'

Des was about to sip his whiskey, but found he was helping himself to a large mouthful instead.

'So you think one or other of us has been left with no security cover?'

'At least one of us is clearly being taken for a ride. Could be both of us for all I know right now. I tell you Des, it looks like we have a serious fraud on our hands.'

The F word dreaded by accountants. *Fraud.*

Des sat silently for a few moments, thinking.

'How much are we talking about here?' Des asked.

A wild look come into Milo's eyes. 'I don't think you want to know. This secrecy thing.'

'Dammit Milo, I know I don't want to know, but you must give me some indication of how much we're out on a limb for?'

Milo put his glass on the table and looked at him, his face blank.

'C'mon Milo, ballpark? How many digits?'

Milo flinched and slowly held up the four fingers of both hands.

Jesus. Eight digits. We've just lost tens of millions on this crazy offshore venture. And I'm the bank's chief risk officer. How did I get sucked in? What now?

Milo watched the shock spread across Des's face, and in silence nodded confirmation.

'So, the question we now have,' Milo began in a low voice, 'is what in the name of God are we going to do about it?'

We. Oh God. So this is the real consequence of agreeing to take that bloody COO job. Think about it later. First, try to figure out if you can do anything to defuse this ticking bomb.

'I suppose Milo, the first thing I think we should do is talk to Arthur.'

'My first thought too, but damn it, he's totally compromised. Des, he's the guy who's dropped us in the shit, by approving the security we now know is worthless.' Milo's head was shaking violently. 'This could end up with us having to sue the bastard.' He scratched the back of his neck. 'I mean even if we win, I doubt if his professional indemnity insurance will cover our loss. And just think of the damage to our reputation if we sue one of our own directors? Des, this is nothing short of a total disaster.' Milo swallowed a large mouthful from his glass and looked at Des, with a frightened look in his eyes.

God, so I can't even turn to Arthur for advice. You're really exposed here Dessie boy. Try to keep a cool head at all costs.

'Good point,' said Des. 'We'll need to inform the board immediately.'

'Yeah, it seems the obvious thing to do, but there are at least two problems. The first is Arthur is a director, and if we tell him, God only knows how he might react. And if we try to have a meeting without him, he's bound to find out and wonder what we're up to. Either way we'd be tipping him off.' Milo waved open hands to Des. 'Can't you see?'

'You said there were two problems?' asked Des, struggling to get to grips with the developing nightmare.

'Yeah. I think we need to have the solution to this figured out in advance of telling the board anything. We need to keep Jack and his bloody pack of spineless sheep firmly corralled. If they're not, they'll fly into a blind panic, and then the shit will seriously hit the fan. Christ, before we know it, we'll have the Regulator down on us like a ton of bricks. We just have to figure out in advance how we're going to divert them.' Milo's eyes remained fixed on Des's, pleading for help.

That 'we' again. Milo it was your crackpot idea to quadruple the size of the bank. But like it or not, you're in it too Dessie boy.

'I see what you mean,' Des admitted, as he wondered where to begin with devising a least worst solution.

Milo rose again, and went over to his cabinet, and poured two more glasses of Jameson.

'The only angle I could think of, would be to see if BWI's legal advisers could come up with something.'

'I'm not sure Milo.' Des shook his head. 'There's a risk you'd be sending them a message we were worried about a loan we were instrumental in them putting on their books. They might hit the panic button.'

Milo scratched his head.

'God, you're right, I wasn't thinking straight. So what do you suggest we do?'

That 'we' yet again. This ain't my problem. Think again, Dessie. Oh yes, it is.

'We'll have to move swiftly Milo. Time isn't on our side to put it mildly.'

'Oh I know. And there's also the not so small matter of me giving an upbeat profit forecast to the market last week. Pushed the share price up to 160.' He looked at Des sharply. 'You do realise we could now be charged with creating a false market.' Milo fell silent for a while and then looked up. 'If this deal goes belly up, when exactly will it hit our numbers?'

'How do you mean?'

'What I mean, Des, is you're our goddamn abacus jockey. Can we spread the loss over a number of years, or would it have to hit the bottom line up front? What's the accounting convention, or whatever you call it, for this sort of thing?' He gulped another mouthful of whiskey.

'Good point. Yeah, there might be some angle there. Just might help soften the impact in the short term.' Mind you, you realise we're into drowning men grasping at straws territory here.'

'So, what do you have to do Des?'

'I'll talk to Billy, our auditor, first thing in the morning. On a no names basis of course. The problem is in Coral's books. Could be a significant help they're not their auditors.'

'God, it would be great even if you could buy us a bit of breathing space. He looked around and reached for Des's glass. 'Here, let's have a refill.'

*****

Des realised he wasn't entirely innocent. He'd missed a number of opportunities to nip the whole Coral business in the bud. And whatever about vacillating when Dawn first raised it and its shape and direction were unclear, he knew full well he should have killed it stone dead at the first mention of the recycling euphemism. All he had to do was to bring his reservations to the board. They wouldn't have thanked him for it of course. But in any event he'd shirked it. Why? Procrastination? Avoidance of confrontation? A conflict of interest? Afraid he'd look foolish challenging Arthur's standing? Or had the risk of damage to his own financial rewards induced him to hang back? While it was Milo who'd offered him the promotion, the seat on the board, the pay rise, the bonus, the share options, he himself could have said no at any point. So had he been bought? Maybe, but for now he'd have to focus on solving the problem.

Much as he might like to deny it, Des realised he was critical to the finding of a solution, even if the problem was not of his making. He understood the imperative of identifying the optimal accounting result. He'd strong doubts he could get away with spreading Milo's damn mega loss over a number of years, but he'd have to try. Any short term respite would help.

He set out for Billy's office. Outside the bank, a sprawling artist on the pavement with drawing chalks shouted: 'Oi, watch it!' at Des as he strode across his reinterpretation of the roof of the Sistine Chapel.

Des glanced around as he walked.

At College Street, Tom Moore standing astride the disused public urinal. Meeting of the Waters. Emaciated druggies, staring vacantly out from under their grubby hoods at Tara Street, their ghostly like presence oblivious to a DART rumbling overhead on the Loop Line. The Liffey reflecting Gandon's Custom House's past splendours. Two boats passing upstream. Glass-topped tourist sightseer, a Garda sub aqua inflatable. Bandaged alcoholic, crabbing with crutch across Sean O'Casey Bridge. Like a character in one of his plays. Caught more than butterflies at Knocksedan. Tourists boarding the Jeannie Johnston. Unseaworthy. Feast or famine. Samuel Beckett bridge. Tramp leaning against parapet. Waiting for Godot? Unwrapping his untouched sandwiches and feeding them to swooping seagulls. Manna from heaven. Bread of Heaven. Cardiff Arms Park. Rummaging in the pockets of his flimsy overcoat. What's this? Mobile phone. Texting. Retrieving large brown bag from behind bollard. Opening cider can. Settling down on hunkers to fruits of his mornings labours. Worthy of his hire. For what we are about to receive.

Des pressed onwards.

Time to start focussing. I must get this right. I've to get the info I need, but without Billy getting suspicious. C'mon Dessie, you're an accountant too, you know how his mind works.

'Like our new offices?' Billy nodded towards the view of the Convention Centre across the river, as he shook Des' hand.

'It's really something. Fantastic view.'

'Not bad, even if I say so myself. We're still settling in here. A great improvement on our rabbit warren on Stephen's Green.'

'Well, I hope you're not going to try and bump up our fees to help pay your rent.' Des forced a light laugh.

'Ah now, don't be like that.' Billy laughed, pointed to a side table by the window, and pulled two chairs out. 'Now, before we start, what can I get you, tea? coffee? Soft drink?'

'A coffee would be great, thanks.'

Billy poured from the sideboard.

'So how are things at the bank?'

Don't frighten the horses. Just ease your way in.

'Great. Couldn't be better. We're busy implementing our Strategic Plan.'

'So I hear. And I hear also you've started a new offshore operation. How's that going, or is it a bit too early to say?' Billy asked, his expression genial.

Does he suspect something? No hint of ulterior motive. Keep calm.

'A bit early, yeah, but the signs are encouraging. Very encouraging in fact.'

'That's great news. If you don't mind me asking, the audit work. Will you be engaging us to do the needful?'

'Nothing personal, but no. We thought the most efficient thing was to use the same firm our partners out there use.'

'Disappointing, but a very understandable decision. To be honest Des, if I was in your shoes I'd probably have done the same.' Billy nodded, accepting reality.

Dessie, you've got to get this right.

'Thanks Billy. And thanks for seeing me. The reason I wanted to talk to you was to understand more fully the flexibility a bank has around reserving profits.'

That's a laugh if it wasn't so serious. It's not profits I want to bury; it's losses.

'Holding back profits instead of declaring them? C'mon Des you know the rules.'

'Sure I know the basic rules. But it's not quite what I'm thinking of. I was thinking in terms of a scenario where if we had an exceptionally good year, to what extent could we defer some profits, you know, as a buffer against a possible bad year ahead?'

Billy looked at him, with a stern face.

'I take it you're not talking about burying profits, not giving a true and fair view?'

'Oh God no Billy, of course not.'

Milo. Thinks that concept a complete joke for starters.

'No,' continued Des, 'it's a theoretical question really. I was thinking more in terms of, how will I put it, not beating the highways and byways to track down every last euro in profits to shovel in at year end, particularly if we were well ahead of market expectations anyhow?'

Which of course is the same thing.

Billy was eyeing him closely.

'I was just wondering,' Des continued, 'what the most prudent approach would be under those circumstances?'

'It's funny you should raise this issue. It's very topical. In the past, our audit guidance notes allowed for some flexibility, or to use your words, a prudent approach, to be taken. However, the guidelines have changed.'

'Changed? How? Why?'

'The ASB, the Accountancy Standards Board, were concerned about banks making provisions for bad debts. Simply put, they felt banks were over-providing for them in good years, and then using these hidden reserves to artificially boost their profits when things got rough. The euphemism is "managing the share price".'

'I've read a couple of articles about "share price smoothing", I think it was called, but I didn't pay it very close attention. Yeah, go on,' Des nodded.

'Basically the ASB has now decided there was too much of this sandbagging of windfall profits going on, so, the new guidelines state the practice is no longer on.'

I know all that. Got to nudge my way into the real issue here.

'I see. But how do you decide when a debt is really bad and when it isn't?'

'Good question. They've introduced a simple test. If the interest and repayments are being paid when they fall due, the debt cannot be classified as being bad. Full stop.'

'Seems like a pretty crude approach. Are you saying there's no room at all to make a judgment call about making provisions?'

'Exactly. Yes, it's a crude approach, but it's the only yardstick we can apply when we're conducting an audit.' He sat back with a self-satisfied look.

Keep going Dessie, you're nearly there.

'I see. By the way, under the new guidelines if a bad debt comes home to roost, can it be written off over a number of years?'

'The rule is clear on this. No, is the answer. You must take the full amount on the chin in the year you become aware it's actually gone bad.'

Bugger. So we're well and truly scuppered.

Des nodded in a disinterested way and then spoke.

'But we've wandered off what I wanted to know about, reserving in good years. Not on, you say?'

'No Des. But you're in a good place. It's better to be worried about your profits being too big than too small, eh?' Billy smiled.

If only.

'Yeah, it's a good problem to have.'

'Des, a word of advice. If you think you won't be able to repeat a bumper year, let the shareholders have the not-so-good news along with the good stuff.'

Bumper year? Blue moon.

'Sounds like good advice, as always. Thanks, Billy, you haven't given me the answer I was hoping to get, but it was helpful all the same.'

'Any time. Glad to be of some use.' Billy smiled as he stood up.

Of some use? No you weren't. You were no bloody use at all.

'And thank you too, much appreciated,' said Des, forcing yet another smile.

*****

'How did you get on? I could do with some good news,' asked Milo walking into Des's office.

Des looked up from his desk and immediately noticed the dark rings around his boss's eyes.

Looks all in, even with the change of clothes. Ah feck him. Let him sweat.

'Get on?'

'Yeah, with your bean counter pals?'

'The auditors? I can tell you they've spent a few bob on that new building of theirs.'

'Never mind their feckin' new building. What did you find out?' Milo's agitated eyes were fixed on Des and eager for answers.

'Not very helpful, I'm afraid. I'd to lay a false trail.'

'Good man. So cut to the chase. What did they say about spreading losses out over a number of years?' Milo eyes pleaded for a positive answer.

'Sorry, a non-runner. There's a new accountancy standard, and under it, there's no hiding. Bad debts must be fully disclosed and recorded on the bottom line once they crystallise.'

'Damn.' Milo sat on a chair and almost immediately jumped up again. 'This isn't good news Des, not good news at all.'

'Well you asked me to check out the facts.' Des waved a hand.

'Shit.' Milo ran his hand through his hair. 'We need to somehow hold the fort while we figure out a solution.'

Holding melting ice cream would be easier.

'Bugger,' continued Milo, pacing up around the room. He then stopped by the window and stood still. After some moments he turned to Des with a strange look in his eyes. 'You said *crystallise.*' What does the word mean exactly in mumbo jumbo accountancy-speak?'

'Basically it means the point at which the auditor believes a debt is obviously bad.'

'But what qualities does it have to have to be regarded as *obvious*?'

'Funny you should ask that because it actually came up in the conversation.'

'Yeah?'

'Billy said the proof is when the borrower misses the repayment schedule of interest, or a due instalment.'

'Really?' Milo began to pace up and down again and then stopped and turned around slowly. The strange look in his eyes had returned. 'Does that mean if the repayment schedule is adhered to, the auditor would not regard the debt bad?'

Des nodded.

'Yeah, that's the logical inference.'

What was at first a hint of a smile gradually broadened over Milo's face.

'You know, we might be on to something here Des, me auld flower.'

'I'm sorry, but I don't follow.'

'Don't worry about it. I think I'm beginning to see my way out of this mess.' He resumed pacing up and down.

'You know Des, I think we just might have found our escape hatch.'

Has he lost it altogether? There *is* no escape hatch. Or is he up to something? Dessie, you got to find out.

Des cleared his throat.

'So when do we tell our board about this?'

Milo walked over to Des's desk, sat down, and crossed his legs. His face was now a picture of calmness. He arched an eyebrow.

'About what?'

He's definitely lost it.

'The problem with the Coral loan.'

'But Des, Coral doesn't lend money.'

'Okay, the loan by BWI then.'

'Des, in this bank, we know nothing about who BWI lends money to.'

'C'mon Milo, that is a bit of a nicety. Coral knows.'

'Maybe, but you don't Des, do you? You can leave it to me to sort out any Coral issues. Me and Jack. Don't forget, the secrecy laws out there don't allow me to discuss anything about Coral with you or anybody else, well, other than Jack, and of course our solicitor, Arthur.' He looked Des straight in the eye. 'Right?'

Ah for God's sake, this is ridiculous.

'But Milo, our board needs to informed about the problems in Coral.'

Milo's face was sympathetic.

'Des, your auditor pals have been most helpful. As I see it, there isn't be any need to escalate matters to our board of directors.'

Des could feel his blood pressure rising.

'Now look here Milo, you can't in fairness fob me off like this. I want to know what you're proposing to do about the problem.'

'Des, please don't speak to me in that tone of voice,' said Milo sternly. 'Just remember I'm the Chief Executive of this bank.'

'But...' began Des.

Milo raised his hand.

'No buts. You can rest assured I'll bring any problems in Coral to the immediate attention of our board, yourself included, should the need arise.'

He looked at his watch.

'Gosh, is that the time it is? I must fly. Bye.'

Rest assured my backside. What the feck is the devious shagger up to now?

Des replayed the conversation over in his mind. Suddenly he felt his heart begin to thump and his hands began to sweat.

*****

'Extenuating circumstances?' said Joan, eyebrows arched.

'Yes, extenuating circumstances,' Des said, collapsing into his chair.

The previous twenty-four hours had been a blur. Joan was in bed when he got home after his session with Milo. He had slept fitfully and then left for work before she awoke. Now he knew he needed to make his peace with her.

'And apologies for missing out on Laytown.' He clenched his teeth and shook his head. 'Now I could really do with a G and T.'

She looked at him for a couple of moments, rolled her eyes, went to the drinks cabinet and spoke over her shoulder.

'Don't worry about it. So what's happened now?'

'Yeah, you've guessed it. Another bloody problem. A ticking time bomb in our new offshore operation.'

'Oh dear.'

'Oh dear is right. I've a serious difficulty in getting to the bottom of it.'

'Well, if you do your best.'

'The sums of money involved are frightening. I'm afraid doing my best isn't going to be good enough. I'm COO of the bank. I also happen be responsible for risk. Anyone conducting an enquiry would reasonably expect me to have intervened by now.'

'Surely there's something you can do about it?'

'I did. I consulted our auditors in an effort to figure out a solution.'

'And were they not able to come up with an answer?'

'That's the trouble. I think they did. Inadvertently.'

'So where's the problem?'

'They mentioned something out of context which I passed on to Milo. To do with recognising bad debts. The bloody fellow has seized on it and I suspect he's going to use it to drive a coach and four through the rule book.'

'I don't follow?'

'Basically I think he's going to corrupt the auditing rules to allow him to "prove", Des signalled quotation marks with his fingers, 'a bad debt is in fact a good one.'

'But how?'

'Auditing rules say a debt is only bad if the agreed interest and repayment schedule is not met. I strongly suspect he's going to manufacture a payment out of somewhere so he can bury the issue out of sight.'

Joan sat looking at him.

'Des, I'm not an accountant, but it seems to me your bank has been operating pretty close to the legal limits for some time. From what you're telling me now, what you're planning to do is simply outside those limits.'

'I'm not planning anything, Milo is. Thing is, while it's certainly highly misleading, technically it may not be fraud. Damn it Joan, if I'm right, he's planning to pervert accepted accounting conventions. And to complicate matters, he hasn't done it, yet, so as of now, there's nothing I can nail him with.'

'I see. Sounds rather challenging.'

'It is. I just can't stand idly by. He's definitely gone too far this time. I feel like a doorman in an asylum who's got his hands tied behind his back. I'm going to have to do something.' He sipped his drink.

'Like what?'

Des brooded.

'Joan, this is it. The last straw. Everything is wrong here. I'm not sure exactly what I should do, but one thing I do know is, I just have to do something.'

Joan looked up, alarm written on her face.

'I hope you don't do anything too hasty.'

'No I won't, but I can no longer postpone it. I need to plot out my course of action very carefully.'

Joan looked at him sitting in silence. Suddenly he sat up with a start.

'Benny,' he said, 'yes, Benny's my man. My first port of call.'

'Benny?'

'Yes, Fr Benedict. In Rossallen. Remember I told you I met my former Dean of Studies at the class reunion? We used to call him Benny. I was sitting beside him at the dinner and I was very taken by his pragmatism. Initially I thought he was for the birds, locked up in there for the past fifty or sixty years. How could he know anything about the real world, I thought. But in fact he was seriously plugged it. Meaning of life stuff. Don't laugh.'

'I'm not. Go on. I'm interested.'

'Anyhow he'd some very interesting things to say about acting honourably and so on. He invited me to drop down for a chat if I ever wanted to kick something around. I feel now is the time to take him up on his offer. Could be just the ticket to set my mind straight.'

'Sounds as if you could do a lot worse.'

'Yeah. Right now I'm flailing about in an enormous swamp and I'm being sucked under. What I need is to get a clear perspective on my bearings and what I must to do to escape. And I've a strong feeling if I have a chat with

Benny, I'll have a good chance of coming away with the right answer.'

'Seems an excellent idea.' She smiled and nodded. 'And you'd have nothing to lose.'

'A wasted trip at most and everything to gain.' He finished his drink put the glass on the table in front of him, and exhaled loudly.

'Right, Rossallen here I come.'

For the first time in months, he felt a cloud was beginning to lift.

Chapter 17

Des heard footsteps on the gravel and looked up.

'Des, so good to meet you again and on such a beautiful day,' said Benny, approaching. 'Isn't it so peaceful here?' Benny's eyes moved around the Rossallen Monastery garden.

They took a seat under an old brick wall which was covered in a profusion of red rambling roses. In front of them a low box hedge surrounded a lawn on which a blackbird was hopping. To one side a stream flowed through a small orchard of ripening apples. On the gravel path an elderly monk was drawing a rake through the small stones in even gentle strokes, and further along another monk was quietly pruning rose bushes.

'It is indeed. You're very good to see me,' Des began.

'I'm only too pleased. Now, you said you'd something on your mind you'd like to talk to me about?'

Des crossed and then uncrossed his legs.

'Well, I'm not sure,' he began.

'Take your time. I've been listening to people's trials and tribulations for nearly sixty years, so I doubt if you can shock me.'

Des looked around the garden not knowing where to start.

'Your reunion last February, quite a memorable occasion,' prompted Benny.

Why did I go to it? This is awkward. I'm not in control here. Still, I'm come this far. No need to be defensive. Just let it happen for once.

'It was alright. But to be honest with you, I wasn't sure I wanted to go to it in the first place.'

'Oh, how come? Did you want to deny your five years boarding with us?' A hint of a mischievous smile flitted across Benny's face.

'No, no,' Des rushed his reply, annoyed with himself for his implication. 'No, not at all. It's well, it's been such a long time. A lot of water under the bridge. I guess I wasn't sure I'd be able to handle it. People go their own way afterwards. Get caught up in other pursuits. Adopt new personae.'

Benny nodded. 'Yes, new identities. It's a survival trait the world over. Now remind me, what have you being doing with yourself since you left Rossallen.'

'After I did my Leaving, I went to university and did Business Studies. That led me into accountancy, and then banking. You'd probably label me as an adventurer in greasy finance.'

'I told you at your reunion I don't put labels on people. Certainly not ones that categorise people by their occupations. Labels can be prisms though which people view someone's life. A lazy way of looking at a person. Can often give a highly misleading impression. I don't judge people either.' He looked at Des. 'So you chose finance. You know when I was your Dean of Studies, I thought you'd be drawn to one of the caring professions.'

'Me? In one of the caring professions?' he forced a short laugh. 'I hardly think so. I don't think I'd have the patience.'

'You might be surprised if you gave it a chance.' Benny nodded over towards the monk raking the gravel. 'You see Brother Francis over there? He'll be seventy-six next January. Does he look to you like someone who fits in here in these surroundings?'

'Perfectly.'

A lady appeared from the building with a tea tray and placed it on a table in front of them.

'Thank you, Maureen,' said Benny. 'We can look after it ourselves.' He turned back to Des. 'You know he only joined the community here fifteen years ago. What do you think he was doing before he came here?'

'I haven't a clue.'

'What would you say if I told you he was a tax inspector? He came here when he retired.' Benny poured the tea.

Des was about to say to Benny he was having him on but suddenly realised this was unlikely. He looked at Brother Francis whose seeming effortless movements brought him further along the path. 'Really? I'd never have guessed.'

'That's the trouble with life today. Mahatma Ghandi put it very well, "There's more to life than increasing its speed".'

It was Des's turn to be amused. 'I didn't expect the opinion from another religious persuasion to be quoted in a place like this!' He waved around the garden.

'It wasn't his religion I was remarking on. It was his wisdom. Wisdom is the first step on the road to self-discovery.'

'Interesting observation.'

Benny picked up his cup and looked at Des.

'But I don't think you came down here to talk to me about religion, about joining up here with Brother Francis and the rest of us did you? How can I help?' He sipped his tea.

'It's just I'm very confused about how I should be reacting to work related issues.'

'Tell me about them. Start at the beginning.'

'Basically, I've a very good job, a job most people in my profession would be delighted to have. I'm number two in a progressive bank. I'm ably qualified. I'm a loyal company man. And I try to always act in a responsible way, and do my duty. And, of course, for this I'm well paid in return.'

'All very positive.' He looked directly at Des. 'I take it there's a "but" coming up?'

Des shrugged his shoulders. 'You're right. I'm not always happy, distinctly uncomfortable in fact, with what's happening around me, some business practices.'

'Business practices?'

'Well, you asked me to start at the beginning. I was very content and on top of my job until I got this new boss some months ago. Then things changed. First he promoted me and gave me additional responsibilities. Initially I was happy and thought I could handle it. But at the same time he launched us on an aggressive expansion programme.'

'I see. Look, you don't have to give me the details, but I take it this, eh, aggressive programme, could lead to borderline practices?'

'That's a very perceptive question. It's often hard to say what the law is at times.'

Benny smiled. 'If it was clear, there'd be no need for courts and judges.'

'My problem is the cut and thrust of winning deals can be the only thing that matters. It's how success is measured. And of course it's what's rewarded.'

'And this troubles you?'

'I feel I've been sucked into doing things I'm not comfortable with, things I feel are just not right. I feel I'm on one gradual incremental slide into a black hole. No one issue is big enough to shout stop over, but when I think about the bigger picture, I get really uneasy.'

'Des, what exactly is it about this bigger picture that disturbs you?'

'Basically corporate decisions get made on the basis of what's technically legal and what is not. Old fashioned values like treating customers fairly just get lost in the ether. You were talking about this in your homily to us at our reunion.'

'Nice to know you were listening to me.' Benny smiled. 'But you haven't explained to me why you feel bothered?'

'Well there may be nothing illegal, or apparently illegal about what we're doing, but I can't help but feel I'm complicit in the perpetration of a serious injustice on people, even if I can't identify who they are most of the time.'

'So your concern is you're playing a part in the perpetration of an injustice?'

'Yeah.' Des nodded. 'I may not always be actively involved in making the decisions to do certain things, but I'm complicit nevertheless, even if it's only a question of doing nothing to stop them. I think part of my problem is I feel obliged to see my employer's strategies are implemented out of a sense of company loyalty.'

'And you think these strategies break a moral code?'

'I think so. I mean I can't just reach for a Moral Code Primer and check off every situation in advance, tick the boxes, before I act. That's really my point. I'm an accountant. I'm trained to operate by the rule book and how to interpret it. But I'm coming increasingly across issues where there aren't any rules. And even where they do exist, it can be all about finding and exploiting loopholes.'

'Exploitation,' Benny repeated, listening.

'Yeah, a culture of exploiting opportunities to make a quick buck. I'm not sure if this is a zero sum game or not, but some people are definitely getting hurt. It may not be always obvious at the time, but there has to be losers. Even a first year accountancy student can work that out.'

Benny chuckled. 'And so could a retired abbot.' He looked at Des. 'Sorry, I interrupted your train of thought. Please continue.'

'I guess one of my basic contentions is most people expect to be treated fairly when they deal with institutions: bank, state, church. But in my experience the soft option for many people working in institutions is to follow the party line and tip-toe around the truth. Trouble is, this can translate into breaking the unwritten trust their clients have placed in them.'

'You feel like a cog in a wheel?'

'Yeah, a fair analogy.'

Benny paused. 'So what do *you* think you can do about it?'

'That's why I'm here talking to you. I feel very confused. It's like looking at a painting from two different angles and seeing two completely different pictures. As I see it, from the outside what we're doing amounts to deceit if that's the right word, but looking at it from the inside, it's just the way things are, the way we do them. The insiders see nothing wrong. And if everyone else is doing it too, the unspoken argument would be one doesn't have a choice but to go along with it, it's what one is being paid for.'

'One doesn't have a choice,' Benny repeated. 'Des, we *always* have choices.'

Benny picked up his cup and drank slowly. They watched the monk who was pruning the roses now pass them with a wheelbarrow full of his clippings which he transferred to a compost heap.

'You know,' said Benny, 'I think you're being very hard on yourself. My advice is for you to consider your own value system, what you really believe in. You did *Hamlet* in your year, didn't you? Do you remember Polonius's advice? *To thine own self be true.* Unless you can reconcile what you believe in with what you actually do, you'll struggle.'

'You're not trying to sell me some retreat time here, are you Father?' asked Des with a short laugh.

'Oh no, but you could do worse.' Benny chuckled. 'I heard a story once about a park attendant who spotted a man sitting motionless on a bench. The attendant watched him for about half an hour and then he approached him and asked him what was he doing. The man said he was thinking. The attendant was puzzled but went off about his business. A couple of hours later he was passing the bench again and the man was still sitting there motionless. So the attendant who was still puzzled asked him, "Who are you anyway?" The man looked at him and replied, "that's what I'm trying to find out".

'Des, from what you tell me, I think your unhappiness stems from the fact you've unwittingly allowed the day-to-day hustle and bustle of your job to cloud your priorities, and your value system has got side-tracked.'

'Side-tracked?' Des looked up sharply at Benny.

'What I mean is one can get so focussed on the immediate issues, one can lose sight of the bigger picture, meaning, your own sense of what's the right thing to do. You could say the reason I chose to live in the community here is so that I wouldn't be distracted from focussing on what I really wanted out of life.'

'Seems like a big call to make,' ventured Des, doubt in his voice.

'It's a question of one step at a time. Look at it another way. Some day when you're a bit older, retired, and looking back on your life, you might ask yourself how you'd like to be remembered.'

Des gave a short laugh. 'That's something I haven't thought about.' He looked up at Benny. 'It certainly won't be as an abbot or a Dean of Studies, like you.'

'The way I look at it, they were just some tasks my community asked me to do for them, and I was happy to be of service. But what I'd like to be remembered for is my ability to listen to people. I don't have a magic wand I can wave for them, but when people like you come with pressing issues, I try to provide them with some pointers as to how they themselves might go about resolving them.'

Benny looked around him for a few moments before continuing. 'But we were talking about you, not me. What do *you* want to see when you look back? Someone who was highly successful in the world of business, obvious status, big money and the rest of the trappings? Or someone who can put his hand on his heart and say with certainty, *I tried to do the right thing, and I behaved honourably*?' He looked at Des directly making sure his message was being received.

'You make the choice seem easy, but implementing it is surely another kettle of fish?'

Benny smiled again.

'I'm sure you remember the part in the gospel about it being easier for a camel to pass through the eye of a needle than a rich man to enter heaven. It shouldn't be taken literally of course. What it's really saying is getting onto the straight and narrow can be seriously challenging for someone who has been successful in business.'

'So what do I have to do?'

'The usual advice for people caught in a pickle such as yours is to point out they have two options. One is to accept the status quo, and the other is to try and change their situation from within.' Benny checked Des was listening. 'It seems to me, however, in your case neither of these will work. In effect, you've been running with the "do nothing" option, and it's caused your present anxiety. And as for the second, it seems from what you're telling me, it isn't going to work because you'll be overruled by the system.'

'So where does that leave me?' asked Des sounding downcast.

'There is a third option.'

'Yeah? What is it?'

'Quit your job. Or at least be prepared to quit.'

Des was flabbergasted at Benny's proposition. His head shot up and he looked at the monk, checking to see if what he'd said was some kind of joke.

'But how could I do that? The bank needs me, and anyway I'm a strong believer in loyalty.'

'Yes Des. None of us likes to kick against the herd. We like the comfort blanket of belonging even if we've joined the wrong herd.' He paused for a moment. 'Des, you've got to realise this might boil down to having to decide which is more important to you: earning power and status, or being true to yourself.'

'The way you put it creates a rather challenging future for me, doesn't it?'

'So, you believe you're a loyal company man.'

'Yeah, I'm pretty definite about that.'

'Company loyalty. It's usually an admirable quality.'

Des looked at him sharply.

'*Usually* an admirable quality. But not always?'

'No, not always.' Benny pronounced the words slowly and deliberately. 'Loyalty is not always a virtue. Take an extreme. Hitler's henchmen in the gas chambers. They were loyal alright, but what they did was hardly the right thing, was it?'

'But if they didn't, wouldn't they have paid quite a high price?'

'Doing the right thing can come at a high price, sometimes what might seem a ridiculously high price. But do you not think being true to yourself is considerably more important than more money? The important thing is not to let your future *happen* to you. Everyone should always take responsibility for their own actions. What I'm saying is by all means try to change things, but be prepared to quit if you don't get your way.'

Des sat, absorbing Benny's words.

'Father I'd love to be able to change things in there, but I'm not the boss.'

'Maybe not, but you can always try. Des, I'm obviously not familiar with your situation, but I suspect your problem is not really with your boss.'

'How do you mean?'

'What I mean is, I suspect what's happened is simply your sense of awareness of what's right and wrong has been heightened by the arrival of your new boss. Up to now you've just gone with the flow, taken the line of least resistance. The arrival of your new boss has merely jolted you out of your cocoon.'

'But if I fail to change things?'

'Failure doesn't come into it. Once you get your value system right, you'll find the inner strength and confidence to follow through. But you must be prepared to move on. You know what the American's say, "You can't beat City Hall". Sometimes the people with the inconvenient truths, the unpalatable truths, don't win the argument. So, if they want peace of mind, they just have to move on.'

'But...'

'No buts, Des,' Benny interjected. 'We're all social animals. We want to be accepted and be part of the crowd. It's what draws us to organisations. In many respects the monastery here is no different. But organisations demand loyalty and discourage individualism. So we must compromise at times to stay on board. But sometimes these compromises can ask too much of us, run against what we believe in deep down.'

'But surely if I left the bank it would mean throwing away all I'd worked for. And it would cost me a fair bit of money as well?'

'Des, doing the right thing can come at quite a price.'

Des laughed.

'Sorry, I was just thinking that's easy for you to say.' Des reflected for a moment. 'But it would be a big loss of face for me. It'd look like I'd been a failure, wouldn't it?' He looked earnestly at Benny.

'Des you have to make up your mind. You face a choice between staying unhappy in your cocoon and all its trappings of success, or you strike out and be prepared to face the consequences of freeing your spirit.'

Des's face clouded.

'Do I have to choose?'

'If you're lucky you may not. But the chances are, you will. There's no point in devoting the rest of your life to trying to beat City Hall is there? Don't forget, they've more resources than you to dig in for a long fight.'

'Yeah, true.'

'The bottom line is you're unhappy because you see yourself living in a business life of falsehoods. If you can't change the situation there, find somewhere else where you can be at peace with yourself.'

'Yeah, I see what you mean.'

'Quitting your job could be a small price to pay for the rewards it will bring you. You have to trust your own judgment in the final analysis.'

'You know, you make it sound very straightforward,' said Des, smiling.

'Actually it is, if you think about it.' Benny nodded.

'Yeah.'

'Des, always remember it's up to you yourself to take charge of your own destiny.' Benny smiled and nodded encouragement. 'If you want to talk again, just let me know.' He rose slowly. 'Good luck, I'll pray for you.'

'Thank you, Father.'

Des watched Benny shuffle away. He looked around him and his eyes were drawn to the nearby stream. He found himself mesmerised by a lone boulder in the centre of it, steadfast in its resistance to the inexorable onrush of water as it pressed and swirled about it.

When he stood up he had a resolute look in his eyes.

Chapter 18

Des was surprised at how calm he felt as he walked down the stairs to Milo's office. He was very conscious he was about to embark on a course of action, the outcome of which was highly uncertain. Apart from the evening he'd proposed to Joan he couldn't recall having been in such position ever before.

'Hi,' said Orla when he arrived, 'he's inside expecting you.' She nodded towards Milo's door.

Des thought she had a curious look in her eyes.

'Thanks Orla.' He nodded.

Tapping lightly on the semi open door, he stepped inside and closed it. Milo was standing by his desk reading a document.

'You wanted to see me?' Milo looked up.

Hooded eyes. Sizing me up. Smells trouble.

'Yeah, something I want to talk to you about.' Des looked at a chair by the desk and then at his CEO.

'Oh, grab a seat.' Milo waved and placed his document on his desk. He sat down himself. 'Now then, how can I help you.'

Cat and mouse. Seize the initiative Dessie, and hold on to it.

'I've been thinking about our Coral conversation and the bad debt.' As he spoke, he could see Milo's eyes on full alert. 'I'm not happy we're going the right away about this, and I want to talk it through with you.'

Milo adopted a puzzled look and let a few moments pass before replying.

'I thought we'd agreed on this. You're not aware there might be a problem. And in the unlikely event that one arises, I'll bring it to the immediate attention of you and our board.'

Okay, if that's the way you want to play it, right.

'Yes Milo, it's where we left it. But as I said, I've been thinking, and I'm not happy to leave it there.'

Milo picked up a biro and began doodling on a pad.

'Maybe you should explain why you're not happy?'

'It's quite simple really. You've already told me, so therefore I'm aware there's a bad debt out there to which we're exposed. I need you to give me the full details.'

Milo sat back in his chair and threw his arms apart.

'C'mon Des, you know I'm bound by the local secrecy laws. I can't discuss with you what may or may not be happening in Coral.'

'Sorry Milo, I simply don't buy that line. You told me there is a problem. I need to know what exactly has happened.'

Milo threw his biro across his desk.

'Des, please be reasonable. This is a very delicate matter. We need to keep things in perspective here. You're a good company man. Surely you don't want to rock any boats, now do you? Eh?'

Trying to play the loyalty card again.

'As COO, I don't believe I can avoid problems by hiding behind some offshore secrecy technicalities. I repeat. I need to know what's going on, period. If this causes you some technical difficulties, then let's work out together how we can surmount them.' He nodded to Milo and sat back in his seat.

'Des, just because you feel you want the information is not a good enough reason for me to give it to you.'

I'm not getting anywhere. So what's new? Time to ratchet things up.

'Milo, with respect, you're not listening to what I'm saying. I didn't say I *wanted* to know what's going on.' He paused for effect. 'I said I *needed* to know. I'm concerned, among other things, my neck is in the noose if the Regulator comes in.'

Milo looked at him and then stood up and paced up and down.

'Des, if I didn't know you better, I'd say you're behaving like a spoilt child looking for his rattle. I understand your predicament, honestly I do. Can't you see I'm trying to act in everyone's best interests here? I can't ignore the legal advice I've been given, even if I wanted to.' He stopped and looked at Des. 'And, I might add, I'm not amused with you coming into my office and giving me a pedantic lecture on the difference between needs and wants.' He sat down, and then almost immediately stood up again. 'Surely you can take comfort from the fact both Jack, our Chairman, *and* Arthur, our trusted legal advisor of twenty odd years, know the status of any lending to which Coral is a party? We're all on the same side here, aren't we, acting in what we believe to be everyone's best interest. Right?'

You could've fooled me.

'Milo, of course I take comfort from that. But it doesn't change the fact this bank's Chief Operating Officer, me, needs to know what's going on. Furthermore, I think I'm entitled to know it, and I intend to find out. Otherwise I would be in dereliction of my duty. Do I make myself clear?'

Milo sat down again at his desk. He jerked his head around the room and then closed and opened his eyes a couple of times. He began to doodle again.

'Des, you disappoint me. I thought I could rely on you to help drive this bank to a new level. That's why I promoted you, that's why I gave you a bigger pay rise than anyone else, that's why I went out on a limb for you to get you co-opted to the board. And another thing. I was rather generous when it came to giving you such a large allocation of our share options pot, an options pot I can tell you I'd to fight very hard for.' He looked at Des, appealing. 'Why are you doing this to me?'

Benny's advice. *Be true to yourself.* Don't waver now.

'I'm not doing anything to you. I just want to know the answer to what I think is a perfectly reasonable question for someone in my position to ask.'

Milo studied him, before answering.

'I'm sorry Des, but as far as I'm concerned, what you're asking is simply *not* reasonable.'

'That may be your view, but it isn't mine.'

Milo sat still and appeared to consider this. 'I see. Des, can I remind you again I'm the Chief Executive. I'm paid to make decisions about how this bank is run, which includes deciding on what information gets disseminated and what does not. On this occasion, I'm of the view it is inappropriate to grant you your wishes. I take it that I make myself clear?'

Des felt his whole being was shaking. He fought to control his voice.

'If that's your view, then you leave me with no option but to request a meeting of the board of directors be convened to discuss the matter.'

'The board?' Milo exploded. His face had shock written all over it. 'Jesus Des, that's blackmail.'

Your word, not mine.

'Milo, I don't think your terminology is helpful in this difficult situation. And I'm sure you don't need me to remind you that any of the directors are entitled to convene a meeting, if they so wish. Please yourself, but I think you may prefer to take the initiative and convene the meeting. If you choose not to, I will.'

Milo glared at him.

'Right, I'll do it, if you're hell bent on self-destruction. I'm sorry you seem determined to go down this route. I only hope you appreciate the implications of what you're doing by choosing to bite the hand that feeds you. Life is a game of consequences you know. I sincerely hope you and Joan can live with the consequences of the crackpot course of action you're embarking upon.'

Des felt his blood pressure rise.

'I'll thank you to leave my wife out of it,' Des replied, as he struggled to keep his voice under control. 'This has absolutely nothing to do with her.'

Milo sat in silence, looking intently at Des.

Trying to figure out another way to make me crack.

Milo cleared his throat.

'You do realise you're making a big mistake here.'

'If I am making a mistake Milo, at least I'm making an honest one.'

Milo glared at him.

'And what's that meant to mean?'

It means it's not a moral failure. But you wouldn't understand that distinction, would you?

'Just what I said.'

Milo looked at him in silence for a few moments before continuing.

'I see. Before I call Jack, is there anything else you wish to raise with me?'

'No thank you, I think I've made myself clear.' He nodded to Milo confirming his determination to press ahead with his course of action.

Well done Dessie, this is what you came to do. At last you've cast your die.

'Yes, Des, you have indeed. I'll be in touch.'

Milo stood up.

'Thank you.'

Des rose and left. He nodded to Orla on the way out and noticed her sizing him up. He kept going. He felt his legs were shaking so badly that he had difficulty climbing the stairs back to his office.

*****

'You're determined to see this through? Joan asked.

They were walking on the Velvet Strand at Portmarnock which was busy with visitors enjoying the warm evening. Here and there children were swimming and playing at the water's edge, pockets of teenagers were dodging among the sand dunes, while adults ambled to and from the farthest end of the beach.

'Yeah.'

'And you've weighed up the possible outcomes, the consequences?'

Des laughed lightly.

'You know, Milo said much the same to me this afternoon. When he was threatening me. To be fair to him, he doesn't do backstabbing. I've said it before, if he wants to get you, he comes straight at you full frontal with a hatchet. What you see with Milo is what you get.'

'So you've worked out all the consequences then?'

'Well until I know how they're going to react, I can't be sure. I think I'm ready for them though.'

'It could get rough.'

'Oh I've no doubt it will. I realise Milo has the board in his back pocket. They can't see beyond the short-term profits he's promised them.'

'And what about the long-term?'

'Oh, he'll spin them some poppycock yarn along the lines that the long-term is just the stringing together of a series of short-terms.'

'It isn't?'

'Not if there's a nuclear bomb ticking away in the middle of it.'

'But surely he's alert to the dangers in all of this?'

'Actually I'm not sure. Milo's not a details man. But at least he realises it. It's why he promoted me to cover his ass on that side of things for him. Now I've jacked up on him, well, we're into unchartered waters.'

They walked in silence for a while before Joan spoke.

'Des, I'm worried for you.'

'Don't be, I'm in a good place. Thanks to my chat with Benny, I've never been in a better place. I know where I stand with myself. That's the main thing. I'll give it my best shot to persuade the board to reconsider the direction their precious bank is heading in.'

'But don't you think they might see your attack on Milo as a personal thing? You know, sour grapes at not having got the top job?'

'They might. But I'm not concerned with what they might or mightn't think. The important thing for me is to be sure of where I stand.'

'Hello Des,' said a man walking in the opposite direction.

Des looked up at the face but couldn't immediately put a name on it.

Who the heck? Got it.

'Dermot,' Des greeted and stopped walking. 'Sorry, you caught me on the hop for a moment.'

Dermot. Well balanced. The very man. What was it he said? Always had a desire to do the decent thing. Why didn't I think of him before?

'Not at all.' Dermot looked at Joan.

'Dermot, this is my wife Joan.'

'Pleased to meet you,' Dermot smiled.

'Dermot was one of my classmates in Rossallen,' said Des, turning to Joan. 'We renewed acquaintances at the reunion back in February.'

'Pleased to meet you too,' Joan returned the smile.

'Well, well, small world meeting like this,' Des nodded.

'It is. Funny thing, I was going to give you a bell,' said Dermot. 'Something I wanted to kick around with you. You mentioned over dinner to give you a call. How are you fixed? Or do the hallowed halls of higher finance prevent you from associating with humble small practitioners?' He laughed lightly at his own self-deprecation.

Couldn't come at a better time.

'Now, now,' Des shook his head, 'totally untrue. I'd be delighted. Will you give me a call in the morning when I've got my diary in front of me and we'll fix it up. That okay with you?'

'Consider it done. I'll be on my way then. A pleasure to meet you, Joan. Enjoy the rest of the evening.' Dermot waved and carried on up the beach.

'Seems an okay guy,' Joan remarked, continuing their walk on the beach.

'I don't know him that well, but I think he is.'

'That's good enough for me.' She slipped her hand into Des. 'How about nipping into that hotel over there and having a quiet drink?' She smiled at him. 'I think you've earned it.'

'Sure, why not?'

Soon they were sitting on the hotel patio with their drinks, looking out at Ireland's Eye and Lambay. The sun was setting, and the north Dublin coast was being enveloped in creeping darkness.

'You're sure you're ready for what might lie ahead?' asked Joan.

No, I'm not. I'm scared. But Benny said to true to myself, and now I've simply got to believe it's the correct way to go.

'As sure as I can be.'

'And you realise you're playing for high stakes?'

With her? With my career? Is she testing me or warning me of something I've missed?

'I know I'm out of my comfort zone, but I think the time has come to jettison my woolly blanket.'

'You realise if it starts to go wrong for them, they'll probably play rough? And it probably won't be the money and perks only, but your banking reputation as well?'

'Yeah,' agreed Des, 'I'll just have to try to be ready for any crap they throw at me.' He turned to her. 'You know Joan, there's just one aspect of this whole business which really concerns me.'

'Yes?' she said, with a wary look in her eyes.

'I don't think it'll come to this, but if I don't get my way with these guys, I'm going to have to walk.'

'They mightn't give you the opportunity. You might get pushed.'

He looked at her.

Is she worried what would happen then? I should know her by now. She's calm, practical.

'Quite frankly Joan, I don't think the niceties of that matter very much, though I will have to negotiate with them and try to make sure I leave in good standing.'

'But do you think you'll be able to live with life outside the bank?'

'I can live with that bit alright. What bothers me is can you? Things will be tighter on the cash front for starters.' He forced a small chuckle. 'No more business class flights to New York either, I'm afraid.' He stopped, waiting.

Now I'll know for sure where I stand.

Joan sat in silence for a moment.

'But we will get by, financially I mean?'

'Oh yeah. I've a bit put by for rainy days. Don't worry, I have my professional qualification. I'll pick up some work easy enough.' He tried to smile reassuringly.

'You know Des, you used to go out to work in that damn bank with a smile on your face every morning. But ever since they put Milo in charge, you've got a haunted look. You've been lost in your own private world.'

Lost in your own private world. Hit the nail on the head. Why don't I give her more credit?

'The job satisfaction has gone out of it for you,' Joan continued. 'You've no reason to be afraid about quitting, and if you don't have to be, neither do I.' She leaned over the table and put her hand on his.

'Thanks.' He looked at her and squeezed her hand. 'I wasn't sure.'

'Des, you must fight for your principles.' She paused. 'You know I lost my way when I went to university?'

'Yeah, you told me before. Opted for the fast lane and flunked Pre Med.'

'It wasn't an episode of my life that I'm proud of.' She picked up her drink and sipped it before continuing. 'The thing is, it was only when I went to work in London and started working in a crap job in a canning factory I came to my senses. Mind you it took some time. I used to spend my days off visiting the local library, and I got friendly with one of the librarians. We used to go for coffee and the occasional night at the theatre. Eventually I began to regain my self-confidence and gradually realised there was another way. All it needed was for me to take charge of my own destiny. So, I came home and apologised to Mum and Dad, and asked them to help me to get back on track.'

Des sipped his drink and remained silent.

'They were very understanding about it all. They forgave me and agreed to fund me to go back to university, but this time I opted for Information Studies. I guess I just needed to prove something to myself.'

'And you got a First Class Honours.'

She didn't answer him immediately.

'Yeah, it's amazing how focussed you can get when you really set your mind to it.'

'Well you certainly proved your point,' Des chuckled.

'You know I think we all may prefer not to have to face our demons, but there are times when the right thing to do is to make a new beginning.' She paused. 'Des, I'm really with you in this.'

She came around the table and kissed him.

Chapter 19

'Hello Billy, is that you? Des, Des Peters here,' he said after he picked up the phone.

'Good to hear from you. How're things?'

'Just fine. Billy. I just wanted to recheck something we talked about the other day.'

'Sure.'

'Do you remember you mentioned a new accounting standard?'

'Yes, I remember. You were asking if it was possible to defer profits into future years?'

Yeah, I was trying to mislead you by laying a false trail.

'That's it, Billy.'

'Yes Des, the new standard is very straightforward really. A bad debt can only be recognised if there's actually a default on the repayment schedule. You simply can't anticipate bad news if it hasn't happened yet.'

'So, the test is, if repayments are on schedule, as far as your audit is concerned, the loan is good?'

'Why wouldn't it be?'

'Yeah. But what if, for instance, the management expressed doubts about it to you?'

'Makes no difference. The standard is clear. The views of management don't enter the equation.'

'So, you won't let me away with any sandbagging of profits on your watch, will you?' He forced a laugh.

'I think Des, we know each other long enough. I wouldn't expect you to engage in any cover ups.'

'Billy, you know me. Thanks, I'm now clear on what the position is.'

'Talk to you. Bye.'

He hung up.

God. That's definitely what Milo is at. The repayment schedule on the Coral loan is probably interest only. A nominal amount due. He'll pull that out of some hat. Or he won't even have to bother doing that if the schedule provides for the interest to be rolled up. Either way, the auditors won't classify it as a bad debt to start with. And so he buries it. At least in the short-term.

*****

The following morning at ten, Des arrived down at Milo's office.

'Hi Orla, Milo wants to see me?'

'Yeah, they're waiting for you in the boardroom.' Des noticed a curious look in her eyes.

They? Boardroom? Red lights flashed at the back of his brain.

He tapped on the door. At the table sat Milo, Jack and Arthur. They rose when he entered.

'Ah, there you are. Take a seat.' Jack waved to a chair on the other side of the table.

Here I am alright. Walked into an inquisition by the looks of it. Three to one. Stacking the odds. Give me a fair trial and then hang me. Keep calm.

'Sure.' Des sat and looked across the table at each of them.

'Shall we begin?' asked Jack.

Des nodded.

'Des, I won't beat about the bush.' Jack looked at the top page in a folder in front of him. 'We're here to discuss this, this bothersome development I think we'd all like to resolve.' He glanced over the top of his folder before continuing. 'Milo's informed us about your conversation. In essence, he says you wish to obtain certain information about Coral he feels legally obliged to withhold from you. Can you confirm to us that's your understanding?'

Des glanced at Milo who sat back in his seat, his face deadpan.

Keep it tight.

'Yeah, that's a fair summary.'

'And you're unhappy with his response and wish to raise the matter with the board?'

'Yes Chairman.'

Jack looked at his notes again.

'Des, I fully acknowledge and respect your right to have a meeting convened to discuss anything you wish. However, my preference is to explore the possibility of dealing with this in a low key manner. So, in that spirit, I've discussed this with the directors, and they've each agreed with my suggestion that an ad hoc subcommittee of Arthur and myself should meet you, and make a recommendation back to them as to how the matter might be resolved. That's why we're here this morning.'

A stitch up. They're pre-empting my right to appeal directly to the full board. War is declared. Okay, if that's the way you want to play it. Amen.

'Fine.' Des looked across the table at Arthur and Milo, and then scratched his head.

Fight fire with fire.

'With respect Chairman,' Des said, looking Jack in the eye, 'if the board has established a subcommittee of you and Arthur to resolve this, why is the Chief Executive attending this meeting?' He paused before continuing. 'Maybe I'm missing something here, but it seems rather inappropriate to me.'

Jack looked to Arthur in silence, but both his and Milo's eyes were fixed on their notes in front of them. Des could feel his hands sweating.

'Chairman,' he continued, 'if the subcommittee is serious about finding a resolution to the issue, I'll have to request you to ask the Chief Executive to leave the room.'

Jack looked again at Arthur, who gave an almost imperceptible movement of his right eyelid in return.

Like a serial dealer at an auction.

'Perhaps Milo, if you wouldn't mind?' Jack nodded towards the door. 'We'll talk to you later.'

Milo grimaced and then glared at Des.

'Not at all.'

He rose, and mustering what dignity he could manage, collected his papers, and left without making eye contact with anyone.

Dessie, you've won that round, evened up the odds a bit, but there's a long way to go with these two jokers.

'Right, can we now proceed with the business in hand?' asked Jack, forcing a smile. 'Des, Arthur and I have obviously heard Milo's version of your conversation. Would you like to give us yours?' He sat back.

'I've no reason to think he gave you anything but an accurate account.'

Jack leaned forward and picked up the folder in front of him. A few pages slipped through his shaking fingers and he gathered them quickly and placed them back.

'So, Milo says you're looking for information about Coral, and he feels that he's legally constrained in giving it to you?'

'Yes, Jack, you said that already.'

He's scared. Keep him on the ropes.

'Quite. I was just trying to ensure we were starting on the same page.'

Ha ha.

Jack turned to Arthur. 'You're our senior independent director, would you like to say anything?'

Forget Jack. Chickened out of the confrontation already.

Arthur sat forward.

'Well, this is a ticklish one Des. I can see where you're coming from, but Milo has a point too. This business about secrecy laws in the West Indies. I know you find it somewhat irritating, but it does rather place us in a bind. We can't condone transgressing local laws because they are inconvenient, you know.'

Going with the party line. Hardly surprising. Covering his own ass for approving the security for the dud loan as well. You're on your own here Dessie, and probably out the door. Fight.

'Excuse me Arthur, but with respect, I've never found complying with legislation either irritating or inconvenient. I think compliance is very much a first principle of good business practice. In fact, I think what you're saying is a somewhat simplistic way of looking at the issue.'

'So how do *you* think we should look at it?' asked Arthur. His pose suggested he wished to fully understand Des's point.

We can both play this reasonable man game.

'I'd have thought you should be saying to yourselves, we've appointed this guy Des here our COO. His function is to ensure all operating aspects of the bank are running smoothly. In the normal course of his duties he has come across an issue with which he is unhappy, so we need to help him with finding a solution.' He sat back with his eyes wide open and his eyebrows raised, his face a question mark.

Arthur took his time before responding.

'Put like that, it all sounds very reasonable, but it still doesn't solve our problem. We've this technical secrecy issue to deal with. So how do you think we should try to square the circle?'

'Forgive me Arthur, but I don't think it is up to me to identify the answer. You're our legal expert. I think it's you who should be advising us as to how we should square the circle as you put it.'

Jack coughed.

'I don't think, Des, that remark is really helpful to us.'

'No, Chairman,' Arthur cut in addressing Jack. 'I think Des has raised a fair question and let me answer it as the bank's legal advisor. The board in its wisdom has decided to establish an offshore operation. Local legislation prohibits, *inter alia*, the disclosure of information acquired by Coral's officers in the course of their duties. In this particular case, the directors of Coral, Milo and you, Jack, are privy to this information, and the law is clear. Neither of you may disclose it for whatever reason to anyone, Des included.'

Arthur sat back, obviously satisfied he'd delivered a knock out.

Don't roll over.

'Yeah, fair comment up to a point,' said Des, 'but you seem to be overlooking one critical thing.'

Arthur looked at him, his eyebrows furrowing. Jack shifted in his chair.

'You seem to be forgetting,' Des continued, 'the not unimportant detail that Milo has already told me there is a specific problem about a bad debt which will impact on our bank here. So, whether any of us likes it or not, I need to know the details so that I can discharge my designated responsibilities to this bank. That's an undeniable fact surely?'

'That's a different matter Des. Milo should not have disclosed to you what he did. But to disclose anything further would simply compound the magnitude of his indiscretion.'

'You say indiscretion, but surely...'

Arthur held up his hand.

'Des, there are no buts here. I'd prefer not to have to be dealing with this, no more than Jack here, but I'm telling you, and I'll be advising the board, we have no option but to fully support Milo's stance on this.'

I'm definitely out the door.

'So what happens now?' asked Des.

'It's up to you really. The board will accept the advice I'll be giving them.' He turned to Jack. 'I take it I'm right there, Chairman?'

'Absolutely correct.' Jack nodded vigorously.

'So you see, Des, it's your call. You feel you're entitled to obtain certain information. However, I'm sure you can make an educated guess what the board will decide. Of course they'll want to know how you intend to respond when they reject your request.'

'Actually, Arthur, I don't *feel* that I've an entitlement. It's a belief I have to do with my understanding of what's expected of any bank's COO. It seems, therefore, you're leaving me with only one option.'

Jack coughed lightly.

'Des, can I be clear on this. Does this mean you are saying you are going to resign?'

'Steady on Chairman,' said Arthur, with a flicker of irritation crossing his face. 'I'm not sure your question to Des is helpful at this point in our conversation.'

At this point in our conversation. So it's settled. You're definitely out on your ass. You knew this could happen, so don't panic. We're into endgame. Arthur's merely teeing up the exit negotiations.

Arthur turned to Jack.

'I don't know about you, but I could do with a cup of coffee.'

Jack turned to Des.

'And you?'

He expects me be the tea lady. Well, feck you. Get it yourself.

'No, I'm fine thank you.'

Jack slowly got up, and called Orla.

Arthur sat back and looked at Des.

'Tell me, seeing we're here to deal with the issue of your, eh, your discomfort with the bank, is there anything else you'd like to raise, anything else you'd like brought to the board's attention?'

Subcommittee. There'll have to be minutes. A written record. Broaden the scope of my reasons for leaving.

'Well Arthur, as you put it like that, I'd have to say that I've been uncomfortable for some time.'

Jack coughed again.

Forget him. Might be the Chairman, but he's a bloody stooge in this. Arthur's running this show.

'In what way?' asked Arthur, prompting.

'Well, quite frankly, I think we have been, shall we say, overenthusiastic, about our methods on delivering on our Strategic Plan.'

'I see. Are we talking here about the Plan itself, or the delivery of it?' He scratched his head.

Aha, trick question.

'It's a bit of both. In my view the Plan is, how should I put it, overambitious?' Des cocked his head and gave Arthur a meaningful look.

'But you supported it Des, didn't you? I mean when it came to the board's discussion didn't you vote in favour of it?' Arthur's glinting eyes showed his determination to stick to his own agenda.

'I did. But in my opinion we've been far too aggressive in marketing it.'

And write that down in your feckin' minutes.

'You think so?'

'Yes. We've gone way over the top in our sales efforts.' Des paused for effect. 'Imprudent I think is the apposite word.'

'I see. Can you give me an example?' Arthur asked in a calm tone.

'Well, take for instance the amount of money now flowing through Coral. I think we could have serious difficulties in framing answers to at least some questions about what's going on behind it all.' Des shook his head.

'What do you mean, *going on behind it all*?'

He's getting interested now. Beginning to realise there could be a serious issue here.

'Let me put a question back to you Arthur. You're a director of the bank here. If the Regulator called you in today and asked you what your understanding is of why people are queuing up in our branches to pour money into the scheme, just how comfortable would you be in framing your answers for them?'

Arthur frowned.

'You're not suggesting we're doing anything improper I hope?'

'No, Arthur, nothing that crude. But I think there is a reasonable expectation a bank like ours would be scrupulous about being in compliance with best practice.'

'Are you suggesting we aren't?'

Des let the question hang for a moment.

'Quite frankly I think the whole question of business risk is an issue which should be prioritised by the board as a matter of some urgency.'

Jack coughed again.

'Gentlemen, we are a sound bank, and as Chairman of the board, I can state categorically...'

Arthur cut him off by holding up his hand. He turned to Des.

'Can you help me here. You're saying people are queuing up to put money into Coral. Just why do *you* think that's the case?'

'Simple. It's because they believe we're offering them a facility to evade tax.'

'I'm not sure *I'd* see it in those terms.'

'Oh come on Arthur. You can look at it in whatever way you choose, but you can be damn sure the man in the street sees it that way. A tax wheeze. Nothing more, nothing less.'

Ball in your court, Mr Respectable Solicitor.

They were interrupted by Orla arriving with a tray of coffee and cups. She looked around the table quizzically. Arthur waited until she'd closed the door behind her before continuing.

'Des, if I read you correctly, the thrust of what you're saying is maybe we should be thinking twice about some of our work practices?'

'What I'm saying is we should, as a matter of course, always do the right thing.'

'And we're not doing things right around here now?'

'No Arthur, I didn't say we're not doing things right. What I said is that we are not doing the right things.'

Arthur paused and looked at Des, sizing him up.

'I'll have to think about your Jesuitical differentiation.' He forced a weak smile before he continued, 'Okay, so what sort of right things should we be doing then?'

'For a start, I think we should be looking at how we conduct ourselves, measure up in the corporate governance stakes, discharge our responsibilities to our stakeholders.'

Des noticed Arthur furrowing his brow. Got him.

Jack laughed lightly.

'Well I for one think we've been looking after our shareholders very well this past year. Why, the share price was at 168 this morning.' He looked at both of them, beaming a self-satisfied smile.

God Jack, why don't you just shut up. You're out of your depth.

'With respect Chairman,' said Des, 'I didn't say *shareholders*, the word I used was *stakeholders*. I'm talking about a broader group of people, who have an interest in our bank as well, people like our customers, our staff, the taxpayer. We have a responsibility to them also.'

Arthur sat forward, shaking his head.

'Des, you talked about looking at how we measure up in the corporate governance stakes. I don't seem to recall this issue ever coming up at the board before?'

'Need I say more?'

'I see,' said Arthur furrowing his brow again. 'So why didn't you bring it up?'

'Because up until lately, there simply was no need. Our checks and balances served us well. It's really only since we started into this Coral business we seem to have conveniently forgotten or overlooked our broader corporate responsibilities.'

Arthur looked at Des, challenging.

'You still haven't answered my question, 'Why didn't *you* bring this up?''

He's trying to skewer me.

Des held Arthur's eyes.

'I've requested a meeting of the board of directors be convened, haven't I? A request which so far has not been granted.'

And Arthur you know why. Because rather embarrassingly for you, you're up to your neck in this Coral mess yourself.

Arthur grimaced and looked to Jack. 'You know Jack, putting it the way Des just has, I think the board needs to spend some time on this.'

'Of course, of course.' Jack nodded.

Des noticed he looked like a man who would prefer to be somewhere else.

Arthur turned back to Des.

'You know, I think you're making a good point here. Whilst our directors were happy to endorse our Strategic Plan, they may not have fully considered all the nuances.'

Nuances. Neat weasel word. The board is totally ignorant for God's sake.

Arthur scribbled on his jotter.

'Right,' he said, 'let me summarise where we are. We've two issues. First, we've to deal with Des's own situation. And second, what we're going to do about this corporate governance question.' He turned to Jack. 'Chairman, I think this subcommittee of ours should make recommendations on both fronts?'

Jack nodded agreement.

Bloody fellow is totally out of his depth.

'Good. Now, this is how I'm going to proceed.'

Arthur reaches for his black skull cap.

'On the first issue, I will, as I stated earlier, be recommending we support our Chief Executive's position, otherwise, I believe we would be falling short in our legal obligations.'

Well Dessie, you knew that bit was coming.

Arthur looked at Des before continuing.

'You've made it clear such an outcome is not acceptable to you, so I presume this moves us into the territory of your position in the bank.'

Nice euphemism for sacking me.

Des waited.

Arthur turned to Jack.

'I think we need to take a bit of time out on this. I'll need to look through Des's employment contract. And I presume you'll want the board to do the right thing. Can we take this offline and come back to Des with our considered proposal?'

So that's how he's going to play it.

'I think that's fair enough,' said Des.

Jack shifted around in his seat. 'But there's just one thing I should mention at this stage. Under the terms of the share option agreement, Des forfeits his entitlement.'

What the hell is he up to?

'How come?' asked Arthur.

'There's a five year qualifying period. To get them he has to be in the scheme for five years, but it only commenced last January.'

'I thought it kicked in in phases, a fifth for each year?' Arthur looked puzzled.

'That's right,' Des interjected.

'But,' said Jack, 'Milo has pointed out to me that Des hasn't been in the scheme twelve months, so he doesn't qualify to participate in the options pot in the first place.'

Milo. The treacherous bastard. Persuaded Jack. Probably promised him some of my slice.

Arthur raised his hand.

'Chairman, I think you can leave it to me to examine all of Des's entitlements, and I will summarise them in my report and recommendation to the board. I take it, Chairman, this is acceptable?'

God he's letting Jack know who's really in charge.

'Quite acceptable, thank you,' said Jack looking less than happy.

Arthur turned back to Des.

'Just to be clear, we'll consider all aspects of your employment contract.'

At least unlike the other pair, he doesn't regard me a complete gobshite.

Arthur continued.

'I'll get back to you on this in a week or ten days. Meanwhile, I suggest we all try to carry on as normal. Okay?'

Carry on as normal. Of course. After all, nothing has really happened? Ha ha.

'Just one other thing,' said Des, 'you haven't said what you are going to do about the corporate governance issue I raised.'

'Thank you, Des. No, I hadn't forgotten. We will of course raise this in our report, won't we Jack?' He turned to the Chairman who nodded in silence. 'My expectation is the board will respond to your suggestions positively. I obviously can't speak for them, but I'd think they'll want to take a closer look at it, perhaps hire in some external expertise to help.'

You mean fix the record to give the appearance you're taking it seriously while you kick the can down the road. To say nothing of generating a nice bit of consultancy fee income for some buddies in that club of yours.

'Well, I'm glad to hear it will be dealt with.' Des nodded his agreement.

A small win, but a win.

'Well that seems to be it for now, gentlemen.' Arthur looked at Des. 'I'll get back to you shortly.' He turned to Jack. 'We need to talk.'

'Okay,' said Des, rising, 'I better be getting back to my desk.'

Hope you don't expect me to bust my ass while you build your scaffold and prepare the noose.

*****

'Well? How did you get on?' Joan asked him when he got home.

'There was a stick-up.' Des flopped into a chair.

'A robbery in the bank?' Her eyes widened.

'In a manner of speaking. I was ambushed.'

'You better explain.'

'Milo wanted to see me. When I called down, he had Jack and Arthur with him. Apparently when I requested a meeting of the board, Jack did a round robin, and they delegated the problem to Jack and Arthur to sort it out with me.'

'Oh.'

'At least I got Milo thrown out of the room and I'm now dealing with Arthur. He's made it clear that they'll support Milo.'

'So, where does that leave you?'

'My mind's made up. I'm not going to concede on my principles, so I'm now heading for the exit. It's all over bar the shouting.'

'I see. And it's the way Arthur sees it too?'

'In effect, yeah. I've to meet him in a week or so to discuss alternative solutions. That's code for agreeing my exit package.' He managed a weak smile.

'Des you're well out of that place. I know it was your career and you care about it, but forces you can't control have changed the rules, and the new ones just don't match your needs. Yeah, a pity, but at least you now know it's time to move on. So don't worry, just finish what you've started now, and I'm with you all the way.' She paused. 'Have you given any thought to what you'll do next?'

'Not really. Actually no would be a more accurate answer. I guess I need to conclude the business with Arthur first, and then I'll take time out to consider my options. I could look for another full-time job, but right now I'm not taken with the notion of working in a place where there's little or no room to think for oneself. I want to be in charge of my own destiny. I might go down the road of looking out for some consultancy work.'

Joan smiled at him.

'Well, good luck with whatever you choose.' She paused. 'So, what do you do while you're waiting for Arthur to come back to you? Click your heels?'

Des laughed. 'In theory it's business as usual, but I can't see myself focusing too much on problems in the bank.' He looked at Joan. 'Oh by the way, do you remember Dermot? We met on the beach in Portmarnock? I'd a call from him this afternoon. We're having lunch on Thursday.'

Chapter 20

A few days later, Alan dropped into Des's office.

'Hi, anything strange?' he asked.

Des looked up, wondering if there was something specific behind the question, but wasn't sure. For a start he'd been mulling over Alan's relationship with Orla. She'd access to Milo's files, so she probably knew of the developments about Des's future in the bank, and if she did, there was a good chance she'd told Alan.

Play dumb.

'No, not really. Just looking through the first cut at last month's figures,' he lied, waving at a file on his desk. 'They make really good reading. The business in Coral is very strong, exceeding all targets.'

'Yeah, I was talking to Ed yesterday, and he seemed to be really chuffed. Mentioned his guys are seriously fired up. Word's got out there, and the punters are producing new business out of the woodwork.'

'These numbers prove it.'

Just then the phone rang.

'Hello, Des here.'

'This is Laurence Swales here.'

'Oh hello, Laurence, how are you?'

'Just fine. Desmond. I wonder if you could drop over here. Something I want to talk to you about.'

Des felt his stomach lurch.

'Sure. When would suit you?'

'How about eleven tomorrow morning?'

'Sure, no problem.'

'Oh, by the way, remember we discussed your suspicions of insider trading?'

Damn.

Des glanced across his desk at Alan.

'I do, yeah.'

'You said you'd looked into it and written a note for your file, didn't you?'

Des paused before answering. 'Yeah?'

'I'd appreciate it if you could bring a copy with you.'

'Of course. I take it that's what you want to discuss?'

'See you at eleven in the morning then.' Laurence hung up.

Didn't answer my question. What the blazes is going on here?

'Everything okay?' asked Alan.

How much did he hear?

'Ah, the Regulator wants to chat to me about something. Probably our last quarterly return. He's fairly new here and still needs someone to hold his hand.'

Get rid of him.

'Anyhow, is there anything I can do for you?'

Alan shifted in his seat.

'No, I was just passing. I better get going.' He rose. 'See you.'

He's lying. Knows about my run in with Milo. Nosey bastard's on a fishing trip.

*****

'Shall we go downstairs to The Vaults?' Des suggested when he met Dermot in the lobby of The Westin. 'The food's okay, and it's not too noisy.'

In the arched cellar, they got a table behind some stacked tiers of long disused safety deposit boxes. Televisions screens beamed in the lunchtime business news, the ticker tape of latest prices flickering along the bottom. A waiter approached and wrote down their orders.

'This place used to be a bank,' said Des. 'Long gone now of course.' He looked around. 'It's reasonably quiet here at this time of the day, but it picks up in the evenings. Particularly on Fridays.' He laughed.

'I can't say I've been here before. But then I've no business around here.' Dermot looked around the bar.

'So, you said you'd like to kick something around?' asked Des.

Their waiter arrived with two smoked salmon salads.

'Yeah. It's just something I'd value your advice on. Thought I'd pick your brains. Can't really talk to anyone in Drogheda about it. Small town. Might as well broadcast it on local radio.' He nodded to Des, seeking acknowledgment.

'Of course, if I can be of any help.'

'It's my business you see. I don't think I told you very much about it at the reunion, but it's a modest accountancy practice. Brian, my partner, set it up. When I left the monastery, I trained there and stayed on after I qualified. I began to generate some new business, and to cut a long story short, he made me a one-third partner.'

'Good for you,' said Des, and pointing towards their salads, suggested they start.

'Yeah. Anyhow, things worked out very well between us. We share the workload, no secrets, and we run a clean practice.' Again Dermot looked to Des for acknowledgment.

'I'm with you there. You're dead right.'

'Anyhow, I could do with your advice on how to handle a development.'

'Shoot.'

'Brian wants out. He's sixty-five and wants to cash in his chips. His wife died a few years ago, and he wants to see a bit of the world.'

'I take it you're thinking of buying him out?'

'Yeah. He's willing to sell his interest to me for a hundred K. It's actually a very reasonable price, not at all aggressive. I'd say he'd get more on the open market.'

'And I presume you're interested?'

'Of course. He's given me first option. Trouble is, I could raise the money all right, but I'd prefer not to. My two kids are coming to the expensive secondary school stage, and I'd like to conserve my fire power.' He looked at Des. 'The thing is, this is a once in a lifetime opportunity. And if I don't take it, Brian might sell it to someone who I mightn't get along with. Things could be difficult if I'm the junior partner.'

'I can see how that could be awkward alright.'

'So what do you think?'

Des laughed lightly.

'I'm curious why you're asking me. You're an accountant yourself, so surely you're well able to assess the situation for yourself. No?'

'A fair point, Des. It's just, well, I'm a pretty cautious guy, and I can't afford to make a mistake. And anyway I have a concern about being too close, and would appreciate a dispassionate opinion.' He chuckled. 'I could try flattering you if that would be of any help?'

'Ah no. No need for that.'

'So, what do you think?'

Des paused before answering.

'My initial reaction is you should take control of the process. I mean, for a start, you've put your finger on a real issue: you need to try to ensure you don't end up in bed with someone who you mightn't get on with.' A fleeting thought struck him about the irony of the advice he was giving and his own current perilous situation. 'Yeah, I'd suggest you should buy out Brian's stake, and once you've got it, find a partner who you think you *can* get on with.'

'I see. But I could still end up in a difficult working relationship.'

'Yeah, but you could reduce your risk by selling just a half share rather than Brian's two thirds. Then you wouldn't be the junior partner anymore. The real trick would be to try and recoup your hundred K for the half share. Have your cake and eat it. Yeah?' Des nodded.

'You know, you might be on to something there. Hmm. And how would you advise me about going about finding my mystery buyer?'

Christ. Why didn't you see the obvious coming Dessie? Think fast. There's a business opportunity for you here. But you're now conflicted. You can't be on both sides of a deal. What would a wise man advise? What would Benny say? Best lay your cards on the table.

He looked Dermot in the eye.

'There's something I wasn't going to tell you because it would be jumping the gun, but it would be wrong of me not to be upfront now. But before I do, I want to assure you the advice I just gave you stands. Okay?'

'You're intriguing me now, but yeah, of course. I value your sage advice.'

'Thing is Dermot, I've to ask you to treat this in confidence for the moment. Right?'

Dermot nodded.

'Strictly between you and me,' Des continued, 'it's highly probable I'm going to quit my job soon.'

'Really? I hadn't realised that. When? Where are you moving to?'

'Of course you didn't know. The whole thing is hush hush. Actually, I'm having a sort of dispute with them.'

'Nothing untoward I hope?' Dermot frowned.

'Ah no... Essentially it's a personality clash about implementing strategy. Dermot, I know I can rely on your discretion in this, right? It's all very sensitive.'

'Of course.'

'Right. You asked when I might be going. It's pretty imminent. I expect we'll reach a final position in the next couple of weeks. Your other question, where I'm going. I'll be perfectly straight with you. I don't know. I haven't lined up anything yet. My intention is to get the first bit over with and then look around.'

'I see. Forgive me, but would you be interested in possibly partnering up with me?'

Play fair.

'Dermot, quite honestly, I don't want to screw you around. I'd prefer not to explore the possibility until I sort myself out with the bank first. I think that's only fair.'

'First? Does that mean you would be open to considering a proposition after that?'

'The honest answer is probably. But don't base any of your plans around me. For the moment, all I can do is restate my advice to you to buy Brian out, and to work on finding a fifty-fifty partner for your hundred K.' Des laughed, 'Or even more if you can get it. Okay?'

'Okay.' Dermot nodded.

Dermot was about to say something when Des cut in.

'I'd prefer if we could leave it there for now.'

'Understood. You know, I really appreciate your advice on this.'

'Sure, glad to oblige. Oh, and good luck.' He stood up and waving at the table added, 'I'll look after this.' They shook hands, and Dermot left.

Des was paying the bill at the bar when he heard a voice behind him.

'Well, if it isn't my old friend, the offshore organ grinder.'

He turned around to see Noel approaching with an enormous grin engulfing his face.

Shit, could do without having to deal with this walking barrel of nitro-glycerine right now.

'I hear Tiger's offshore milking machine is churning on overtime these days? Shipping out speculators' ill-gotten euro by the container load?' Noel mock laughed.

Des automatically looked over both his shoulders.

'Ah ha, we've struck a raw nerve there again, have we?' Noel added through his grin.

'C'mon Noel, enough of this tomfoolery. Alan told me you were a serious journalist.'

'Between you and me, I find if I act the fool, I can sometimes get the other guy's guard down. Mind you, the competition isn't too hot. A lot of them are lazy buggers and don't dig too much behind the press releases we're flim-flammed with.'

'Surely any journalist worth his salt will do his homework before he files his story?'

'Oh yeah.' Noel smiled. 'But the economics of running a newspaper come into play. There are times when editors don't want to risk offending their advertisers, particularly the big hitters, by running with stories too close to the bone.'

So much for print and be damned.

'Must make it very difficult for some of your colleagues.'

'Ah, there's always an outlet for us guys.'

'Yeah?'

'Did you ever wonder where the satirical mags get their stories? Sure they run with the stuff our guys think is too hot to handle.' He winked at Des.

'You mean you...' began Des.

'Wink nod say no more. Let's just say you don't think humble hacks like me can survive on the paltry wages our unions have negotiated for us, now do you?'

Des fell silent for a moment before responding,

'Anyhow, what are you doing here? Is this place not a bit off your beaten track?'

'Ah no, nowhere is off *my* beaten path. Let me ask you a question,' Noel said in a conspiratorial tone. 'Why did *you* come here?' He held up his hand. 'Let me guess. It's because it's quiet, the tables are a good bit apart so you can't be overheard, the lighting is low so you can't be seen very well. Sure isn't it the ideal place to have a clandestine meeting? You get the drift? It's why I like to pop by. See who's scheming what.'

That knowing smirk again.

281

'But surely if you can't hear what people are actually talking about?'

'Building a good story is like assembling a jigsaw. You see two guys huggermuggering in a corner, you've got a few pieces, who they are, what's the connection, the possible reasons they're meeting, and so on. Okay, you don't hear what they're talking about, but you've still got something to work on. So, you've still got to figure out what the missing pieces might look like. You see part of my job is really detective work.'

'If you don't mind me saying, it sounds a bit fantastical to me.'

'Maybe to you. But you see I've got a lead. Then I follow it up with a couple of phone calls. Get me drift? The jigsaw begins to take shape.' He looked around him and back at Des. 'Do you mind if I have a cup of coffee?'

I'm stuck with him. Might as well be polite.

'Sure.' Des ordered.

'Yeah, it might sound a bit fantastical to someone in your position, but, for instance, what would you say if I told you I'm working on a story about a guy who's having a major row with his board of directors about his organisation's activities?'

Des felt a queasy pang hit him.

It's just coincidence.

'Oh I suppose such things happen. It's not after all unusual for people to have differences of opinion in the corporate world, is it?'

'No, but the guy I'm writing about isn't in your normal corporate set-up. He's in a bank. There's a difference. And his row is around how they present their profit numbers.'

Don't worry, he's just on a fishing exercise.

'Surely all companies are always seeking ways to increase their profits?'

'Of course, Des. But I was talking about the tricks they're using to get there. Of course all bankers do it.'

'Ah, steady on. Surely you're stretching it?'

'Well if they're not at it themselves, they're complicit. They know this jiggery-pokery is going on. Same thing.'

'Jiggery-pokery you say. Do you mean illegal stuff?'

'Oh God no Des, nothing as crude as that. No, I'm talking about more subtle ways of conducting their business. Usually it's legal, but barely. I'll put it this way. Do you think the average guy in the street who walks into a bank would have a reasonable expectation he's getting a fair deal?'

'Of course.'

'And tell me, do you think he always gets it?'

'You're framing your question as very black and white, but in the round, yeah.'

'But you have reservations, right?'

'Well, banks, like any other business, are there to earn a profit for the shareholders.'

'Earn a profit for the shareholders, you say. Might that be more important to them at times than treating their customers fairly or being a good corporate citizen?'

'Well...' Des paused.

'Ah ha, you've answered my question. C'mon Des, we're both big boys. One doesn't have to be a genius to work out all banks have an inherent conflict of interest in their dealings with their customers. They won't admit it of course.'

'But.'

'No wait Des. When conflict of interest is mentioned, people get excited and say it shouldn't exist. That's bullshit. Life is riddled with them. I've a conflict of interest right now as we talk. For instance, I could be heading for Kerry to see my mother for the weekend. Or out chasing a new lead. Or, I could do what I'm doing right now: having a friendly cup of coffee and a chat here with you. Know what I mean?' He winked.

Watch this bastard. Friendly cup of coffee and a chat my backside.

'The real issue,' Noel continued, 'is we all have to recognise a conflict when we have one, and then decide how we're going to manage it. For instance, take that story about the banker that I'm working on. I'll have to make decisions on certain aspects of it.' He sipped his coffee, watching Des over the rim of the cup as he did so.

Don't show any interest.

'Noel, I'm sure you're well able to handle it.'

'I've to decide how to position the story. How and what I'm going to expose.'

Expose. Oh God.

'Well good luck. By the way, how does it end?' Des fought to control his voice.

Noel sipped his coffee again.

'I don't know yet. As I say, it's like putting together a jigsaw. I haven't got all the pieces yet. But I'm pretty certain I'm onto a real scoop.'

Definitely he's trying to sucker me into this.

'A scoop?' Des proffered mild interest.

Noel put down his coffee cup.

'Yeah, a scoop.' He slowly raised his eyes to meet Des's. 'You see my guess is my banker friend will get totally pissed off with getting the run around, so he'll come to realise his only option is to blow the whistle on the whole shebang.'

No way am I going down that route.

'Doesn't strike me a very prudent action for a responsible banker to consider.'

'Maybe.' Noel picked up his coffee and sipped it, his eyes all the time firmly on Des. 'Yeah', he continued, 'maybe. But I think Des you're pushing it with the respectable banker terminology. Rather an oxymoron in these Celtic Tiger days don't you think?' He smiled. 'Anyway, my money is on my pal getting so frustrated with being fobbed off with threats and promises, and putting up with bureaucratic arse covering, he'll eventually come to realise turning whistleblower is the only way he can redeem himself.'

'Yeah, maybe.' Des did his best to sound dubious.

'And if he's any sense, he'll use me,' Noel continued. 'He knows I'm the best in the business, the only guy who can guarantee his side of the story, with a full and fair and accurate report. Means the public will be able to grasp the essence of what *really* has been going on.'

'You make it sound like a bit of an art form. Fair play to you. How do you do it?'

Noel touched his nose. 'That's *my* secret Des. You have to learn how to crack secrets if you want to survive, don't you?' He winked.

Crack secrets. He's talking about Coral. How the hell did he find out?

'I see. And what happens if you don't get your scoop, your banker friend doesn't blow his whistle? I mean, why would he?'

'Oh he'll blow it alright. His sense of frustration will drive him to wanting to put his story out there. I can see the banner headlines already.' He laughed.

'But maybe he's not the type who'd want banner headlines? He might find it distasteful, might he not?'

Noel held Des in a steady gaze. After some moments he reached for his coffee.

'Maybe you're right there, Des. But my guess is, even if you are, my man will still believe it's in the public interest to speak out.'

'It seems to me it would be a pretty dramatic step to take all the same.'

'Ah no, I wouldn't call it a dramatic step. No, if I've my man figured out correctly, in his book it would go under the heading of "more in sorrow than in anger". He'd justify it to himself as his contribution to the common good. And to be fair to him, it would be.' Noel paused. 'Yeah, it'd definitely be a contribution to the common good.'

He's trying to manipulate me. Still, he has a point.

'Yeah, an interesting theory you have there I suppose. And if you get your pal's co-operation you should get the banner headline.'

Noel shrugged slightly.

'Even if he doesn't co-operate, I'll soon have enough of the story and be able to run with it, even without him. You know Des, one of the things about doing a jigsaw is you don't have to have every last piece of it in place to get the picture. I'm nearly there, and I expect to be asking my editor to hold the front page soon.' He looked at his watch and stood up. 'Got to go. Good to talk to you, and thanks for that.' He turned to go and then turned back. 'Oh, and thanks for the coffee as well.' He winked. 'You know where to find me, don't you?'

Des watched him leave.

He nodded to the barman and ordered a large brandy.

Chapter 21

The following morning Des was sitting in Laurence's office, watching him read his file note on his investigation into Orla's share purchase.

Why didn't he ask me to send that document over in advance? Maybe he's deliberately trying to put me on edge? Either way, don't forget Arthur's advice when you consulted him about this: *just answer the questions you're asked.* No need to volunteer anything extra.

Laurence reread the report, and eventually put it down on his desk.

'Your analysis and conclusion seem pretty clear,' he said, tapping it with his index finger.

'Thanks.' Des nodded.

'But you obviously felt the need to look into things.'

An apparent statement, but really a question.

'Once I realised a staff member had been dealing in our shares ahead of the Stock Exchange announcement, I thought it was wise to have a look.'

'Were you suspicious?'

Not half. But just answer the question.

'No, I wouldn't say suspicious. I just think it good practice to clarify things if there's potential for ambiguity. Tie up any loose ends.'

'And I take it you're now fully satisfied there was no abuse of insider information?'

Apart from Alan telling Orla between the sheets. But you don't know for sure Dessie, do you?

'My file note shows I didn't find evidence of anything untoward occurring.' He nodded at the document.

'I see.' Laurence picked it up and looked at the second page. 'You like to tie up loose ends, you say.' He looked over the top of his glasses at Des, his face expressionless. 'I see from this you pulled your Chief Executive into your investigation. Did you regard him a loose end?'

Des half shrugged, half nodded.

'Why did you draw him in? Had you a specific reason?' Laurence continued.

Something funny's going on here.

'Sorry, Laurence, I don't follow you. I didn't draw in Milo as you put it. It was simply when I asked Orla why she bought the shares, she said it was because Milo advised her to. So, I thought I should clarify with him what he'd actually said to her.'

'Well your note is clear and conclusive. I think we can move on from that matter.'

That matter. Sit tight, there's a but coming.

'But, there's something else we need to talk about,' said Laurence.

'Yes?'

'I've been given to understand, informally of course, you're considering your position with the bank. Can you confirm if this is correct?'

Milo, the bastard. Must've tipped them off. Bad mouthing me in here to boot. Laurence is fishing for my side of the story. How much does he know? Just keep it as tight as you can.

'Yes, I can confirm I've discussed it with a subcommittee of the board.'

'I see.' Laurence sat back in his chair and studied Des. 'As the Regulator, I'd like to understand why you're thinking of leaving your senior position at one of our banks, particularly at a time of remarkable growth?'

Tell him? Tempting, but just because Milo's into calumny isn't a sound reason for me to do the same. Only fair to wait until Arthur gets back to me. I can always pick up the phone later.

'Quite frankly, I'm not convinced my personal needs are aligned much with those of the bank anymore.'

'I'm not sure I follow?' Laurence narrowed his eyes and shook his head.

'You've seen the bank's Strategic Plan. It's pretty ambitious, so the implementation of it will call for a rather aggressive marketing effort. I just don't think I really want to be part of it.'

'Why not?'

'Well, it's a shift in direction to the one we were going in before. I guess I've just run out of commitment.'

'I see. You say a shift in direction. You're an accountant by profession. Would you say you don't find change easy to take?'

Is this some kind of entrapment?

'No, Laurence, I wouldn't say that at all. Indeed in my profession one of the things clients complain about is we bring in too much change. You know, accounting standards for instance. Constantly changing. No, I'm not against change as such at all.'

'Fair point.' Laurence acknowledged and paused again. 'Your running out of commitment wouldn't arise by any chance from the fact you lost out on the Chief Executive position when it became vacant last November, would it?'

Getting too close for comfort. Give him the Kerryman answer.

'Why should it?' said Des, managing a frown.

'Oh, I don't know. We're both men of the world Desmond. A personality clash perhaps?' A sly smile crossed Laurence's lips.

Milo. The bastard.

'Well, okay. Of course I was disappointed to lose out on the top job. But I wouldn't regard it as the end of the world. A personality clash? Maybe. But then Milo isn't the type of person I'd normally socialise with. Mind you I

don't really socialise with any of the people in the bank.'
Des spread his hands and shook his head.

'Desmond, you'll have to help me here. I'm still struggling with why you are considering your position at the bank. Has a particular problem being identified?'

'Do you mean is the bank breaching some of your rules or regulations?'

'Well has it?' asked Lawrence leaning forward.

'No, not that I'm aware of.'

'Did your bank break any limits we set for them?'

'No.'

'Did your bank carry out any activity which should have been authorised by us but was not so authorised?'

'No.'

'Are you aware of any legal issues?'

'No.'

'Have your auditors raised any concerns?'

'No.'

'Has there been any disagreement at board level about strategy?'

Uh uh. Getting bloody close. Wait. The subcommittee isn't the board.

'No.'

'It seems to me, Des, you're confirming you aren't aware of any instance of something happening which could be construed as a breach of any law, rule or operating regulation?'

Des nodded.

'So Desmond, and please correct me if I'm wrong, your eh, difficulty, is you've a personal view on how banking should be conducted which is at variance with your bank's strategy?'

Don't be vindictive, but you got to make certain your name is kept clean.

'No, I wouldn't put it in those terms. It's as I said earlier. Our Strategic Plan is fine in itself, but delivering success will require a rather robust approach to the market, and I guess I'm a rather conservative type. I've thought long and hard about it and have come to the conclusion the right thing for me to do at this stage is to step aside.'

Because as Benny succinctly put it, you can't beat City Hall.

'A pity but understandable. But if it comes to you leaving, we'll be sorry to see you go.'

'Yeah, I'm sorry too.'

'Thank you Desmond, I think that will be all.' He rose. 'Let me see you out.'

*****

Des and Joan were finishing their dinner and he was telling her about his meeting with Laurence.

'If you ask me,' said Des, 'the real problem with regulatory types is they tend to put too much focus on the rule book and whether there are any infringements. This can mean they're in danger of missing the bigger picture.'

'But isn't that their job,' said Joan, 'to see the bigger picture?'

'Yeah, but it's not as simple as that. You can have a situation where each element of a system is present and correct, each box ticked if you like, but if you step back and take a helicopter view, an alternative picture can begin to present itself, one which will lead you to pausing for thought.'

'I'm not sure I follow.'

'Take the bank. You could look at each individual step of a transaction and put your hand on your heart and say no rules or regulations have been broken, so therefore everything's fine and dandy. Trouble is, another person considering the same facts, but from a more holistic perspective, could conclude they weren't. The tricky part comes when you begin to factor into the process the soft behaviour stuff, which is not captured in the figures, stuff like the culture and ethos of the organisation. Now you're moving from the tightly defined world of box ticking, to an amorphous universe and the language that goes with it. And then you begin to realise that one man's prudence is another man's dead hand of bureaucracy, and one man's so called creative marketing is another man's recklessness.'

'I see,' said Joan, 'but if they're meant to see things that way, why don't they?'

Des shrugged.

'Of course they should, but bureaucracies have an aversion to setting precedents, and they convince themselves that the easiest way to control risk is to stick to the letter of the rule book. Anyway, right now it seems to me that the Regulator simply doesn't have the resources to deal with the booming economic activity.'

'So why doesn't someone higher up do something about it?'

'Higher up? Who? There isn't the political will for a start. Call me a cynic, but I doubt if politicians want to do anything that might interfere with their new pet, the Celtic Tiger as it stalks the land dishing out largesse, is there?' He picked up his wine glass. 'Look around you. Everyone is making pots of money. They're living in a fool's paradise, of course.'

'Maybe you're right. The property developers seem to be doing alright out of it.'

'They talk about greedy bankers.' Des threw his eyes at the ceiling and shook his head. 'Sure they're in the halfpenny place. What about the builders and tradesmen manically digging for gold in the street, most of them squandering their bonanzas on apartments in the sky, in places they couldn't find on a map if you asked them. The farmers doubling their acreage with their motorway monopoly money. Public servants with their benchmarking find the lady deal. Ah, don't get me going. And you know, there's still plenty left to throw a few euro to keep the social welfare brigade at home watching their free TV, so they won't use their free travel cards to come up to Dublin for a day and march on the Dáil. Everyone is winning. Or at least think they are. That's the ultimate irony of it.' He shoved his glass away from him and threw himself further back in his chair.

Joan watched him and started to smile.

'I take it you're not about to change your mind and decide to buy a holiday home?'

'Dead right, I'm not. Anytime you want to go away for a break just say so. It's not necessary to buy a bloody country in advance you know. We can afford to pay our way as we go.' He paused before repeating, 'Joan, we pay our way.' He watched her absorb what he'd said.

'Thanks, and that's good to know. But if it's all so clear, why do so many people think buying something abroad is so attractive?'

Des laughed.

'Greed. Remember the seven deadly sins? This country is consumed with greed right now from top to bottom. Everyone is happy to delude themselves they're a millionaire. It's only on paper of course, but they can't see it because of their avarice.'

'So why doesn't someone in authority do something about it?'

'Ah ha.' Des grinned. 'Exactly. There's nothing in it for the politicians to encourage the Regulator to slam on the brakes. I mean the government is more popular than ever right now. Turkeys don't vote for Christmas.'

Joan sipped some wine.

'So you got nowhere with Laurence. You were saying earlier he knew you were leaving?'

'Yeah. I don't know how. Alan was in my office when he rang, so he probably tipped off Milo. Either that or he told Orla, same thing. Anyway it became clear Milo had been in with him and got his retaliation in first. Told

Laurence we were having a serious difference of opinion.'
He sipped his wine, and then muttered. 'Bastard.'

'But it's true, isn't it?'

'Yeah. But I think Milo could've waited until we'd agreed a deal before shooting his mouth off. What really bugged me is he'd obviously told them my nose was out of joint because I didn't get the CEO job.'

'Well...' began Joan, and let the rest of her obvious comment remain unsaid.

'Okay, I guess you could say it's true, but only up to a point. However, the upshot of his shit spreading is I look pretty flakey in their eyes.'

'Which is why Milo did it of course.' Joan pushed her wine glass across the table. 'Just a small drop.'

'You know,' said Des, pouring, 'it's funny in a way, but for the first time since I joined the bank, I didn't feel like defending it.' He looked at Joan. 'It's a strange, strange, feeling.'

'Do you not think it might be because you have, to use your own words, "taken control of your own future"?' She nodded to him inviting his recognition of the change.

'Yeah, you're right I suppose.'

'Anyway, so where does this leave you now?'

'We're into endgame. I'll play my cards as best I can and live with the consequences.'

'You do that.' Joan nodded and smiled. 'Oh, by the way, how did you get on with Dermot?'

'Oh yeah. Very interesting lunch.' Des reached for his glass. 'His partner is retiring and he needs to find a new one. Quite a coincidence, but it could suit my book very nicely to cut a deal and buy in.'

'Really?' said Joan. 'So you might be able to walk from one job into another? That's great news.' She was smiling now.

'Steady on. It's only a maybe and it mightn't happen. But for now, my total focus is on finishing this thing with the bank once and for all. I up-fronted my situation and told him I'd get back to him when the fog has lifted.'

'You think you might be able to agree something?'

'If I was a betting man I'd say probably, but who knows? His offer may not be on the table by the time I feel free to engage with him. Either way I'm looking forward to starting afresh.'

'Good.' She sipped some more wine.

She's hedging. Something on her mind.

'And tell me,' she said, after some moments, 'have you thought about the reaction there might be to you leaving the bank? You know, some people might think you're a failure in some way? You've thought about this?' She was looking at him closely.

'Quite frankly I'm not particularly interested in what people think, as long as my name isn't tarnished. As far as I'm concerned, I'm doing the right thing and now it's time to move on. That to me isn't failing. It's winning.'

'You know, Des, I'm really happy for your sake you've taken control of this.' She sat back and studied him for a moment. 'So when you do your deal, what happens? Presumably there's a notice period?'

'That's just a detail to be worked out. Both sides will want a quick painless break as soon as possible, but we'll have to work out the practicalities. Three or six months should do it I'd say.'

'And a big party?' Joan tittered. 'I presume everyone will want to go through the pretence that you're going is unfortunate, but they really wish you well?'

'Yeah, something along those lines.' Des frowned and took a drink. 'There's at least one potential fly in the ointment though.' Des paused before continuing. 'I'm anticipating a row over my share option entitlement. Milo's doing his damndest behind the scenes to cut me out altogether.'

'But surely what you're entitled to is set out in black and white?' asked Joan looking puzzled.

'Ah, there are rules alright. I'll have another look at them but they don't specifically legislate for this situation. There's certainly a basis for strong disagreement about how they should be interpreted, but that's just my opinion of course.'

'So what are you going to do?'

Des reached for his glass.

'Simple really. The qualifying period for my full entitlement is five years. By the time I've worked out my notice, I'll be in the scheme twelve months. So from a purely fairness and justice point of view, I should get a fifth of my full entitlement. That's what I'll fight for.'

'And if they don't give it to you?'

'If Arthur starts to behave dishonourably or bully me, I just might consider whistleblowing.'

'Whistleblowing?' Joan put her glass down and drew her head back sharply. 'I don't understand the ins and outs of it all, but wouldn't it be a rather drastic step to take?'

'Joan, my priority is to negotiate an honourable deal, and in my book whistleblowing is incompatible with that. It would be like throwing a grenade over my shoulder as I walked out the door, after they'd fulfilled their side of the bargain. But if they try to browbeat me or diddle me out of my rights, well then, it's an option I intend to hold in my back pocket.'

'I hope you know what you're doing. You're the one who'll have to live with the consequences.'

'Yeah, but as John Wayne put it, "a man's got to do what a man's got to do".' He chuckled.

'Des, this is serious. Whatever you do, I hope you realise that when you walk away it's essential for your own state of mind you're able to put all this behind you.'

'Don't worry. That's precisely what I intend to do.'

'It's just...' She paused.

'Just what?'

'Well, if you start this whistleblowing thing, it could well put your fresh start, as you call it, on ice for quite a while.' She looked at Des who was silent. 'Just think about that before you make up your mind. That's all.'

'Rest assured, I will.'

Joan picked up her glass again. She watched him sitting motionless in his chair.

'And you've no reservations about walking away from the big money Milo and the rest of them are making?'

Des broke into a broad grin.

'Joan, let me tell you something. Apart from you, I've got something that Milo will never have.'

'And that is?'

'Enough.'

She looked at him, a soft smile playing in her eyes and on her lips.

Chapter 22

Des stood looking out the window of the boardroom. Across College Green the sunlight glistened on the granite of the portico of the Bank of Ireland. It also caught the right temple of Thomas Davis' effigy, highlighting the seagull droppings on his cropped hair. A cluster of blue and yellow buses, released by the College Street traffic lights crept onto the Green beneath the flinty reflections of Edmund Burke atop his lofty plinth. On the traffic island, Henry Grattan's petrified hand waved adieu to his forgotten parliament, while Oliver Goldsmith looked on in stoic silence, from his deserted village green.

There was a gentle knock on the door and Arthur came in, all smiles.

'Des,' he said, walking across the room and shaking his hand, 'and how are you?'

You couldn't care less.

'Fine thank you,' Des replied, nodding slightly and adding with a thin smile, 'obviously prefer if we didn't have to have this meeting, but here we are.'

'Fully understood. But let's sit down anyway. These things can be a bit awkward. Between ourselves, I'd much prefer not to be here myself.'

But you can console yourself with your fee clock running, can't you Arthur?

'Anyone joining us?' asked Des.

'No. I'd a chat with Jack and we decided I should meet you one-to-one. So, let's get started, shall we?' He waved to the chairs and they sat.

Watch this slippery eel.

Des nodded.

'Okay, let me summarise where I think we're at. If you feel I'm not representing the position fairly, just say so. We can then move on to considering the best way forward. Right?'

'Sure Arthur, go ahead.'

'Right. First I want to make it clear I'm wearing two hats here, both as a director and as the legal advisor of the bank. Understood?'

Des nodded.

'That means, among other things, if you feel at any stage you might like some legal advice, you appreciate I can't act for you?'

My heart bleeds for you. You mean you can't run a fee clock for me as well?

'Understood.'

'Good. Now, let's see if we agree on the issues we're trying to resolve here. First there's this business with the Coral loan. You wanted more details, and the bank won't give them to you.'

'Correct. I believe I need to know them.'

'Des, off the record, I don't think you'd want to.' He leaned closer and dropped his voice. 'Strictly between you and me, we've discovered the borrower has mortgaged the same property to at least four different banks.'

God. Just when I thought it couldn't get worse. At least that's one dunghill I won't have to clean up. Wait. Why is he telling me this? Trying to get my guard down by portraying he's on my side?

'Sounds pretty serious.'

'I know. It'll all come out in the wash eventually.'

Des shrugged his shoulders.

Arthur clasped his hands and leaned slightly forward. 'Anyhow, the directors have now discussed your request. The bottom line is, they've agreed to take my advice, meaning, the bank should be scrupulous in its compliance with the local secrecy laws.'

'I see.'

'Des, to be crystal clear on this, the board is supporting Milo's stance. In a nutshell, you will not be getting the information you requested.'

Board put under three line whip to tow the party line. Inform Des. Arthur ticks his first box.

'Right.'

'The other substantive issue you raised was in relation to what you termed our corporate governance framework.'

Don't tell me you're actually going to do something about it?

'That's right.'

'Personally, I think you've made a very valid point. I, sorry, I mean Jack and I, the subcommittee, have decided to take this to the board.'

Too late now to do me any good of course.

'I wouldn't be surprised,' Arthur continued, 'if they decided to engage consultants. Anyway, the good news is your recommendation has been taken very much to heart.' Arthur smiled to Des.

No, procrastination. At least twelve months before anything might begin to happen.

Des nodded acknowledgment, his face expressionless.

'Before I get to specifics,' continued Arthur, 'I'd like to take you back to the visit you paid to my office just after Christmas last year.'

'Yeah?'

'You were enquiring about insider trading.'

'That's right.'

'Is there anything,' Arthur paused, 'anything further you'd like to tell me about the reason you called?'

The wily fox is trying to find out if I've some compromising info up my sleeve.

'Not really. I'd a bit of a concern, but I took your advice. I talked to the relevant people. Nothing significant emerged, so I just took a note for the file as you advised. Funny you should mention it though. The Regulator wanted to see it the other day.'

'Oh?' Arthur flinched. 'And did they raise any further questions with you?'

'No.'

'Good.' Arthur exhaled slowly.

Get Des to confirm insider trading time bomb defused. Arthur ticks his second box.

'So, that leaves us with the business of your general discomfort with us. It seems to me there's little point in beating around the bush here. Can I be frank?' Arthur straightened himself in his chair and eyeballed Des. 'You said you believe Milo's strategy is inappropriate?'

'No, I didn't criticise the strategy. My issue is around the way it's being implemented. My discomfort is based on my belief that what we're doing is bordering on reckless trading.'

'Reckless trading?'

'Yes Arthur, reckless trading.'

And you can put I said that in the minutes of your subcommittee for sweeping-embarrassing-stuff-under-the-carpet.

Arthur sat back and studied Des for a few moments. 'I'm not sure how familiar you are with the law in this country, but are you aware that reckless trading is not a crime here?'

'It's not?'

Arthur looked at Des, his widened eyes patient.

'No, it's not. Maybe it should be, but it isn't. Let's not split hairs here. I'm trying to resolve this ticklish problem we have. The issue I'm trying to resolve is the bank's two most senior executives are at loggerheads. And as you know, after due and careful consideration the board appointed Milo its CEO, not you.'

Go on, make a pompous speech out of it. I'm not the sensitive type.

'Des, the board's primary duty is to deliver the best results, profits, for our shareholders. To achieve this, we've approved the Strategic Plan put forward by our

CEO. I don't have to remind you but you were part of the unanimous decision. The board now wants the Plan implemented in full. Given you have an issue with this, it clearly means we've to go our separate ways.'

Not one of them has a bit of backbone in them to challenge anything.

'So,' continued Arthur, 'we're simply left with how you want to play it. As promised, I've gone through your employment contract and I think it might be easiest if I tell you what I've in mind, and then you can let me know if it's acceptable to you?'

Arthur ticks his third box. Jesus falls the third time. Pilate washes his hands and prepares himself for the crucifixion scene.

'I'm not entirely clear what the choices I have here,' said Des.

Presumably two: none and feck all.

'Well let me outline the bank's offer to you then.' Arthur smiled a sickly smile.

At least he's spared me putting on the black cap.

'I can see you're wary,' Arthur continued. 'Fully understood. I'd be too if I was in your shoes. But I'd like to propose what I think will be an acceptable solution.' He looked at Des, nodding slightly.

Don't emote. Make him sweat.

'Sure, go ahead.'

Arthur took a file from his briefcase and read from it.

'Under your contract of employment, there's a three months' notice clause, so that'll bring you up to the year end. We'll obviously pay you your salary until then whether you work out your notice or not. In the meantime, we'll be reassigning your duties.' He looked up at Des for affirmation he understood.

Straightforward.

Des nodded.

'In addition, and as a gesture of good faith, we're offering you a consultancy contract for a further nine months, during which we may call on you for services from time to time. Your existing salary will continue to be paid for the duration, which adds up to two hundred K in all from now. In the event you're not free to provide the time due to other commitments, we'll still make the payment.' Arthur looked at Des.

Sounds far too good to be true, so it can't be. Must be a snag. Got it. They'll continue to own me. Trapped. Say nothing until you see his full hand.

Des nodded.

'Des, I understand you will be fifty in January, right?

'Yeah.'

'As a further gesture of our good will, the board is prepared to arrange to pay your full pension from that date, rather than delaying it for ten years until you reach the normal retiring age.' He looked up at Des again.

The carrot and the big stick. Don't yield.

'Sorry, Arthur, but I'm unclear on something here.'

'Yes? What are you unclear about?' Arthur asked with a frown.

'This pension business. Surely what I'm entitled to is between the Fund Trustees and myself?'

'That's what I said.'

'No, Arthur, you brought the bank into it. If I'm not mistaken, the bank has nothing to do with my pension.'

'Well, technically speaking, you're correct, of course.'

'So why are you talking about it at all? I mean as far as the bank is concerned, if I leave, I leave?' Des shook his head looking puzzled.

'Des, I'm trying to resolve our difficulty in an amicable manner, and I just thought it worth mentioning the bank would use its good offices to, shall we say, encourage, the Trustees to pay you the pension at fifty rather than sixty.'

Jeez, Milo'll pay anything to get me out of here.

'Thank you for the clarification,' Des replied, keeping his face blank.

Put this on hold. What else has he up his sleeve?

'Finally,' continued Arthur, 'there's the matter of your share options.' He looked up from the file and paused. 'We touched on this the other day. I've looked up the rules of the scheme, and I'm afraid there's a five year qualifying period. Milo tells me he confirmed this directly to you at the time.'

Vindictive bastard. Don't let him leg you over.

'Ah come on,' Des raised his voice, 'surely the board isn't going to go along with Milo's narrow interpretation of the rules?'

Arthur held up his hand. 'Steady on Des, they aren't entirely clear, and the board's referred them to me to give a legal opinion.'

Encouraging. A hint of some give?

'So what exactly are you saying to me?'

'I've looked at the situation very carefully, and I believe it might be possible to identify a basis for me to arrive at a more favourable opinion from your perspective,' replied Arthur, pokerfaced.

Wants me to concede something?

'Yeah?'

'However, before I reach a final position, I'd like to know how you intend to behave towards the bank after you leave?'

Hidden agenda? Time for tip toeing.

'I'm not sure I understand?'

'Come now Des, do you intend to leave us on an amicable basis?'

'Sorry, of course I do. Why do you ask?'

Arthur looked at Des and allowed a silence to develop in the room.

Let him break cover.

'Des, I believe you know a certain journalist, Noel Nash? You've been talking to him recently?'

Whistleblowing. How the hell did he find out?

Des nodded, as he fought to suppress a surge of anxiety move over him.

'Des, I hear Noel likes to specialise in sensationalist stories, encourages loyal staff in organisations to turn whistleblower and spread malicious gossip about their organisation to titillate his readers. This is, of course, good for headlines and selling newspapers, but does nothing for the reputation of the organisations concerned, nor indeed for the whistleblower in question.' He looked closely at Des before adding. 'Particularly if it can be demonstrated nothing illegal has occurred.'

He's tying this into the options. Negotiating. Play him along some more.

'Are you suggesting...?'

'I'm not suggesting anything Des. I'm merely trying to point out, if anyone should consider going down that path with our bank, there could be significant unpleasant outcomes for the individual in question.' His eyes were cold and held Des's as he spoke.

The bastard is threatening me.

'Sorry, I don't follow you?' He looked at Arthur, his face showing no emotion.

Arthur continued to hold his gaze in silence for a number of moments.

'Des, there can be particularly serious consequences for a whistleblower if he'd signed a contract with an all-embracing confidentiality clause in it.'

'A contract with an all-embracing confidentiality clause in it?'

'Yes Des. Like your original contract of employment.'

Shit, I did?

'But that was years ago. And in any case, it can only be a general catch-all clause.'

'Yes Des, catch-all.' He looked at his file and picked out a document. 'Yes, here it is. This is your signature here, isn't it?' He pointed to the bottom of the final page. 'It's a pretty standard clause in bank employment contracts of course, but well, it's clear you agreed to treat information on all bank related matters you receive in the course of your duties in strictest confidence.'

He's trying to put the frighteners on me with the mailed fist. You got to find out what's in his gloved hand before you react.

'But it was a long time ago,' said Des.

Arthur's smile appeared almost imperceptibly at first, and then spread until it seemed to cover his entire face. It reminded Des of Paul Newman in *Cool Hand Luke,* just before he revealed his house of aces to win the jackpot.

'It was Des, but when you signed it, you weren't under duress. You're a principled man who believes in fair play. I'm sure if our situations here were reversed, you'd be the first to expect me to honour my end of the bargain, wouldn't you?' He raised his eyebrows, questioning.

Thinks he has me cold.

'So where does that leave us?' asked Des.

Arthur coughed.

'Let me put a hypothetical question to you. Let's assume for a moment someone in a senior position in a bank signed such an all-embracing confidentiality clause, and then decided to renege on it by going down the whistleblowing road.' He paused to emit another staged cough. 'If such a hypothetical situation were to arise, I presume you'd understand, it would be the duty of whoever the bank's legal advisor was, to strongly advise the board to vigorously defend its reputation, by pursuing the said whistleblower for flagrant breach of contract? And let's also assume the bank's legal advisor's advice also recommended they sue the whistleblower for reputational losses, plus, *plus*, exemplary costs and damages which would, of course, be considerable. Well into seven figures I'd say. So in such a hypothetical situation, do you think such action by the bank would be unreasonable?'

Hard ball him.

'Would that not be a question for a court of law to decide?' asked Des.

'Of course it would. But Des in our hypothetical scenario, if the whistleblower couldn't prove any law had been broken, and let me remind you, reckless trading isn't a crime, and all that was involved was baseless allegations and hot air, well, in my professional opinion the outcome would be a foregone conclusion. So, to answer your question, I believe the bank would win punitive damages against the whistleblower in question.'

Arthur sat back and sized up Des before continuing.

'I'm sure you appreciate, even in the unlikely event our hypothetical bank lost in a lower court, it wouldn't hesitate to use its financial muscle to appeal to a higher one. I don't think I need spell out to you, such an outcome would result in financial ruin for the whistleblower, to say nothing of him being made a public laughing stock.'

He paused again for effect.

'If you ask me, Des, if I was the solicitor acting for our hypothetical whistleblower, I'd certainly be advising him it could be a most foolhardy and financially ruinous course of action to pursue.'

'I see,' said Des, waiting.

'So do we understand each other, do we?' Arthur moved his head backwards and peered at Des.

'You mean about my intentions?'

It was Arthur's turn to nod.

Play the long game.

'Well, I hadn't really thought about it.'

'Perhaps now is the time to do just that.' Arthur smiled and raised an eyebrow.

Not his kindly uncle smile this time. This time it was saying, time to make your mind up, Sunshine. Okay, time to flush him out.

'You haven't told me yet your opinion on my options entitlement or what your proposition is.'

Arthur looked at him with uncertain eyes.

'I'd prefer not to go into that until I knew which way you were going to jump with this whistleblowing nonsense. But I believe you are a man of integrity.' He paused before continuing. 'In fact it's because I've always regarded you as a man of integrity, I proposed you to be a director of the bank in the first place.'

Whoa. What's going on?

'Sorry Arthur, but Milo told me he proposed me.'

Arthur chuckled softly.

'Ah, Milo. He just loves his little games. No, he didn't. I did. I wanted you as a counterbalance to him on the board. Looks like it's not to be any longer.'

Christ, Arthur's straight and has been on my side all along. Well, well.

'Looks like I misunderstood,' said Des.

'Yes, seems so. In fact, maybe we all misunderstood. You see the board was seduced by Milo's promise to get the bank into the First Division, and let's just say those of us who'd reservations were simply outvoted. But then,' Arthur shrugged and added with a wry smile, 'I like to remind myself from time to time, there are always consequences. Life is a game of consequences.'

So I'm learning fast. Even Milo said it.

'You mean you supported me for the CEO job?'

Arthur sighed. 'I think that's all water under the bridge now.'

God, I've totally misread him. What else have I missed along the way?

'So let's get back to the share options,' continued Arthur. 'I've to advise the board on what I believe you're entitled to. As I said earlier, strictly speaking under the scheme rules the answer is none. However, it seems to me we could, under certain circumstances that is, factor in your appointment to the board.' He raised his eyebrows to Des, questioning.

An invitation to treat.

'And what might those certain circumstances be?' asked Des.

'In my opinion it is incumbent on members of our board to demonstrate their adherence to the highest ethical standards at all times.' Arthur paused to check Des was listening closely. 'And all times would include a commitment to uphold them even after they departed from the board.'

Get him to spell it out.

'And this translates as?' asked Des.

'It means,' said Arthur, clearing his throat, 'if you are willing to sign an agreement to the effect you will continue to be loyal to the bank, and not engage in any activity such as whistleblowing which could be considered injurious or embarrassing after you have left, then I will recommend you be awarded three fifths of your options, which is calculated on the basis you had a legitimate expectation of being a director for a three year period.' He sat back and waited.

Three times what I hoped to get! Six hundred thousand shares at 90. Price now 185. He's put over half a million on the table, even if it's still only a paper profit. Christ, just shows how seriously worried he is.

'I see,' said Des as evenly as he could.

Arthur closed his file, clasped his hands to his chest, and sat back.

'Des, let's cut to the chase. As I see it, you have two choices. One is to accept what I genuinely think is my very generous offer.'

Keep him off balance.

'And my second choice?'

Arthur slowly unclasped his hands, sighed, and sat up straight again.

'Should you decide not to sign, we would, of course, honour the three month term of your employment contract. If you feel you're entitled to anything else you'll have to pursue us in the courts, though personally I doubt if you'd get anything.'

'But...' interrupted Des.

Arthur held his hand up.

'Des, I haven't finished. In addition, should you decide to pursue this whistleblowing, well, let's just say you can safely assume we would use every possible means at our disposal to protect our good name, that is, by *every* possible means.'

Meaning, you'd screw me to the wall.

'I see.' Des sat back, non-committal.

'I sincerely hope you do.' Arthur put on a friendly smile. 'Look Des, I know this is very difficult for you. I explained I can't advise you, even if you wanted me to. But would you mind if I offered you an opinion, and I ask this as the person who proposed you for your seat at the board table in the first place?'

Trying flattery now.

Des nodded.

'Can I suggest you look at this objectively. Things haven't worked out for you. That's unfortunate, but it's a fact. You have, in my view, showed extraordinary courage in taking this on, but it's over. The package I'm offering you is the decent thing for the bank to do by you. If anything, it's more than fair and reasonable. It gives you the opportunity to begin again.' Arthur folded his arms and sat back before continuing. 'If on the other hand, you choose to go down this whistleblowing road, what would you achieve? Okay, sure, you'd have your day of glory. Sure, the journalists would hail you a hero and you'd be the toast of the media for twenty-four hours. You'd get to see the bank's dirty linen washed in public, and some of the solids might even stick. You'd probably even embarrass us. And some others as well. If you're hell bent on that, fine, go ahead.'

'Do you mind if I ask you a question Arthur, off the record of course?'

Arthur smiled, a patient of-course-I-can't-expect-you-to-know-all-the-rules-of-this-game, smile.

'Des, until we reach an agreement, this entire conversation is off the record.' He nodded. 'But sure, you have a question?'

'I'm curious to understand how happy you yourself are with all of this? You've your own reputation to protect. I mean, you're now aware what's going on falls somewhat short of best practice, shall we say. Just how comfortable are you yourself with that?'

Arthur sat silently looking at Des for some moments before he responded.

'Des, I deal in legal and economic facts, not moral judgments. And I don't think my personal views are relevant to what we're discussing here. But let me say this. I've been listening very carefully to all you've said, and you can take it I'll be recommending to the board a full review takes place of all of our operations. It's my expectation this will lead to certain changes in the manner in which we conduct our business in the future.'

Expectation. Not, intention. Everything will change.

'So, you expect change?' asked Des.

'Yes, most assuredly.' Arthur put his forearms on the table and leaned forward. 'Look Des, for God's sake, the bank will sort out any issues it has. It has to. If you think about it, it doesn't really have any options. But it's time now for you to look out for yourself. The bank's pocket is a lot deeper than yours. If you take them on, your costs will far exceed any money you may or may not get from those options. You'll be broke. And the yapping press will continue to hound you mercilessly from your hall door to the court room and back, and they won't let your phone lie silent either.'

Fair comment.

'So, ask yourself this,' Arthur continued. 'Do you really think you'll achieve anything tangible that won't happen anyway? And what will it cost you, even apart from the money? You'll be a pariah. Nobody in the industry will touch you. And three or four years of your life will have gone up in smoke. Don't you think life is too short to pursue such a pointless exercise? Are you really willing to ruin yourself for a fleeting day of glory in the media?'

Arthur paused, his eyes appealing. 'Des, don't let your heart rule your head.'

Stop messing about. It's a fantastic offer. Much better deal than you'd hoped for. But get in the driving seat.

'I think we have a deal,' said Des. 'I'm sure we both want the parting to be amicable.'

Amicable. What a lovely euphemism. At least I didn't say honourable.

'You've made the right decision.' Arthur smiled.

'Thanks. Oh, by the way, I'll just settle for what I believe I'm legally entitled to.'

'I'm not sure I understand?' Arthur looked sharply across at Des.

'In my book, I'm due my three months' notice pay, and the three years share options. I'll settle for that.'

'And the pension, of course,' added Arthur.

Don't be beholden to him.

'I expect the Trustees will pay me my entitlement.'

'As you wish. And I'll get you your consultancy contract to you in a day or two.'

'Thanks Arthur, but no thanks. No need.'

Arthur looked surprised.

'No? But we're offering you a six figure golden handshake. It's free money.'

Feck off money you mean. Only place where's there's free cheese is in a rat trap.

'Thank you for the offer,' said Des smiling, 'but I'd prefer a clean break.'

He rose and left the boardroom.

Chapter 23

'You still there?' Des asked on the telephone.

'Oh, sorry, I was just taking in what you said,' Joan answered with a catch in her voice.

'It *is* okay with you, I hope?' he asked, tentative.

'Of course it is,' she said, after blowing her nose, 'I'm just so relieved. I wasn't sure you'd see it through.'

'Well, I've agreed my deal. I finish in three months.'

'I'm so happy for you.' She sounded confident now. 'Well done. So your meeting went the way you wanted?'

'Well, let's say I've had easier ones.'

Talk about an understatement.

'Des, you've done the right thing. You should be really proud of yourself. I know I am.'

He heard her blow her nose again.

'Sure?' he asked.

'Of course I'm sure. Why wouldn't I?' She laughed. 'My old Des is back again.'

'Yeah, and it sure feels good.'

'And the whistleblowing?'

'Nah, it's not going to happen. Mind you, Arthur knew about the possibility, and as it happened, it helped sort out my share options issue. I'll tell you about it later.'

'That's terrific.' She paused. 'So what are you plans now? I hope there's room in them for me?'

Des smiled to himself.

'There's always room for you in my plans, now more than ever. Say, why don't we start with dinner in Guilbauds tonight?'

'Sounds good. I'll already looking forward to it.' She paused again. 'Des?'

'Yeah?'

'Love you.'

'And I love you too. See you later then.'

He hung up and sat back, his mind a riot. He suddenly realised how selfish he'd been. He hadn't given her much consideration during his fixation in his battle with Milo. He'd put her through an emotional wringer. What had she said some time back? *Maybe you didn't hear me.* She was right of course: he hadn't been listening to her. He felt a pang of guilt. She'd been encouraging him all along to think for himself and take responsibility. She'd seen what he hadn't seen: that he'd been seduced by it all, the power, the glory, the business and social standing, And the money. She'd also seen the price he was paying. He should have trusted her judgment more. Why had he underrated her? She'd wanted him to quit all along. A surge of emotions engulfed him. He owed her everything.

He recognised the chat he'd had with Benny had been the catalyst for the change though. It was now clear to him how loyalty could be blind and needed to be tempered with a questioning mind. He'd tried to put his concerns on the table but had been frustrated on all sides by bureaucratic evasion and over emphasis on due process, conformity and quasi legal technicalities, with each step justified, every box ticked. Everyone had executed their respective jobs as they understood them, but they lacked any appetite to engage in moral or ethical discourse: they did not see such considerations as part of their remit.

Staying and fighting on was, of course, an option, but it was clear to him now that by walking he'd made the right decision, even if it had come at quite a financial cost. But then it was a price worth paying to escape from what someone once called a fur lined rat trap. He smiled to himself at the thought when push had come to shove, Arthur had felt so threatened by the possibility of whistleblowing, that he'd ended up offering a better deal than Des had thought possible, even if it the money was only on paper. And not only that, but Arthur had committed the bank to cleaning up its act.

The markets would whisper, of course, once word of his departure came out. They'd say he hadn't the bottle for the heat when it came on, that he was at heart a wimp, that he couldn't stick the pace. In short, he'd be branded a failure. But Benny had warned him: standing up for what you believe in often comes with a high price.

He stood up and walked to the window and looked out. A strange feeling came over him. A cloud had lifted and he was somehow outside his own body looking down at himself. He saw a person newly energised. He recalled Benny quoting Polonius to him: *to thine own self be true.* He shook himself and smiled.

With a spring his step he left his office. On the way down the stairs he paused by Orla's desk and told her he'd be gone for the afternoon. He stepped out onto College Green, where he was immediately engulfed by the din: buses, taxis, cars, pedestrians, cyclists, a kaleidoscope of movement, colour, clamour. A clutch of workmen in high visibility yellow jackets were attacking a stretch of the footpath with jackhammers, pickaxes, and shovels.

At the bottom of Grafton Street he waited at the traffic lights. Couriers on motor bikes zigzagged between the chaotic traffic. He glanced up at the statue of Edmund Burke and allowed himself a chuckle. What would the man of letters make of the sophisters, economists, and calculators, scurrying by in front of him in their pursuit of commercial gain? At the front gates of Trinity College he slipped his way through the groups of students and tour bus touts, and ambled under the Front Arch and past the Porters' Lodge.

Shut off from the commercial bustle, the activity of Freshers' Week on the cobbled stones of Parliament Square seemed like a different world. Students armed with bright new shoulder bags were renewing acquaintances after the long summer break. By the

Examination Hall enrolment booths: rugby and running clubs, drama and debating societies, philosophical and political groupings, vied with each other to attract new members. Students were conversing, enquiring, learning, and experiencing.

By the Campanile, he paused to glance at the monument to Lecky, ruminating on the ethical problems of everyday life. With a wry smile he wondered what he'd make of issues in banking in the Celtic Tiger era. He walked on past the Old Library where a group of elderly tourists were queuing to see the Book of Kells. Outside the New Library, clusters of students clutched their beakers of Lavazza, posturing with their precious opinions and airs of nascent self-importance.

In College Park a cricket match was in progress beneath the watchful willows along by Nassau Street. Young blades in whites bowled and batted, seeking to impress the girls in short skirts, stretched out on the grass by the boundary, who in turn feigned not to notice them. Smaller clusters lounged across the railings of the rugby pitch, engaging in mild banter as they idly watched the players mime their way through their moves.

He moved out onto Westland Row and ascended to the platform where he boarded the DART. From the elevated loop line he watched the car ferry crabbing out from its dock onto the relentless flow of the Liffey, and eastwards towards the Baily lighthouse.

At Howth he alighted and walked along the pier and breathed in the ozone. In the still September air, the deep green sea was barely ruffled. He eased himself onto a welcoming bench and gazed at the brightly coloured sailing boats moored to their shimmering reflections.

Further along the pier, a flock of gulls were scavenging in a discarded fish box. One of them broke free with a herring grasped firmly in its beak, and flew to a spot near where Des sat, and proceeded to enjoy its unexpected repast.

Presently the other gulls spotted their sibling and with loud shrills descended upon the carcass of the fish. With a twinkle in his eyes, Des watched the victor hop, hop, hop away from the offal, and with a brief glance over its shoulder, launch itself from the pier wall and into a slow languorous glide across the harbour. He continued to watch the gull as it gave a joyous scream, flap its wings and bank as it passed the lighthouse, and soar high into the afternoon sky.